Bring Him In Mad

RUSSELL CROFT

ISBN: 1481025465
ISBN-13: 978-1481025461

For my Father and Mother, James and Kath.

A LUNACY INQUISITION

I remember the day on which Windham's trial began most vividly, because it coincided with another momentous event. It is nearly fifty years ago now since Queen Victoria's beloved consort, Prince Albert, died unexpectedly of typhoid fever while still in his prime. His death fell on a Saturday evening in the middle of December, 1861. Those of us residing in London were awoken from our beds in the early hours of Sunday morning by the great bell of St Paul's tolling to mark his passing. This was joined, one-by-one throughout the day, by the bells of all the City churches. On the Monday morning shops opened half-shuttered, and no fabric was displayed of any hue but black. Coaches went abroad with their blinds tied down, and their horses tossing dark plumes. *The Times*' leader writer was so beside himself as to beg to know of his readers, "How will the Queen bear it?"

But on that same Monday morning, a lively spirit that belied their black mourning attire was evident among a large crowd pressing against the public entrance to Westminster Hall. The Hall led to the Law Courts, and there, in the Court of Exchequer, what *The Daily Telegraph* had trailed in a superheated headline as "The Extraordinary Proceedings in High Life" were about to start. With the doors thrown open at ten-thirty, the mob surged across the medieval hall's hallowed boards making a racket that rattled its antique rafters. They squeezed through the narrow entrance and constricted passages of the adjoining court building, elbowing one another aside in the dash to claim a premier vantage on what promised to be a prize spectacle. At the Court of Exchequer threshold, uniformed janitors struggled to distinguish the properly accredited from the prurient *voyeur*. Lawyers and jurors advanced their credentials alongside suburban excursioners and skiving mechanicals. Soon every space in the cramped courtroom was taken, with the doormen scarcely confining an overflow to the corridor.

Fingers jabbed and necks craned as the onlookers tried to catch an unobstructed view of the accused. Chatting to his counsel at the front of the courtroom the young man in question appeared affable and composed, though slightly bemused. Once the general clamour had, with difficulty, been calmed, a clerk announced the party who was to preside. This official, a so called "Master-in-Lunacy", emerged berobed and bewigged from a side door to take his place seated behind a stoutly panelled desk sited on a raised platform. He nodded to the clerk to have the jury sworn in. Still in their outdoor hats and coats, for the room was draughty and less than warm, the twenty-three "good and lawful" men of Middlesex wedged into the box were no common jurors. They were "special" ones, each of whom had to be of outstanding place and position to try this case. Having taken their oaths and overseen their election of a foreman the clerk moved, at a signal from the master, to particularise the cause against the accused.

A petition had been presented to the Court of Chancery, the clerk said, alleging that the accused, named a "supposed lunatic" therein, was unable to conduct his affairs or see to his person by reason of his being of unsound mind. The petition had therefore prayed that control of his affairs and person be taken from him. This petition, the clerk went on, bore the signatures of fifteen of the supposed lunatic's well-connected relations, who included a Major-General, a Marquis, two Honourable Lords, a Dowager Countess, and a Captain R.N. Finding a case made out by the petition, the clerk explained, the Court of Chancery had issued a writ for a *Commission De Lunatico Inquirendo*, or Lunacy Inquisition, to be held to enquire into the true state of mind of the supposed lunatic. Today's hearing, he added (to further inform the gathering) constituted the commencement of that inquiry.

The accused sat calmly through these preliminaries and gave no outward sign of the lunacy alleged. Those alleging it were formidably arrayed, though of the shadowy but influential fifteen who had brought the lunacy petition only one was present. He was the Major-General, the leading petitioner, who sat with his arms folded, staring up at the skylight. The fifteen were represented by a trio of barristers, numbering a venerable Queen's Counsel as well as two juniors, seated in their fancy dress on the counsels' bench next to their client, the general himself. Behind them a second bench boasted several attorneys and their runners and note-takers, being men from both the accusers' Aylsham solicitors and their London trial agents. Not yet present, but primed to appear for the petitioners, were dozens of witnesses. These included two highly distinguished "alienists" (as psychiatric practitioners were then commonly known), ready to stamp the lunacy charge with the imprimatur of science.

The subject of all this unwelcome attention, William Frederick Windham, was otherwise a man of enviable position and fortune. On turning twenty-one (just recently) he had inherited the extensive Felbrigg estates in Norfolk, and so become their squire. Windham was the happy recipient of rents from thousands of fertile acres spread across North Norfolk, and hundreds more scattered about Essex and Suffolk. He had it in his gift to appoint rectors to several rich parish livings. Felbrigg Hall, his ancestral seat, was an ancient and noble mansion, brimful with pictures, bronzes, furnishings and diverse articles of taste acquired over centuries by those bearing the illustrious Windham name. The house was set in swathes of undulating parkland, which included a charming flint church housing memorials to assorted forebears. The estate woods that fringed the park were both pleasant to traverse and laden with valuable uncut timber.

Windham's father, who had died some years before the son inherited, had had no use for the county society to which his standing qualified him and had husbanded the land instead. All commentators measured him a fine, improving custodian, and he had passed affairs on in good order. But those who had known the old squire also considered him to have been truculent and bothersome, and an eccentric of the first rank. Windham's mother, Lady Sophia, who was still living, came from the notoriously peculiar Hervey family of Ickworth in Suffolk, hereditary earls, and then marquises of Bristol.

Looking back over the half-century or so that separates me from the time of the trial, it seems to me that Windham was called to privilege when it still had an unalloyed lustre, still attracted an unquestioned deference, that has today grown cloudy. I write these lines in the first decade of the Twentieth Century, but it was then the "Merry Sixties" of the Nineteenth, when flaunting wealth and taking pleasure unashamedly, often indiscriminately, was in the fashion. Many a landed gent grazed the attractions of London or the Continent, high and low alike, assured that bountiful rents were pouring into his bailiff's coffer back home. Roystering swells would go for thrills to the flakier quarters of the metropolis, like the East End's docklands, accompanied for safety by a tipped detective policeman and a brace of uniformed drones. Our now departed Queen Victoria had still been in her first flush of vigour when her "angel" Albert was wrenched from her side. Even the then Prime Minister, old Lord Palmerston, who had been a noted libertine in his regency youth, would affect spry virility whenever the occasion warranted it.

These should have been palmy days for the likes of Windham. But just as society's surface glitter hid extremes of squalor and deprivation in the population at large, so the coach of his fortune had become mired deep in the Norfolk mud. He was on trial for madness, with his liberty and property at stake. His trial was to be followed with a relish not confined to those who packed the courtroom throughout the thirty-four days of its sitting. The general public fastened onto the affair to help it through a cheerless winter, and before it was ended the entirety of Windham's life of twenty-one years to date had been eviscerated for an entertainment.

Led by the high minded *Times*, all the London newspapers carried verbatim transcripts daily (and these not tucked away on the Law Report pages either), and they were matched by the periodicals in passing pious or satiric editorial reflection. Interest was enhanced, as the inquisition dragged on, by the widespread perception that here was a lunacy trial turning itself into a kind of lunacy. In a cavalcade of glare and grime, a host of characters lit up its scenes. There were truculent tutors, tradesmen waiting on tick, biddable railway officials, garrulous policemen, grasping mercenaries, and eminent mad-doctors. And there was a young woman, of a certain type, whose close involvement in the matter was guaranteed to spice its savour still further. Though Windham did not lack for failings, the one that damned him in the sight of many observers was that of falling for a woman generally considered irredeemably debased. It seems to me that notions of madness are all too easily inoculated with notions of immorality, in any age.

Few of today's readers will be able to call the affair distinctly to mind. It caused a great stir in its time, but is now almost completely forgotten. Yet I witnessed its events at first hand, and played my own small part in their unfolding. And a recent personal tragedy has returned them to the forefront of my thoughts. As I look at the browning press accounts, and curling, fading, papers that I have kept from the trial, I see "Mad" Windham's face looming up afresh from my memory. It strikes me that a salutary tale abides in these fragments, and I mean to tell it here without sparing the intimate details at which some contemporaries affected to take fright. I will also relate how my place in the business has coloured my own subsequent life.

George James Phinney, Solicitor (Retired)
August 1909.

THE CALL OF THE FOOTPLATE

"Get into your carriages ladies and gentlemen, quick quick", the guard cheerily cajoled the boarding throng as he passed down the smoky platform amongst them. It was on a sunny afternoon in the far-off spring of 1861 that my part in Windham's story began. My train from London had halted at Ipswich and I observed the guard, at first idly and then with growing interest, from the open window of my compartment toward its rear. Guards on the Eastern Counties Railway normally maintained an imperious detachment when it came to passengers, especially with regard to those of the poorer type, but this one was assisting travellers of every kind aboard in an extravagantly courteous and attentive manner. He helped threadbare parties and their battered boxes into third-class with the same solicitations that he lavished on squeezing ladies and their voluminous crinolines into first. Everyone was treated to a gracious bow and a "Good daaaaay Sir", or a "Good daaaaay madam", all delivered in a fruity rustic burr, and no one was required to consult purse or pocket for a compensating tip.

As the guard drew nearer, I noticed some more surprising curiosities about him. He wore the regulation greatcoat, embroidered on its sleeves with the company initials "ECR" and his serial number, and round his shoulder he had the company's pouch and belt, worn sash fashion. But where the greatcoat stopped a pair of distinctly tailored trousers began, and where they ended there emerged a pair of well-made boots. Instead of the customary rough cloth, his throat sprouted a velvet cravat threaded through a silver band, and beneath that I detected lapels of fashionable cut and dimension. Perhaps the man had paused to pilfer a gentleman's outfitter on his way to work? He was better turned out than I was, but back then I would no more have been ranked a gentleman than would a common railway guard.

I was then a very junior solicitor, whose own suit would not have been fashioned in one of the West End's finer arcades. Nor would the Red Lion Square place of business of my then employer, Messrs Praed & Pumicestone, have been counted as one of West London's classiest addresses. Still less would our average client have been numbered among the fabled "top ten thousand" then often cited in the press as constituting "society". It was also true to say that I was, at the time I am describing, somewhat becalmed and adrift in what seafarers call horse latitudes, or the doldrums. Paradoxically, this was the case despite the fact that, far from being placid, my life was generally very exercised indeed. Samuel Praed, to whom I had been articled as a solicitor and whom I had revered as a gentle mentor, had died two years previously, leaving Patrick Pumicestone as my sole principal. Mr Pumicestone, however, only graced the firm's office intermittently, claiming it as his higher calling to swim in the social stream and tickle the gills of prospective clients, thus leaving much of the actual work to me. As the train waited to depart Ipswich that afternoon I was on my way to a bit of legal business at Norwich, which would necessitate an overnight stay. I was only enjoying the luxury of a first-class cabin because the client who was subsidising the trip was uncommonly liberal with cash expenses. Though still incontestably young I felt my brow prematurely corrugated by pressing cares, and in this supposed guard I saw someone of a similar age to myself who seemed to be having the most uninhibited fun.

He was obviously an impostor, but that did not prevent him from blowing the whistle to start the engine once the platform had cleared and the doors had been slammed shut. He did this with a wave and a final shout of "Time's up...time's up...". I did not wonder that the Eastern Counties had the dire reputation it did, if it allowed any untutored fellow in a swiped greatcoat to officiate over its proper functioning. Only the previous year they had had a terrible smash at Tottenham, which had left engine, tender and coaches disarrayed on the platform in a fog of smoke, steam and debris. It was reported that the company's own accountants had recently refused to sign their books off, on the basis that mis-statements therein amounted to a deliberate perversion of the facts. So slow and inefficient were their trains said to be, that a story was doing the rounds that a Bethnal Green costermonger had raced an Eastern Counties train with his donkey and barrow, and won. Any teller of this yarn would crown it by proposing that a statue of the donkey be erected in front of the company's Shoreditch terminal in London, to advise its patrons what was in store for them if they ventured inside and bought a ticket.

Amusing though this sort of thing was, the three hours that it had already taken to shunt us from Shoreditch to Ipswich did seem excessive, and those three hours were due to be supplemented by two more before my journey was done. And this was the express train running to timetable! As was usual at that time of my life I was struggling under a weighty burden of work, and so, when I felt the first jolt of resumed motion, returned my attention to the papers I had been perusing before we stopped. But as we jerked and chugged, picking up pace out of the station, I became aware of the compartment door opening and someone jumping in along with a great concentration of smoke. In that state of perpetual near exasperation experienced by those who grind out a living between the law office and the courtroom, I was ready to perceive any intrusion as unwelcome. I looked up, and, as the smoke cleared, saw that the guard was settled opposite me on the first-class upholstery. He beamed affably, undoing the belt and coat buttons to get comfortable. When he had done so, I saw that the underlying costume was indeed one of quality, but that it was also rather less sleek and more crumpled than its extremities had announced.

Catching my eye he said, "You'll understand that I must see to it that these railway fellows do their work properly" by way of explanation. He had ditched the rural burr in favour of a more cultivated accent, but I noticed that it came out in a rather thick and slurred fashion. "I'm William Frederick Windham of Felbrigg Hall, up near the coast past Norwich," he said, "and I'll be pleased to make your acquaintance." He offered me his hand, and as I took it I offered him my own name in return.

Observing him now at close quarters, I saw a fairly thick-set young man of not displeasing features, with black hair parted in the middle and plastered down to either side. He had large, watery eyes. He also had a peculiarly small mouth, with a harelip that exposed several front teeth of the upper row. The moustache that he wore to disguise the deformity was too weedy to effectively do so. I later learned that he suffered from a congenital condition passed down from his mother's side, wherein the small mouth housed an unusually large tongue and a misshapen palate. This malformation plainly accounted for his awkwardness of speech, and contributed to an awkwardness of appearance and manner. It is unfortunately the case that many people, some of them even practising physicians and some of them otherwise quite refined, will think to diagnose mental maladies from such purely physical signs. A harelip is not the best equipment in life, inviting the ignorant, as it does, to take one look at the sufferer and remark to their fellows, "There goes a fool."

Having exchanged introductions, polite convention would allow that I carry on working and ignore him for the rest of the journey. But this particular intruder really was rather intriguing. So, instead of casting my eyes down again to my work, I found myself saying, "Forgive me for being curious but I see that you are dressed, at least in some respects, in the ECR livery. Are you employed by the company as some kind of observer of works?" I made this enquiry while not thinking for a second that it was so.

"Oh no, I'm a gentleman of leisure and only supervise works on my own estate", he replied. "The actual guard is a friend of mine who doesn't mind it one bit if I wear his coat and do his job for him while he takes a snooze in the van. They're made to work such terrific hours that they often nod off when they shouldn't. And their wages are so sinful that a small douceur here and there isn't sneezed at, so they can get something extra for the family. I said I'd work the train down as far as Ipswich, so he can take it on now, while I put my feet up here, and converse pleasantly with you."

"Forgive me again, but why would a man such as yourself work a train any distance?"

"Why, for the sheer lark of it. I know how to take charge of a train on the footplate too, and it amuses me more nearly than anything else I can think of."

I was halfway fascinated and halfway appalled. "But what of safe running? The results of a lethal machine being entrusted to unlearned hands must surely be horrific?" My instinct for litigation was bristling.

"Not at all. I've been about the railways for years and know the form as well as any regular."

"And what of the operating company, don't they take a disapproving view?"

"Well some gentlemen get up to much wilder frolics than I do, and some have longer reaches too." I took this answer to imply that a railway board might not be immune to improper influencing by their social betters. "You see," he added, "some very respectable men might feel that a spree on the way back from town, one, say, involving a crate of fizz and some girls they've just met, is best conducted in the privacy of a guards van."

So contrary was all this to the dull world of my habitation that I found it oddly enticing. "How did you come across your hobby, if I may call it that?"

"I'm inclined to put the original blame on my father", Windham replied magisterially. "He bought me a set of toy trains in my boyhood which got me in the way of it. I used to play with them in the kitchen while the servants were about their chores, opening and closing the doors and shouting out the names of the stations. I'm an only child, you see, and haven't been much blessed with companions."

This poignant note prompted him to offer me some reflections on his background and upbringing. I abandoned thoughts of working, stowed my papers in the bag next to me, and listened as we juddered and clanked though the Suffolk countryside.

My travelling companion spoke affectionately about his father who had apparently died when he was only fourteen, but who sounded to me neglectfully indulgent. As well as the toy trains, the father had had a little costume made for him in the Windham livery of blue coat, dress buttons, red waistcoat, and red plush breeches. Apparently the boy nearly wore it out before it became too small for him, carrying meals to the dining room with the domestics and serving at table as they did. Though he had more uncles and aunts than he could mention, they seldom visited and most had known little of him since he had been swaddled in nursery petticoats. They disapproved strongly of landed heirs given to waiting at tables, and, as he picturesquely put it, would rather ride three times round the park than raise their hat to him nowadays. It struck me as a very strange nurturing indeed, apparently conducted more by the occupants of the stable and the servants' hall than those of the main house. I surmised that this fact explained the fluency in Norfolk vernacular that he had demonstrated on the platform.

After the father died it seemed that Windham's mother, Lady Sophia, of whom he talked lovingly but who sounded a cold crow in my estimation, had promptly brushed her sleeve of him. She left fusty old Felbrigg Hall shuttered and sheeted and decamped to the sunnier and more artistic climes of Torquay, where she was remarried to an Italian music teacher almost half her age and less than half her station. Not feeling equal to the care of her son, who was by his own admission now hopelessly unruly, she abandoned him first to the savage tumult of Eton, and then to the governance of a series of so-called tutors who taught him nothing. It was only on his most recent, twentieth, birthday that Windham had been freed from what he described as their "strangulating superintendence."

"It was at Eton that I started slipping my minders and getting in thick with the porters at Windsor station", he said, returning at length to the railway theme of my original enquiry. "I was very ill-behaved there I'm afraid, and beaten badly for it too. 'The influence of terror' one master pleased to call a birching, though I suppose it was no worse than others endured. They called me 'mad' Windham at Eton, and not, perhaps, without cause. Bit-by-bit I got bolder in my escaping, at first hopping just a few stops in the van, and then jumping all the way up to London. I often gave the tutors who governed me after Eton the slip too, and made for the nearest station whenever I could. After that my hobby, as you have put it, was set. There's a rare freedom to it, and a rare companionship, do you see? It's made me friends all over the place, and there are plenty of railwaymen on this line who are glad to see me coming."

He rolled his head with a smile redolent of naïve self-satisfaction. No doubt operatives in need of "douceurs" would indeed welcome a benefactor's coming.

"But I'll not be carefree when I'm twenty-one in August and come into my inheritance." Clouds were occluding his hitherto sunny mood. "I'll have to play the mildewed squire then, to humour my relations and the rest of the mouldy gentry. Some people of my acquaintance think that there are things a gentleman just doesn't do, things which unfortunately account for almost everything I've ever done or said. Especially the many times I've forgotten myself and been a fool, or worked myself into passion, and then rued it."

"We are all," I said, "surely entitled to our due portion of foolishness, so long as we do not bear any malice."

"I swear that I bear no malice to anyone at all, but sometimes think I shall go melancholy mad with this world."

A curtain of pause fell on this unsettling revelation. There were times then when I felt much the same. Since Mr Praed's death there had been an understanding that I would, at some as yet unspecified juncture, succeed him as partner to Mr Pumicestone. Meanwhile, in lieu of the money contribution normally attendant on the grant of a partnership, I was to labour all hours for little more than bed and board. Our business premises doubled as the downstairs of the Pumicestone residence, and I was their upstairs boarder. Outside of the not invariably joyous company of my principal and Felicity, his daughter, recreational release came my way seldom, and in short measure.

But the Red Lion Square household was the only family I then knew. My parents, who had secured me my employment there, had passed on in quick succession soon after. And, like Windham, I am an only child.

By the time we reached Stowmarket, Windham's spirits had lifted again as our conversation swayed this way and that. But some little while into the halt he sat up abruptly saying, "Pretty doings on foot over there, my friend", and looking outside to the platform. I followed his gaze and saw that a young girl, simply dressed, with a basket and a bonnet, was striving to progress further along the train to board it, but was being persistently hindered by some coarse-grained, gnat-faced ninny. He was exhibiting the most disgraceful conduct, pushing up against her, stepping on her toes, and talking in her face. Every time she broke away from him he swivelled round and harried her anew, volubly incited by a knot of his cronies some paces distant. Anyone could see that the girl was frightened, distressed, and close to crying, but no one stirred to her rescue, not even the several railway officials who were lolling around the vicinity. As the fracas drew level with our window, we became conversant with the tenor of her tormenter's patter.

"A plain faced dollymop like you," he was drawling lasciviously, "should count herself flattered when a gentleman so good looking takes an interest in her, and not push him away." The girl was in truth quite pretty, but to admit as much obviously found no place in this man's style of courtship.

On hearing this, Windham could sit and watch no longer. Buttoning and buckling himself back into the guise of a guard, he leapt forth onto the platform urging the tough to desist. But his strongly built antagonist was obviously no stranger to roughhousing, and showed himself disinclined to take orders from guards, whether real or pretend ones.

"Get out of my lane, loony face," the tough ejaculated, "you look soft in the nut."

Then he advanced on Windham, throwing determined punches that missed striking their weaving target by mere slivers. Faced with such unbridled aggression, Windham managed to slap an ample palm on the man's face and thrust him forcefully into an iron pillar. At this point I, who had been cringing in my seat at the escalating disturbance, suddenly found it within me to act. I jumped down and grabbed the girl's wrist, pulling her into the compartment. Windham followed, and having banged the door to, fumbled a skeleton key from his pouch and turned it in the lock, shutting the miscreant out.

He, meanwhile, had launched himself at us and the velocity of his pursuit pressed him flat against the door, his features squashed to the window in a mask of grotesquery. Frustrated in his games and looking foolish in the sight of his mates, he pummelled the window and the side of the carriage and let rip a foam of foul language. Windham dangled the skeleton key defiantly at him by its ring, which only served to amplify his rage. The screams and shouts of onlookers could be heard from outside and one game old cove had begun beating the man rather ineffectually with his stick from behind. For a moment I thought that the window must shatter beneath the barrage, and that the accredited guard must still be slumbering in his van. Then at last the laggardly fellow materialised and came to our aid by blowing his blessed whistle. The train lurched into thankful motion, leaving the author of the rumpus stranded impotently outside. We three clustered together at the window, anxiously watching his dancing form fade to nothing.

It must have been simple relief at our salvation, rather than any hilarity inherent in the situation, that caused all three of us to sink to the cushions laughing. This we continued to do for some time. Once the cog of our cacophonous merriment had wound itself down, the girl was at pains to assure us that she was no man's "dollymop", as the ruffian had alleged. This demeaning epithet has now largely passed out of common usage, but was then used to describe a girl of humble situation whose response to pinched times was a resort to part-time prostitution. Now that she was safe from him, the girl seemed more concerned that we should not attach merit to her attacker's allegation than she was still rattled by his assault. I told her of my profession and offered to write to the Eastern Counties complaining of their staff's shameful inattention to the outrage. But she considered that it would do no good, as these things were wont to happen all the time. And, after all was said and done, her honour had been defended by an Eastern Counties guard had it not? Neither Windham nor I wanted to push her off this happy, but deluded, pedestal. She was, in any event, gratified that his presence appeared to officially sanction her sitting in a first-class coach for perhaps the only once of her life.

We learned that she was called Kitty Kelding, was a live-in servant at a big house near Stowmarket, and was on her way to visit her people who had a smallholding near Diss. Taking a backseat in the conversation I marvelled at what rapport Windham, the moneyed heir, had with this simple person. He did not care to assert his position as a gentleman. Slipping back into the Norfolk vernacular, he conversed easily with her as they exercised a common interest in country matters. They discussed the husbandry of sheep in relation to black ones, white ones, and ones with no tail. They highlighted points of note in the passing landscape such as market gardens, crop rotations and the fecundities of differing types of soil. They chattered sagely of livestock and produce. The girl was easy company and had some amusing anecdotes of her life in service to tell. I think we were both genuinely sorry when she got down on our arrival at Diss. Glowing with gratitude she gifted each of us a kiss on the cheek, and then floated off to find her father who was waiting to collect her in the dog-cart.

Windham and I sat in silence for most of the remaining pull to Norwich. As we drew in, he wistfully remarked that the likes of Kitty Kelding were not reserved for him.

"For fellows of my station there's 'right' girls and there's 'wrong' girls" he lamented. "And nice girls like her are always 'wrong' ones, while the 'right' ones aren't always that nice, worst luck. The young ladies I'm supposed to be charming turn-tail at the very sight of me in any case."

As we stood saying our goodbyes under the station's front arches Windham said, "Look here Phinney, we've had a jolly little escapade together and it would be a pity to end a friendship before it has properly begun. My uncle Charlie, who's been away soldiering in India these last few years, has just got back to England and is coming to Felbrigg tomorrow. He's the only one of my aunts and uncles who's ever had any time for me, and he'll have some daring doings to recount. We're throwing a bit of a homecoming celebration for him. You might totter along yourself when your business in Norwich is ended? You'll stay the night too, of course. We'll take that as given. I'll pick you up myself from this very spot. Shall we say at half-past two?"

Though I was immovably due back at Red Lion Square the next night and could think of no arguable cause to not be, I straightaway assented to this proposition. Parting from my new friend I bespoke a fly to remove me to the Norfolk Hotel, up in the main town, where I passed the night.

The next morning I appeared in a professional capacity at a Lunacy Inquisition taking place on the hotel premises. I should mention that paupers are committed to public asylums every day of the week on a doctor's say-so, and the law thinks nothing more of it. But to take control of the means of a propertied patient, at that time, the law decreed that he must endure a public hearing to determine his state of mind.

Though still in place as I write, this pantomime has now withered on the vine and been replaced by a cheaper, simpler, and above all private, mechanism that is generally preferred.

The inquisition that had brought me to the Norfolk Hotel was really the purest formality. Its subjects were a brother and sister of middle years, who had spent most of their lives in a nearby asylum. That they would never be able to care for themselves outside its walls was beyond any reasonable person's doubting. The hearing was only required so that another brother could take charge of some property they were due to inherit. My client, this other brother, was not present and had instructed me to appear there to represent his interest, but as I expected I had no great call to intervene.

Matters commenced in a barrel-vaulted hall upstairs at the hotel. As was the usual form at these things, a crowd of locals had turned out hoping to witness some display of deranged histrionics. They were all very festive and jolly to begin with, while the brother and sister sat there quietly holding hands as if a pair of death-masks at a banquet, unable to answer any of the questions put to them. But as the anticipated spectacle failed to catch hold the spectators grew silent, then restive, and then trickled off in ones and twos downstairs. The participants were left alone in the echoing hall to complete their doleful business. Both brother and sister were found to be of unsound mind, and the entire proceeding was disposed of within the hour.

A MISSHAPEN OAK

With the inquisition ended, I visited a telegraph office near the Norfolk Hotel to inform my client of its outcome. I also sent a telegraph to my principal Mr Pumicestone at Red Lion Square, saying that I would be detained an additional night in Norfolk courting a wealthy prospective client. Though this was a perfectly reasonable excuse on the face of it, touting for work from Windham was not the real reason for my failing to return to London straight away. The simple fact was that the events of the previous day had stirred an unaccustomed levity into my spirits. A fresh breeze had blown into my previously becalmed sails, and I was anxious that they should billow out still further. I was, surely, entitled to pursue my own fancy once in a while?

The Eastern Counties Railway penetrated Norfolk no further than Norwich at that time, so that any traveller for points beyond would be obliged to ride the rutted road by stage coach. As the day was clement, I planted myself on a bench outside the station to await my lift to Felbrigg as offered by Windham. Whilst waiting, I sifted half-heartedly through some legal papers in attempted recompense for my impending dereliction of duty. I could not settle to them, however, and found myself watching the world go by instead. Numerous persons and goods were set down or picked up in every variety of conveyance, and I was diverted for some time by a fussy gaggle of passengers from the London train boarding a ramshackle old coach.

In the calm, warm air I began to feel dozy. But my reverie was abruptly broken by a shout of "Make way for her Majesty's mail", and the sight of a black and scarlet Post Office mail-cart swerving too swiftly onto the station forecourt.

My alertness increased with the realisation that the cart was heading directly for my resting place, causing some dilatory individuals to jump hurriedly from its path and curse its driver. In view of yesterday's abnormalities I should perhaps have predicted it, but I was nonetheless surprised when the cart pulled up sharp in front of me and I saw William Windham seated on its top-board with its reins in his hand. Next to him was a long, thin man with a drooping moustache. This companion wore a red frock coat with bright buttons and braided cuffs, topped by a polished pot-hat with a gold band around it, which uniform marked him out as the proper Post Office driver.

"Halloo there, Phinney", Windham called down to me. Then, seeing me look sceptically at the cart he added, "You didn't think I'd roll out the livery carriage to pick up a halfpenny scrivener like yourself did you? Heave your bag aloft old chap, and clamber aboard."

Undeterred by his suggestion that I was a cheap copyist rather than a time-served solicitor, I manhandled my bag onto the roof as directed. Windham then gave me a hand up, and I squashed beside him with some difficulty, so that we were perched there three in a row with the regulation man at his far shoulder. Windham introduced him as "My good friend, Mr Green." As I shook hands with him, the fellow bore solemn witness to the fact that Mr Windham had always been a very good friend to him and his family too.

"So your hobbies run to driving mail-carts as well as locomotives", I remarked to Windham. "Is there no sprung vehicle that you would not take charge of?"

"None at all. And I wouldn't hold a lack of springs against any contraption either."

"And would it be futile of me to argue that postal vehicles are best driven by legitimate postmen?"

"Altogether futile. And I really wouldn't give the matter a second glance. After all, Mr Green is here to correct me if I go astray. I latched onto him when he passed by Felbrigg first thing. He runs his round as regular as clockwork, and as you can see it has brought us here in time to collect you. So now we have you, we'll be away, quick quick." At this Windham stirred the cart's pair into action, and we were off.

As we drove along the road pointing northward to the coast, I asked Windham about the military relative whom he had mentioned as being due at Felbrigg today.

"Uncle Charlie? Why, I've followed his adventures from boyhood, and he's sailed the seven seas to ever so many faraway places. He's a Coldstream Guardsman, and he looks flush in the full dress kit with his bearskin on. He's a general too, don't you know? And he's been showered with all kinds of medals and honours, from the French and the Italians as well as our lot. He even got a medal from their Sultan for when our army saved the Turks from the Russians."

"He fought in the Crimean War then?"

"He not only fought in it, but he was acclaimed a hero there!" Windham rolled his head and beamed at the glory he plainly felt this reflected upon him. "The so-called 'Hero of the Redan'. "

Few readers will be old enough to remember that benighted Black Sea war against Russia, which had ended five or six years previously. I recall hearing about it as it happened, and learning what a shocking travesty of arms it was widely thought to be. I will not drown you in the detail, but suffice it to say that it was a terrible conflict. In the days when I met Windham you still saw sad, derelict veterans begging for alms at roadsides in greatcoats of filthy red. And some of them were even genuine!

"What noteworthy act did your uncle perform in the war to be garlanded a hero?" I asked Windham.

"Well, when the big attack on Sebastopol came at the end of the campaign, he led a storming party with carefree abandon against a bristling fortification. It was called the Redan, and he butted his skull against it like an old tup. He rallied his men time and again, and crossed to-and-fro over the ditch and parapet for reinforcements, waving his sword through a hailstorm of rifle and grape-shot."

"Did he carry the position?"

"Oh no, but that hardly mattered a jot. He was specially mentioned to the Queen in the commander's despatch, and immediately made up to Major-General. They had an engraving of him on the *Illustrated London News* frontispiece, with laurel leaves around the border and a breathless account of his conduct."

In fact, as I recall reading about it, the final attack on Sebastopol failed across the board, but next day our army found that the besieged Russians had packed their kit and gone home anyway along a causeway across the bay. The town was ours for the taking. Our sore pride at not having won it through force of arms needed a poultice of heroism applied to mollify it, and I daresay that those who had behaved with the most insensible gusto fitted the condition.

"And he was afterwards granted an Ovation through the streets of Norwich," Windham continued, "like a conquering Roman general in olden times. The whole town turned itself out, and it was quite a triumphal procession. Uncle Charlie had me ride with him in his carriage through the packed streets, escorted by troop formations and big guns. It was quite a gala day, and there was cheering all the way from the station to the Guildhall. There were flags and banners draped about the lamps and houses, and soldiers on horseback galloping everywhere. At the Guildhall dignitaries presented him with the Freedom of the City, and a jewelled Sword of Honour, got up by subscription of the gentlemen and yeomen of the county. There was a banquet at St Andrew's Hall afterwards, with all sorts of top-hats present, and there was a great din when Uncle Charlie's health was drunk. I never heard more noise in St Andrew's hall."

I noticed that Windham's speech grew steadily more slurred as these memories aroused him to excitement. He had also begun driving more furiously than was comfortable in the un-metalled conditions, so that we were now barrelling unsteadily along the narrow and irregular country lane. I looked over at Mr Green, but he was a vision of taciturnity and unconcern.

"Won't you spare the pair a touch, Mr Windham", I appealed. "We don't want to get ahead of Mr Green's delivery schedule for the next town do we?"

"No, that's true", he said, pulling them back to a trot. "We're not due in Aylsham for a bit. And do call me Willie, as my friends are wont to."

Readily assenting to this, I asked him to return the favour by calling me George. I then enquired how his uncle's fortunes had fared once the tinselled hour of his fame had faded. "You say he's just back from India," I observed, "was he there to suppress the mutinous sepoys?" This was a reasonable supposition given that the Indian Army's mutiny that almost overthrew our oriental empire was then only a few years ended.

"He was sent there about that business, yes, and it was he who defended the bridge at Cawnpore while the commander marched up-river to relieve besieged Lucknow. You may remember reading about it in the papers? The Gwalior Contingent of mutineers swooped down on him thousands strong, and he had only a few hundred with which to check them. But he sallied out of his entrenchment and gave them a blow which fair staggered those sepoy gentlemen. The bridge was not lost and the army's supply line was saved."

As it happened, I did remember reading about this and was now able to place his uncle Charlie in my mind. But the press accounts had this General Windham disobeying orders by leaving his position to attack the mutineers, and not being mentioned in despatches as a result. An odour of disgrace clung to the affair, and clearly the uncle's return was not going to be celebrated by popular acclamation this time around. I did not say this to Windham, as I did not want to prick my companion's balloon of simple adoration for his relative.

"It's been so long since I've set eyes on him", Windham enthused, "that I'm skipping like a spring lamb at the prospect." He went on to enumerate other instances of his uncle's pluck and *élan*, and, as he did so, he inadvertently picked up the pace of his driving again until it grew quite unnerving.

Such was the condition as we entered the small market town of Aylsham. Nearing the market square, there was a blind bend which Windham took at rather a lusty stretch.

"Steady on, Mr Windham", counselled Green, and I nudged our driver's arm to get him to slow down.

But, coming out of the kink, we hurtled towards a stationary wagon which was carelessly blocking the road in front of us at right angles, where it gave onto the square. The wagon had "Wombwell's Menagerie" stencilled in gaudy letters on its side, and its roof was packed with tied-down baggage and equipment on which a number of dirty children were lounging. Its front-board was crewed by a rough-hewn middle-aged man, a hardy looking youth, and a sinewy elder woman. On its lowered tail-gate a stout woman, wearing an apron and a shawl and displaying brawny bare arms, was making up an as yet unlit brazier. She was clearly preparing to cook, when they got into position for camping, and she was surrounded by assorted articles of kitchenware. The whole equipage groaned under the weight it was bearing, which was enhanced by the bulk of a hairy camel who eyed our approach lugubriously from through the bars of a portcullis.

Calculating that Windham would be hard put to stop before hitting the obstruction, Green shouted "Make way for her Majesty's mail," which was plainly the regulation warning. He also got to his feet and signalled wildly.

This had the rough-hewn man in charge of the van frantically snapping the reigns and cracking the whip, so that it cranked ponderously into motion and lurched forward. But this upset the brazier and several of the items around the tail-gate, and they went bouncing and clattering to the ground. The woman contrived to hold on and stay put, but I need hardly say that her kitchen goods spilled onto cobblestones that were swimming in refuse and horse dung. Now seeing a gap open up behind the wagon, Windham managed to steer us toward it and squeeze us through. This unfortunately necessitated our ploughing right through the fallen kitchenware, crushing and grinding several objects into the dirt. A section of ripped tablecloth wrapped itself around our cart's axel, and dragged us to a halt on the wagon's far side within the market square. The hairy camel crossed its pen to eye us anew, while chewing upon something nutritious.

Showpeople are seldom accorded a temperate reputation in the popular mind, and these representatives of the breed did nothing to counteract that conception. The calamity was greeted with exclamations of anger and threat from the extended family that had sustained it. Several of them, led by the rough-hewn driver who appeared to be their patriarch, jumped down and examined the upturned brazier and the battered and shattered things strewn across the cobblestones. Then they glared over at us and began advancing in our direction, clearly intent upon a hostile collision. A group of bystanders scurried out of range.

"Who's going to pay for this lot?" enquired the chief of them, with a composure that was of itself a menacing display. A conciliatory atmosphere was not helped into being by the whining and yelping that the upset had incited among various wild beasts. I could now see that a number of similar vehicles, each containing at least one exotic creature, were drawn into an incomplete circle at the centre of the market place, within which a stage was being erected. This was, I supposed, how Wombwell's were given to presenting their menagerie show. I realised that the vehicle we had disturbed had, before our arrival, been queuing to take its place there.

Green went forth to parley with the man, gamely pointing out that the smash had been occasioned by his own fault in blocking the roadway, and that he must, as a consequence, take any loss out of his own pocket.

Debating the legal niceties did not appeal to the showman. "I'd sooner take it out of your hide, Mr Postman", he said, and knocked Green down with his fist.

Windham ran at him demanding to know, "Who is interfering with my friend, Mr Green?" But he too was knocked down by the man's fist.

It seemed that one was to be implicated in some kind of rumpus every day one spent in the company of William Windham. I was not, and am not, physically brave, but felt that in the circumstances I had no option but to take my companions' part. I did so and was duly knocked to the floor myself for my pains. The dispatch by their leader of all three of us was taken by his followers as their cue for a general free-and-easy at our expense. They laid into us with boots and fists and anything else to hand. The stout woman who had been on the tail-gate bashed me over the forehead with the lid of a tin pan, and I felt blood trickle from it.

Windham sustained a nasty nick from a spoon jabbed at his cheekbone.

Green, who had also shipped some injuries, rallied us to our feet and under his direction we attempted to retreat, holding onto each other for support, to the post-office which was only a few doors distant. But our assailants hemmed us against an intervening shop front and Windham, in the act of retracting his fist for a blow, crashed his elbow through its window. It was an apothecary's shop and the action dislodged several glass vials and vessels containing luridly shaded tinctures, which shattered on the tiles of the shop floor.

Suddenly I heard the crack of a horse-whip and a booming cry of "Thunderation!" I saw that a military figure in full dress uniform, his head topped by a bearskin, was bearing down upon the commotion astride a ferociously snorting bay. He sported the handlebar moustache and side-whiskers so favoured by officers at the time, though the expanse of the combination only served to emphasise how sunk back his eyes were in their sockets. His skin was weathered brown and leathery, and the fact that he was well advanced in years only enhanced the degree of mastery he conveyed.

"Get about your business you quarrelsome savages," he commanded the mob swirling around and worrying us, "get on your way I say." He addressed them while twitching the horse-whip in a manner designed to make even their very bravest flinch from its sting. These were hard people, accustomed to settling disputes in hard ways, but this mounted apparition fidgeted them and they backed off quickly, and then melted away. Our deliverer dismounted, and then handed the care of his horse to an ostler's boy before striding stern-faced into the apothecary's shop.

We reached the sanctuary of the post-office where the postmaster's wife and daughter, who had viewed the disturbance with alarm, occupied themselves tending to our wounds and soothing our nerves with words of sympathy and comfort. Hot water, liniments and bandages were produced, and a pair of tweezers was put to work picking glass out of the elbow of Windham's jacket. There was much shaking of heads and clicking of tongues on the subject of travelling people and what they were, or rather were not, good for. I managed to quash talk of involving the magistrate as I had no wish to be detained here giving an information, and still less desire to appear in the local press as party to an affray. Cuts and bruises to my face would already require explanation when I got back to the premises of Praed & Pumicestone.

Our martial saviour, meanwhile, had presumably been squaring the shopkeeper for the damage enrolled, because he was restoring his wallet to a tunic pocket as he joined us in the post-office. He removed his bearskin and sat on a stool with his elbows resting on his knees and his face cupped in his hands, contemplating Windham critically.

"I'm sadly disappointed in you, Willie", he said at length to his nephew (for he was, as you may have guessed, none other than Windham's returned Uncle Charles). "I'm sadly disappointed that my homecoming after all these years is greeted with the sight of your participation in a public brawl. Because I dislike the tremors of steam locomotion I have ridden hard all the way here from London so that we may be soonest reunited, only for me to find you sullying yourself by association with the lowest elements imaginable."

He held up a hand to cloak Windham's attempted interjection of explanation. "That you should trade blows with gutter showmen is bad enough," he continued, "but that you should do it in the neighbourhood of Felbrigg, and in a market square at that, can only redound to the dishonour of the family name throughout the county. I don't give tuppence for a bunch of tinkers, but your entanglement with them will be broadcast far and wide."

He sighed, before resuming. "And I've had other bad reports of you while I've been abroad. Accounts have reached me of your clowning on the railway, and dressing up in workman's garb, and carousing all-hours with social inferiors. What were you doing just now at the reins of a post-cart in the society of a deliveryman, and lord knows whom else?" He gestured in the direction of Green and me, between whom he seemed to draw no meaningful social distinction.

"I perceive that in my absence you've grown up like a misshapen oak might do, with all its limbs flung about it at wild angles. It is to be regretted that all your peculiarities have sprouted out this way and that, unguided and unchecked. I cannot hold myself forever at the ready to gallop forth and rescue you from the consequences of your own folly. You will be squire of Felbrigg before the year is out, and it strikes me most certainly that you must undergo a thorough overhaul of your sensibilities before you may be equal to that charge. That I have not been on hand to steer your past life to the good is a matter for my deepest shame. But I am resolved, at any rate, to ensure that your future life will not be warped similarly misshapen."

Though the general seemed to be expressing himself more in sorrow than anger, it was clear to me that his disapproval was nonetheless deeply wounding to his nephew. Still shaken by the fight, Windham looked crestfallen to have the object of a lifetime's veneration upbraid him in such harsh terms. "I fully admit my every fault, uncle," he said weakly and in a very slurred voice, "and will do whatever you prescribe to make good."

"Very well then", returned the uncle in a lighter tone. "It had occurred to me before my return, and indeed before my witnessing the disgraceful exhibition just gone by, that you would benefit from emersion in the finishing school, if I may term it thus, of a London season. You are not the first heir to need the rude bunions of his miseducation clipping off, and the

London season can be a wondrous professor of manners. It is, fortuitously, just now getting under way."

Then as now, the London social "season" began in spring when society's upper ranks quit their country estates and converged on the capital. It ended when the onset of the game shooting season in August occasioned a reverse migration.

"In point of fact, Willie, I have already engaged for you a set of chambers suitable for a gentleman in St James's, run by a couple named Lewellin. There is a bedroom and a private sitting room, and the terms provide for full board. Now that I am come home I have taken a house for your aunt and myself and your cousins at Montagu Square in nearby Marylebone, so we need not be strangers to one another."

"You desire me to leave Felbrigg?" Windham received the idea with dismay.

"I more than desire it, I require it. And I also require you to undertake a study in self-improvement while you are away. I will not countenance your mixing in low company or making a pastime of loose living. Your rooms on Duke Street will be close to the gentlemen's clubs in Pall Mall and the vicinity of St James's Square. Round the corner on Piccadilly is the Egyptian Hall, and over the way from there are the Royal Society and the Burlington Arcade. Breathe in the air of edification that such temples of culture exude. Observe the grand mansions peppering Piccadilly all the way to Park Lane, even the one that belongs to that petrified old dandy Palmerston who so hobbled our fortunes in the Crimea."

He adjusted himself on the stool and rubbed his palms over his knees, which looked like they were giving him some discomfort. "In truth," he resumed, "you would do far better by attending to the example of that real prince of affairs, the late Duke of Wellington, whose house stands proud at the Hyde Park end of Piccadilly. 'Number one, London' they used to call it, when the town started at the turnpike there. Would that I could have served with 'old nosey', but that generation was long past before my career had begun. Like Wellington before Waterloo I have been a crude soldier all my life and have passed all my nights in a bivouac, as it were. But you are heir to Felbrigg, Willie, the very dearest place in all the world, and you should aim for greater learning. You should not, at the very least, jeopardise its sylvan groves through the pursuit of inane tomfoolery."

General Windham accompanied this injunction with a very solemn stare.

"Of course, Uncle Charles", said Windham resignedly. "I will strive to gratify all that you instruct."

"Your ready compliance does you credit, my boy. I will write out some introductions for you to produce to worthy parties of my acquaintance. I will also entreat your aunt Marie, the dowager Lady Listowel, who resides in Mayfair, to guide your enlightenment. Promenade yourself daily amid the equestrian throngs at Hyde Park. Attend *levées* and *soirées*, dinners and balls, and see if you can put yourself in the position of making polite and formal house calls. You might take yourself off to the Exeter Hall, or some other house of public benevolence, to hear someone of moral authority spout off. Attend a programme of Italian Opera at Her Majesty's Theatre, or some novel theatrics at the Lyceum. I am, as I have freely admitted, an ignorant solider who knows nothing of cultured things, but I counsel you to make familiarity with them your dedicated purpose.

"Oh yes," he added, rummaging about in his whiskers, "busy yourself at the higher end of the matrimonial mart, and see if you can find a well-bred young lady with whom to adorn Felbrigg Hall."

Windham looked singularly unenthused by this last suggestion. "When must I go?"

"You may leave it a few days, while you assemble your travelling kit and say your farewells."

With this General Windham bade his nephew *adieu*, nodding cursorily to the rest of us there assembled, and set out to gallop the remaining miles to Felbrigg. We chattered intermittently while the women finished ministering to our injuries. Once they had done so the postmaster sent out for a trap for Windham and me to complete our journey to Felbrigg in, it being generally agreed that we were done with unorthodox transportation for the day. We shook hands warmly with Mr Green who lived in Aylsham and was, not unnaturally, inclined to duck his outstanding duties of that day and stay put. Windham apologised profusely for landing the postman in the wars, while Green was equally profuse in desiring Windham not to trouble himself unduly about it.

When the trap put us down at Felbrigg Hall, just as dusk was descending, I was struck by the modesty of its setting. Though the house was large enough to be the seat of a local grandee, it was no grand palace. I had imagined fancy fountains and formal gardens, but instead found that the rough pasture which constituted the parkland swept almost up to the front door. Indeed, from where we were deposited some little way from it, we were obliged to cross a patch of grassland through a small group of cattle, dodging their pats, to reach the entrance. The frontage of the house bore a kind of ancient bark-like render, bits of which had fallen away to expose flinty stonework beneath, giving it a mottled appearance in the failing light. I looked out over the park and saw that it was dotted with fenced copses and fringed all round with woods. This was an earthy place for certain, and when Windham heaved the door open the house vented vapours of manure, damp soil and stale lamp-oil.

My companion had been uncharacteristically subdued on the last leg of our journey, no doubt musing over his impending exile to the metropolis. He now apologised to me that the house was very primitive in its appointments, and lamented that I was to expect neither gas nor running water on tap, never mind any other modern conveniences. He asked if I would not mind sitting in the hallway while a room was readied for me, and then he disappeared for some time, before returning with a venerable woman whom he introduced as Mrs Jeffery the housekeeper. "I'll let you alone to spruce yourself up for tonight's festivities", he said. "Jeffy will see to everything you need."

Once he had gone, the housekeeper examined me closely by the light of the lamp that she carried, the mansion's interior being remarkably dim.

"Willie is very much taken with you, Mr Phinney", she said after apparently satisfying herself as to my appearance. "I know nothing of you or your family so you must forgive me in questioning it, but I do hope that you're worthy of his affection. He's not always the best judge of a character, and there are some who aren't slow to latch onto his weak spots. I understand that you met him while he was acting the giddy goat on the railway. You don't go in for such silly skylarking yourself I trust?"

I replied that I was a solicitor and assured her that we were not given to playacting and dressing-up, vices that we left to our wigged and tasselled brothers-at-law, the barristers.

The housekeeper managed a pale smile at this, which was more than the quip honestly merited.

"I've been in service here for a very long time," she said, her face resuming its previously anxious expression, "and I have known Willie all his life. He still trusts me as he did when he was a child, and I can truthfully say that he has always treated me as a confidential servant. You must forgive him his eccentricities, Mr Phinney. His late father was hasty and passionate with him, and his mother was woefully inattentive oftentimes. Mr Jeffrey and I have not been blessed with children ourselves, but I would venture to say that Willie's Mama, Lady Sophia, has misplaced something essential to motherhood's calling. Sometimes the parents indulged their boy, and sometimes they were very severe. You see, Mr Phinney, he would be blamed at one time for what was ignored at another."

She lowered her voice and leaned toward me conspiratorially. "And at one time, when he was little, his mother took to coming to meals with a little whip in her hand to flick him with when he was displeasing her. And that's a fact! Sometimes when she didn't want the bother of him she'd have the kitchen girls upstairs to dance and romp about to amuse him, while she played the piano out of his sight. And though there were other youngsters belonging to good families about the neighbourhood, I never saw any of them here at Felbrigg. He had no playfellows, so was mostly left to amuse himself. I'm not certain that he's ever had what you would call a proper friend to this day."

The housekeeper straightened up and resumed a normal tone of voice. "So I ask again that you allow for his eccentricities." She considered for a minute and then enquired, "You live in London do you not?"

"Yes, I live and work at Red Lion Square."

"Is that anywhere near this address his uncle would have him banished to?"

"Not so far distant."

"He sorely needs a good companion, and in London he will need one more than ever. I am greatly afraid for him there. Base temptation lurks round every corner, from what I'm given to understand. So if you are to be a friend to Willie have a care and see to it that you are a true one. Look out for his interest would you, Mr Phinney?"

I pledged to her that I would do everything for him that I could.

Mrs Jeffrey then showed me to a room off an upstairs corridor, and I was pleased to find a warming fire in its grate and a jug of hot water steaming on its sideboard. She told me that there would be some guests and some dancing later in the general's honour, and informed me of the hour by which I might think to dress and descend. Then she left me.

While washing and dressing I reflected on the happenings of the past two days, and the comments the housekeeper had just made. Windham had not known many playfellows and neither had I. We were far apart socially, but would soon be residing close by. I was, on the other hand, rattled by the fighting in the market square and anxious that such episodes should not find a regular berth in my life. The world that I had entered with Windham was outside my customary field of experience. Perhaps it was a world best dipped into and then quitted at the first chance? I reasoned that future contact from Windham was in fact unlikely, given our differences in status, and resolved myself content that after this evening our friendship should lapse.

Having straightened myself out on this point, after a fashion, I descended the stairs and followed the sounds of laughter and chatter I heard until they led me into Felbrigg's Great Hall. In the bright lantern light with which the room was illuminated, a gathering of those ladies and gentlemen who presumably constituted local society was assembled. They were dotted about, eating and drinking, in talkative and congenial groups. One length of the room was lined with trestle tables, bearing gloriously presented sweetmeats and elaborately moulded confections of jelly. Halfway along the display was a sizable ceramic punch-bowl, decorated with oriental characters and pagodas, with the handle of a ladle protruding invitingly from it. In the alcove of a floor-to-ceiling bay window at the far end, a small orchestra was setting up, and bunting was draped across the room from lintel to lintel. Bunting also graced several very large but very gloomy examples of country house portraiture, investing them with a much more cheerful aspect.

I stood uncertainly at the door, absorbing the colourful spectacle. Then I spotted Windham waving at me to join him, and a grizzled but benign looking man, where they were seated on the cushioned surround of another broad bay. Once I had crossed over to them Windham introduced the other to me as Mr Jeffrey, bailiff to the estate and husband of the housekeeper. The two of them were apparently supping their way through their own exclusive pitcher of punch sited on a little table at arms reach, and Windham poured me a cup from it and recharged theirs. He was telling the bailiff about the incident at Aylsham, which both of them were treating as an occasion for guffaws. It may have been due to a sudden release of tension, or to the unaccustomed effect of liquor splashing around my insides, but I was soon laughing as heartily as they were.

When he had finished telling his story Windham looked at me with a more serious expression. "We had a lucky escape from a very nasty scrape, didn't we George?"

Indeed we had, I agreed. Reversing myself on an instant, I now hoped that our friendship might endure.

The rest of the evening spreads out in my recollection as something of a smudge. I went on carousing with the heir and his bailiff, and helped myself to food from time-to-time. At length the tables were cleared away, the floor-rug was rolled and folded, and the miniature orchestra began to play.

We joined in with the dancing, which was conducted with such verve that the floorboards bounced in tandem with its cadences. Examining the glowing folk about me, I realised that these people formed no local "society" as I had first supposed, but were instead tradesmen and tenant farmers and their wives, daughters and sons. A lot of whooping and shouting went on, and during one dance Windham jumped about, walked backwards, and beckoned to a girl on the sidelines to come across to him, and then kissed her on the forehead when she did. He then trod upon one man's toes, apologised, then swore, and when someone afterwards trod upon his toes took up his foot in his hand and hopped across the floor. All this was received with gales of hilarity, and Windham played up to it as the most magnanimous of hosts. These were more boisterous revels than I had ever known, and I was gripped by a sense that I had neglected, up to that time, to address the task of properly living.

But such expansive feelings were not universal in all quarters. General Windham, now in civilian evening dress, did not present himself until late-on despite being the subject of the jollification. He received the welcoming accolades given to him by his nephew and some others with a tolerable grace, but took no part in the dancing. He passed most of the remaining proceedings seated at the centre of a staid little group that included someone Mr Jeffrey told me was the family solicitor, a Mr Portal. The General starred intently at his nephew's somewhat exaggerated antics, looking haggard and cross.

THE PRETTY HORSEBREAKER

The atmosphere at the Pumicestone dinner table next evening was far less exuberant. Mr Pumicestone, his daughter Felicity and I sat in the little dining room at Red Lion Square, mostly in silence, being waited upon by Anna, the house's maid-of-all-work. There was also a cook, who went home after she had seen to the meal, and during business hours we had a hall-boy in the offices on the ground floor. Though unfashionable our part of Holborn was at least respectable, inhabited as it was by middling tradespeople and those pursuing the lesser professions. Our household was more prosperous than those of many neighbours in not needing to sub-let its top floors, but it was about average in having just the one live-in servant. It was a narrow town-house in the elegant Eighteenth Century style, located mid-terrace towards the small square's south-eastern corner.

I had awoken at Felbrigg to a throbbing head and an upset stomach, and had endured the bone-shaking journey home in pronounced discomfort. Before departing I had spoken briefly to Windham, who had seemed unafflicted by the previous night's excesses, and who had pledged to inform me once he was installed in London. I had no appetite for dinner and the fumes from the gaslight caught in my throat and made me feel queasy. All I wanted to do was excuse myself and retire to bed, but knew better than to interpret the fact that Patrick Pumicestone was saying nothing for the time being as signifying that he had nothing to impart.

We adjourned to the front parlour after dinner. My principal persisted in wearing the sort of swallow-tailed counting house coat that even then belonged to a past generation, and he flicked its tails to either side as he sank into his armchair. He was a bulky man, with thinning grey hair and a sallow complexion. What thatch he held onto stuck upwards and was overdue for a trim, and his general turnout was a rumpled one. His daughter, in contrast, though no natural beauty was neat and possessed of youth's bloom. She might have used this to greater effect, however, if she had managed to illuminate it more often with bursts of cheerfulness. She settled herself recumbent on the sofa and propped a volume from the circulating library in front of her face. Her eyes were chestnut, and her hair was of an auburn shade. Just as there was an understanding that I would at some unspecified time become a partner to Mr Pumicestone, there was an understanding that Felicity would at the same unspecified time become my wife. I was no longer certain that either of us was in full accord with this plan.

Though the evening was mild a fire had been set in the grate, the heat of which only served to increase my discomfort. As Mr Pumicestone was in no hurry to arrive at the point in hand, and his daughter projected a frosty detachment, we remained in silence for some time. He examined today's paper in detail, successively folding and refolding its leaves and rotating it this way then that.

After studying the Court Circular page he remarked at last in Felicity's direction, "It seems, my dear, that our George Phinney revolves in only the topmost social circles this season. We might expect to see his name sometime soon in the press as an honoured guest at some high-blown function. He has been in Norfolk courting a prospective client named Windham of Felbrigg Hall, when we thought he was only up there on an everyday lunacy inquisition. I know all this because his telegraphic message of yesterday told me as much."

Felicity went on reading her book and made no pretence of listening, but her father continued to aim his remarks in her direction.

"George also told me in his message that he was planning to pass last night at this man Windham's country retreat, and was therefore obliged to absent himself from his work here today. Now then, my dear, who might these Windhams be and are they worthy of George's stay at their house?"

No response being forthcoming from his daughter, Mr Pumicestone continued along his merry way. "Well now, I have ascertained from my own researches that they are no breed of straw-men. This William Windham's mother was born Lady Sophia Hervey, one of the daughters of the Marquis of Bristol who is recently deceased, and the present Marquis is an uncle no less. And one of his aunts on his father's side is the Dowager Countess of Listowel. That's only an Irish peerage with no House of Lords seat, but it's a peerage all the same. All–in-all, it's fair to say that these Windhams are most handsomely connected. They make the bill-discounters and commissioners of works who are the best class of patron we generally drag in appear small beer indeed. George deserves our congratulations for whistling them into the Praed & Pumicestone fold and closing the gate. Wouldn't you agree, Felicity?"

She peered round her book at him with a studiedly expressionless face, and then returned her eyes to her reading.

"But the one essential that George's message is lacking," Pumicestone continued worrying away at the matter, "the one fact that it does not contain, is the precise nature of the legal conundrum in question. One is left wondering as to what business this Windham consulted him upon as they were sequestered together in the comfort of his mansion last evening. George must have made a very favourable impression on him. Perhaps the young squire wanted his advice on how best to market the estate shooting rights, or on how to go about twisting the arm of Lord Palmerston for a dukedom? One is also left to speculate as to where this consultation might leave the local firm of solicitors that the Windham family has doubtless retained since the time of the flood. One marvels that a London courtroom hack proves so much the better oracle to a country gentleman than his local chap."

I lacked the energy to muster a fighting opposition to this satiric tirade. There was an occasional table to Pumicestone's right hand, and from it he lifted and inked a pen and raised it to the top of a clean sheet of paper. He then wrote various details thereon by way of a header. "Let us proceed to particularise," he said with a look of mock expectancy, "the lucrative legal instructions that George has returned from Norfolk with; instructions that justify his bunking off a day's work here and obliging me to give up a day at my club to wait on clients."

"Oh Papa, you're rather sticking it to him aren't you?" Felicity interjected irritably before I had a chance to reply. "And it's becoming tiresome too. Talk about something interesting, or pipe-down and let me read my story."

"If I 'stick it' to him, my summer rose, it's because he has grave responsibilities, and not the least of those to you. If he is to be admitted as my partner and is to enter an...", he searched for a suitable word, "...altered relationship with my daughter, then he must be fastidious at all times in discharging his duties."

"We know all that, Papa, and you do contrive to make George and me sound so romantic" returned

Felicity, exhibiting an ability to rival her father in the sarcasm steeplechase. She lowered her book to her lap. “Why don’t you ask the poor lamb what he has really been doing out in Norfolk, and where he came by those scratches and bruises that he has tried so artlessly to disguise?”

The borrowed compact that I had dabbed here and there at Felbrigg that morning had clearly been wasted on her. Pumicestone examined me and perceived the blemishes for the first time.

“He prides himself on his honesty,” Felicity asserted, “so we may take what’s written in his telegram, as far as it goes, as undiluted fact. As to the rest...” she flapped the back of her hand at her father by way of authorising him to resume his interrogation.

“Where did you come by those knocks then, George?” her father obliged her by asking.

“In a fight.” This reply of mine made them both sit up.

There was now no option but to furnish some account of my adventures. “I did indeed stay at Felbrigg Hall on the invitation of its heir Windham,” I elaborated, “but did so purely as his guest. He did not entrust any legal work that I could mention to my safe keeping, nor did he hold out any prospect of his doing so at any future date.”

“Never mind all that frightful dustiness,” said Felicity, leaning forward and showing a glimmer of concern, “what about the fisticuffs?”

“Well, Windham was sprinting me from Norwich to Felbrigg in a public vehicle...”

“A what?” asked Felicity.

“It was a postman’s mail-cart.”

“Oh, I see.”

I proceeded to put as favourable a slant on the incident at Aylsham, and my meeting Windham in the first place, as their circumstances and my enfeebled condition would permit. Though it disclosed nothing of any businesslike substance, Patrick Pumicestone nonetheless took a verbatim note of my answer, as was his practice when he was in a contentious mode. Occasionally he would add some annotation to his note, presumably by way of private commentary, or underline a particular word or passage. When I explained that Windham had jumped into my compartment in the guise of a guard, Pumicestone repeated my words back to me ostentatiously as he recorded them.

"It's all quite clear to me now, George," was Felicity's comment when my narrative was concluded, "that this man you've fallen in with is as mad as a firefly, and he's led you astray. We really must arrange for you to be supervised by some responsible party next time we let you go out and about. Who knows who you might take up with?" She gifted me one of her rare smiles. "Still, you're back now and restored to your senses so far as one can judge it, and we must be grateful for that." She yawned and resumed her reading.

Her father was less content. "Make sure that you acquaint me of the fact if this Windham character renews contact", he directed. "If he shows any sign of having any worthwhile patronage to throw our way then grab at it. If not, then you must cut him off." He then allowed me to at last creep up to my bed, wherein I fell asleep instantly.

A few weeks of being steeped back in my wearisome routine later, Windham did get in touch and I did acquaint my principal of it. The heir of Felbrigg sent me a telegram saying that he was lodged at the St James's address that his uncle had secured, and inviting me to call round the next evening. He also proposed an outing to the park.

One of the grand pastimes of the "season" was to promenade around Hyde Park, weather permitting, either up and down Rotten Row on horseback or along its driveways in a carriage. This was considered to constitute a far more glamorous spectacle than its equivalents at Longchamp at Paris or the Unter den Linden at Berlin. And you may recall that it was one of the activities General Windham had recommended his nephew to engage in during his sojourn in London. I had viewed it while out strolling in the park on a few occasions, but had never imagined myself as the sort of person who would participate in this equestrian pageant. It reached its height at six in the evening on a fine day in the season, and Windham's message fixed the hour of our meeting at five.

Having rounded off my work on the day given with some business at Whitehall, I crossed Horse Guards and St James's Park on my way to the appointed address. The terraced house, at number 35 Duke Street, was respectably presented and looked recently erected. Brightly striped awnings hung from every window. I pulled the cord and the door was answered by a man who introduced himself as its landlord, David Lewellin.

"Mr Windham is our most prized gentleman guest," he said after I had given my own name and the reason for my visit, "and he told us to watch out especially for your coming. Any friend of Mr Windham's is by his very nature a friend also to us. Augusta...Augusta," he called, "Mr Phinney the lawyer is upon us."

His wife bustled down the passage exclaiming, "Is that Mr Phinney, the brief?" They invited me in with a good deal of show and fuss, as if I was the most important person they had had in the house all year. I did not trouble to tell Mrs Lewellin that only barristers might correctly be termed "briefs", and that even then the usage would be woefully colloquial.

The interior was scrupulously clean and sprucely furnished, though there was a vague overhanging whiff of disinfectant. Given this, I noted the somewhat rakish appearance of its proprietors with a pinch of surprise. David Lewellin was dressed in working corduroys, with a handkerchief knotted around an unshaven neck.

Perhaps he had been at some labouring job in the garden before I arrived? Augusta was a redhead wrapped in several coarse shawls, and her tiny forearms supported a number of unruly bangles. Slight in stature, the pair stood at almost precisely the same height.

As they showed me busily up the stairway Mr Lewellin confirmed, in response to my enquiry on the subject, that the house was fairly recently built. He added that it had, at least in some respects, been constructed in accordance with their very own specifications. "We wanted gas mantles in every room and corridor," he said, "and we've got them. And we wanted a flushing water-closet, and we've got that too. It's quite some crib."

"And we've got hot and cold water on tapped flow," Mrs Lewellin chipped in, "except during the company's night time dry-out. You can pour yourself a bath down the passage even while you're lying in the tub, without having girls to-and-fro with buckets. Not that we don't have enough girls to see to it of course."

"Benjamin Disraeli himself stayed in the house occupying the plot before ours did back in the thirties," Mr Lewellin asserted, "and we're all for Mr Disraeli."

"And now we've got Mr Windham," his wife took up the theme, "and we're all for him too. Since he's been with us we've had some mighty jollifications together. Isn't that true, Mr Windham?" She knocked on a half opened door off the first floor landing while at the same time peering within, "are you at home?"

Windham's face appeared round the door beaming out at us. "My dear Mrs Lewellin," he said inviting us into his sitting room, "and my good friend George too." He patted my shoulder and squeezed my hand. "Well well, now we are reunited we must have something together to mark the occasion. Will you take a glass of fizz, George? Of course you will. Mr Lewellin my dear Sir, would you be so good as to fetch one of my best necks of champagne from the cellar; of course you and Mrs Lewellin must help us in draining it too."

The couple protested that they could not bring themselves to bung up a private celebration with their presence, but when Lewellin returned from the cellar he carried four glasses not two. The conversation that ensued was rather too voluble for my tastes, though I was soon slightly anaesthetised to it by the champagne. I was glad when Windham ended it shortly by asking Lewellin to arrange for our transportation to be wheeled out front. Bearing in mind the happenings at Aylsham, I was less than reassured when we got outside to discover that the vehicle was a racing phaeton. With an open twin seat suspended between two big wheels at the rear and two small ones at the front, it looked an ideal chariot for catching a spill in. You could see why it appealed to Windham, who had no doubt specified it to Lewellin as the type to hire from the livery stable.

My friend and I exchanged glances. "I'll drive today, if you don't mind", I proposed, though I felt a bit light-headed. All his instincts plainly rebelled against bequeathing me the reins, but he governed them sufficiently to nod in companionly acquiescence.

As I piloted its pony along Piccadilly at a steady pace I asked, "How are things coming along in London?"

"Very well, my dear fellow. I'm getting to know my way around, and this chap Lewellin seems to have the gift of arranging for anything to be done." This sounded ominous enough as far as it went, but Windham suggested worse with a wink.

"How fares your uncle's direction that you devote yourself to a season of cultural pastimes? What of the *levées* and *soirées*, the forays to see museums and hear men of high morals hold forth?"

"I would mark my efforts to date in that relation as no better than evens."

"Where have they fallen short?"

"In that I have not attempted to do any of those things at all. And as my uncle neglected to mention," Windham indicated behind us with his thumb, "at the wrong end of Piccadilly resides the Devil's Acre." He was referring to the Haymarket area, that notorious blister on the West End where it was all dives and divans and soiled doves. I knew of its existence and would not have conceived of straying there even as a sightseer. I also remembered my promise to Mrs Jeffery to try and keep Windham from harm.

"You're surely not going to waste your time here in a season of dissipation?"

"Am I not then?" he replied enigmatically. "But don't worry; our mission this evening is entirely in line with Uncle Charlie's wishes. He wants me to see his sister Marie, my aunt who's the widow of the Earl of Listowel. I never met him and I haven't seen her for ever so many years and don't suppose she'll recognise me, but I thought you might like to meet a titled lady. No doubt she's enlisted in my uncle's campaign to keep me on the straight and narrow. We're to rendezvous with her carriage in the park, somewhere near that old house of Wellington's that my uncle thinks so fondly of."

We had by now reached Hyde Park Corner and were caught up in a great mass of traffic and a great racket of hooves and wheels grinding over the granite sets. There was a current of traffic striving to exit the park through one carriage archway, and a counter current striving to enter through another. A third tendency sought merely to carry on past in either direction. An equestrian statue of the Duke of Wellington stood on top of a huge arched pedestal, which was opposite the park entrance and the duke's former residence of Apsley House. His outstretched arm pointed far away in an entirely different direction, possibly to the site of one of his battles. Equally jumbled up in the jam were solitary riders and every variety of carriage with their drivers, and salary men sitting back-to-back on the knife-boards of omnibus rooftops. Somehow the blockage remained fluid enough for me to edge us by degrees into the park, all the while ignoring Windham's suggestions that I cut in here or there to steal a march on some sluggard.

Once through the arches, Windham looked about for a sighting of his aunt's carriage. There were some, but not her one, parked at the end of sandy Rotten Row, which was reserved for riders and their mounts. These were present in an astonishing variety and profusion. As far as I could see along its great length, Rotten Row was a bobbing flow of glossy top hats and fancy velvet caps. All of their wearers set about the business of being seen in society with poise and solemnity. There were lordly young ladies cantering side-saddle, and galloping young bucks, and nurses trotting with their little charges on ponies, and prancing old aristocrats. All the riders were groomed to perfection, to say nothing of their majestic mounts, and everywhere sunlight glinted on spurs and shiny boots. We moved on past the end of the carriage drive that led to the Serpentine, which was clogged with a string of drags and four-in-hands and a stream of pedestrians. It may have been down to the "fizz", but being on show in the park at the reins of a nippy phaeton puffed me into thinking myself the regular swell.

We soon identified the Listowel equipage from its livery, and saw that it was drawn up opposite the giant statue of ancient Achilles. This figure was fashioned from melted down cannons captured in Wellington's battles against the French, and it posed in a warlike posture with splayed legs, and sword and shield in hand. It also stood completely naked.

I plugged the phaeton into a nearby space, and once Windham and I had got down handed the halter to one of those tattered types who would pop up whenever an animal needed minding in those days. Lady Listowel was reclining in a large landau with its top down, attended by two grooms in comically outdated costumes sitting stiffly on its rearward rumble. They wore the tricorned hats and knee-britches and hose of a bygone era, and their shoes sparkled with silver buckles. The driver, seated rigid and straight-backed, was similarly costumed, except that he had on a rounded hat, crimped at the edges, which looked medieval in conception.

"It's so frightfully crowded today we couldn't find anywhere else to stop." Lady Listowel made this remark when the needs of introduction had been met and Windham and I were positioned opposite her in her carriage. She was rouged and lacy in an aristocratic fashion. "Now we have to endure the sight of that horrid thing", she said of the Achilles statue. "You'd think that a public subscription would be got up to at least have a fig leaf put on it."

As he had predicted, Windham's aunt had not recognised her nephew straight away, and she showed no sign of pleasure at being seen entertaining either of us. When he had introduced me as an attorney, she scanned me sceptically as if disbelieving that it was physically possible for such a nonentity to draw breath in her carriage. Perhaps it would have been even less agreeable if we had been observed on the front stair of her town-house. The conversation was stilted to an acute degree, and consisted mostly of Lady Listowel telling Windham what he should and should not do while he was in London.

"Here are the private cards of some of my lady friends," she said to him at one point, "who have daughters of marriageable age. I trust that you will approach them, if approach them you must, with the utmost circumspection. Your Uncle Charles said that you were to have some introductions in order that you might finesse a travail of courtship, but it is against my better judgement. There is certainly a better class of filly on show in London in season than in the sticks the rest of the year round, though my own view of your chances here is that the lower you set your sights in terms of a girl's looks the better they will prosper. I can see that you have grown up to a limited degree, but there remains much room for improvement in your general deportment and demeanour. I do think that you might use your handkerchief from time-to-time to hide that unsightly deformity, and to wipe the flecks that gather at the corners of your mouth. And you really might serve your cause better back out in Norfolk. I'm sure that there are plenty of plain young ladies waiting to be partnered to Norwich quarter session balls?"

"It is not by my own choice that I am presently unavailable to partner plain girls at Norfolk balls." Windham's relative was obviously irritating him considerably. "Uncle Charlie decreed my banishment."

"Indeed so, but you must try and conduct yourself correctly while you are in town. If you will call at one of the addresses I have furnished then do so strictly between the hours of two and four, when the young ladies and their mothers may be expected to be 'at home.' And even then, do no more than leave your own card. Do not expect to be invited within, and do not expect any invitation to issue at all within at least the ensuing week. It is much the pity that I have to spell these refinements out for you, but you remain a primitive in social matters."

As Lady Listowel continued to outline the applicable courtship protocols, my attention faltered and then drifted off from listening to her altogether. But then it was seized by a most compelling sight.

Directly across the way from us, and directly beneath the statue of the indecent Greek, an open barouche had drawn up which contained a striking young woman. I say "contained", but it would be more accurate to say that she was "arranged" in the conveyance. She was more recumbent than seated, and the voluminous blue crinoline robe that she wore appeared inflated around her like a gas balloon. Before she had set off it must have needed someone to tuck it in and press the door closed against it. Her gown was braided charmingly in gold at the cuffs and at the corsage, which followed faithfully the curvature of her bust. None of the shapeless and flattened ladies drapery of today could excite half the wonder of this fetching garment. It framed her diminutive form so very well. And she was so fascinating to watch in what seemed her state of perfect repose. Her head floated above the blue waves of the robe, and her complexion was creamy white. Golden hair protruded from under a blue and white velvet cap, enlivened to one side by a pink rose, and above that sailed a parasol. The whole ensemble appeared one of natural grace, though doubtless the effect was really the fruit of much labour.

Forgive my overwrought prose, but you may suppose that I was much taken with her. Observing her closely, I noticed that she attracted a considerable amount of discreet attention from both sexes. It slowly dawned on me that she was actually holding court, with the opulent carriage for her throne room. Passing young men would slow their pace and shoot her diffident glances, before spurring their beasts on. More mature gents in dark frock coats would circle expectantly in her vicinity, affecting indifference but desperate to snare her vision. At once one of these might catch her eye, raise his hat, and know by some secret sign that he might approach, but just as soon be dismissed. Another might make three or four passes by, always just missing the inviting line of her eye, and never quite drawing close. One favoured suitor made so bold as to tether his horse and stride to the very gate of her carriage. He was rewarded for a while with sunny smiles and chatter, before an ever so slight frown informed him that the audience had reached its close. Well-heeled women, on the other hand, observed her performance with perceptible disquiet.

All the while I had been watching this spectacle, Lady Listowel had proceeded to lecture her nephew. I now looked at his countenance and saw that his eyes were dilated and his jaw had dropped slack. His expression was entirely vacant. I had been riveted by the vision in blue crinoline, but he was mesmerised by it. His aunt at last realised that our attention was glued elsewhere and turned her head to follow our gaze.

"I wonder," I blurted out without really meaning to be so gushing, "what might be the wellspring of such ebullient waters?"

"What indeed", agreed Windham. "She must have torrents of the very finest blood."

On hearing this, Lady Listowel heaved with derisive laughter. "I wouldn't give a farthing a bucket for that slattern's blood. Do you think her people came in with the Plantagenets? Why, you're nothing but a pair of credulous young pups."

"Who is she then? Windham asked, still transfixed.

"She calls herself Agnes Willoughby," his aunt supplied the answer, "but it's generally known that she's actually a 'Smith' or a 'Jones' or some such. I can't speak to her parentage precisely, but everyone knows she was born a common peasant girl. They say her father was a village sawyer and her mother was a milkmaid. It is part of her calling to pretend much, but there's no substance to any of it. She may not patrol the Haymarket at midnight or dance with jolly jack tar at his dockside revels, but she's a girl of accommodating morals just as surely as those women are. They term her sisterhood 'the pretty horsebreakers.' I don't know all their names, apart from hers and that of Catherine Walters whom they call 'Skittles' for some ghastly reason. Anyway, they're all at each others' throats. They're every one of them harlots, and if I had my way the whole troupe would be turned out of the park tomorrow." She tossed her rouged and lacy head in the direction of the gates.

You may think it shocking to hear such forthright language coming from a Dowager Countess, but she was raised in the more forthright regency age and was obviously much exercised on the matter. There had been a lot in the press lately about the so-called "pretty horsebreakers." The term had apparently first been applied to attractive women hired by livery stables to ride their most imperious beasts in the park by way of self-advertisement. Whether any of those women currently attracting the epithet had ever done so I cannot say for certain.

There had recently been an entertainingly fake correspondence on the subject in *The Times*. Someone had written to the editor, supposedly on behalf of "seven Belgravian mothers", and this letter had become generally known as "the Belgravian lament." The correspondent had purported to be the aristocratic mother of seven girls, "in running" to be married off. She wrote to complain that wealthy heirs were not interested in her or her friend's well-bred daughters because they preferred the company of pretty horsebreakers, who neither expected nor demanded marriage. Then someone purporting to be one of those wealthy young heirs (signing himself "Primogenitus") wrote in reply. He confirmed that he was not interested in boring old aristocratic girls and the marriage machinations of their mothers. Pretty horsebreakers shone far brighter and were more appealing in every regard, and through his association with them he proposed to postpone indefinitely the catastrophe of marriage. I subsequently learned that the true author of "the Belgravian lament" was a journalist named James Matthew Higgins, who did this sort of thing a lot. His best known pen-name was "Jacob Omnium", and he had a fetish for spurious groupings of seven at the time. I suspect that he also authored the "Primogenitus" response.

"But how can anyone with her obvious grace and style be anywhere near the sort of harlot you allege?" Windham protested vehemently to his aunt, as if someone dear to him had been slandered.

"Really Willie, you're every bit the imbecile you were as a child, and I'm sorry to detect that you still haven't mastered the art of speaking clearly without slurring. Harpies like her don't live by way of the one-off douceur as does the street walker you envisage. Her only requirement in a man is that he must be able to stand her ever more expensive gifts. One must pay for the carriage, another must subsidise driver and groom. She looks to a third to furnish the costume. Despite the cheap gaudiness that you confuse with style, society does not know her and our drawing rooms are swept mercifully clean of her presence. She most likely inhabits a miniature villa in some neighbourhood where nobody in the swim of things would live, and has a yappy little dog she's christened 'Fluff'. When she sits in a box at the opera it's rented for the night, and so are the brilliants beatifying her scrawny gizzard. When she has the sheer brass-neck to ride out with staghounds, because some simpering young dummy thinks it'd be 'going the pace' to ask her along, she flops down at an hotel rather than at the host's place. One doesn't mix a wine of price with the *vin ordinaire.*"

Hearing this, it struck me that it must have taken great courage and self-possession on the part of this young woman to brave the disapproval of those like Lady Listowel who were assured that they were "Ladies" by divine right. Like the statue Achilles' outsized musculature and pantomime sword, all their breeding could not prevent a feral pigeon like Agnes from soiling their garlanded heads.

"And of course she has no fine sentiment in her whatsoever" Lady Listowel rattled onward. "I have heard that she found out that one lord she was entertaining had no cash and had outrun the constable. He came to great grief and had to enlist in the Royal Artillery. It wasn't likely that she would take any interest in him after that, and she let him enlist without demurring. She wasn't going to waste her time traipsing after a full private. People of breeding can see through a pale *demi-mondaine.* You men let your taste be tipped by any sulky sparrow, but cultivated Ladies can see beyond your lustfulness and their loathsome pretension."

"I don't give a damn about people of breeding," Windham returned with palpable anger, "and don't see why a man shouldn't prefer a horsebreaker if he wants one, or she him. And I'd be glad to learn how you can talk of 'fine sentiment' when you and the rest of the family stopped me from seeing Adele at Antingham? It seems that I'm encouraged to partner a plain protestant girl to a ball, but when it comes to someone of perfectly good family who happens to be Roman Catholic I'm to be put off." His aunt's strictures had clearly loosened a cause for deep rancour within Windham's remembering.

He turned to me indignantly, explaining, "I met this sweet young thing, Adele, while out riding in Antingham parish near Felbrigg. Her horse became restive, and as she had no servant with her I rode up and assisted her as any gentleman might. I got the animal by its bridle and settled it down, and prized the stone that had occasioned the upset from its shoe. I visited her several times afterwards as a friend, and she was kind to me. We might easily have become sweethearts. But then my family got wind of her people's religious disposition, and warned them off. I heard soon after that they had moved away from the district for good."

"No one's going to apologise to you on account of that, Willie", his aunt retorted icily. "We sought merely to prevent you from sullying the purity of your heritage."

"Do you see it, George? I'm forever the idiot to be talked down to and have things settled for him over his head. I'm forever to be told to wipe my mouth so as to not embarrass anyone. How would it be if I were to settle my own affairs for once? How would it be if that pretty horsebreaker over there and me were sweethearts? Why don't I wave to her now, and see if I can't attract her attention?"

"Don't be so wilfully absurd, Willie", said Lady Listowel, assessing her nephew's threat as mere bluster. "You wouldn't dare make such an atrocious scene."

She was probably right, but I was in no doubt that if someone in her company did wave to a despised horsebreaker then it would be a sin beyond her forgiving.

"Why don't I go over to her, right away?" continued Windham, his diction slurring terribly in his agitation. "So what if she lacks all 'fine sentiment', she can hardly have less of it than my family, who are supposed to be the ones that cherish my feelings closest to their hearts."

Lady Listowel looked coldly at her nephew. After a while she said in a chilly tone, "I think that you and your little office clerk friend can get down now, Willie. And you can return those address cards to my safe keeping before you go."

Windham duly restored the cards to her outstretched, gloved hand. We did get down, and after she had let her nephew know that his Uncle Charles would hear the facts of the encounter, we watched the Listowel equipage trundle off.

Windham gazed across at the so-called pretty horsebreaker. "Why don't I go to her now?" he recited softly, as if in a trance.

"Women like that aren't meant for ordinary mortals" I counselled him, sagely.

But I did not like the fixed look in his eye. I saw then that he was awfully suggestible, and that he needed to have a care what he wished for in case it came to pass. Needless to say, the exotic object of his interest showed not the tiniest flicker of noticing either of us.

AN ASCOT INTRODUCTION

The locomotive powers of steam notoriously collide with what is respectable, and drive it out. Though salubrious no doubt before the South-Western Railway planted its terminus here, the tall terraces lining the Waterloo Road were now mostly decrepit, and the narrow byways off it forbidding to say the least. Down one of these a scruffy knot of loungers was visible, likely to size one up for who knows what bullying if one strayed off the main drag. I was walking from Waterloo Bridge toward Waterloo station along with a variegated crowd of excursioners, all intent on swapping its smoky vicinity for the fresh air and country climes of Ascot Heath.

Some little time after our evening in the park, Windham had proposed that I join the Lewellins and himself for a jaunt to Ascot races, and I was due to meet them with a view to catching the ten-fifty a.m. down train. Mr Pumicestone had reluctantly consented to my vacating the required working day, on condition that I did not let the chance to importune Windham for business slip. We both knew, however, that a gentleman of Windham's lineage was unlikely to entrust any London legal business he may have to a middling firm in the vicinity of Red Lion Square. He would sooner look to the more exclusive localities of Grey's Inn and Bedford Row that bordered it, or to chambers elsewhere in the metropolis known to minister to the gentry.

As I met my party by the stairs leading to the main line ticket office as prearranged, David Lewellin asked me "Have you walked it all the way over here?" He was decked out in a loud bottle green suit and matching bowler hat, though he was still unshaven. "If we'd have known you were on foot," he added, "you could have had a chair in our growler."

He referred to the four-wheeled hackney carriage for which this was the going slang. It seemed not to have occurred to him that his plan would have involved my walking, or going by hansom, all the way to his house in the first place. I had actually boarded an omnibus of the fancifully named "Favourite" line on High Holborn, and had got off on the Strand side of Waterloo Bridge.

Lewellin's wife Augusta had on a canary yellow crinoline with a bright pink bonnet, and she had a multicoloured shawl draped around her shoulders. She was also carrying a wickerwork hamper, and the two of them looked as pleased as punch.

Windham appeared downcast on the other hand. "Good to see you, George", he greeted me. "I've been a bit out of sorts lately and hope today's jolly will blow the cobwebs off."

I asked him what had occasioned the slippage in his spirits.

"It's that horsebreaker woman he saw in the park the night he was in company with you", Augusta Lewellin interjected. "He's imbibed a passion for her, and thinks he's in love. He told us all about it." She nudged his ribs with her elbow and let out a rather smutty chuckle.

Her husband let out a similar one, before adding, "But he's in a fix for the lack of an introduction to her. Wouldn't you know that the people he knows aren't the same as the people she knows?" He accompanied this with a raised eyebrow, which intimated that he knew very well what sort of people were what.

"Do *you* happen to have her card handy in your pocket-book, Mr Phinney?" the female member of the partnership enquired rhetorically, this time nudging me in the ribs. At this insinuating witticism both husband and wife guffawed.

"But we shouldn't make fun of the poor love", Mrs Lewellin continued. "We've nothing but fondness for our Mr Windham, and think that nothing that comes his way can come fondly enough. That's why Mr Lewellin suggested this day out you see."

"I said to him," Lewellin confirmed his wife's account, "you'll find balm for your upset in a dose of Berkshire breezes, Mr Windham. You know that a woman like her would only drive you dog-mad, so you should be glad you've got no way of making her acquaintance. Forget her, Mr Windham, I said, and spend the day backing some decent nags."

"Oh, I intend to do that." Windham seemed to perk up a little at the prospect.

"And it's Ladies' Day at Ascot," Lewellin went on in a suggestive tone, "so you might find your luck's in somewhere else."

"Let's go up and get our tickets then", Windham said with sudden animation. "We're all to ride first-class, and it'll be my little treat."

"But the victuals for the hamper are already on your slate", Lewellin objected.

"And you came across for hiring the growler too", added his wife.

Windham brushed their objections aside as we joined the tide of racegoers surging up the stairs and into the ticket office. It was very crowded in there, and demand for the festival was so great that one booth was selling tickets to Ascot alone. The Lewellins' staunchly expressed opposition to Windham standing all of our fares evaporated as we neared the window.

When Windham had paid our way, all we had to do to find our train was manoeuvre ourselves from the booking office to the adjacent platform where it stood. But so dense was the crush that we only just got into the first-class portion at the rear of the train before the guard whistled for steam-up. The second and third-class coaches were fully filled, and specials were apparently being laid on at regular intervals to provide those still left on the platform with their bounty of open carriages and hard seats. Though more prosperous citizens preferred to travel in their private vehicles whenever they could, even the first-class coach we entered was not far short of being full up. With a certain amount of badgering existing incumbents to shuffle along, we succeeded in seating ourselves in a foursome with the Lewellins facing Windham and me.

The heavily loaded train ground and squealed across points as it cleared the station. Once it had picked up pace and was going at a good chip along tracks elevated above suburban rooftops, I thought to question Windham. "Your head's not really been turned by that woman in the park has it, Willie?" I said.

"I'm sorry to say that it has."

"But you've not even seen her at close range, never mind managed to actually converse with her. And if your aunt is right about her then she's only after men for their money. Surely the fact that you've got plenty of that for her to go at should persuade you to avoid her, not court her?"

"Mr Phinney's trodden on something there, right enough", Lewellin seconded me sagely. "Show a dash of good sense, Mr Windham, and keep a closer watch on your purse than you do on the likes of her."

"I don't know why everyone's in such an uncommon rush to call her a soiled dove", Windham countered bluntly but in good part. "We only have my aunt's say-so for that proposition, and she's a snob who sees no use in anyone beyond money and position. Besides, those things do not necessarily do any good to a person. I should know. Sometimes I wish I hadn't been born to property and then there'd be no one to offend, and my choice of lady friend would be of no consequence to anyone. And who says she *is* right about Agnes?"

"Well even if she's not," said Mrs Lewellin, tossing in her pennyworth, "it sounds like it would take a very dashing gentleman to sweep such a lady off her feet."

"And am I not the most dashing of gentlemen," replied Windham, clutching his lapels and rolling his head in a show of comic complacency. "Who knows what heights I'll scale in my forthcoming life? Maybe I'll be a general or an admiral, or a lord high potentate of some foreign place. Then I'll have my own railway line, and my own station right up by Felbrigg gates. Agnes Willoughby will be the lady of Felbrigg, and when she pleases to go up to London they'll clear the line all the way to Shoreditch, and I'll work the footplate with a fireman friend of mine and have us there quick quick."

We laughed at this little fantasy. "Oh you're a wonder, Mr Windham", commented Augusta Lewellin.

"Still, I suppose you've probably right to caution me against her", her lodger resumed with equanimity. "I'll just have to forget about horsebreakers, and get on with enjoying the day. And what of you, George", he enquired of me. "I fear I've neglected so far to ask. Have you a nice, homely lady friend who keenly awaits becoming Mrs Phinney?"

"Well I have, in a manner of speaking." The question was unexpected and perplexed me into hesitancy. "But she's not always that nice...though sometimes she is a bit...and we're not betrothed...or more strictly speaking we're not betrothed now, but we may be in the future. She's called Felicity, if you want to know, but..."

"He seems certain of the girl's name, if nothing else", Lewellin interrupted facetiously.

"It warms my heart to hear a young man so steadfast in love", contributed his wife, and they all three howled with laughter.

"Sounds like we'd both better keep off the briar patch of romance today", said Windham, patting me consolingly on the back.

I would gladly have done just that, though I suppose that I did deserve having the question turned back on me once I had quizzed Windham on his feelings for the lady in the barouche. I gazed out of the window, and on consulting myself considered that my own feelings were about as foggy as the billowing exhaust smoke. Certainly my statement about Felicity had been clear only to the extent that it described my ambivalence with precision.

When my attention returned to the general discussion, I heard that the Lewellins were tracing out the course of their own romance.

"I had just handed the Queen back her shilling, and Augusta was in domestic servitude when our paths first crossed", Lewellin was explaining. "I'd had my fill of military discipline, and she'd been bossed about in service scarcely less. We resolved to see to it that we would never again be beholden to any master or mistress for our living."

"So Davie hit on the wine trade for a vocation," Mrs Lewellin took up the narrative, "and our larder has never once been bare in the happy years that have blown by since. He's ever so clever when it comes to juggling bottles and crates."

"There's an especial knack to the profession," Lewellin lauded himself modestly, "and I'm just one of those that's naturally blessed with it. Let me give you an example." He leaned forward confidentially on the couch, pressing his palms together. "A while back I had fifty necks of malmsey on the rack for a rum cove up in Islington. Well, he tried to bilk me for the price of it so...."

An exhaustive account of the ensuing saga followed, which I shall not attempt to reconstruct beyond recording that it cast its teller as the very wiliest of businessmen.

By the time he was finished, the blocks were grinding us to a halt at Ascot station. As the stop was sited some distance from the racecourse a short country hike was called for, and so we disembarked and joined the colourful procession of fellow celebrants headed for the festival. While we were channelled at one point into snaking along a path through knee high crops, Lewellin discoursed to me on the rigours of self-made fortune. He did so with the implication that, as men who worked for a living, we bore the same stamp of worldly mankind. Meantime Windham took the hamper, and lent his arm to his landlady so that she could direct her efforts to lifting her encircling crinoline free of the muddy terrain. Soon, a milling mass of people greeted our sight at the entrance to the racecourse. We had to weave our way to the gate through tract-peddlers and the like, with their dismal warnings that attending a race meeting would tip all concerned into the torments of hell.

"Let's get our cards from this Molly" Lewellin suggested, approaching one of the dishevelled gipsy girls that sold them inside.

"First up is the Norfolk Stakes," he observed once we had our race cards, "which may be of particular interest to you, Mr Windham, given that you are yourself a good old Norfolk pudding?"

Windham chortled, and took this jest in good heart.

"It's five furlongs," Lewellin continued, studying his card, "and there's a good sized field we can look up and down before venturing a selection." He took out his watch and examined it. "Shall we go straight to the paddock and peruse the contenders? Over there in the far corner, by the big clock?"

I looked out from our position across a teeming landscape. To one side, the pinnacles of enough tents to house a campaigning army poked above the *mêlée* of merriment. To another, the grandstand towered in receding layers above the finishing post. All the way to the trackside rail, carriages were cluttered in disorderly ranks; some bearing the parties they had transported here, feasting and drinking with their roofs for a table.

The clock Lewellin had mentioned was a landmark visible from a long way around and, there being general consent to his plan, we set out toward it through crowds that grew ever denser. At one moment the Lewellins were close by us, but at the next they had become detached in the throng. It was understandable that they would lag behind given their burden of the hamper. But on reaching the paddock rail at the appointed spot, Windham and I looked about us and saw no trace of the lodging house proprietors. The passage of five or ten minutes still failed to disgorge them. It seemed that they were mislaid, picnic hamper and all, which we agreed was the greater shame because we were both getting peckish.

"We'd best not budge for a while in case they find us", Windham proposed. "What in the world can have become of them? Still, never mind, I daresay they have business of their own. Let's see this race out anyway, and if they've not come by then we'll move off in search of luncheon."

I agreed to this sensible proposition. The hour of two was just striking, which was the signal for the runners to be led out to begin their circuits of the paddock for the benefit of eagle-eyed connoisseurs. I watched the horses complete several revolutions, to the accompaniment of Windham's observations upon each in my ear. One was "an elegant little bay", another "a handsome looking chestnut", a third "a clever black hunter". While this was going on, I became conscious that a stout man, with florid jowls and round tinted spectacles, was lurking uncomfortably close behind us and listening in. His fidgety demeanour telegraphed his intention to press himself upon us.

"But see that grey mare," Windham tugged at my sleeve, unaware of the looming presence, "the one that's plunging and prancing. She's got a gleam in her eye and a spring in her step. I tell you truly, George, she's the winner! Wouldn't you concur?"

"Forgive me for remarking on it, my dear Sir," the stout loiterer presumed to intrude before I could respond, "but I'd have to say that she's a narrow, melancholy specimen, unlikely to reward anyone's trust." He said this with a bland bonhomie which sounded to me a shade forced.

Windham turned to face him good humouredly. "Why, she's the best looking horse in the field. Surely you can see that?"

"Not a bit of it", the presuming fellow persisted. "Too strong willed by far, and not the kind of prospect on which a shrewd chancer would pin his hopes. I think you'll find that those in the know agree with me." He raised the tinted specs to his forehead and trained his binoculars on a bookmaker's scratchboard. "Oh yes, there she is. She's *Flying Star* and she's thirty to one. Those odds proclaim that she hasn't the twinkling of a chance. I can promise you that picking her would be like asking one of the thieving vermin that infest this heath to pick your pocket."

"So you say", Windham returned, apparently not averse to joining in with this style of banter. "But my pocket's not so easily pilfered. I'll lay out a sovereign in cold blood on her to win at any odds."

"You'd only come off crabs."

"Would I indeed? Who are you on then?"

"I'm for *Skirmisher* the black hunter, who's favourite to win as it turns out." He then lowered the binoculars and replaced the tinted specs. "I can see you're a brother in 'the fancy' though, and that affords us every margin for amiable disagreement. Let me to introduce myself. I am James Roberts, a gentleman of Piccadilly." He lifted his topper to reveal a bald pate, fringed by a crescent of long hair.

'"Why, what a noteworthy fact", replied Windham. "I myself am residing near there at Duke Street until the season's out. Just off Piccadilly."

"Well then," returned this Roberts fellow, "we're as good as neighbours to one another. My own house is at the Park Lane end, where we have all sorts of knobs virtually next door. Of course mine isn't as palatial a residence as those of the titled aristocrats, but it does tolerably well for me and my twin boys Ferdinand and Augustus. I'm a widower you see." He gave over his card.

"I'm so sorry to learn that", said Windham, presenting his own credentials in return.

"A specimen of our noble squirearchy," Roberts observed, "how wondrously elevating!" With this kind extravagant effusion, the interloper expressed himself rejoiced to make my friend's acquaintance. But when I presented my own card he glanced at it blankly, as if he would happily suffer my not being present. I put up with this in order to avoid retarding Windham's gregarious nature. I was unable to square this man Roberts, who struck me as being at best a boor in gentlemen's clothing, with someone who might inhabit one of the capital's most prestigious thoroughfares. Still, the fact was easily checked and so it would behove him little to lie.

Windham asked me if I wanted in on *Flying Star*, and in a spirit of good-fellowship I decided that I would risk a sovereign backing his tip, though I thought the punt to be profligate. When we went off to the betting-ring to place the wagers we found that Roberts was still with us, still arguing the case for favouring *Skirmisher*. He remained with us as we put our money on our choice at a gaming-booth. He was still at our shoulder as we advanced as near to the trackside as we were able to witness the race. His attentions were becoming limpet-like.

Our vantage was too poor to afford us a clear view as we were hemmed in by a cordon of lofty persons, and we heard a good deal more than we saw. We gathered from those about us that there were several false starts, before both flags went down together and the field streamed away. For a while the only sounds to be heard were those of tense mumblings and murmurings, and exhortations to success hissed through clenched teeth. Then, as the rumble of approaching hooves mixed with a rising tide of roaring voices, Windham pointed out the blue and white cap of *Flying Star*'s jockey hurtling by at the head of the pack. Our joint gaze fixated upon it until it could be seen careering past the post, the winner by a neck. Windham and I jumped up and down and raised a mighty cry of elation, bashing each other on the back. I must say, however, that I did not fully believe in this lavish good fortune until the number of our horse was hoisted onto the board as the conqueror.

Roberts was unconcerned, grateful even in defeat. "Good win, Mr Windham," he conceded, rubbing his hands oleaginously, "capital triumph indeed. My pick was nowhere to be seen."

It certainly was a good win. Instead of losing a sovereign I had gained thirty, which was an unheard of cash sum for me to have at my personal disposal, and so had my friend.

"You look like gentlemen in need of relaxation and refreshment after such heaving excitements", Roberts speculated once our celebrations had calmed. "Look here," he proposed, "I happen to have my own on-course marquee. I can vouch for it being an infinitely superior destination to any other you might fall into hereabouts. Come over there with me if you will, and let me spread out the cloth of hospitality."

It was hard to resist this generous offer, especially as the luncheon we had intended to enjoy was gone. In my giddiness at our lucky punt, I pushed any doubts I may have entertained to the back of my mind. Windham was more than willing to go along with this questionable individual also, and so we collected our winnings and followed him as he led us into that region of the racecourse that resembled a tented maze. We found that a carnival atmosphere prevailed therein. There were jugglers, performers on stilts, and children standing on stools trilling simple balladry. Everywhere there were tooters outside this or that establishment puffing up the merits of wandering in. Dozens of tents and booths were fitted up for the sale of liquors and foodstuffs, while others were offering dancing, or entertainments of a fairground character. Some of these were of the innocent "throw a hoop and win a prize" variety, but other establishments promised the baser thrills of pugilistic violence. Indeed many of the places were so vilely peopled as to forbid one's entry at a glance, and some of the drunkards who swayed across the congested pathways of grass were already bloodied from fighting.

Roberts sailed carelessly through all this, and hurried us to a patch where the tents were bigger and more widely set apart. Two blunt bruisers dangled at the entrance of what I took to be his marquee, smoking clay pipes. They nodded at his approach, and stood deferentially aside. It was brightly lit and done out like a Thames pleasure steamer inside, all gilt mirrors and potted palms. To one end a miniature band in full dinner dress was grinding out tunes from a podium, and a well-dressed but not wholly steady collection of revellers was jigging along to them. Round the bar there was a crush of girls in gaudy ribbons, moustachioed moochers in floppy suits, and other persons of louche appearance and apparel. White-bibbed waiters, and waitresses in stripy gowns and florally adorned caps, were gliding to-and-fro between tables, several of whose occupants had left decorum behind. There was also a certain amount of licence on display in the relations between men and women. I had never seen the like of it before and should rightly have been horror-struck, but instead I experienced a surge of fascination. I saw that Windham's interest was also hooked by the benighted scene.

Our host had the grace to appear fleetingly embarrassed at the environment he'd landed us in, or perhaps he was just good at conveying that impression.

"Gentlemen...gentlemen..." he said, surveying Windham's expression carefully, "we can't have you exposed to this noisy exhibition. The victuals I promised will be much better partaken in the select, where you can stretch out your legs as well."

Roberts led us to the far end of the tent, where a tall screen embroidered with gold trellis cut a section of the accommodation off from the rest. He parted a panel of it and let us into a snug. A small bunch of swells, who looked like stock-jobbers or the like, were sitting around a young lady who was reclining on an ottoman and was clearly the centre of attention. She was dressed in a close fitting black riding habit. Some rather more showily-dressed girls were disported about the swells, draped around their shoulders, or nesting in their laps, and all present were drinking and very jolly. But they quietened down the moment they became aware of Roberts' presence. He clicked his fingers, then indicated the outside of the screen with a jabbing thumb and all but the figure on the ottoman made haste to be gone.

On her way out, one of the showily-dressed girls suddenly stumbled in my direction and pressed herself against me. She encircled me with her arms and kissed me on the lips, whispering, "Come along, my darling one." The smell of drink hung heavy on her breath, and she was surrounded by the fragrance of a perfume that failed to mask the stale underlying odour of her unwashed person. It occurred to me that the showy clothes and spangled adornments were probably only hers on hire for the afternoon, and that this was her place of business. I was certainly not her darling one.

Roberts untwined her arms from me and propelled her roughly toward the gap in the screen, which she passed through unsteadily and without a backward glance. As she went, I caught the distinct reflection in one of the gilt mirrors of a man's face on the other side of the screen looking in my direction. It was a thin, purposeful, clean shaven face and its all too sober and steady gaze was trained directly on my reflection. I was disturbed by the sensation of having seen him sometime before. But he stepped coolly out from my line of vision without betraying any twitch of recognition. I wondered whether the giddiness of my win had made me into fortune's fool, but then just as soon forgot the phantom sighting.

The last of the swells to go was extravagantly moustachioed and clad in a flamboyant check. He snatched a hurried conference in whispers with the lady in the tight black habit, before sauntering out swinging his stick as if he had reckoned on this moment for his departure all along. The lady remained lolling on the ottoman, the topper and cane that went with her outfit housed on a nearby low table. She was pale and dazzlingly pretty, with golden hair gathered at her neck in a silken net. Her face was small, round and doll-like, and her eyes were of the deepest blue. I confess that I could see every point of the attraction. As Roberts was now pleased to inform us, she was Miss Agnes Willoughby.

It was not hard to see that Windham, who did not need anyone to tell him who she was, was in a state of advanced agitation.

"You'll understand," said Roberts after telling her who we were, "that I have any number of practicalities to see to at the front of the house. Miss Willoughby here is a lady of considerable accomplishment, gentlemen, and I feel sure that I can entrust your amusement to her capable hands. I will arrange for refreshments to be sent in. So do forgive me...". He raised the specs and then lowered them.

He then gestured for us to sit down and, once he had seen us settled, backed out of the snug with a bow and a twirl of his hand. Two waitresses appeared almost immediately, laying a buffet before us and thrusting glasses of wine into our hands. Our hostess, who already had a drink on the go, invited us to tuck in, and then watched us do so with a detached sort of beatific expression. Reclining languidly there on the ottoman, she looked petite and demure and inscrutable.

When we had finished eating, she moved on to the serious task of making light conversation. "Well now Mr Windham, or perhaps I may take the liberty of calling you 'William', what brings you and your charming friend out to Ascot today?" Her voice was melodious and as smooth as molasses.

"We're just here for the sport of it, you know? And you really must call me 'Willie'," Windham responded, the slurring of his words proclaiming his heightened agitation. He knew very well that this interview with Agnes was good fortune come upon too easy, but at the same time he wasn't about to look a gift horse in the mouth.

"Very well then, 'Willie' it is", she said, dispensing him a faint, but encouraging smile. "I always say that Ascot attracts a much more select company than does Epsom. It's always so much more fashionably attended, wouldn't you agree?"

"Yes...yes it is...very much so", he did agree.

From far away I heard the cry, "They're off", to signal the commencement of the next race, and thought to myself "so they are too." But just like the Norfolk Stakes earlier on, the conversation proceeded to rack up a series of false starts as Windham's composure appeared irreclaimable.

"You're a Norfolk gentleman then, Willie", Agnes said at length, resorting to a statement of the obvious as conversational primer. "It must be awfully nice out there in the country?"

"Nice? Yes, yes it is nice. Awfully nice," he blathered in response.

"Especially so, now that we're having such fine weather?"

"In fine weather it certainly is splendid."

"It is most clement today", I took it upon myself to say, trying to get a conversational look-in. But Agnes did not care for the interruption, and let me know it by shovelling a scowl in my direction.

"I was referring to weather conditions in Norfolkshire, not to those hereabouts", she corrected me primly. She then returned her attention to Windham, favouring him with another slight little smile. "Do you have a nice big house out there, and are the lands extensive?"

"Oh yes. My father is gone along home several years ago, but he left me with any amount of property though. I'm to come into it when I'm twenty-one in a few months time, and when I'm twenty-nine there's ever so much more bunce due to me."

"Indeed so. Do take another glass of wine, Willie dearest." She was sufficiently solicitous as to rearrange herself upright, and lean forward to pass him the bottle.

"One is so in need of enlivenment on a warm day, if only to keep oneself awake", she disclosed, leaning back. "I'm from the country myself. Hampshire as it happens. And my father is gone along home some time ago also, so we may very well have much in common. He was a village parson, you see, a very respectable man, who was known about the entire county, and who kept us wanting for nothing. My mother had passed away before him, and when he died he left me hundreds a year by will to see to myself and bring up my two little sisters, Thirza and Emmeline. Their safe launch upon the stormy sea of life is now entrusted by providence solely to myself."

"Lovely girls, I'm sure," Windham purred in his state of distraction, "so very lovely. And I weep for your father and mother."

"It rejoices my heart to hear you say it, Willie dear. But there was a lawsuit and a villain robbed us of all our father's money." Agnes put her head in her hands. "My father had been quite blameless in the whole business. We would have been destitute had not a wealthy gentleman swept us up in his arms and given us shelter in his grand house as if we were his own daughters. But then he seduced me, and that is the only wrong act I have ever committed, and we had to leave. Now we must seek protection wherever we can find it." She lowered her eyes sadly to the ground, where a fancy rug was unfurled beneath her bare feet.

Cranked by this performance to the very edge of his endurance, Windham rose halfway from his seat blurting out: "I will be your protector; we will be married the very day that I come of age."

Agnes raised her head slowly, obviously incredulous at what she had just heard, as was I. She scanned his features acutely, perhaps suspecting a satirical motivation for his outburst, but perceiving only innocence.

"Married? Don't jump out of your cot, lovey," she at last said, twittering with laughter. "Let's just get squizzled sloppy for now." With that she collected the bottle and recharged our drinks.

We remained with her for I do not know how long. When she decided that the time had come for us to go, she said goodbye to Windham with a great quantity of show, promising that he would hear from her directly. Her farewell to myself was also pleasantly done despite her earlier shortness, which aroused in me a rather pathetic glow of satisfaction. We then exited the tent sharply, and whiled away the rest of the afternoon watching the remaining races, and losing several of the sovereigns we had previous won. When we finally gave up the course evening had come, and we strolled contentedly back to the station.

Standing on the platform, Windham recognised one of the guards from the days when he was a homesick Eton scholar and would ride up to London in the van. My friend went over to the railwayman, and they were soon absorbed in reminiscent conversation. As they talked, I saw a brougham draw up, and a man get out, then help a woman down after him. The next train up to town was just then approaching and they hurried up the stairs to the platform to catch it, the man leading the woman by her hand and both of them very high-spirited. The man was the moustachioed swell from earlier on, clad in his distinctive check, and Agnes Willoughby was the woman, now wearing her riding topper and carrying her cane.

They arrived in time to board the train, and leapt into a compartment together and slammed the door behind them. I watched the swell take a key from his pocket. Then he looked this way and that and locked the door from the inside, before removing his jacket. He was undoing his necktie with one hand, and pulling down the blinds with his other, as he thus closed them off from my sight. They were unobserved by Windham and the railwayman, who were still chatting, and I do not think that they saw me. The guard then parted from Windham to take charge of the train, at which my friend and I clambered aboard, the whistle blew, and we departed.

AN ARTISTIC CONVERSATION

Our audience with the pretty horsebreaker at Ascot had a decidedly unsettling effect on me in the days immediately after it. I think I had, up to that moment, assumed that women who led scandalous lives would bear some obvious mark of moral degradation upon them. They would, perhaps, betray their shame through some mournfulness of expression or vulgarity of attire. Agnes Willoughby, on the other hand, bore nothing of the kind, and instead showed every sign of vivacity and conviction in her vocation. She seemed to me, who knew no better at the time, to be entirely pleasing herself, and that was something I could not persuade myself to condemn. A shimmering aura of her lodged itself in my youthful mind, and served to amplify my discontent concerning my relations with Miss Felicity Pumicestone.

We seemed to be locked in the dreary abode of routine. We only really met at meal times, or in the arid expanse of evenings spent with her father. Whatever the time of day, our exchanges often struggled to attain the commonplace let alone glide to the heavens. We seldom shared any thought or experience that was genuinely noteworthy. Practically the only outdoor activity that we regularly undertook was on a Sunday, after morning chapel, when we would hack out together for an hour on hired mounts. We resembled two stuffed owls perched side-by-side beneath a glass dome on a sideboard, unable to face one another. This state of affairs pained me and I was no longer content to let it remain that way. And so it was that one morning, several days after encountering Agnes, I thought to put a suggestion of a novel character to Felicity.

The two of us were alone at breakfast, her father having left for his club where it was his habit to cloister himself on three working days of the six that made up each week's allocation. As usual we were breakfasting across from each other over the little table by the parlour window on the first floor, overlooking the gardens in the middle of Red Lion Square. The terraces that surrounded them were still neat and trim in the classical manner, if not quite as well maintained as they would have been in their heyday. But the gardens were blooming, and I was bolstered in my intention to put a modest proposal by the sight of the flower beds in their colourful array.

"What would you think, my dear Felicity," I ventured to break the silence between us to say, "if I were to suggest that we pop out together this afternoon and see if we can't find some lively entertainment to immerse ourselves in?"

"Pop out together, for entertainment, today?" It was a token of how staid our relations had become that such an apparently unassuming proposal aroused her incredulity. "But you have your office business to attend to and I must see to the house."

"Well, to dispose of your first objection I am pleased to relate that your father has granted me the afternoon off." I explained that I had received an anxious sounding telegraph from Windham, first thing that morning, begging for my attendance in a professional capacity at his lodging later on. His uncle and the family solicitor were apparently planning to descend upon him to advance some legal proposition, and he thought that he might benefit greatly from my presence. Before going out Mr Pumicestone had acceded to my request for daytime off, in lieu of evening working, on the basis that my acquaintance with Windham might at last be about to bear professional fruit.

"And as to the second obstacle you mention," I continued, "I feel sure that your customary command of domestic matters permits that you may leave the house for two or three hours or so untended."

"I trust that that is indeed the case," she was not so easily bamboozled by flattery, though I was right to say that she was a more than capable manager of the household, "but we never go anywhere in business hours."

"We never go anywhere much out of them either."

"Perhaps that's for the want of your asking." Felicity observed me sceptically, but not without a glimmer of interest. "Something's come over you, George, since you met that peculiar country squire." She pulled a face at the thought of him, and drained her teacup as if to cleanse her palate of it. "And I'm not at all sure that it's an alteration to the good."

"Let us assume that it is, for the sake of argument."

"Perhaps we'll allow that it maybe, for the time being." She gazed out at the gardens, no doubt thinking of how to place herself in relation to my proposal. "Let us also allow, for the sake of argument," she resumed, giving me one of her rare but welcome smiles, "that I am willing to consider frittering away a working day on a frolic. What do you have in mind for it?"

Naturally I had given this question a modicum of forethought, intending that whatever it was should be invigorating and out of the ordinary. When I had rendered a (highly selective) account of my day at the races to Felicity, I had noted that she enjoyed hearing of the triumph against the odds of *Flying Star*. I knew that she took pleasure in riding, and I made the leap of assuming that a show featuring horses would tickle her also. This had led me to search for something of that sort, and I had identified what seemed like a strong possibility in that morning's press.

"There is a 'carnival of equestrian performance'," I replied, reading from the appropriate notice in the newspaper covering the empty plate before me, "advertised to take place at Astley's Amphitheatre in Lambeth, just the other side of Westminster Bridge. The show will apparently include what is described as 'an astounding performance' by a tribe of mounted Arabian artists, thirty in number. It claims here that they will attempt 'a variety of novel and extraordinary feats that have never before been seen in Europe!' What do you say to that? It might be quite thrilling."

"I say that I will not go anywhere near it at all. It is certain to be noisy and smelly and grating on the nerves. Not to mention obliging one to beat the rabble of thieves and rogues it is sure to attract off with an umbrella. I never do feel myself properly safe south of the river."

Miss Pumicestone reached over to confiscate the newspaper from my place and examine the "public amusement" pages on her own account. I chided myself for having thought about the matter, yet still managed to hatch a project so painfully misjudged. Perhaps I should have entered into a more scientific survey of her likes and dislikes?

"How about this then?" she said, after scanning the columns of type up and down, and dismissing a number of possibilities. "There is to be an exhibition of works by the noted artist E.A. Seafield at the Hanover Gallery, on Hanover Square off Oxford Street. He's the one who does those 'Hearthside' scenes of domestic life in the penny illustrated press. I quite like them. It says here that the full size canvasses on which the 'Hearthside' engravings are based will be hung, together with 'a wholly new work that will confound the expectations of the artist's curious public.' What audacious puffery! We have to go and see it after hearing that, George. And the showing is to be accompanied by a 'conversazione' with the artist himself being present, so that should be lively enough for you to be going on with."

The concept of the "conversazione" was an overblown one that event promoters of the time had concocted to elevate what was generally no more than a public discussion. I did have a passing familiarity with Seafield's output, and if I had been asked to comment upon it would probably have argued that it suffered most from being overly sentimental. The chance of being able to tell him so to his face, however, did nothing to lean me in favour of attending the occasion. An artistic exhibition struck me as being rather far removed from the "frolic" that Felicity herself had invoked. But in proposing that we step aside for once from what was for us the stultifying and the everyday, it seemed that I had succeeded in engaging her enthusiasm for something. That, in turn, engaged mine, so that I did not really care what we did so long as she wanted to do it. And the promise, held out by his notice, that the artist had broken controversial new ground was at least mildly intriguing.

"Very well then," I granted, "Mr Seafield's exhibition it is. Shall we have a hansom scoot us round?" Our household did not count a horse and carriage as part of its inventory, nor did its retinue number a coachman or groom.

"It'll be more exciting if we don't, and less of an expense too. Though I'll have to get out of my crinoline and into petticoats if it's to be the omnibus", she declared, rising from the table. This was a wise precaution for a woman who did not want to flaunt an immodest amount of herself in public to undertake. The steel-hooped undergarment that was the crinoline gaped ungovernably when the wearer climbed on or off an omnibus platform, and only the most hardened exhibitionist would attempt to scale the vehicle's back ladder with one on.

We parted to attend to our several affairs during the remainder of the morning, having agreed to rendezvous downstairs in the hall at midday. When that hour came we fell in nicely arm-in-arm together, to amble along our terrace to the nearest corner of the square. From there the narrow Red Lion Passage led into Red Lion Street, which in turn gave out onto High Holborn. This was the main shopping street of our quarter, and it was also the main drag along which omnibuses heading to Oxford Street ran.

After only a short wait, an omnibus of the "Citizen" line came careering along. As I hailed it down it swerved precariously through lanes of traffic to join us at the kerb, its iron shod wheels gouging a noisy path across the street paving. I got on and handed Felicity up behind me, and we stooped inside to grab two adjacent seats that were vacant. In those days these saloons were insufferably cramped due to their beggarly dimensions, and everyone inside sat sideways on, staring at each other. The conductor swung onto his foothold halfway up the back ladder, and banged on the roof to tell the driver that it was time to push on.

When we reached it half-an-hour or so later, we found that the atmosphere inside the Hanover Gallery was significantly more fragrant than that of the omnibus car had been. The smattering of patrons already present at the gallery was also a notch upscale from those populating the omnibus. The artist himself was not yet in evidence, there being just a few well-dressed couples wafting from picture to picture, and a few solitary gentlemen hovering about here and there. The hanging room was large and well-lit, being overarched by a cavernous glass and iron roof. Some greenery overflowed from picturesque pots placed in tasteful positions. As we advanced tentatively inside, the planks of the varnished wooden floor creaked slightly under the pressure of our footfalls. So hushed was the ambience that one felt it would be an offence to let one's voice rise above a whisper.

At the room's centre was a table, draped in a patterned cloth, which supported an urn, several cups and saucers, and some fancy pastries adorning decorated plates. Felicity and I agreed, by hand signals, that we would make a bee-line for these refreshments. But as she poured us each a cup of tea, we could not help laughing at how the trickling of the liquid seemed to mock the reverent grandeur of our surroundings. When our laughter seemed to mock it further and some of the patrons peered disapprovingly at us, it made us laugh all the more, so that we were obliged to stifle our amusement by pursing our lips. In doing so we leaned into each other in an affectingly intimate fashion.

The tea episode set a satiric tone for our perambulation of the exhibition. Although Felicity had earlier expressed a mild liking for Seafield's "Hearthside" studies even she, seeing the paintings exposed one after another to the critical eye, could not deny that they were mawkish creations. Their organising principal was an idealisation of hearth and home, and they were characteristically set in some rustic cottage or garden. In one composition a floppy-eared dog with a glossy coat gazed adoringly from its fireside repose at its plump and complacent master, at leisure in his rocking chair. In another, cherubic children radiated simple delight as they ate an alfresco picnic from a rough but well provisioned cloth, watched over by horny-handed but tender elders. We found ourselves suppressing sniggers over each new sugared confection that hove into view.

We entertained ourselves like this for quite some time, and became rather oblivious to anyone else. While we thus circulated around it the gallery slowly grew more populated, and it gradually became apparent that our mirth was no longer the sole source of disturbance.

The sound of muffled, but unmistakably agitated voices alerted our attention to a huddle that had formed around a canvas far larger than any of its fellows. We decided to potter over there and investigate, and as we drew near saw that the grouping was made up of a number of older persons crowding in on a tall, thin young man. Given that he was most certainly not striving for anonymity in his personal get-up, the young fellow could only be Seafield, the exhibitor himself. His long, thick black hair and beard combined with an incredibly patterned waistcoat as if to proclaim him the soul of creativity. As they were highly respectable those around him were striving to confine their protests within limits, but a marked strength of feeling was seeping through nonetheless.

"It seems," Felicity observed, "as if the painter has been granted his wish of confounding the public, or at least some of them. I wonder how he likes it? That must be his new work. Let's get closer in and see what there is to take umbrage about."

Detecting our approach the artist decided for reasons best known to himself to appeal to us, or more particularly to Felicity, against his detractors. Perhaps it was because we were so much younger than they.

"Oh what pretty eyes you have, my cuckoo", he declaimed rather alarmingly at her over the hats of the others. "I could see them from half-a-mile off. You would make for such a model as would have any painter worth his palette in a swoon."

Those crowding in on him turned their heads to see what sort of woman could incite such outrageous patter. I chose not to take offence at the man's undoubted presumption, on the basis that his words probably amounted to no more than his normal brand of tradesman's puff. Looking at her now he had said them, though, I had to agree that Felicity's brown eyes were sparkling handsomely, and that her shape would not disqualify her from sitting as a studio model.

"This young lady," the artist continued to address

those in front of him, "will, I feel certain, find no difficulty in seeing the matter at issue in the same light that I do. Make a pathway for her to come through." He mimed a swimming motion to induce the onlookers to part and give her an unencumbered passage to the picture.

Though she was clearly embarrassed to be at the centre of this perhaps oppressive attention, she stepped up gamely nonetheless. I stayed where I was, deducing that I was watching a showman in action and not wishing to queer his pitch. It was notable that with one flourish he had managed to quieten the naysayers, and somehow bamboozle them into having this unknown young woman for arbiter of whatever was in dispute.

"Tell me, my dear," he directed the question at Felicity, "do you perceive, as some of these cultured folk would have it, anything immoral in the scene depicted before you? Can you interpret its meaning for us?"

The painting in question was a monster in its proportions, taking up an entire facet of wall. But apart from it being larger than they, there was little to distinguish it at first glance from the other compositions. A small drawing room interior was pictured, which was laden with all the chintzy paraphernalia of everyday domestic life. Scattered about were numerous knick-knacks and embroidered fabrics, and on the mantelshelf there ticked an ormolu clock. Several generations of the same family were portrayed assembled around a comforting fire, in varying states of dreamy, one might almost say dopey, repose. An old man was snoozing with his head on his chest, while a younger one did the same with his legs outstretched. A matronly figure was knitting from a workbox full of woollen balls which a little girl lolling on the floor was leaning sleepily against. They were apparently meant to be a comfortable, if not an unduly prosperous lot.

A boy was shown placed slightly apart from the

others on an upright chair by the window, with his legs curled under him. He was fixed in the act of holding open a fold of curtain so that a glimpse of the outside world was let in. Through this aperture it could be appreciated that the room overlooked a bustling dockside scene, where a square-rigged ship was being loaded in some hurry by the light of blazing *flambeaux*. It was clear that the vessel was soon destined to depart for who knows what destination. The heavens above were covered in blackness, though a patch of cloud shone silvery with the light of the moon concealed behind it.

I could not divine where any point of morals entered this visual equation, and waited with apprehension to see what Felicity would make of it.

"Well," she began uncertainly, "it all looks very homely and nice, and then it acquires a sort of nautical twang." She angled her head this way and that as she struggled to find anything in this formulation to expand upon. "Hold on, I'll get it in a minute." More peering at the canvas from odd angles ensued. "The boy," she said at last, looking to the artist for confirmation, "is perhaps bored and listless, and yearns to be anywhere other than where he is; possibly outside on the quay?"

Seafield nodded encouragingly, and pointed to the caption adorning the gilded frame at the painting's foot.

"The Adventurer Awakes", she read. "Oh I see it now", she exclaimed after some further consideration. "The boy is entranced by the urgent prospect of travel and adventure that he sees in the dockside *tableau*."

Seafield nodded again and lifted his palms by way of coaxing her to further leaps of insight.

"And that prospect is contrasted in his mind with the cosy but stupefying world that he actually lives in...so much so that he wants to run off to sea...this very night!" She beamed with an endearing satisfaction at having got the conundrum right.

"Quite so", piped up an elderly lady who was

peeking at the offering with distaste though a pair of *pince-nez*. “It is no less than an incitement to the young to abandon those who have succoured and nurtured them, on any casual caprice.”

This brickbat was received with an up-thrust of approving voices, a baritone one of which could be heard complaining, “And to think that it is ‘Hearthside’ Seafield himself who promotes this artistic mummery. It is youth’s bounden duty to remain at home, and provide for their seniors in the event that they are ailing.”

“Is it really?” the artist returned, urbanely. It seemed to me that he was thoroughly enjoying himself. This was, I supposed, the sort of spat he expected of a *conversazione*.

“Well, I must tell you all,” he advised them cheerily, “that I have lately attained an advanced sphere of thinking that quite leaves my old output behind. In point of fact, I would go so far as to say that it renders everything I have done prior to this new composition utterly redundant. I reject the tyranny of the circulating libraries and the illustrated press that would have me repeat myself endlessly. They say that I must do as I have always done, but see, I have jilted them in their strictures. I will not suffer their petty censorship.

“And now,” he turned back to Felicity with a deft spin of his wrist, “will you complete your appointed task, my fine and valued critic, by informing us whether this picture’s message is, or is not, an improper one?”

Her eyes shot upward in concentrated deliberation. “If I truly comprehend the message, I cannot condemn it as an improper one”, she eventually concluded. “I take you to be saying that the boy must not waste his existence bound to insufferable dullness, but must follow his own lights even if they turn out to be misguided. The painting is, I think, in every respect an admirable one.”

Seafield was so pleased to hear this that he acted

out the actions of applauding her. I had not hitherto rated Felicity as an artistic commentator, and was proud of the assurance with which she had performed. The rest of them, however, were not so impressed and her judgement set off a babble of dissenting voices. Seeing that she was becoming hemmed in by their critical ardour Felicity reached out her hand to me, and I grabbed it and pulled her away; though not before the artist had seized his chance to bid her *adieu* by planting a kiss on her forehead. We were as one in being ready to leave the conversationalists to it, and so we hastened to the exit before anyone else lobbied for Felicity's opinion on cultural affairs. Once through it we rushed to the garden opposite, in the middle of Hanover Square, where we tumbled onto the grass in a very hilarious turn of mind.

The day had dispelled some blockage between us, and we sprawled there on the lawn for a long time chirruping brightly about nothing whatever. When we got up and were making our way back to Oxford Street, a summer shower caught us, and we took refuge in a coffee house. Sitting on a cushioned window bench watching the world get drenched, Felicity leaned her head over to lay it on my shoulder.

"I'll talk directly to papa about your entering the partnership, George," she promised, "and then you may pose me a certain carefully considered question."

Nothing further needed, for the time being, to be said. On the omnibus back she led the way by ascending the ladder to the roof, despite there being space for us inside and there persisting a gentle fall of rain. "The adventurer awakes" she halloed down at me, as she swung from the handrail and braved the precarious rungs. We sat side-by-side up top on the knife-board, facing the bustle of a teeming Oxford Street pavement. Our talk was of travel and strange places in the world, and of desiring to explore some of them while we were yet young. When the shower dispersed, and the sun returned, the breeze on our faces was tremendously fresh. I put my arm around her waist, and felt that our spirits were singing.

By the time we reached home we were pleasantly mellow, and we took off our outdoor things in the hall. Anna, the maid, appeared to ask after our pleasure, and we said that we would like to take tea in the front parlour. She informed us that Mr Pumicestone and another man were already up there with a pot, but that she would supply us with fresh cups and hot water.

This gave me cause to fear that something was not in good order. My principal never normally returned from his club before six and it was not yet four, and he never normally brought anyone home with him either. He drew a strict demarking line between his home life and his life at the *Gibbous Club*, of Staple Inn Passage off High Holborn. This unassuming institution made no claim to rival the famous names of Pall Mall, such as the *Reform* or the *Athenaeum.* It catered for a certain class of practitioner in the "noble" professions like medicine and the law, and for ranking police officers and lesser government officials. What they did there all day I could hardly imagine, but it appeared to operate mainly as a mart for the exchanging of business. Mr Pumicestone was fond of telling me that the firm would sink without the work his contacts there generated, and it was an argument with which I could not in honesty quibble.

When we got upstairs and opened the front parlour door we saw Felicity's father and the visitor sitting upright in the armchairs and looking ill at ease and frightfully solemn. My own mounting unease was accentuated by the fact that Pumicestone made no move to introduce the other, but instead trained a withering scowl upon me. I felt my cheeks flush and my neck prickle as I recognised the thin, purposeful, clean shaven face of the stranger. It was the one that I had observed reflected back at me in the gaudy gilt mirror at the racecourse marquee. Seeing it afresh, I was now wise as to whom it belonged to. It seemed that the questionable events of that day were also due to be reflected back at me.

It is strange what kind of inconsequential fancy floats across the mind when it is under gnawing duress. Paralysed at the parlour's threshold, I cast my gaze around the room and noted that our furnishings and articles of ornament were remarkably similar to those we had just seen depicted in the contentious painting. Indeed, we too had an ormolu clock balanced on our mantelshelf. Hearing its movement cut through the charged silence of that moment, it occurred to me to reflect, "There is music in the ticking of a clock." The room might be conventionally furbished, I considered, but it did exude the comfort of familiarity and the certainty of home.

"Is something amiss papa?" Felicity queried him, intertwining her fingers sympathetically with mine in the face of her father's show of hostility toward me. "You're awfully soon in getting home. And may we have the luxury of knowing whom our visitor is?"

"He is Inspector William Holden of "C" division, the Metropolitan Police, and he is a friend and fellow patron of my club." I remembered that I had some time before been fleetingly introduced to this man at some formal occasion that I had attended with my principal.

The officer nodded respectfully at Felicity and me. "Good day to you, Mr Phinney...Miss Felicity." His manner was calm and polite. But Mr Pumicestone did not seem disposed for the moment to enlarge upon the meaning of his presence, and continued to cast the scowl in my direction.

"Really father, you are being quite mysterious and more than a bit disagreeable", Felicity said impatiently. "Come on George, let's sit ourselves down and find out where this little tea party is tending." She was outwardly sanguine, but her squeezing at my fingers betrayed her anxiety nonetheless.

She led me across to the settee, but her father

tried to arrest her progress, saying, "What we have to ventilate is not fit for your hearing, my dearest. It concerns George only. Would you oblige me very much by leaving us alone for the time being?"

"Not fit for my hearing?" she replied, now audibly cross. "I will hear everything of consequence that is said in this house, and what concerns George most definitely concerns me too." She reversed herself defiantly onto the settee, and pulled me down after her as she still had hold of my hand. Despite the apparent intimacy of this coupling, the joyous spell that had grown up between us that day had already been broken.

"So let it be then, my love; have it as you will." Pumicestone was more resigned then thwarted, knowing that once roused his daughter was hard to put off. "But if you stay, you must be ready to learn something that strikes to the heart of our happiness."

"What manner of thing could that be?" Felicity gripped my hand harder and pressed up against me. That her father was not making ready to take a note, nor indulging in his usual elaborate verbal preliminaries, told both of us that he was in an exceptionally grave frame of mind.

"May I be allowed to step in, Sir, before our feelings run away with us?" Inspector Holden had decided that the time was nigh to intervene. This was turning into a very different kind of *conversazione* from the earlier one.

Anna then breezed in with a tray, and there was a brief intermission while she apportioned the cups and replenished the pot. A slight tremor in her pouring hand, and a faint clattering of the cups in their saucers, demonstrated her awareness that something unwanted was going forward. Once she had retreated, an ill-tempered grunt from Pumicestone authorised the inspector to say his piece.

"You see, Mr Phinney," Holden commenced, looking me straight in the eye, "the police division to which I am assigned covers an area that includes several of what we term the 'noisiest' parts of West London. By this we don't just mean that they are loud, Sir, though they are, but that they are obvious hotbeds of vice. It is common knowledge that the most prominent of these is to be found at the Haymarket and in the area that surrounds it. The streetwalkers there ply their trade so visibly that many tourists are persuaded to visit the locale solely in order to view the depravity at first hand."

"I cannot conceive of there being any good reason for you to be telling us this", Felicity objected.

"Hear me out, Miss." He took a sip of tea, and then rejoined his narrative train. "But it is fair to say that not all practitioners of vice offer themselves up for inspection in so visible a fashion. Some of them operate from highly exclusive residential addresses, where they are hard to locate and weed out. Some set up purportedly legitimate watering holes at festivals held beyond London's boundaries, such as at Ascot at race time. Now then, I am required by law to inspect the night houses of the Haymarket and I do so quite openly in uniform. However, as regards what we may term these more concealed places, I often find it expedient to survey them in what we describe as 'undress'. I had occasion to be doing just that last week at an Ascot pleasure tent, one that was in my estimation no less than an outdoor brothel under sail. It was in there that I saw someone who bore an uncanny resemblance to yourself, Mr Phinney. And that someone I saw appeared to be in thick with some very unbecoming individuals."

Bubbles of misapprehension rose to the surface of my mind like froth in a jug. I opened my mouth to try and forestall him with an explanation, but Holden gave me a significant stare that made me clamp it back shut.

"There's really no need for you to say anything, Sir", he counselled me. "I am not here in an official capacity. How you pass your hours of recreation is entirely your own look-out. But I do feel that it is my place to warn you to think hard about the sort of circles you choose to revolve in. You see, I observed that you were escorted into the place by a gentleman named James Roberts, a most pernicious brothel and gaming house proprietor better known to us as 'Bawdyhouse Bob'. We have our eye on him in connection with several rackets and swindles, about which we think that there's no night-soil without there's his foul reek. Forgive my vulgarity, Miss Pumicestone, but it is all too often a vulgar currency that I must treat in."

She was plainly too dazed by what she was hearing to make any comment, so the inspector resumed. "And I also observed, Sir, that you were then ushered by this Roberts into a private snug where you were entertained by Agnes Willoughby, a notable, one might even say a celebrated society prostitute. She has been one of Roberts' instruments since she was seventeen, when we understand she started out by patrolling the card tables in one of his gambling dens, distracting the young men at their play. But she has scaled the heights in his service since then. He is what we may term her pander, or to put it more crudely, her pimp, and she is by dead reckoning not the chastest of the chaste these days. I am sure that on the afternoon I am describing nothing indecent did take place, but you and your companion, Sir, a Mr Windham, remained supping with her, and were friendly, for a good stretch longer than simple politeness might dictate."

Holden paused again for a slurp of tea. "You must appreciate, Sir, that I am not repeating these unsavoury facts in order to gratify some malign purpose of my own, or to subject you to persecution. Far from it. It is my duty to Mr Pumicestone, and more particularly to his daughter, that forces me to share these confidences, however unwillingly they are wrung out of me."

He presaged his final disclosure with a great gulp

of tea. “And there is just one more detail that I must divulge for the sake of completeness. It is that you seemed, Mr Phinney, to be on very familiar terms with another loose girl who was present, judging by the nice kiss and embrace with which you greeted each other.”

At this, Felicity let go of my hand and separated herself bodily from me. I could see that she was struggling hard to prevent herself from crying.

Needless to say, I strained every sinew in presenting my own account of the items against me. To her credit Felicity received my efforts attentively and, I am convinced, strove to believe that my part that day was one of total innocence throughout. But in the end it was not a particle of use my protesting. What was inescapable was that everything described had indeed taken place. I had, at the very least, gone to a bawdy house and consorted with villains, and remained there long after I knew such to be the case. This was behaviour that could not be squared with respectability.

Her father was implacable, but I believe that I would have had a faint chance of convincing Felicity were it not for that damning marquee embrace with the showily-dressed girl. Once I had thrown over the unequal attempt at persuasion, she pledged me her continued civility while we remained under the same roof. She would however be obliged, she said, if I were to begin searching without delay for another residence and situation.

A CELESTIAL SIGN

Fifty years ago, London was not the insatiable monster it has since become. There were no underground lines reaching outlying suburbs, no tram lines, and motor vehicles had not yet been invented. West of Kensington and Holland Park there were cottages and green fields and market gardens. Fulham and Walham Green and Earls Court, which are now continuously built up and joined on, were separate villages then, and Hammersmith was an independent township. Sussex House was a sizable mansion, set in open country to the south of Hammersmith, and surrounded by spacious grounds. It was once the residence of the Duke of Sussex, one of George III's sons. It has long since been demolished and replaced by terrace housing, and traffic now thunders past its former site along the Fulham Palace Road.

On the evening of my day of romantic triumph, then disaster, I was being driven through the gateway to Sussex House in General Windham's carriage. Having received Felicity's banishment order, I was wondering whether my own residence would soon be something more akin to a fireless garret in a rookery than a stately mansion. The carriage was a choice one, the sort that our maid Anna might have described as, "a proper posh trolley" if given the chance to peek into it. As well as myself it contained the general, Windham my friend, and Mr Henry Portal of Messrs Portal & Merritt of Aylsham, hereditary Windham family solicitors. I had first spotted the latter, briefly, at the homecoming party at Felbrigg. When I had joined them earlier at Windham's lodging as my friend had requested, General Windham, who had settled for civilian attire on this occasion, had declared that he was on the way to a pressing engagement. We would all have to come along with him, he had insisted, and the legal proposition that was due to be discussed would have to wait its turn until later on. I thought this was all very irregular, but it was hard to resist being steamrollered by the general. All the way there, he remained tight-lipped about where we were going and whom we were going to see.

I knew nothing of Sussex House then, but as we crunched along its driveway I could see that it was at the centre of a little society of its own. A number of figures were dotted about the woodland and gardens that surrounded it, apparently strolling at their leisure. There were trellised walkways, and a small group was gathered on benches in an arbour of hedging around a sundial. Nearer the house, games were underway on a croquet lawn and a tennis court. Several blocks of outbuildings were grouped to one side, and we passed a bustling stable range. The driveway terminated in a broad oval, fringed by fuchsia bushes, in front of the porticoed main entrance. Here the coachman parked to let us off, and the general strode to the door with Mr Portal in tow, and tugged the rope. From where Windham and I were standing, hanging apprehensively back, it looked like the proprietor had answered the door in person, as greetings of mutual respect and cordiality were exchanged.

General Windham signalled us impatiently to come forward and we all stepped into a lofty vestibule, into which shafts of orangey evening brightness were being projected through a fanlight. The floor was laid with alternating tiles of white and black, and a wide stairway rose from it to a halfway landing, before sweeping back on itself to reach the next level in two cantilevered sections. There were a series of recesses containing posed statues, reminiscent of classical antiquity.

"Mr Portal has already had the pleasure of his acquaintance," the general announced, "but I'd like you to meet Dr Forbes Benignus Winslow, Willie. This is my nephew William, doctor. Oh, and this man is called Phinney." Portal and the general were not overjoyed by my inclusion in their party at Windham's behest.

Doctor Winslow was bald, rotund and jowly, yet fastidiously shaven and groomed. "He owns and supervises this establishment," the general informed us, "which is for the male inmates only. And he has Brandenburgh House over the lane from the gatekeeper's lodge, which caters for the poor afflicted women. Sixty or seventy patients in all, is it doctor?"

"That would be about right, at the last count."

Though no exclamations of distress could be heard, and though the place was ostensibly as placid as the Hanover Gallery had been, it was now apparent, nonetheless, that we had come to a lunatic asylum. Windham and I exchanged astonished looks, but his uncle brazened out the incongruity of having fetched us here. "How has Freddie been?" he asked of the alienist.

I had already heard of Winslow, partly because he was an assiduous seeker after publicity, but more particularly because of his close involvement with the law. He was well known as a prosperous psychiatric physician, with consulting rooms in prestigious Albemarle Street, and he had written copiously on multifarious aspects of mental illness. I had, at some point, had cause to look up his grand opus, *On the Obscure Diseases of the Brain and Mind*. But it was so dense and prolix that I had failed to hack a path beyond the introduction. He frequently appeared as an expert witness in lunacy cases, and had long been a pioneer of insanity pleas in the criminal courts. So much so that he was widely accused of being too eager to diagnose derangement, and of confusing the downright wicked with the mad.

"Much as usual, general," the doctor responded, "he is flat...utterly flat. I am afraid that it's all the same to him these days. He greets silence or argument, company or isolation, sedation or stimulation in the same unerringly blank spirit. Of course we try him on potations and preparations, and infusions and distillations, but the most that any can achieve is to arouse his irritation, which is, I suppose, better than getting no reaction from him at all."

"Forgive me, but might we know whom we are speaking of, doctor?" questioned Windham irritably. "I have to say that my uncle has not seen fit to put my friend and me in the frame."

"It is mine to explain, doctor", said the general. "You see, Willie, I come here to visit an old friend named Freddie, whom I have known since I was a young officer in the reign of old King Billy. Your own presence here, and that of Mr Phinney, are quite incidental to that purpose. Given the nature of his confinement, discretion prevents me from disclosing his family name, which I may only state is an aristocratic one. We were newly gazetted ensigns in the Coldstream Guards when we first met, stationed in the Portman barracks off Oxford Street. But he became embroiled with a scarlet woman and the affair ended as messily as could be imagined.

"I will tell you how it happened before we go to him, but I must sit while I do." The general lowered himself stiffly into the corner of a settle which rested against the left hand side of the hall. "I have difficulty in standing for too long, gentlemen. One day in the Crimea I was fetched a kick on the shin by a charger which hurt me most severely, and the pain of it persists to the present. Sit here beside me, Willie. You've always liked a good tale, haven't you?"

"You seem to forget how long you have been abroad, uncle. I am no longer an infant to be distracted by stories."

"Quite so, Willie. Of course you're not. Do stay with us doctor." The general was accustomed by his calling to arranging people, and he waved at some chairs for Portal, myself and the doctor to draw up and occupy. Windham did go where he had been put, despite his protest.

"Our commissions of ensigncy," the general resumed saying when we were all seated, "were paid for in cash of course, as the idiotic purchase system that still constricts our military effectiveness prescribes. I ask you, does it make sense for promotions to be bought and sold like a sabre or a sash, regardless of ability? It's enough to frighten the horses from their oats."

This iniquitous system, whereby rank was a marketable commodity, had only another decade to run before it was done away with by Mr Gladstone's first government.

"Anyway," he reflected, "I mustn't prattle on about soldiering like the music hall martinet. Our ceremonial duties at the royal palace were not overly demanding and much of our time was spent footloose and carefree. You may say that the West End was our youthful stamping ground, and we would amuse ourselves thereabouts handsomely. Freddie was blessed both with winning features and the personal gifts necessary to launch him upon a dazzling career. We became firm friends. He was a lively and outgoing spirit, occasionally wilful and cussed; though these are flaws that many of us might lay claim to. The loss of his parents, when he was at a tender age, meant that he had inherited a not inconsiderable fortune by the time I came across him. Their loss, perhaps, also tilted a temperament predisposed that way toward bouts of morbid gloom.

"Well, this girl that I mentioned was of good looks and high charms, but no apparent fortune. She fluttered about our social circle without anyone being quite sure how she entered it. I believe that she was called Maud Kemp, though it goes against the grain to dignify her with any gentle name. Freddie soon grew tremendously enamoured of her, and their relations developed so immoderately that those of us who were his friends began to see something obsessive in the ardour of his attachment. His mood was inordinately afflicted according to whether he was in high or low favour with her, and she seemed to know it and play on the fact.

"But as it happened, a chance sighting by one of our brother officers revealed that she kept company with a police-court *habitué* named Franklyn Duce, an infamous orchestrator of sexual swindles and other assorted corruptions. I refer here, gentlemen, to the sort of practice whereby a married man, for instance, is introduced to a young lady in the apparent privacy of a room rented by the hour. He later receives a letter threatening exposure, on the word of the girl and some planted third party, if specified payments are not forthcoming. Sometimes mention is made of a photographic reproduction. I believe that this strain of criminal infection is still rife, is it not Portal? Or is the country solicitor innocent of such 'lays'?"

"They are not unheard of even in Norwich nowadays," Portal proffered in a loamy Norfolk tone, "and there are countless different trips the blackguards have to set their mantraps." Looking at his weathered, whiskery face, and his fustian brown suit and bowler hat, it was hard to consider Portal innocent of anything.

"Quite so. And as we feared that Freddie had been marked down for one duping or another, we had no choice but to inform him of his *amour's* criminal connection and prevail on him to end the affair. I regret that his friends had to wrestle with him most officiously in the matter, and must say that he resisted us mightily. In fact, hearing the unwelcome intelligence about Maud Kemp nudged him into a frenzy of vacillation. First, he broke it off with her. Then he begged himself back, which she only allowed in exchange for a promise of marriage, given, as it turned out, in the hearing of a hidden witness. Next, she goaded him, through a series of infelicitous provocations, into finally breaking it off. Once he had done so, he found a solicitor's letter nesting in his pigeon-hole claiming damages for breach of promise to marry. Whether it would have sunk or swam in a courtroom, I can only leave it to the likes of you lawyers to argue. The point was that the publicity would have been ruinous either way, and so the suit was vacated by means of negotiated settlement. Though the sum arrived at was steep enough, the money was the very least of it to Freddie. The harm done to his soul was, however, profound and lasting.

"There followed a deterioration, by stages, in his state of mind, which was most immediately apparent in his sliding standard of cleanliness and dress. Prior to this, he had always been correctly, on occasion flamboyantly, decked out. Corrosion seemed to eat into his very props. At first there was a keen intensity to his distress, and there were manic interludes accompanied by false behaviour and notions. Attempts proceeding from argument to refute whatever false notion he was espousing from time-to-time, reinforced by praise and encouragement, only served to rivet it more strongly upon his mind. But later, the manic episodes went into a decline, and are now seldom evident. He has long been so resolutely indifferent, that mention even of the girl's name elicits not the slightest response. He was committed soon after the settlement of the suit, on the ground of 'mania and melancholia intermitting, attributed to a disappointment of the affections.' He's been an inpatient ever since at various establishments, and been in the care of Doctor Winslow from when he opened this house, upwards of twenty years ago."

The general placed a paternal hand on the knee of his nephew, adjoining his on the settle. "You see, Willie, this fellow Duce had measured Fred up feloniously from the outset, and the Kemp girl had never given a hatpin for him. It behoves young men who stand in the path of fortunes to be watchful as to whom they consort with. This especially applies to young heirs who are smitten at the sight of horsebreakers in the park."

He looked reproachfully at his nephew. "It saddened me to hear about your rudeness to your aunt in Hyde Park the other day, and I trust that you are ready to make amends for it?"

"I am sorry that I lost my temper with her", Windham conceded. "What would you have me do?"

"Compose a letter of apology to your aunt for your incivilities. If she is content with it, then I will consider the offence spent."

"Very well, uncle."

"But you must also think hard about how you deport yourself generally. It is all very well to look at a pretty girl, but you must be able to recognise those who would prey upon you, and hold them at bay. And it has to be said that young men who are already prone to wayward and unaccountable actions must be particularly wary. As I have stated, it is my belief that Freddie was predisposed to psychological upset. So you see, Willie, that ill-judgements, particularly those in the sphere of romance, can have unexpectedly dire results, as they did for poor Freddie. He will never know ease of mind again."

The general paused gravely for his words to sink in, then removed his hand from his nephew's knee and patted it a couple of times in a sudden show of bonhomie. "Still, if your mind did cave in there are worse places than this to find yourself quartered. Isn't that so, Doctor Winslow? You believe in humane treatment of your patients, do you not?"

I had noticed that the doctor had been observing Windham closely while the general spoke. Winslow had positioned his chair so that he was placed opposite my friend, with the light playing upon his subject's face. I also noted that Windham was twitching uncomfortably and fiddling with his cufflinks, now it was apparent that our being in the asylum was no accident.

"Humane treatment is beyond question our fiery beacon," replied the doctor, "as I trust you gentlemen may infer from the tenor of these surroundings. It astonishes many who come here to learn that not all mental institutions, including those maintained at the public expense, are as monstrous as popular novelists would paint them. Most establishments these days, god willing, bear no comparison to the madhouses of yore, run by indifference for profit. We reject the old resorts to physical punishment, solitary confinement and mechanical restraint, and are not content to merely keep order. We do not go in for indiscriminate applications of bleeding, or blistering, or emetics. We decline to administer to the unsound of mind the lacerations of the scarifying instrument, or the stripes of the lash. We hold fast to the first tenet of pastoral care, that corporal punishment is to be strictly avoided."

"Decent handling is all well and good so far as it goes," Mr Portal objected, "if it can be afforded. But I can't see where it gets you in terms of a cure."

"Our doctrine accords a high therapeutic value to kindness and good living in and of themselves", the doctor reassured him airily. "In our scheme of things, the patient is to receive every encouragement to freely pursue the occupation or recreation of his choice. You will find that there is no want of stimulation here, and our attendants positively strive to engage their charges' interest. We have a walled garden, and a producing farm. You will have seen our grounds for rambling in, and our installations for sporting pursuits. There are regular entertainments where the otherwise segregated sexes from both of our houses may mingle and mix. We have afternoons of tea and cake, when there are special amusements such as plays and shadow pantomime displays that the patients themselves put on."

"But do games and parties, and tea and cake, make for sufficient correctives by themselves?" Portal persisted, unconvinced.

"Many minds are indeed recovered, and lives restored, by dint of these methods alone, Mr Portal. Humane treatment, however, though undoubtedly a prerequisite for a cure, is no guarantee of it. We also use medications, and certain other procedures as appropriate. You see, each of our patients has his weak place, his twist, his hobby, and we have to delve around to discover what will unlatch it. Some instances will always prove to be irreclaimable, as, sadly, has Freddie's. Come, gentlemen, let us go and see what humour he is in tonight, and you can observe some of the communal parts while we are in transit."

We got to our feet, and Winslow ushered our party through a wide double doorway. Once inside the chamber beyond, it was not hard to see that this had once been a royal duke's mansion. The chamber took up a whole corner of the house, and had the dimensions of a stateroom. There were long, lancet windows at regular intervals, and a gigantic marble fireplace. Various heraldic motifs and designs were worked into the cornices, which were meticulously and ostentatiously crafted. The carpeting was regularised with elegant designs and opulent pigmentation. It was noticeable, however, that the quality of furniture and ornamentation did not keep pace with that of the decor. This was down to the hazard of breakage, I first thought, though the dozen and a half persons inhabiting the space did not look bent on destruction. But on giving it deeper consideration, I understood that the sort of delicate items, such vases and figurines, which one would normally associate with the grandeur of the setting, were irrelevant here. It was the purely functional to which merit was assigned.

A pair of uniformed attendants acknowledged our entrance with polite nods. The patients, however, who were clad in everyday clothes rather than any institutional gown or smock, barely registered our coming. Numerous books and games were strewn about, and two groups were sitting cross-legged on the floor, the one playing at draughts and the other at bagatelle. A solitary man was lying flat out sketching on a pad, whether from life or from his imagination I could not say. In a nook there was a grand piano, and other musical instruments were scattered around in positions that suggested recent employment. One fellow was picking out a primitive tune with his thumb on a sort of zither, and the notes chimed with the twittering and scratching of several caged birds. A few persons, it was true, were doing no better than sitting and staring into space, and one or two looked wholly unapproachable.

Winslow continued to enlighten us concerning the curative process as he led us through a series of similarly imposing apartments, one of which was given over to a billiard table.

"And don't suppose that we strap them in a strait-waistcoat, and lash them to a pallet the moment they are out of sight at night", he advised us smilingly, when describing the sleeping arrangements upstairs. I supposed that this was the sort of black humour that went along with his occupation.

"Though they do share bedrooms, sufficiently few patients are allocated to each as to avoid the creation of a dormitory ambiance. They have access to modern plumbing at all hours of the day or night, and our attendants are forever on hand to assist those that need it."

Eventually we were conducted into a long, low glasshouse, populated with fascinating botanical exotics as well as a host of fibrous and leafy palms. "Fred's generally in here about this time" was the doctor's stated hypothesis, as he peered into a series of natural pens formed by the foliage of the larger plants. Sure enough Winslow soon located his quarry, sitting on a low restraining wall behind a curtain of green fronds. “See here, Fred. Charlie Windham’s come to visit.”

Looking through the foliage one could detect that the man’s grey hair was shorn short and shapeless, and that he was wearing corduroy trousers and a rough woollen shirt. He seemed overdressed, and a muffler was wrapped round his throat even though the glass house was to me uncomfortably hot. His face was parched, cadaverous, and inexpressive, though, on perceiving the general, he tilted his head toward him by an almost imperceptible fraction. Even this microscopic motion seemed to have cost him the profoundest exertion of the will. His skin was stretched taut across his bones. He was the bare ghost of a man.

“Leave us alone, now,” the general requested, stepping into the circle of vegetation, “and continue your tour.” He squatted down on the wall next to Freddie and turned to face him, clutching his elbow.

We explored further regions of the house in the care of Dr Winslow at some length, so that it was dark by the time we returned to the vestibule to rejoin the general. He had by then ended his interview with Freddie and resumed his place on the settle. We departed, and wished the doctor a good evening. Once more in the carriage, we were returned to London by the light of a candle-lantern swaying from a hook on the roof. General Windham was subdued as we travelled, and not disposed to conversation. His head sank back to the rest, though in the semi-darkness I could not discern whether he was awake or asleep.

After we had rolled some distance in silence, Mr Portal addressed Windham who was facing him across the cabin. “There was one saving grace to Mr Freddie’s case, you know Willie, and it was a nice legal point that was at issue.” He stroked his whiskers and glanced at me. “You might find this instructive yourself, Mr

Phinney, as a fellow practitioner, though I don't have you down as a land estate lawyer. Being from the town you'd be more of the courtroom body, I'd surmise."

I had passed a long day, and was weary and wanting to be untroubled. My anxieties about Felicity, and whether anything could be saved in her respect, were at the forefront of my thinking, and I regarded instruction on arcane points of land law as inessential at this juncture.

But Mr Portal was not averse to their intricacies, and he rehearsed an explanation that I shall not trouble to reproduce verbatim. The gist of it was, however, essentially simple. He contended that Freddie's swindlers had been prevented from winning a greater sum from their subject because, as he had no right to sell or mortgage any part of it, his inheritance had been legally shielded from their avarice. Thus, though Freddie had been cleaned out personally, his family estates had been saved to finance him in the physical, if not mental, comfort that he enjoyed at Sussex House. And as Mr Portal put it, "It's not cheap to keep a man there by any means; four guineas a week, despite the doctor being the soul of humanity."

The rustic solicitor then proceeded to contrast this fortuitous state of "Mr Freddie's" legal affairs at the time he was duped, with the opposite condition that he ascribed to "Willie's" position now. If Willie were to be swindled as Freddie had been, then the entirety of Felbrigg would be open to attack. The solution he proposed was that Windham should sign some legal documents, when his impending twenty-first birthday rendered him of age to do so. By these he would renounce the right to control Felbrigg and determine whom it passed to after his death, but he would still live there and receive all the income its lands generated. Any legitimate children he had would still inherit after him. In technical terms, he would give up the "tenancy-in-tail" that was due to fall in on his birthday and become instead "tenant-for-life." Portal pledged that he and General Windham would see to it, as legal trustees of the Felbrigg settlement, that he would receive a significantly greater income by dint of recompense. Here then, at last, was the advertised legal proposition, lent weight by the sorry fate of "Mr Freddie."

"I only ask that you give the proposal fair consideration, Willie", said his uncle, now alert and leaning in from the shadows. His sunken eyes looked strained and careworn in the wavering pool of light.

"It affords you the great boon of offloading the responsibility for managing Felbrigg to Mr Portal and myself. You know very well that business is not your strong suit, and that you are prone to erratic episodes of unwisdom. The contemplated readjustment would free your mind of practical burdens, and, at the same time, boost your income handsomely. We could see to the signing of the documents as part of your coming of age *fête* at Felbrigg, and thus add to the festivities of that occasion."

Windham looked overwhelmed, and at a loss to know how to respond. It seemed that various emotions were fermenting in his breast.

"I may sometimes appear fierce to you, my boy, and I can only regret it. But since the untimely death of my beloved brother William, your poor father, I must watch out for your welfare. It remains, I fear, a forlorn hope that your mother Lady Sophia will ever offer any useful contribution to your upbringing. So you see that it falls to me to protect you from marauding blackguards, and from your own weaknesses. And it would be to the destruction of all right feeling if I failed to act as I saw fit in preserving Felbrigg intact for future generations of our line. I judge that you yourself will rest easier for knowing that the estate is kept safe and sound. Don't give me your answer now, but promise to think on it faithfully and advise Mr Portal in due course."

"I will give the matter every consideration, as you have requested me to."

At length we were set down on the pavement outside my friend's Duke Street lodging. As we watched the rear of his uncle's carriage fade towards Piccadilly, it seemed that Windham was simmering fit to explode. He spluttered incoherently, then burst into merriment, and then looked awfully sad. He was so disconcerted as to sit down on the kerb, with his boots in the gutter. I joined him there, in sympathy.

"Did you ever witness such a blatant morality play?" he enquired incredulously of me.

"A cautionary tale, certainly," I replied, catching onto his meaning, "with the pairing of Duce and Kemp for its villains, and poor Freddie for its fated victim."

"Yes, and the madhouse for a backdrop. Uncle Charlie has acquired a taste for theatrics in the orient. He drives us all the way to Hammersmith accidentally-on-purpose, just to put me to such an awful spooking that I might be prevailed upon to disinherit myself. He seems to have caught a bad dose of dyspepsia out in India. Since he's returned he's grown the same bump of dictating to me as the rest of my family have. I'm perfectly able to look after myself and have no intention of giving up the same rights to my property that my father had. What did you make of the solicitor's proposal?"

I outlined my view that such an arrangement would be entirely suitable for a hopeless wastrel or an invalid, but that it would be quite wrong for a person of sound heart and mind to subscribe to it. I said that I considered the scheme to have been advanced in good faith, but I advised him to resist it resolutely.

He thanked me for coming along, and asked after my own welfare. I then gave him a précis of my time with Felicity earlier that day, and he commiserated with me over its *dénouement*. He proceeded to make the sort of optimistic noises about my domestic situation that one would hope a friend might attempt. He was less receptive when I disclosed Inspector Holden's view of the true nature of Agnes Willoughby, and of her association with James Roberts, otherwise known as "Bawdyhouse Bob".

"It may be that Agnes is in some way beholden to Roberts as the policeman says," Windham stated, clutching his lapels and rolling his head as he did when making a declaration, "but I am convinced that she wants no more than to be shot of him, along with all else that is unsavoury in her existence."

This assessment was, to me, so unrealistically optimistic that I was unable to return my friend's favour with noises of reassurance.

"Possibly," I said, "but I think that you would do better to erase her from your mind, rather than bank upon such an unlikely occurrence."

"I suppose that I would", he replied.

"And though you may baulk at your uncle's interfering, let's not forget how a combination of womanly wiles and criminal cunning did for his old chum Freddie."

"No doubt you're right." His expression as he said this suggested that he held fast to the opposite opinion.

Then, noticing that we were still sitting on the kerbstone he added, "I think that we are due a round of conviviality after this evening's dispiriting excursion. It's late now, but I know of some places round the Haymarket where they keep it up all night. I suppose you're far too respectable to accompany me there?"

Until recently, this would unswervingly have been my position. "Not a bit of it, Willie," I said, despite being markedly jaded, "lead the way."

So he did, and we walked up to Piccadilly without bothering to call in at his lodging. "Incidentally," I enquired as we went, "what did the Lewellins say happened to them when we missed each other at Ascot?"

"They said that they had run into an old friend who they hadn't seen for a long time", Windham explained. “And once they were done nattering with him they couldn’t find us to save their lives, though they searched high and low. Strange to say, they also made themselves scarce earlier on when my uncle showed up.”

We turned right, along Piccadilly, and walked past the tall town houses and glittering emporia that lined it. At its far end, past the circus at the foot of Regent Street, we came upon the equally showy underside of the metropolis that flourished at the top of the Haymarket. It was by now just gone midnight, and revellers who had been turned out of the nearby dancing rooms and saloons were swelling the already teeming pavement life. The excitement of liquor and a rollicking spirit of good fun blended uneasily with an undercurrent of hostility and desperation. All types and classes were represented in loud and extravagant profusion, and it was clearly an open forum for casual prostitution, beggary and theft. One wandering damsel with a scarred and blemished face was crying so that her make-up ran, while a squadron of braying swells mocked her affliction. Some of her sisters in flaring colours hurled the abuse back, and violence did not seem too far distant. I felt some creature of indeterminate provenance tug at my sleeve, and I yanked it free. In contrast with the ordered serenity of the place we had just returned from, this scene was rather the madhouse.

Windham hurried me through it and onward down the Haymarket, weaving between further inebriated and licentious hordes.

“A good number of the drinking dens hereabouts are flash houses,” he remarked knowledgably, “the haunts of criminals, and so best avoided. But through here we can find a nice little haven.”

He led me off the street, along a narrow passage that gave onto a large courtyard enclosed by crumbling brick terraces. The sign, “beds to let” was prominent above several of the entrances. As an unsteady couple were attempting to enter one of these, the girl dropped her bonnet onto the dirty flagstones and keeled over while stooping to retrieve it. The man got hold of her by the waist with one arm, and hauled her through the door like a puppet, leaving the bonnet on the floor. It did not seem a promising place to locate a haven.

"Here we are," said Windham, heading for the entrance of a decrepit looking dive, "this is Cauty's Chop House." Much to my surprise, the atmosphere inside was warm and welcoming. A large gasolier, suspended from the ceiling, was burning brightly, and the highly diverse clientele appeared equally lit-up. The proprietor and a good number of the patrons hailed Windham as a boon companion, and a pack of them shuffled along to clear space for us at a table. We had barely taken up our places, before a quart of beer and two pint pots were slammed down. This quart proved to be only the first in a procession of the same, and it was not long before we joined our fellows in having a mixture of fun and folly etched on our faces.

We were served with a repast at one stage, consisting of roasted pork, declared to be country bred, and piles of cauliflower and potatoes. The night was punctuated by bursts of singing and dancing, to the lively accompaniment of a piano and a fiddle. A sentimental tune of the time, *The Rose of Daplemore*, was fetchingly rendered at one point by an angelically sweet girl, who was compelled by popular acclamation to give it repeated recitals. At another point a policeman walked in, to be received with a cry of "Here come the Bobbies", and a hearty round of guffaws, at which he merely shrugged and departed. The entire company was as merrily made up as harvest-bugs at harvest time.

But there is always a reverse facet to unrestrained libation. Deep into the early hours, my friend turned maudlin when describing emotions that he took to be ones of love for Agnes Willoughby. I tried to tell him that he was experiencing nothing more than a foolish fixation, but in so doing fell into the trap of turning maudlin myself over Felicity. When we at last agreed to be off, I fear that we had both swallowed a stiff draught of pathos.

Back at the top of the Haymarket, the revellers were still going at it hot and thick. "Well old fellow, we have been jolly together", Windham said, his spirits abruptly reviving. He then approached the policeman we had seen earlier, who was leaning against a railing looking bored, and offered him half a crown for the loan of his whistle and chimney-pot hat. The officer readily accepted, whereupon my friend clapped the hat on his head. Assuming the voice and manner of a policeman, and thumbing his lapels, he approached a school of streetwalkers gathered close by and announced, "You're all very naughty girls, and if you don't move along, quick, quick, I'll have you in the lock-up as fast as pharaoh." He swayed and wagged a podgy finger at them, and then blew the whistle.

They giggled and swished their satin and paid no heed to his instruction.

Returning to address the custodian of public order, Windham shook hands with him energetically, enquiring as he did, "My dear Mr Moppet, have you seen my fancy girl?" The officer just laughed and took back his whistle and hat, though he stowed the half crown in his tunic pocket.

"It's alright old chap," my friend slurred, "I'm only chaffing the Bobbies; they know me well enough."

As we staggered away, it was possible even in our befuddled state to dimly perceive that other pedestrians were looking up at the heavens and pointing. In fact, a couple of little parties of folk had had their coaches pulled over and halted, so that they could climb down and do the same. Far overhead, a comet was floating as bright as bright can be, with a long tail spluttering behind it like a gas jet. Windham suddenly came over all solemn. He knew that the odds of courting Agnes were against him, he said, making an effort to clearly enunciate his words, but had he not won, despite long odds, when wagering on *Flying Star* at Ascot? The flying star that we were now witnessing was assuredly sent as a celestial sign, he gravely alleged, directing him to press his suit and win her. For myself, I considered that nothing could be less of a certainty in the matrimonial stakes.

THE ITALIAN OPERATIST

Sometimes a woman is called an "actress" with the term being intended to suggest that she is actually a member of an older profession. When I next saw Agnes it struck me that there was much of the actress about her. She had her stage name (if Lady Listowel had been right about "Willoughby" being an assumed one) and she had her own vantages from which to present herself for public admiration. At one moment she might lounge in an open carriage at Hyde Park, while at another she might grace the luxury of an exclusive, but prominently placed box at the theatre. The Italian operas staged at Her Majesty's Theatre were then ranked amongst the most desirable occasions to be seen at in the season, and Agnes had invited Windham and myself there to see a thing called *Lucia di Lammermoor.*

Having arrived at its stated hour and presented our invitation at the main entrance, we were ushered up to the passage outside her box where Agnes greeted us. She wore a white silk dress cut very low, with a diamond studded necklace adorning her *décolletage.* A black velvet mantle was around her shoulders, and a tiara atop of her golden tresses sparkled with tiny jewelled stars. She presented the back of a gloved hand to be kissed. "Delighted..." she breathed, though I suspected that for her the prospect of an evening in our company was an essentially humdrum one.

Her Lady's maid, who had on an ostrich feather hat in the style of the French Empress Eugénie, was despatched to fire up the lamps in the enclosure. The usher then held its door open, and Agnes swept regally into the ensuing blast of light, with Windham and me following. She did so to the accompaniment of a restive murmuring round about. Many heads protruded from adjoining boxes, and those opposite, anxious to inspect her and know whom she was entertaining tonight. Extravagant bouquets awaited her within the sumptuous interior of the box, bearing ribbons and messages inscribed in swirling hands.

In the old auditorium of Her Majesty's, which was erased by fire some years later, the private boxes were stacked in six tiers. These snaked along both its sides, and faced each other more closely where they curved inward to fringe the stage. Our hostess's box was a particularly visible one. It directly overlooked the stage from the second tier up, and its situation had plainly been selected to show its proprietress off to maximum effect. The stacked tiers put me in mind of a dovecot, with each compartment a hutch housing a number of well-groomed and bespangled birds. Several of the necks popping in and out to examine Agnes would have been titled ones, as there was an immense assemblage of the fashionable and the aristocratic present. While Windham revelled in the stir her entrance was creating, bowing ostentatiously to startled onlookers as if he were the object of their attention, Agnes affected complete unawareness of it.

Unfortunately, there had been no element of affectation in Felicity's reaction to my sloshing in from the Haymarket at six in the morning a few days earlier. When I had at last risen from my bed, after midday, she had confined herself to a glare that needed no accompanying comment to convey the depth of her disgust. Her father had required no recourse to thespian skills either, when expressing his own displeasure at this fresh dereliction on my part. I fear that the night out had done my cause at Red Lion Square not the slightest good, and had instead reinforced their growing impression of me as a debauchee in training.

Once the ripples excited by her entrance had calmed, Agnes introduced her maid as a French *mademoiselle* named Trinette. This young woman stayed silent, and sat unobtrusively in the shadows toward the back of the box. Presumably to facilitate social interaction the chairs were not fixed to the floor, and our hostess placed Windham next to her and me at one remove. Receipt of her invitation had put him into such ecstasies that my attempts to talk him out of going had been half-hearted at best. I had resigned myself to attending in the part of second fiddle and first chaperone.

"I do hope that opera is to your liking", Agnes said, addressing us both but patting the back of Windham's hand where it rested on the cushioned rail. "I can't claim to possess a shred of Italian myself and seldom have the faintest idea what's going on. But that doesn't seem to be any great disadvantage. It's usually a good spectacle, and the costumes are always nice. They'll put it on before too long. In the meantime you two will have to be my own little bit of theatre." Her faint smile as she said this seemed to challenge us to entertain her.

But our initial efforts in this regard proved unimpressive. Windham seemed unable to do anything other than grin idiotically, and I found myself bereft of anything topical to say.

"We don't have operatics in Norfolk," my friend at last managed to utter, "so I really can't say whether it's to my liking or otherwise. We generally go in more for things in the agricultural line."

"I couldn't afford the price of it if you hadn't been so kind as to invite me, Miss Willoughby", I chipped in lugubriously. "And I've had to hire a very expensive evening suit."

"What a pair of prunes", she chided with a chirruping laugh. "You might manage to be more conversational than that." Then, turning her head in the French girl's direction she added, "Mix us some cordial and ice would you, Trinette my love."

The maid did as she had been requested. When she had stirred and handed out the glasses, her mistress examined them and pronounced, "These drinks look appallingly slack. I think they need a sprinkle of stiffening." She then produced a flask from under a flounce in her gown. "Let's make the spoon stand up in them shall we?" she suggested, splashing a generous tot of brandy into each. "Here's how!" she toasted us, lifting her glass then draining it.

I took a sip of mine and found it more than stiff enough to be going on with.

"Forgive my ignorance concerning this evening's musical diversion, Miss Willoughby," Windham said, gulping heavily on his own drink, "but can you fill us in on the general drift of what we have in store?"

"Do call me Agnes, Willie dear." This was a special concession that did not apparently extend as far as myself.

"I understand that it's a tragedy about doomed lovers," she set out to explain, "but then again what opera isn't? It's supposed to be set in Scotland, at a place called Lammermoor, though you'd think that the Italians of all people would have enough romantic tragedies of their own to choose from without filching foreign ones. You'll have to read the programme for yourself if you want to follow the finer points of the story. I generally don't bother."

"Is anyone famous in it?" Windham wanted to know.

"Ah yes. The male lead is called Antonio Giuglini,

whom they say is quite a sensation. I'm looking forward to seeing him. They call him 'Cherub', reputedly on account of his babyfaced good looks. And the heroine is impersonated by Miss Marietta Piccolomini, whom they say is a very delicious creature but no great shakes as an artist. The whole company are fresh in from Italy, and booked to play out a European tour."

"There is one thing I can say for sure about the opera", Windham volunteered in the mock pompous way he had about him, the rush of drink having infused him with a surge of confidence. "You see Agnes, before I was banished to London, my uncle Charlie gave me a list of dos and don'ts to observe while I am here. George will bear me out on this, because he was present at Aylsham on the occasion it was given. And it just so happens that Italian opera was one of those very things that my uncle said was safe for me to attend. Indeed, he positively encouraged me to do so. So, while I do not appear to be in his good graces in general, as matters stand, I can congratulate myself on doing the right thing by him for once tonight. He says that if I follow his strictures it will improve the quality of my mind, which he apparently finds wanting. But we'll have to see whether or not the opera turns out to have the desired effect."

He darted his head from Agnes to myself and back again, laughing uproariously, and we both joined in. Agnes then retrieved the flask from its locker in her drapery, and administered another shot of invigorating liquor.

"Tell me, Willie dearest," she taxed him playfully, "does this uncle of yours always issue you with a schedule of approved pastimes before you go a-wandering? He sounds a frightful pest."

"Not normally, but it's usually him that's been away not me, so he's not been able to."

"And do you comprehend enough Italian to enable the improving effects of the opera to soak their way into your head?"

"Not a word of it. I have some French and German because several years ago one of my tutors, a chap named Bathurst, led me on a trip to Brussels and on up the Rhine. But like you I haven't a morsel of Italian."

I also lacked the linguistic wherewithal to enable me to properly follow the forthcoming production, but Agnes was not about to ask me how I was placed.

"Oh you're quite the traveller then, Willie", she cooed. "I had no idea. I've never crossed from England's shores myself, but if there's one place I'd really like to visit it would be Paris. I've heard it said that they appreciate a good horsewoman at Longchamp like nowhere else in the world. Isn't that so, Trinette?"

"Yes, Madame." The maid nodded, swishing her ostrich feathers against the crimson and amber damask that papered the compartment's walls.

"And their manners are refined to such a height that they make most of our countrymen look like hobbledehoys. I would so adore it if I could make a great splash over there."

"You're a good horsewoman?" Windham leapt at the intimation that they had some pursuit in common. "I had you down as more of a one for being driven in a carriage."

"I flatter myself that I can decorate a carriage as daintily as the next girl, but there's not a horse alive that I cannot bully or persuade."

"Do you like to gallop fast, on a loose rein over rough ground?"

"I like nothing better. I go out with the Royal Buckhounds when I can wangle an invitation, and we tear off through the woods jumping over fences and fallen trunks."

"Why, you must come up to Felbrigg someday soon. We have any number of the most wonderful woodland rides, and you'd find them all very daring. Riding, and driving traps, are about the only things I'm good at. Oh, and I'm also good at driving trains. I don't suppose you've ever managed a train from the footplate?"

"I can't say that I have. But do tell."

"Well, sometimes I've been gone from Felbrigg on the eastern rail lines for days on end, and only eaten one jar of pickled cabbage in all that time. I've often come home dirty, all covered with soot and black as a sweep. And one time I came back with no cravat or collar on, and only one sock. I got it in the neck that day from Jeffy, I can tell you. She's my housekeeper you see, and tries her best to look after me. Some hope. I never was in such a state in all of my life, but I can honestly say that I more than enjoyed it."

"It sounds ever so thrilling", Agnes said. She was pressed very close to him, and now placed a hand on his shoulder in a seamless manoeuvre. "Is there one thing that you would really like to do, Willie?" she said, leaning into him and speaking softly in his ear. "I mean something that really appeals to you, just for the sheer dash of it?"

"Go kite flying on Hampstead Heath", he replied after only a few seconds contemplation. Then, after a few seconds more he added, "Or better still, go kite flying along Oxford Street on horseback, skipping over the dung heaps and weaving through the carts and omnibuses."

"How marvellous!" Agnes looked genuinely taken by this proposition. "And you could jump up from the saddle to the roof of a shiny coach, and leap from one liveried contraption to another chasing the kite. And you could cock-a-snook at the poker-faced grooms and footmen on their rumbles, and tie them all up in kite string. Then dive back into the saddle and make off."

"We could do it together one of these days?"

"Of course we could."

At this point the brandy flask remerged, and a double ration was dolled out. There was a pause in the conversation while it was drained, and when Agnes resumed speaking it emerged that she had a kite of her own to fly.

"And there's something else we might do together, Willie," she intoned sweetly, "if we were ruminating one day in the region of Oxford Street. It would be the tiniest little something, just as a token of your esteem. You see, I've reached a bit of an impasse with Mr Emmanuel, a jeweller on Brook Street. I'm afraid that one of his salesmen has been dunning me for the price of a pendant that I've had on tick, and he's getting to be rather a nuisance. The sum involved is a meagre one. It's not that I can't pay him, but rather that I don't care to be harassed. I'm sure that a gentleman like yourself would never stand that from a tradesman. And there is a wonderful diamond and emerald trinket in his display that I've had my eye on. If we were to go over there one evening and see him straight, we could have supper afterwards at my nest, *tête à tête*."

This idea commended itself unequivocally to Windham. "That would be ever so excellent", he said gushingly, and not without his characteristically excitable slurs. Then he curbed himself and assumed a wise expression. "Of course we must look carefully at any articles before we buy them, as I would want to lay out as little as possible on mere workmanship. But precious stones are, needless to say, always valuable in themselves."

"It's so reassuring to find a man who knows his mind in relation to retail matters."

"Forgive me for being so forward as to mention it," I interjected, "but surely the cost of a few baubles is as nothing to someone such as yourself, Miss Willoughby, who can command a box as luxuriant as this one? It must notch up a fabulous amount to hire for the season, and the going rate to nab the freehold must be in the thousands of guineas. And surely it's not right to put a material price on someone coming round to your house for supper?"

The moorings of my tongue had been untied by brandy, and I was annoyed on my friend's behalf by Agnes's unashamedly mercenary approach. But if I am frank I must also admit that I was irked by the marginal role she was allotting me in the conversation, and I yearned to attract her attention in my own right.

"Yes, the items of jewellery I speak of are of no great value, as I have said", she replied, undeterred and smiling beatifically.

"Then why not settle the monetary accounts yourself, rather than troubling Willie to answer for them?"

"You really are uninformed, Mr Phinney, on the niceties of social interaction. I can only put it down to your revolving in somewhat limited circles. It's a well known fact that enabling those with inherited wealth to pay for this or that trifle affords them no end of satisfaction. It informs them that they have been planted in the earth to serve some higher purpose, and fills them with a warming glow of delight. And aside from that, it's such a civilised way to cement a friendship. You would go along with that, wouldn't you Willie?"

"Nothing could be more pleasurable to me," he concurred oleaginously, "than to furnish you with something that you truly care for."

"But then you ask him to come back to your 'nest', alone, if he does so", I persisted in exasperation. "Where's the correctness in that?"

She lifted her eyes to the heavens, obviously thinking me a piteous plank. "Don't you think that correctness puts such a brake on anyone having any fun, George? I can see that you're not the type for whimsical kite flying."

"She's got you there, my friend", Windham said, chuckling. It was indeed easy to feel trussed-up in the gossamer thread of her light and carefree evasions.

The sound of the orchestra tuning, which had been swelling in the background for some moments, now reached a crescendo and then abruptly tailed off. The chattering audience fell silent with it.

"Off we trot", whispered Agnes, withdrawing her hand from Windham's shoulder and turning to face forward.

The conductor assumed his place at the front of the pit and raised his baton. The music he then set in motion began in a quietly meandering sort of a way, until a couple of staccato blasts from the horns heralded the opening of the curtain and the commencement of the first act.

When they came on, all the male players were costumed like cavaliers, with long hair and feathered hats and pointed beards. Though the women were dressed in crinolines, they had elaborately lacy collars and cuffs. Despite these allusions to Civil War times, the substance of the plot had more of a medieval flavour to it. Consulting the programme to brief myself, I ascertained that it revolved around two Scottish families, named Ravenswood and Lammermoor, who were locked in a feud. I was at one with Agnes in finding the twists and turns taken by events too trying to fully delve into. But the scenario, in essence, was that the hero Edgar and the heroine Lucy shared a love across the chasm of their families' mutual distrust.

First, there was a scene involving a guard troop that took place in some ruins. This included an extended passage wherein characters stood around telling each other about things that had previously happened. The focus then shifted to a fountain, whereon Miss Piccolomini entered as Lucy, in tandem with a female friend, to a bubbling harp accompaniment. The celebrated soprano really was a tiny person, though her voice was sweet and she was as nice to contemplate as Agnes had led us to expect. I was unable to detect any artistic deficiencies that may have been evident to a more expert observer. She did seem slightly nervous though, but foreign performers were reputed to go in awe of London audiences and critics at the time. These were reckoned to regard any success enjoyed outside London as immaterial.

The music and acting were passable enough without being truly enthralling. What did engage my interest, as the concoction proceeded to brew up, was the increasing boisterousness of the crowd's involvement in it. Given the elevated social standing, or at least the considerable wealth of most of the clientele, I would have expected them to receive the recital in a thoughtful and measured fashion. But far from this being the case, the action was repeatedly interrupted by outbreaks of shouting and applause as if it were being mounted at a penny gaff in the East End. The spectators did fall short of fighting and hurling fruit peel, as the patrons of such cheap theatres were said to, but sometimes sections of the audience looked ready to stampede out of their location and invade the stage. And the players themselves had no qualms about stepping out of character, when the audience demanded it, to bask in any gust of appreciation that wafted their way. When one song or another found particular favour, this was so thunderously expressed that the singer was obliged to repeat it.

Windham found this disorderly aspect highly entertaining, training his opera glasses more often at the onlookers than at the stage. Agnes, however, looked at nothing in particular. I noticed that her fair complexion was slightly downy, and not as clear as it seemed at first sight. A scattering of dark moles could be perceived around her neck, and at its root her hair was not perhaps quite as golden as advertised. But I found these bodily flaws wholly endearing, and fancied that I perceived a less blemished personality underneath. She was very young to attract the worldly kind of celebrity that she did. And she had a girlish practice of narrowing her eyes and biting her lower lip whenever her mind was far away. It seemed to me that she was immersed in other preoccupations.

The Edgar character, played by "Cherub" Giuglini, did not appear for a good while. When he did bound on, to a vociferous reception, Agnes's demeanour underwent a profound alteration. She sat up in animation, and became glued to his every movement and utterance. She watched him with such enraptured concentration, that one would be forgiven for supposing him her sweetheart or her betrothed. For my own part, I was inclined to yawn at the very sight of him. He had a moustache and wavy hair, parted to one side, which stuck out slightly behind the ears. Though small, he looked tall next to Miss Piccolomini. I did not think him notably distinguished of countenance, but then again I was not Agnes Willoughby. To me his deportment betrayed signs of vanity and petulance, and his performance appeared wilfully mannered and melodramatic.

Perhaps these were the very qualities that Agnes found compelling. She sat forward on the edge of her seat with her elbows against the cushion, as Edgar and Lucy combined to render an amorous duet at the end of the act. This they did right in front of our situation, where the stage lighting was such that we must have been as generally visible as were the dramatic protagonists. As he sang, Giuglini became aware that Agnes was gazing at him, and their eyes met. Then, bit-by-bit, the focus of his outpourings of romantic ardour seemed to shift from Miss Piccolomini (as Lucy) to Agnes, as herself. Soon he appeared to be serenading the petite woman in the box alone, and from her tender expressions she appeared to be responding to every word as if she perfectly understood each one.

The audience reacted to this upturning of dramatic convention with a blend of cheering and exclamations of affront. In their turn Agnes and Giuglini milked the uproar they were causing, whilst poor Miss Piccolomini ploughed on as best she could. The first act, as written, was due to climax with Edgar and Lucy swapping rings as love tokens. But Giuglini ostentatiously offered his ring up to Agnes, before slipping it onto his colleague's finger. And then, when the lovers had finished bidding each other a touching farewell, he made a show of blowing a kiss to Agnes before scurrying off. The sound of the machinery drawing the curtain down was drowned out by cross-currents of huzzas for the performance and protests at its perversion.

When the furore at last dwindled to nothing, Agnes laughed off her antics with Giuglini as a bit of fluff. Then, soon after the interval had begun, an usher opened the door a sliver and beckoned Trinette into the passage to confer with him. The maid returned to implant some fact in her mistress's ear, whereupon Agnes excused herself saying she would be back before the start of the next act. Windham struck up a conversation with Trinette in broken French, and while he was thus distracted I decided to go outdoors and take a breath of air. The atmosphere within was nauseous and stifling, and I was slightly addled by the brandy.

I descended to the arched promenading colonnade, open to one side, which then skirted Her Majesty's Theatre at street level. Much of this was destroyed in the subsequent fire that I have mentioned, though a section of it has survived and can still be traversed to this day. The old theatre was a terrible loss because it was such a beautiful building. It had the simple rectangular shape and pristine marble lustre of an ancient Greek temple, and was far superior to the fussy confection that stands there now. It was at the bottom of the Haymarket where it adjoined Pall Mall, down the slope from the "Devil's Acre" where I had made a glutton of myself some nights previously. I assumed that the contagion of vice from that source would not penetrate as far as this cultural bastion. But when I reached the colonnade it was after lamplight, and I saw several satin-clad women patrolling there in a workmanlike fashion.

I walked on a stretch to discover some solitude, and leaned against one of the arches that divided the promenade into segments. There was a refreshing summer breeze. But after a few moments, I became aware that a man and a woman were having a hushed conversation on the far side of the arch, and out of my sight.

"How are you faring," the man was enquiring, "in curing our fat country ham into fit condition for the slicer?"

"Oh, well enough," the woman replied, "he's quite a sweetheart really, and very suggestible with it."

"Well, you're not short on the requisite materials to do the job, and you've always been a clever modeller. He's a cub to be licked into shape, just like any other. He's got the money, and he's got piles more to come. I wouldn't have marked him down for your special attention, were I not certain of your achieving a return that will amply remunerate us for our trouble and outlay."

"Don't fret about that. I already have him booked in to pay a call on Emmanuel the jeweller."

"I don't expect to fret," said the man slowly, "and don't take kindly to being made to."

"I'd best get back in now, so he won't be missing me."

"Stay a while." The man paused deliberately, and I had the sense that he had bodily blocked her departure. "You see, sometimes I *am* driven to fret over you, my pretty seraph."

"There's really no need to."

"I think that there is. You know that I slip into the theatre on occasion to see what's what?"

"Yes. I've seen your dark specs glinting between the pillars at the back."

"Well, I did so just now before the intermission, and was frankly perplexed by what I witnessed. Perhaps I misinterpreted the orientation of matters, but it didn't look to me as if your attention was wholeheartedly devoted to the task at hand. Correct me if my sight has undergone a deterioration recently, but from where I was standing it looked as if you were flirting with some Italian operatist. And it was so openly done as to be beyond reasonable denial. Now, I say that it's unhealthy for you to indulge in romantic distractions."

"Oh that. It was just a bit of showy fun, and there's not the least harm in it. And besides, the more outrageously I flirt with someone of Giuglini's celebrity, the better it is for my reputation. Why, it's as good as having a sandwich man pad round Leicester Square with my portrait on his boards. I would've thought you'd commend me for my publicising acumen."

"Don't think to be glib with me, my little glow-worm. When your pretty light goes out no one will look at you, whether in the flesh or on a placard. I strongly advise that you take my lead in the conduct of business meantime, so that you may have some fund put aside against the future days of your unwatered spinsterhood. And my advice in this business is as follows. The operatist, Giuglini, whom you've obviously taken a shine to, is known in every continental land as a busted flush. In fiscal matters he is a counterfeit. He squanders everything that comes his way and holds onto nothing. Do not beguile your time in chasing after an empty vessel."

"I'll beguile my time however I like. You've become very vexatious of late, Bob. I'm going inside."

She then vented a little cry of anguish, which made me think that this time he had prevented her departure with some insidious act of violence.

"You know that I can hurt you so it won't show", he affirmed. "There will be no outward mark of rough handling."

I heard the steely slither of something being withdrawn from a sheath, and a gasp of alarm. "Then again, I can hurt you so that it will show if you earnestly desire it."

"You're cracky", she said. I think that he must have put a blade to her throat, causing her to speak hoarsely. "There's no rest with you when your mood's turned curdled."

"I don't think you've seen my mood turn properly curdled yet. Nowhere near it. There's a rare treat for you in store. I don't run an agency for the lovelorn, so listen to this. Have no dealings with the swaggering operatist, either privately or in public", he directed. "Now get back upstairs and wet-nurse the Norfolk bumpkin."

"Oh how the charm drips from you," she returned, "in a great big dirty puddle."

Just then, her mentor noticed something else that demanded his executive intervention. "What are you squawking geese doing down here during the intermission?" he enquired.

I poked my head around the partition to see a portly figure, who was wearing round tinted spectacles, waddle toward a collection of satin-clad strays.

"Get up to the balcony right away," he chivvied them, "do you want to lose out on the whole night's trade?"

The figure was James Roberts, also known as Bawdyhouse Bob. Though he might not go so far as to sit with her in her box, it was clear that Agnes was never far beyond his controlling range.

She took her chance to break away from him, and vanished through a side entrance. I followed some moments later and re-entered the box to find her sitting there serene and imperious, with not a flounce out of place. A consignment of champagne and *canapés* had been delivered while I had been absent. Agnes was tucking into both, and chattering to Windham as if nothing grisly had occurred.

When the performance resumed I studied our hostess with renewed curiosity, anxious to learn whether she would obey or defy her mentor's ban concerning the "operatist." We had retired to the rear of the enclosure, where we were no longer on view, to enjoy our refreshments. There we remained while the plot placed Giuglini, as Edgar, offstage for most of the next act. By the time he returned, his beloved Lucy had been tricked into marrying someone else, thinking him faithless. His return coincided with her wedding feast, whereon he seized back his ring from her and threw her the one she had given him. I think it probable that Miss Piccolomini had remonstrated with Giuglini during the interval, because in this half he was a picture of concentration upon his labours. And the occasional glances that he did shoot in Agnes's direction failed to find their mark because she was still seated out of sight, shunning exposure. I could not say whether she meant to placate Roberts, or tease Giuglini, by thus remaining inconspicuous.

Whichever it was she now appeared fully absorbed in the drama, which was cranking up towards its conclusion. There were some interesting storm effects in the third act and a lengthy solitary spot for the Lucy character, after she goes mad and kills her bridegroom. Miss Piccolomini was quite affecting in this, and executed some vocal gymnastics with considerable aplomb. Her movements were at one moment lithe and leonine, and at the next wilfully clumsy and idiotic. Passages of calm and rationality gave way to tempests of anguish. She dropped to her knees and berated the heavens, and then she sunk spread-eagled to the floor. She tore at her locks and scratched her nails along the boards. Then she flopped backward in a heap. All this led me to reflect, however, that real madness was more likely to resemble the silent agonies undergone by Freddie than the histrionics of this display.

Lucy eventually falls down dead, and on hearing of her demise Edgar kills himself also, after a passage spent in a graveyard contemplating mortality. I thought that Giuglini threw an awfully good death in the end, and it seemed that Agnes thought so also. Her attention had been consumed by him as he bestrode the final section of the opera.

His character's passing marked the end of the piece, and Agnes now hastened back into view at the front of the box to join in enthusiastically with the applause. As Giuglini saw her reappear, he touched his heart and bowed conspicuously in her direction. The players were obliged by the volume of acclamation to return for numerous curtain calls, and during each one Giuglini did not omit to acknowledge Agnes. But at length they returned without him, and though the crowd took to stamping for him to come on he did not.

It became clear why he had abandoned his fellow players when he suddenly burst from the corridor into our box. He was breathless, and still in the pantaloons and lacy frills of his cavalier costume. The sight of this drove the house insensible with delirium. He knelt and kissed Agnes's hand, then straightened up and held it.

"You are the famous Miss Willoughby," he suggested, "and I have tracked you to your cupboard."

"In person."

"Are you as bold as they say?"

"Every bit."

"Tonight the caravan of our troupe rolls on to Paris. Do you travel with it?"

"Trinette," she said by way of an answer, "go back home and pack my compartment portmanteau."

Agnes and Giuglini then sailed out together, hand-in-hand, with the French maid fluttering along in their wake. Windham watched her ostrich feathers flap down the passage with a look of profound dismay on his face at the turn events had taken.

GREAT HEIGHTS AND DEPTHS

The Paris of those days purported to be the most luminous place in all the world. It was widely held to radiate everything that was enviable in art and architecture and gastronomy and apparel. This was the dizzy age of the Second French Empire. The Emperor, who styled himself Napoleon the Third, was nephew to the infamous Napoleon Bonaparte who had turned Europe on its head half-a-century earlier. The current Napoleon had restored the Bonaparte dynasty of late, and he and his Empress Eugénie exuded a stylish modernity that made competing royalties look stiff and staid. At the Emperor's decree, crumbling acres of his capital were being swept away and refashioned into the sweeping boulevards that have so beautified it.

Our periodicals and illustrated press made sure that we in England were kept abreast of all the latest Parisian innovations. Though I was not even slightly interested in any of these, I did take to inspecting the relevant publications for news of Agnes and Giuglini. I even went so far as to call in at Groom's coffee house, when my work put me in the neighbourhood of Fleet Street, to thumb through the various titles shelved there for general reference. And news of the starry couple's exploits was to be had, especially in the dedicated theatrical organs. It turned out that Antonio Giuglini was regarded by those in the know as the leading operatic tenor of his day. He was in the French capital to fulfil a series of fully subscribed engagements at the Imperial Opera, on the Rue Le Peletier. Considerable interest was aroused in him, and in the captivating Englishwoman who followed his every performance from the best spot in the house. She was there on evenings when the Emperor and Empress enlivened the Imperial box with their presence, and she was said to have attracted no less ardent attention than they.

It was reported that she was taking singing lessons herself, with a view to duetting with her beloved operatic cherub. They shared, it was said, a suite at the Hôtel Meurice opposite the Tuileries Garden, a scandalous fact that most Parisians declined to disparage. This was apparently a high-class hostelry that prided itself on catering to English sensibilities. The couple also paraded their attachment freely about town. They consumed the cuisine of celebrated chef Adolphe Dugléré at Les Frères Provençaux in the Palais Royal. They went to the Café Anglais, located on a corner of the Boulevard des Italiens, which was reported to be a chic and fashionable eatery where the furniture was of walnut and the mirrors of gold leaf. They often dined there, in the declining light, on pavement tables in company with a coterie of equally stellar persons. On one occasion Giuglini took his place at table in a fur-lined cloak, wearing the sombrero, sash and boots that befitted the role of a brigand he was then playing. Agnes appeared beside him in the swirling dress of a gypsy temptress, with big round earrings and a broad-brimmed hat.

At the Jardin Mabille, which had a thoroughly *risqué* reputation, the pair swilled quaintly named drinks, and then entered energetically into high-kicking dances in the glittering outdoor ballroom. They visited the Parisian houses of *haute couture*, unrivalled in setting the fashions, and Agnes made it her practice to model every novel outfit and accoutrement. She did not, of course, neglect to be seen riding about the Bois de Boulogne, a woodland area recently landscaped and made into a park by order of the Emperor. And, on the promenade of the Hippodrome de Longchamp, she made sure to display her considerable talents as a horsewoman. There were hints of arguments and passions and of artefacts being hurled and smashed, but one would expect no less from those taking life at their clip.

This was not the regulation style of things at Messrs Praed & Pumicestone. As the weeks succeeded one another, I began to think that the matter of my ejection from Red Lion Square had been quietly dropped. There had, at the very least, been some sort of stay of execution. My principal's attitude to me was taciturn, occasionally tending toward the antagonistic, despite my efforts to be emollient. I found it hard to gauge Felicity's true temper, however, as she stuck to her resolution that a superficial civility would reign while we shared the same address. Since they had been treated to Inspector Holden's revelations concerning events at Ascot, they had not desired me to attend Sunday chapel with them as had previously been the case. Mr Pumicestone rented family seats at an Independent congregation housed on nearby Kingsgate Street, and both father and daughter set some store by their religious observance.

By mutual consent, Felicity and I had also discontinued the leisurely hack that we used to take together after chapel. But on returning from Kingsgate Street one Sunday, she proposed that we did ride out after all. I guessed from her irritable demeanour that some blunt words had been exchanged with her father. I fell in with her plan, and so, once we had assumed our riding apparel, we went round the corner to the leasing stable. This establishment was in French Horn Yard, which was halfway along a narrow back lane that led through to High Holborn. The area hereabouts, squashed between Red Lion Square and the main drag, was crowded with dingy lodgings and tenements, and was not one where we might comfortably linger. It was arguably a candidate for some Napoleonic remodelling.

Mr Tredgold, the yard overseer, had a clapboard shack for his office, just inside the arched entrance and underneath a swaying sign depicting the eponymous coiled brass instrument. Observing our approach through the shack's grimy window, Tredgold shook his head discouragingly at us.

"I've nothing in the docket book for you youngsters today", he said, rifling through its leaves as we stepped into his headquarters. "You should have tipped me off you were coming." He had a curly grey beard and was clad in a massive leather apron and a stiff muffin hat.

"I'm afraid I've let your *Pandora* go out with Mr Fitzjames, Miss Felicity. And as to your usual girl, *Dione*, Mr Phinney, she'll be halfway to Chatham with the sailor's mission by now." We each had a favourite mount that we were content with, and which we usually managed to reserve ahead of time.

Noting Felicity's disgruntled expression, Tredgold raised himself up from his paperwork and studied a blackboard behind his desk. "Well now, let's see who's still in the hotel. There's *Rhea*, though she's feeling feeble this week, and there's *Hyperion,* but he tends to tire and drag his feet. Then there's *Atlas*, though you know he's got a bit of a temperament on him, Miss, and can be fractious and insubordinate."

"I'll take him, if there's no *Pandora*", Felicity pronounced curtly. "At least he has some pluck."

"Very good, Miss." He scored a mark on the blackboard. "Oh, and there's *Hermes* whom I think you've had before, Mr Phinney. Will he serve you alright?"

"He has, as you suggest, proved amenable in the past, so I'll make no objection."

"Right you are then." He made another chalk mark.

The overseer then led us out of the office and across the cobbled yard in a sprightly, but bow-legged kind of amble. We passed the selection of second hand coaches which constituted the carriage hire pool. Some chickens had taken up residence in an old hansom, which was resting on its forks and looked as if it had not been trundled out of its stall for years. This was not a scrubbed and gleaming West End livery emporium.

Once we had reached the stabling range, Tredgold chivalrously invited Felicity to go in before him. As she did, he raised an expressive eyebrow at me and pointed at her back behind the palm of his hand. It was, I think, his commentary on the unsettled state of her temper. He then summoned one of the ostlers who were working in the stable to see to my mount's saddlery and tack, while he assembled hers in person.

"Mind how you go", he said by way of a send-off when all was set and we had been shouldered aloft. Then, beckoning me to bend across the horse's mane and present my ear to him, he delivered a parting shot. "See if you can't cheer Miss Felicity up", he suggested softly. "It's a crying shame to see that girl discontented."

We clattered out of the yard and quit the Holborn locality at a brisk trot, before meandering through Russell Square and the quiet byways of Bloomsbury. We were aiming for Regent's Park, the usual setting for our canter, which was closer than Hyde Park and rather more restful and sedate. It was our practice to take a turn around its outer rim, before meandering back. But in order to reach the park we had first to ford the "great excavation" that was then in full swing.

These works were occasioned by the building of London's first underground line, the Metropolitan Railway, which was due to connect the overground termini of Paddington and King's Cross. However convenient this facility would prove to be for travellers, the method chosen for its construction could not have been more disruptive. Both Marylebone Road and Euston Road were being dug up and gouged out along their entire courses. The tunnel that was to carry the tracks was being laid within the resultant ditches. Once a particular section of tunnelling was complete, it was roofed over and the roadway restored above it. The public nuisance caused was intensified, in many individual cases, by the demolition of scores of inconveniently situated houses.

A temporary bridge had been erected over the works at Portland Road, where one of the new underground stations was to be sited. Felicity and I rode up the earthen ramp that approached the bridge, and then advanced as sure-footedly as could be managed along its rattling timbers. We halted halfway across to gawp at the mammoth spectacle, and to gauge its progress since we had last passed by. The gash of excavation ripped open the roadway for as far as could be seen in one direction and the other. Different sections were at differing stages of completion, some being newly hewn while others were in the process of being covered over. In the cavernous drop below us, the brick-lined walls of the tunnel were open to the elements. We could see where the platforms of the new station were to be positioned, because there was a greater separation between the walls at this point. The brickwork was also more ornate there, and contained arched openings to passageways that existed as yet only on the contractor's drawings.

As it was a Sunday, a strange calm hung over what was otherwise a scene of gigantic enterprise. Huge spoil heaps were banked to either side of the excavations, spilling almost into the stuccoed porticoes of stately terraces. Wooden walkways weaved over the spoil's humps and hillocks, and several gantries spanned the divide, supporting frames and pulleys. All sorts of hefty lifting machines, and vast stacks of implements such as shovels and axes, were scattered about. A cluster of navvies was lazing over tea and smokes in a town of tents on the northerly bank. This was a highly exclusive part of London, and those residents who had ventured out, in their pristine Sunday finery, tacked gingerly around the aggravating obstructions. One elderly couple, obliged to negotiate a bulge of spoil in order to exit their own residence, wore the wretched expressions of ragged scavengers on a dust heap.

"What horrors they have lived to witness", Felicity remarked gloomily, before nudging her horse to walk on.

Once we had cleared the far end of the bridge, we rushed eagerly for the lush greenery of the park. Our route along its outer carriageway took us past the grand Regency terraces that lined its perimeter. At last we could have an unimpeded canter, and enjoy the breeze and the gentle bounty of the surroundings. Felicity appeared a shade more at ease as we rode along to reach the park's further corner. At this juncture, the carriageway cut off to the left and intersected the Zoological Gardens. These were widely regarded as a premier public attraction, though I had never paid the shilling required to experience them at first hand. Judging by the panoply of strange noises being emitted, they housed a fabulous menagerie. The squawking of parrots, and that eerie cry that peacocks make, were the most salient sounds to be heard as we passed through. The passage was separated from the Zoo by walls to either side, so that nothing could actually be seen of the animals' accommodations.

Despite the unconcern she had affected towards partnering him, I knew that Felicity did not get on famously with *Atlas*. Though he had been ostensibly well-behaved so far, I had been able to perceive that his underlying disposition was in fact mutinous. It may have been the piercing sounds from the aviary that finally impelled him to play up. Then again, it may have been the sight of a giraffe sizing him up disdainfully from over a wall. In any event, Felicity's mount now began to demonstrate the indiscipline that Mr Tredgold had highlighted. He bucked his head and weaved his neck, and skittered senselessly sideways. Felicity, whom I can picture now in her light coloured habit and pill-box hat with its cockade, struggled against him crossly. I cannot say how women in those days contrived to control a horse while being perched side-saddle, still less how they avoided being thrown off at full pelt. But when *Atlas* took to prancing and capering in a totally giddy manner, Felicity lost her temper and spurred him into a sprint.

Instead of continuing straight along with the carriageway once we had passed the Zoological Gardens, she hauled *Atlas* off it in an apparent fit of brain fever. I was astonished to then observe them spring, with the force of a catapult, across the canal and over the main road that marked the park's northern boundary. I did not know what aberration of mind had gripped her, but saw no choice but to harry *Hermes* into pursuit. Felicity hurtled headlong up Primrose Hill, without pausing to admire the blooms of that variety that brightly adorned it. She then descended its further slope and dashed along the track that led out to the country beyond it, with me still pursuing. We passed a cricket pitch and a bowling green and a small woodland copse. We then sped even further onward, braving two ribbons of London development that stood in our way, and attracting stern looks from strolling suburbanites. Avoiding Hampstead village along a southerly flanking route, we navigated a level-crossing over the Hampstead Junction Railway. Felicity was then obliged to slacken her pace, but only slightly, as she exhorted *Atlas* into the exertion of scrambling up the rise of Parliament Hill.

When they had attained the summit she jumped down, flushed and excitable, and holding her newly quiescent charger by his reins. "There now," she pronounced wildly as I pulled up beside her, "all he needed was a full-necked gallop to straighten him out."

"And what possessed you to give him his head?" I enquired, more curious than disconcerted by her uncharacteristic behaviour. "You hared off as madly as some ripe 'fellah' on a glee club outing."

Her face suddenly clouded and her eyes welled with tears. "What possessed me," she replied, "is that father would have you out of the house by a week tomorrow. He wants to engage a new junior, someone connected to one of his clubroom cronies, to take your room and fill your position. I know that *I* said you should go, but..." she tailed off.

Then she staunched the saltwater and composed herself. "I am cross with him for obliging me to tell you, rather than having the gumption to do so himself. And I am furious with you for shattering our contentment in the first place."

This disclosure was not softened by it being expected, and I found myself almost physically winded now it had actually come. So much so, that I dropped my horse's reins and flopped down to the ground. *Hermes* wandered a little way off, trailing his reins behind him and nuzzling amongst the tussock-grass. What really thumped me in the chest was the knowledge that Felicity would not have announced my banishment simply on her father's say-so. The resolution clearly carried her personal endorsement, however reluctantly she had arrived at it.

Felicity settled herself on the turf a few feet away from me, and we both stared out morosely towards the river for some time. Parliament Hill is the highest point for a long way roundabout, and the whole of London, as it was then, was spread out before us. It was a cloudless afternoon and so we could see the steeples and towers, and the chimneys and rooftops, poking up through the abiding smoke drifts. The cross and ball on the dome of St Paul's were distinctly visible. I even fancied that I observed the masts of ships, crowded together like matchsticks on the Thames and in the teeming dockland basins.

Contemplating my predicament, it occurred to me that there was a multitude of worlds down there. And there were multitudes more to be gained across the seas and the oceans. It was surely insufferable to be forever confined to one tiny speck on the globe, and to be forever in thrall to one enervating occupation. My daily courtroom round often goaded me to a state not far short of stupefaction. There was scant satisfaction in conspiring with one party to grub money from another, or in conspiring with the other to withhold it. I thought of Agnes in Paris and of how she seemed licensed to flit carelessly hither and thither (though her chosen profession did, of course, more readily permit of foreign travel). Perhaps it would be a blessing for me to be bounced out of my accustomed inertia?

With this in mind I grandiloquently proclaimed, "The adventurer awakes", to Felicity. I accompanied the statement with a sweep of my hand, thinking to thus encompass the myriad possibilities represented by the panorama. But the display of bravado fell woefully flat.

"That's all well and good in the imaginary land of a painting," she replied, "but few of us actually spend our time petrified in paint."

I let a little dust settle on this dismissive remark. Our joyous afternoon at the Hanover gallery now seemed very far distant.

Then I broached a highly pertinent enquiry. "You don't really think me guilty of a vulgar dalliance with that girl the police inspector mentioned, do you? As I have assured you, I had never seen her before that day at Ascot, and I have certainly never seen her since. She thrust herself upon me quite unexpectedly, and no part of it was by my own volition. No part of my being in that tent at all was by my own volition, come to that. I just got caught up and whisked along."

"What kind of a person would I be if I didn't believe what you said to me in good faith?" she returned with an asperity of feeling. "Of course I accept your explanation. I don't consider you a bad man,

George. I don't suppose that you go around drowning old ladies in treacle." She summoned a faint smile upon saying this, but withdrew it almost instantaneously. "But you did allow yourself to get 'caught up and whisked along' in something you shouldn't have. You broke bread with criminals known to the police. It was negligent in the extreme, and it leads me to wonder what other improprieties you might get inveigled into. I honestly shudder at the prospect."

Felicity twisted some strands of grass this way and that in her lap. "And I can only deplore your recent descent into drinking. You know how strong our people have always been for temperance, but now you seem to have well and truly caught the carousal bug. It wrenches my heart to hear you come in late and unsteady, and I dread to envision the palaces of poison you've been frequenting. It's all the same to that Mr Windham, your moneyed playfellow, who needn't so much as chip a twig to earn his livelihood. But Papa says that you are all too often dull and inattentive to your labours nowadays. My mother abominated inebriation and all its consequences, and yours would have set her face as flint against it."

This stark assessment contained much that rang true. My night of carousal with Windham at the Haymarket had not proved to be a one-off, and the quality of my wakefulness had indeed waned of late. Felicity was also right to say that my mother would have disapproved of this, though it was unbearably affecting to be put in mind of Mama in relation to my current shortcomings. Before their untimely deaths, my parents and I had resided a few doors along from the Pumicestone house so that Felicity and myself had been acquainted from infancy. It was poignant for us to recall that both my parents, and Felicity's own mother, had been carried off in the same epidemic of cholera, that insensible assassin, which had struck our locality seven years before. The medical authorities had concluded that bad water was to blame, and our families had drawn their supplies from the same afflicted pump. Mercifully, there had been no repetition of the outbreak since we had been plumbed into the mains.

"Perhaps I would be less susceptible to what you term the 'carousal bug'," I blurted in an ill-considered reply, "if those lost persons who were dear to us were still present today."

"Don't be so unspeakably blasphemous", Felicity retorted sharply. "Your idiocies are your own and don't belong to phantoms. You should have a care for those who *are* still with us. I don't think you realise just how great a shock it was for my father to have a stain upon his household honour brought to his attention in the sanctuary of his club. You know how jealously he regards his standing there. And furthermore, he maintains that your continuing presence in our house undermines his quiet repose at chapel. He fears that the minister has started to look at him askance."

She paused, whilst winding the grass strands some more. "I do not go along with Papa upon this point. He sometimes inflates his worries to an almost hypochondriac extent. But I am in accord with him when he says that it is for the best that you should depart."

Felicity paused again. "That is to say, I am in accord with this view, unless you are able to offer me two most earnest assurances before we leave this hilltop."

"What might they be?" I asked, although I could predict them accurately enough.

"You must pledge your absolute abstinence from drink and warm company. And I include your friend Windham, and the horsebreaking woman, in the latter category."

"I'm afraid that I cannot pledge so much."

She gazed lengthily at the impressive visual prospect, then removed her pill-box hat, adjusted its cockade, and restored it to her head. It sat well upon the auburn sheen of her pinned and braided locks.

"I think," she said at last, "that you have a modest sum set aside from your father's inheritance that might serve to keep you for some little duration?"

"That is so, though the sum is small enough." The bulk of the money that came to me on his death went into buying the articles of clerkship that allowed my qualification as a solicitor.

"Very well, George, my father will write you a favourable letter of recommendation, addressed 'to whom it may concern.' Let us return these weary beasts to Mr Tredgold's hotel."

With this we remounted and rode, at a rather less exacting pace, down the hill and back into town to the stables. The silent excavations looked even more forlorn the second time around.

Tredgold, who was standing in the yard as we entered it, faced *Atlas* down and caught him by the halter.

"There's been a gentleman in here asking after you, Mr Phinney", he reported as we lowered ourselves from our saddles. "He said his name was Windham. When I told him you were out riding and would be gone for a while, he said he'd wait for you in the French Horn Inn." The overseer relayed this with a note of surprise in his voice. Though no doubt one of its patrons himself, Tredgold did not reckon on his customers meeting friends in the public house that abutted onto the stable yard. "Well I told him it was a roughhouse, but he would go in there all the same. Then some time later he came out again. He's down in the dumps by my estimation, and doesn't know whether he's coming or going."

"Where is he now?" I enquired.

"He's resting in the *Queen Charlotte* over there, and I can't tempt him out. But I don't think she's going to take him anywhere."

Tredgold pointed to a particularly old and battered hire coach of that name which was occupying one of the carriage stalls. You could tell that she had once been a majestic conveyance, perhaps belonging to a swish hotel or a swanky town house. But it was impossible to say precisely where, as her livery was worn and scuffed beyond recognition. The aged carriage was in an advanced state of dereliction. Weeds were growing from her guttering, and in places panels were broken or missing so that her stuffing and slats were exposed.

Looking closer, I was able to observe a stiff figure slumped on the faded and threadbare upholstery inside the *Queen Charlotte*. Though it was indeed him, the figure was so pallid and lifeless that it might have been a wax-work model of my friend Windham. His cheek was pressed against a window-pane. His eyes were open, but his face was expressionless.

"So that's your precious Mr Windham?" Felicity observed angrily. "From the way he's slouching I wouldn't be surprised if he was dead drunk. He's sagging like a sack of potatoes. And it's a Sunday, and we're well within the hours of daylight. I'll give him a piece of my mind."

Mr Tredgold raised his expressive eyebrow and trained it on me. It was designed to inform me that I had made a very poor fist indeed of cheering "Miss Felicity" up.

She strode over to the coach and threw the door open, then she climbed onto the cushioning on all fours and smelt his breath. She lifted his limp head toward her and examined its features. Tredgold and I followed her, and arrived just as she replaced it and reversed out again. Windham's eyes swivelled uncertainly as he beheld us, and he appeared confused and unaware that he was waiting on my arrival. In fact he seemed to be in an utterly plethoric state, as if numbed by dropsy or narcotics.

Felicity's disposition revolved, on a sixpence, from outrage to alarm. "He's not remotely drunk," she said briskly, "but he is ailing. Have you got something to revive him, Mr Tredgold?"

"I might be able to locate a drain of pale in my office", the stableman responded cautiously, knowing her attitude to intoxicants.

"Well go and get it." It seemed that her absolute aversion to alcohol had been temporarily suspended in the circumstances.

"Certainly, Miss." Tredgold went off in his bow-legged lollop, and returned directly with a bottle of pale brandy whose liquid level was at half-mast. Felicity withdrew the stopper with her teeth and climbed back into the upholstered relic, before tilting the bottle to Windham's lips. By stages she induced him to imbibe a little, and his face gradually assumed a more human aspect. She then withdrew the restorative, and herself, from the carriage and invited him to follow.

"Good afternoon, Miss" he said, dazedly, without making any move to get up. Then he saw me too. "Oh there you are, George. I have been looking for you. I wanted to have a talk. I have been out for hours walking round and about, and I fetched up at your porch. I met a very charming girl there who said that I might find you here. Are you going to introduce me to this other charming lady?"

It was remarkable that his customary slurriness was now largely absent from Windham's speech. Instead his words emerged slowly and with an unnatural clarity, as if each syllable required the utmost definition if it were to be formed at all.

"She is Miss Felicity Pumicestone, the daughter of my employer, and it would have been our maidservant, Anna, whom you encountered at the door."

"Anna was it? Oh yes, she is a most delightful girl and we had a terrific conversation. We talked about the glories of summer. And we spoke of the trees and flowers in the garden of your square. Very colourful they are, though I was only able to name a few of them by variety. I did better in naming some of the birds that we saw fluttering around. I told Anna of the Pantheon Bazaar, over in the West End, where they have ever so many singing and fancy birds that you can buy and keep in a cage in your parlour. She said that she might go there one day and nose about, but didn't think that she would ever bring a bird home as the endless twittering might wear her nerves down. And she said she did not think that birds should really be caged anyway, which I considered a noble sentiment."

His face knotted, as if with the strain of maintaining a coherent line of thought. "Things *are* generally colourful in the summertime, I find, though it does get beastly sweltering hot here in London. I do not sleep as well here as I do at home. The salubrity of the air is somehow better out in the country. So much fresher, do you see? And Felbrigg is near the coast, so the cooling sea frets float in. My housekeeper, Jeffy, Mrs Jeffrey, always keeps a cheerful flower garden along with the herbs..."

He suddenly winced with emotion and his eyes filled with tears. "I really am the most worthless fellow that has ever lived" he stated starkly, as if it were a point of incontrovertible fact. "Everything I say is the purest nonsense and everything I do is the grossest folly. I advise you to pay no heed to me whatsoever. I do not deserve the consideration of decent humankind."

His large eyes looked out at us, plaintive and glassy, from inside the coach saloon. Shreds of torn silk dangled from the decrepit ceiling around his head.

"Oh come now, Mr Windham," Felicity said, "things surely can't be as dire as you make out. No one is beyond the consideration of decent folk."

"It's kind of you to show concern, Miss Pumicestone, and I appreciate it, but I fear that it is misplaced in my case. I am a burden to my family and anyone else unfortunate enough to draw close. I have never been anything but a trial to my mother. She left me for an Italian singer, just as Agnes has. Only a fool would expect someone like me be held in genuine affection. Women care nothing for me, they only want my property."

These words put me in mind of the day that Windham and I had first met on the Eastern Counties train. He had said then that his mother had run off to Torquay with a young Italian music teacher after his father's death. He had also said that he sometimes felt that he would go "melancholy mad" with this world.

"I am sure that there are plenty of people who hold you in genuine regard", Felicity sought to reassure him. "What about all those good folk at your country estate? I expect they'd brim over with gladness at the chance to toast your returning. You've said yourself that it's fresher out in the wilds. Why don't you go home to Felbrigg and find succour among those who truly know you?"

"I would dearly love to go home," Windham replied with an agonising effort, "but cannot bear for my friends and neighbours to see how wretched I truly am. And besides, if they toast me it is only because I am born to be squire and not for myself alone. It is better by far that they are rid of me."

Seeing his head press back vacantly against the window-pane Felicity directed Mr Tredgold to summon a cab, and she instructed me to see Windham returned to his lodging in it.

I had been aware that my friend's spirits had been tumbling of late, and could precisely date the onset of that slide to the night that Agnes had eloped with Giuglini. But he now seemed to be in total mental disarray. All his vital juices had been leeched from him, as if in a bloodletting. All his daring had been drained away, and his mind had become polluted by self-doubt. His whole system had been lowered very much, and he was in as deep a trough as that being scraped from the earth to make way for the Metropolitan Railway.

THE GONG AND THE MALLET

No pageantry accompanied my departure from Red Lion Square. I picked my hour of parting to be such that no awkward farewells would have to be navigated. Felicity, I was sure, felt that way about it as well. And I had no desire to meet the new office junior, whom I imagined would be as keen as mustard. I had Mr Pumicestone's letter of recommendation in my pocket, together with his closing gratuity in a modest sum. Though lacking a settled and decisive plan of action, I did have a new accommodation address. When I had escorted Windham home from the French Horn stable, his landlord Lewellin had offered me the let of a room that had recently fallen vacant. And so it was that I took up residence in St James's at No. 35 Duke Street.

The Lewellins ran a lively household, which was attended by ceaseless comings and goings. My allotted slot was on the first floor, across the corridor from Windham's own chambers. Being only a single room it naturally attracted a lesser rental than his suite, but on moving in I discovered that the terms were not as attractive as they had first been advertised. As I unpacked my belongings, David Lewellin informed me that he charged out an extra element of "personal attendance" at three shillings and sixpence a week. This, he explained, encompassed grooming and valeting in general. He did, he said, see to these things himself as a favour to all his "gentlemen guests". He also provided them with their baths, by appointment, at an extra "shilling a dip." Windham suggested that I might share my meals with him in his sitting room, and I was required to notify Mrs Lewellin of my needs in this respect first thing each morning.

My chamber was very constricted, being no bigger than a lumber room really, and I discovered that privacy was hard to come by. Both of the Lewellins blew in and out without giving much thought to knocking. Though their attentions came larded with a layer of practiced deference, an underlying note of insinuation could often also be detected. When I said that I was going out for a walk, for instance, they might jovially contrive to suggest that I was bound for some prearranged debauch, rather than merely taking a turn around the block. Husband and wife fluttered about their charges persistently, enquiring whether they were in need of this or that. Mr Lewellin was given to implying that there were no limits to what he could arrange for an agreed outlay. Having been accustomed to residing in a small household of essentially reserved persons, I found it wearying to acclimatise to my new landlords' familiarity.

There were four other boarders besides Windham and myself. Two Scottish brothers named Campbell occupied an upper floor. They were described to me as being merchants in the East India trade, and they worked long hours at a City office. They were also devoted to rackety home entertaining, and had a lively procession of business associates up and down the stairs and across the landing. Then there was a shy young man called Corbellis, who was a clerk at the War Office. From the few occasions that I met him on the stairs and we exchanged some rudimentary chat, I learned that he had ambitions to go into the law and was squirreling his earnings away against that eventuality. When I told him that I was a litigation solicitor, he looked at me disparagingly and declared that he was reading for the bar. There was also an extraverted older gentleman, a Colonel Broughton of the Royal Artillery, who boasted that he had been born at an Elizabethan mansion into a family of Staffordshire gentry. A shifting population of servants furnished these residents with full board. This included cleaning and laundering, and providing them with such meals as they and their guests pleased to eat indoors.

I soon became aware that things were less rosy between the outwardly bluff Lewellins than they cared to let on. So far as one could tell, the tiffs that could sometimes be heard leaking from their private apartments were grounded in two principal aggravations. The first of these concerned the overly friendly relations that Augusta Lewellin openly enjoyed with Colonel Broughton. They would often go out together for the day as a twosome in a trap. And they would, on occasion, lurk conspiratorially about the house, laughing inordinately over some shared nugget of amusement. The second area of contention was less concrete, but seemed to revolve around visiting members of Mrs Lewellin's clan. Augusta's maiden name was Dignam, and when her young unmarried sister, Eliza Dignam, spent a few days at the house the girl was instantly put to work stripping beds and cleaning. She was a redhead like her sister and she was sweet-faced and personable, but her brief presence occasioned fierce disputes between the Lewellins. There was more domestic strife after Mr Lewellin turned away a beggar who called at the door, who had apparently been his wife's brother, Conway Dignam. And the couple's relations with their servants were so choppy that there was a rapid turnover in the household positions. Yet despite all this, they possessed a remarkable gift for maintaining that everything was sweetness and light.

It took barely a week of exposure to these conditions for me to feel utterly dejected. I had made the most terrible mistake. Far from my being "bounced out of inertia" into fresh fields of possibility, I found myself drifting into a paralysis not unlike Windham's. And I am afraid to say that his state was worsening all the while. Nothing stimulated him or excited his curiosity. He would mope about all day like a lost soul, and could not settle to any rational distraction. I got the impression that he experienced even the faintest alien sound as jarring and discordant. His nervous fragility was such that the blare of a German band striking up from across the street, or the din of voices ringing shrill from the landing, would oppress him horribly. What scant conversation he did manage picked repetitively at the sorry delusion that he was good for nothing. Melancholia had even stolen his zest for nights of revelry. We stopped going out to the Haymarket on an evening and became, I fear, very thin companions to one another.

His decline was punctuated by successive visitations from his Uncle Charles, Doctor Winslow, and Mr Portal. The latter pair took to calling repeatedly, but I was not made a party to any of their consultations. So far as I could piece the facts together from his fractured and indifferent bulletins, Windham had submitted himself to the alienist's care and received from him a therapeutic programme. He had also agreed to embrace the proposal concerning Felbrigg that Mr Portal had outlined on our return from Sussex House. Windham was as a rag-doll in the hands of his uncle's agents, and it was disheartening to learn of his meek reversal in the matter of the estate. This, to me, symbolised how far his spirit had ebbed.

Once he had been "put under the mad-doctor", as the Lewellins termed it, they clucked over him so incessantly as to smother any spark of independent action. Doctor Winslow left regular instructions with them prescribing the optimum balance of his diet, his hours of waking and sleeping, and the manner of his hygiene. The doctor had also presented some herbal preparations for Mr Lewellin to use in his bathing, and some medicinal additives for Mrs Lewellin to blend with his food. These remedies only seemed to me to make him duller and more debilitated. Their administration also gave his landlords a licence to keep him under a drastic regime tantamount to detention. I found myself increasingly shooed out of his chambers on the ground that he needed to shelter from disruptions. I then had news from Mr Portal that "the patient" was not well enough to go to Felbrigg, on his forthcoming twenty-first birthday, for the time honoured investiture ceremony. He would instead be escorted on that day to the offices of Messrs Outram & Co, Portal & Merritt's London agents, where he would sign the papers enacting Mr Portal's proposal into existence.

But one morning, over an early breakfast, I managed to cheat the cordon that surrounded him so far to coax Windham outdoors for the first time in days. As he was so enamoured of trains, I suggested that we proceed to a mainline railway terminus and while away a few hours watching them come and go. The most convenient station for the purpose was Euston Square, home of the London & North-Western Railway. To my delight he consented to the idea of going there, which I thought stood a real chance of having a beneficial effect upon him. The fact that he had agreed was of itself encouraging. Indeed my friend's temper, as we set off walking, impressed me for the first time in weeks as being better than that of an invalid. We strolled up to Piccadilly and hired a hansom there. Though still subdued in comparison with his normal self he responded to my conversational forays, as we drove through the busy streets, with a refreshing alacrity. The cab let us down by the lofty stuccoed terraces of Euston Square. A short walk from there along Euston Grove, past the two big railway hotels that flanked it, brought us to the station.

This splendid edifice was (and remains) one of the jewels of our railway establishment. The entrance to its courtyard is guarded by a huge Grecian arch, and at its centre is a massive Great Hall, classical in design. Inside, this has a high iron gallery all around and a double flight of stairs at the far end, sweeping up to the company's offices. A giant statue of George Stephenson, the great railway pioneer, occupies a high plinth near the staircase. As we entered it I contemplated the hall with awe, and marvelled at the scale of an enterprise that could afford for such a vast space to be purely decorative. Windham was visibly taken with it also, rolling his head back to examine the coffered ceiling and follow the continuous run of windows beneath it. Though travellers were gliding this way and that, with porters wheeling their trunks, they were not a throng, and the prevailing atmosphere was calm and unhurried. Light washed in from all angles. It was more like a large recital hall than a railway station, and the gentle patter of footfalls and chatter combined to produce an almost musical echo.

Having absorbed its grandiose but serene charm, we passed through one of the several arches that separate the Great Hall from the booking office to its right. This appendage (which is matched by a twin leading off to the left) has a gallery and a glass dome, and is hardly less magnificent than the central structure. We obtained our platform permits there, before going through the barrier into the smoky plumes of the train shed. I bought a newspaper from a kiosk, and Windham saw to the supply of some coffee from a stall. We then sprawled on a bench overlooking the departure platform for Scotland, and leaned back to observe the traffic.

After a period in which little more than minor manoeuvring went on, an express train reversed into the station and shunted slowly into position before us. The platform indicator slats stated that it was the morning departure for Edinburgh, due to be off shortly at ten a.m., and those who had been awaiting it busied themselves with boarding.

As the passengers and porters fussed over stowing baggage on the rooftops, my attention was drawn to a theatrical notice in the newspaper. It stated that a certain Signor Antonio Giuglini was booked into the Queen's Theatre, in the Scottish capital, to give a short season. This was to commence that very evening with the staging of a production entitled *Norma*, set in the historic era of Roman Gaul. The notice announced that Giuglini was to sing the leading part of Pollione, a Roman proconsul, opposite Miss Marietta Piccolomini's Gaulish high-priestess, Norma. And where Giuglini appeared, it seemed to me, so was Agnes Willoughby also likely to be present.

"Have you ever washed up in Edinburgh on your travels?" I enquired of Windham, nonchalantly.

"To those of us who know their railways," he corrected me, "the direction of travel to Scotland is technically 'down' not 'up'. It's dictated by the direction in relation to London, as a glance at any edition of Bradshaw's guide will reveal. And I have been to Edinburgh as it happens. I once spent a week there with the last of my so-called 'tutors', a chap called Peatfield who was by far the pleasantest of that lot. We had a nice stay and tripped across some amusing entertainment. Then we went on to Glasgow and from there to Dublin by steamer. Why do you ask?"

"Well, I've never been there myself, but I do gather that the city boasts some very particular attractions around this time of year."

"What leads you to suppose that? What sort of attractions?"

I handed him the paper so that he might scrutinise the theatrical notice for himself. Once he had read it he looked over at the blackened locomotive as it wheezed and hissed, impatient to be off. Then he looked back at me, suggestively.

"I have been quite ill of late," he said in a most earnest tone, "and think that you have not been too well either. But the time has come for us to get better. They say that travel can be the best form of convalescence. Shall we go to it?"

"I am not unreceptive to the proposition," I granted, "and am given to understand that the Scots are a most hospitable folk."

The harebrained scheme was minted between us in the space of a moment. We got up and arranged for the purchase of two tickets, and we then returned to the platform and boarded the Scotland-bound train.

You may judge me harshly for indulging Windham thus in his obsessive regard for Agnes, especially after what I had overheard at the Italian Opera. But when I had told him of this, he had responded that her break with the Bawdyhouse man that night absolved Agnes from involvement in any plot to mulct him. Indeed, he had contended that she could only have been forced into such a plan unwillingly in the first place. Dubious though these assertions were it was my honest opinion that, in his existing condition, any emphatic action was preferable to continued indolence. And this consideration was not entirely selfless, as the need for positive exertion applied equally to myself.

I was to have plenty of time to weigh the wisdom of this decision in my mind, as the journey before us was scheduled to last for almost twelve hours. We were quiet and reflective for much of this time, dozing intermittently in our compartment and passing the newspaper from one to the other. The train stopped at Leamington, then Birmingham, then Wolverhampton, then Crewe. There was a short rest at Preston, while we got down for refreshments at the platform buffet. Carlisle was the last halt before our destination, and beyond there we crossed into the endlessly bleak border terrain along the Caledonian line.

It was soon after dark, and just before ten p.m., when our train met the buffers at the old Caledonian

Railway terminus at Lothian Road. Far from being exhausted by our journey, we experienced an accession of energy on being released from it. The weather had turned wet and squally, but we won a cab almost straight away. It whisked us past the densely-packed dark stone tenements, through the Grassmarket and up onto Nicolson Street. Then it dropped us there outside the Queen's Theatre. Inside the theatre's bright and inviting vestibule, we made straight for the glazed pay-boxes. The oily-haired young chap manning the one we chose was amused by our improvident appearance, questioning whether we seriously expected to be admitted dressed as we were. We had not, of course, had the chance to pack any formal apparel, or indeed anything at all. He also pointed out that the performance was well into its second act, and that our interests would therefore be best served by our returning at the commencement hour on another night.

Leaning into the window, Windham informed him confidentially that we were not concerned with the performance as such. Our main preoccupation, he stated, lay more in the direction of sighting the famous Miss Willoughby. Was she in the house tonight?

"Oh she's here all right", the booking clerk divulged with a lascivious grin. "If it's an eyeful of the delectable Miss Willoughby you're after then you must surely have it. I'll let you in at the pit price and you can stand wherever space permits." He gave us the requisite entry tokens, together with a mental map of where Miss Willoughby was located.

We entered the packed theatre just as it was reverberating to three crashing strikes of a gong, struck one after another. Squeezing in to lurk at the back with a lot of others who had failed to assure their places in advance, we saw that the stage was rapidly filling up with chorus performers. The scenery indicated that the action was set in a woodland clearing, and it seemed that the strokes of the gong were intended to summon a gathering to what was a sacred arbour. Helmeted warriors were filing on holding spears, accompanied by garlanded druids of both sexes in long white robes. Standing out amongst them, dwarfed by the gong itself and with a mallet held high in her hand, was the tiny shape of Marietta Piccolomini. She was in the guise of Norma, the high-priestess of druids, and it was obviously she who had called the warlike assembly into session. Her robe was differentiated from those of the ordinary priestesses in that it tended to flatter her figure. It was gathered in around her miniscule waist, from which an elegant bustle draped to one side. Her dark hair was roundly plaited on top, and hung long at the back.

Riding the swelling orchestra she was rendering a stirring call to arms, presumably against the hated Romans. This was being echoed in approving responses from the chorus of druids and warriors, with the latter thrusting their spear points upward in a belligerent display. Then, an off-stage commotion presaged the arrival of another group of warriors, carrying a bound and struggling man wearing a Roman toga. He was Antonio Giuglini in the role of Pollione, the proconsul. This representative of Gaul's oppressors was then tied to an altar, amid a bloodthirsty clamour for his immediate death. The high-priestess swapped the mallet for a sword, and advanced upon the Roman with the apparent intention of killing him. She put the sword to his breast, but pulled back at the last moment against the persistent urgings of her followers that she press ahead. She then dismissed them from her presence with an impassioned sweep of the weapon, and they all trooped off obediently.

Now alone with the sacrificial candidate, Norma moved to untie him. Thus freed, Giuglini swung himself off the altar and readjusted his toga, which did not seem to sit very comfortably around his shoulders. His sandals looked unimpeachably Roman, but it must be said that his moustache did not. From the way that their ensuing exchanges alternated between the tender and the fiercely reproachful, it was plain that their characters were estranged lovers. And from the uninhibited way that the audience was expressing its partisanship, it was clear that Giuglini's character was the undisputed villain of the piece. No doubt he had been untrue to her. First it seemed that Norma was going to kill herself, which the audience disapproved. Then it seemed that Pollione was going to be the one to end it all, which they resoundingly applauded. At this stage I managed to make out Agnes, sitting in the box where the clerk had said she would be, in company with a clutch of other well-got-up persons. She was wearing a golden gown and a furry white stole. Behind the faintness of her fixed smile, I thought that she looked bored enough to be contemplating her own suicide.

The scene between Norma and Pollione moved to its climax with the high-priestess dropping the sword and retrieving the mallet. She was apparently intent on striking the gong again to reconvene the druidic hoard, doubtless to convey her decision regarding the proconsul's fate. But, preparatory to doing so, Miss Piccolomini drew back the mallet too far and too forcefully. Perhaps she had Giuglini's unprofessional behaviour on the night he first glimpsed Agnes in her mind. Or perhaps she was just completely transported by the cresting drama. In any event she slammed the mallet hard into Giuglini's fleshy nostrils, which began to spout a bloody cascade.

"Oo, she's bopped him on the boko", Windham observed, not entirely sympathetically. Some sections of the audience laughed, whilst others sucked sharp intakes of breath.

Once the shock permitted the tenor to comprehend what had befallen him, Giuglini became too incensed to maintain the pretence of character. He shouted something foul-sounding in Italian that was probably not as written in the libretto. Then he raced angrily to the wings, with his palms clapped over the dripping organ. Miss Piccolomini stood stock still in a shocked fashion, and the conductor waved the musicians to a discordant halt. There was a confused hiatus, with a hubbub of startled voices, before the curtain was hurriedly lowered. After a few moments an extremely well-dressed and suave gentleman, with a colossal floral buttonhole, appeared out front to introduce himself as Mr Mapleson, the operatic impresario. He announced, in an accustomed and silky tone, that there would follow a short, unscheduled intermission. He also beseeched the ladies and gentlemen to keep to their seats in the meantime. Everyone immediately got up and started circulating.

"There she goes", said Windham, looking up at her box where Agnes was on her feet and making ready to leave it. "She'll be wanting to be beside her cherub, backstage. Let's see if we can't find some passage there ourselves."

"We'll never get through the stage door," I said, "as there'll be some brawny commissionaire put there to stop us. How about we go up to the front and see if an opening presents itself?"

We did so, and reached the stage in time to see the musicians beneath it retreating into the bowels of the theatre. There was a bit of a drop down to their pit, but nothing too vertiginous.

"Shall we chance it?" I said.

"I think that we must", returned Windham.

"Very well then, here goes."

Saying this, I vaulted over the partition into the pit with as much grace as a drayhorse, and Windham followed suit. We overturned a couple of music stands which we fumbled to set upright, though I fear that the scores became irredeemably dishevelled. In the overall *mêlée* nobody took any notice. We then trooped after the tail-end of the orchestra through an open doorway. This led us into an ill-lit underground passage which had a series of changing rooms leading off. It seethed with a mass of displaced players, conversing in a babble of different languages. Half-naked warriors smeared with woad chatted to frock-coated bandsmen, whilst white-faced priestesses conversed with their grey-bearded counterparts. A line of warriors was lounging on the floor, with their backs against the wall and their spears tucked between their knees. Nobody seemed in the least put out by the interruption, and the news of Giuglini's misfortune was being received with heroic equanimity.

We elbowed a course along the passage, apologising as we went, and finally located the room bearing Giuglini's nameplate. The door was ajar, and agitated parties were constantly spilling in and out. We edged inside to behold a spectacle that was far from tranquil. The great tenor was sitting with his back to the mirror, puffing feverishly on a cigar and fulminating against all and sundry. His wavy hair was in a tousled jumble, and his toga was bloodstained all down its front. A make-up girl was dabbing at his nose, when he would let her, and another was trying to repair his face as a whole. A third was trying to persuade him out of the toga, while a collection of costumiers was ransacking cupboards to locate its replacement.

Giuglini, who could perhaps be forgiven for being scratchy in the circumstances, was batting heated Italian back and forth with Miss Piccolomini. She was acutely embarrassed and contrite, and kept dropping to her knees with her arms stretched wide in supplication. The tenor was also gesticulating wildly, and repeatedly getting up and down, which was not helping those whose task it was to restore his theatrical mask. At the same time Mapleson the impresario was endeavouring, with the ardent encouragement of a jittery man whom I took to be the theatre manager, to induce the wounded campaigner back into the fray.

"Pardon me, Mr Mapleson," Giuglini responded to his entreaties in an affronted voice, "but I will not be taking to the stage again tonight." He wagged a forefinger from side-to-side to illustrate his reluctance. “For me, the piece is contaminated beyond all sufferance.”

Miss Piccolomini interjected with a renewed torrent of staccato Italian.

“Si...si, Marietta,” Giuglini replied, “enough of this now. I forgive you. I would forgive you anything after your rendition of *Casta Diva* tonight. It was exquisite beyond expression. Now let me treat with Mr Mapleson.”

“Hear how they bray for you, Antonio”, the impresario told him, referring to the shouting and stamping that was stoking up in the auditorium. Mapleson was no doubt well-used to stroking sensitive personalities. “They will not let you go. No, you must get back on.”

“On the contrary,” Giuglini returned, gesturing with the cigar at his female opposite number, “they bray for her, and demand that she go back on.”

He pushed the hand dabbing his nose away from him, and grabbed a sponge to see to it himself. “I give you my solemn oath, Mr Mapleson, that I will never perform Pollione again. It is not a noble role and the public will despise any man who plays it, no matter that he is a great singer. The damnable Roman’s only talent is for fornication, and his airs are all high-flown twaddle. I have never cared for the antiquated ass, and now his own gods have proven me right. No, this piece belongs to Norma. She is the hero. She has all the best arias. It is for Marietta to receive the braying, not for me.”

He blew her a kiss, and she curtseyed in recognition of his forbearance. Just then, Agnes Willoughby entered the already over-stuffed dressing room.

“Oh Antonio”, she exclaimed. “How are you? I’ve been ever so worried. I’m sorry to have taken this long, but all the lobbies are full and the crowds have detained me.”

She reached out a hand to caress his injured face, but he slapped it away.

"Here is the true mistress of mischance", said Giuglini, jabbing his cigar in the direction of Agnes and becoming angry again. "She has put a jinx on me. I will call her 'Little Miss Jinx' from now on. Through all these summer days that she has dogged me, I have known only bad luck."

As he did not elaborate on this proposition, his listeners were left to speculate as to what heinous misfortunes she had brought down upon his head. "And now look," he raged, "at what her ill-starred presence has caused fate to deal out to me."

He withdrew the sponge to exhibit his livid nose to Agnes, and he glared at her accusingly. "I should never have taken up with this unholy trollop. I swear by the Blessed Virgin and the Italian Nation that I will never perform again so long as she is near by."

A united Italy had just been proclaimed following the amazing martial exploits of Signor Garibaldi and his Red Shirts. This fact might have accounted for Giuglini swearing by his new nation, but not for his irrational desire to blame Agnes for something that could not possibly be her fault.

"I see that you thank me not for my love for you, Antonio", she replied with quiet composure. "You must think that it's a tribute to your genius, I suppose."

Uninterested in the relations between the lovers, Mapleson was keen to return to the pressing matter at hand. "How much must I stop from tonight's receipts, Antonio," he wondered aloud, "to have you see the performance through to its conclusion? Shall we say twenty-five pounds?"

The great artist's forefinger wagged from side-to-side once again. "I have sworn off it, solemnly."

"Well strictly speaking, Antonio, you solemnly swore off singing Pollione again, rather than concluding tonight's recital as such."

"Perhaps." The singer shrugged his acceptance that this might indeed be so.

"Shall we say forty pounds, and I'll arrange for the mallet to be locked in a strongbox and drowned in the Firth of Forth?"

An indifferent flap of the hand notified the impresario of his client's acceptance. "Look sharp," Mapleson said to the circling greasepaint and wardrobe hands, "let's buff Signor Giuglini up to a brilliant shine."

As they converged around him Agnes was cut off from her cherub, and for the very briefest of instants she looked lost and uncertain. But then she spotted Windham and myself, and latched onto us gratefully.

"Well, if it isn't Willie," she said, "and Georgie too. What a pleasant surprise. I was just thinking of scooting back to my hotel for a tipple, as it happens. Would you two care to escort me there, and we can have one together? I have a carriage waiting outside."

She extended an arm for each of us to take, and, once we had, she steered us out of Giuglini's presence.

"One has to make allowances for the artistic creature", she alleged as we moved towards the stage door. "They forget who they really are and can't help dramatising. And they're all incorrigibly superstitious. It's the agony of being forever gawped at by the public and dazzled by the limelight. It sends them funny. He'll eat his words in the morning and split his stays trying to please me."

Once outside, we halted under an awning as a heavy rain was in progress. The brawny commissionaire, whom I predicted would be there, proved to be the opposite of obstructive. He whistled Agnes's carriage along from the waiting line clogging the side street, and held its door open for us.

"Back to Slaney's, Danny, if you would be so good", Agnes directed the coachman.

"When did you arrive in Scotland?" Windham asked her, as we edged out into the traffic flowing down to Princes Street.

"Antonio and I got in yesterday from Paris. We took the night steamer from Boulogne."

"Where are you staying?"

"We're in a passable little *pension* on St Andrew's Square, though it's not a patch on the Meurice at the Tuileries. And the climate's not what it is in Paris either, being that it's so northerly here. But Antonio has his commitments to fulfil. Where are you berthed, Willie?"

"Oh, we haven't booked in anywhere."

"Nowhere at all?"

"That's right. We set off this very morning without having planned to, and we've only just arrived."

"That sounds charmingly foolhardy. What made you do it?"

"Well we, or more particularly me, dearly wanted to see you, Agnes, and George was more than agreeable to coming along. We read that Giuglini was here tonight, and thought that you might be with him."

"Oh, how sweet you are." Evidently Agnes did not find it strange that mere acquaintances should traverse the length of the land on the off-chance of finding her.

Windham trained a devoted gaze upon the pretty horsebreaker. "It upset me to see him mistreat you, just now", he confided.

"I wouldn't necessarily call it mistreatment", she replied. "It's just what one comes to expect from a man of his temperament. He's childlike, and one has to humour his caprices," she frowned and bit her lower lip, and looked out of the window to contemplate the rain, "to a limited extent."

Our carriage reached Princes Street, and then headed up into the Georgian New Town. Danny the driver let us off by Slaney's Hotel on St Andrews Square, and Agnes asked him to wait on her convenience. The linkman scurried out carrying a broad umbrella with which he sheltered Agnes on her voyage from door to door.

We went into the hotel in a warm spirit of fellowship. Agnes declared that our reunion called for some bottles of “fizz” to be cracked open, and she suggested that we retire to the select lounge to empty them.

But as we entered that room, we saw that it had occurred to another party to sit there and place a similar order. This patron was Mr James Roberts, a supposed gentleman of Piccadilly. He was occupying a corner table, with a bucket containing a bottle set in ice on a stand beside him. There were two clean glasses placed upside down on the cloth. It was clearly destined to be a trying night for Agnes as regards men.

“There you are, my dear”, observed Bawdyhouse Bob blandly, clicking his fingers for a waiter to approach and broach the bottle.

“Have you had a dandy little dawdle in Paris, my dove, seeing all the sights and the suchlike? I heard that you were due back, and thought that we might mark the occurrence with a splodge of champagne. Slide over here and be companionable with me,” he patted the place next to him on the banquette, “there’s a good girl.”

Agnes’s face froze, and she became soldered to the ground. Her former mentor addressed her as if she were quite alone.

“You can be as coy as you like,” he continued, “I don’t mind. But we both know that you will come to me in the fullness of time.”

He motioned for the waiter to upturn the glasses and fill them with sparkling wine. He then motioned for the underling to hop-it.

“The trouble with Paris,” Bob resumed languidly, “as you will certainly have discovered, is that it’s villainously expensive. And the trouble with the operatist Giuglini, as will also have become apparent to you, is that he gambles all his cash away. I think that I did warn you about this. It wouldn’t surprise me if *you* have been obliged to underwrite the expenses, which is rather getting things the wrong way round for a person in your profession.”

He wheezed dryly at this hollow witticism and lit a cigarillo. "Indeed, I am inclined to speculate that the matter of finance is something of a sore point for you just now. In fact, I would go so far as to guess that you are in need of some good, honest toil to repair your solvency. I am a magnanimous provider, and am willing to overlook your recent disloyalty and take you back on my books." He patted the vacant seat again and smiled horribly. "Can a kind employer say fairer that that?"

Agnes still did not move nor reply. Windham and I were too confounded to know how to act.

Bob shrugged his shoulders, but he would not let up. "It's a pity you've been out of town these past few weeks, because I've never had such a popular filly. It's not as if your face is lacking an aesthetic aspect. Why, I've had a queue down the alley asking after you all the while."

He lifted his tinted specs and locked his stare upon her. The eyes were intensely narrowed in their puffy sockets, and the expression was downright nasty despite the studied geniality of his patter. He replaced the lenses after a moment or two and dipped into his pocket to pull something out in his fist.

"Well see here," he said, "let's stop playing around and get to the pith of it. I've brought you a little present, to celebrate your return to the paddock."

Agnes advanced a short way toward him, in curiosity.

Bob opened his palm very slowly to reveal a glinting bracelet, which he held up and rotated between his fingers. "Here you are my flighty glow-worm. Come and get it."

Agnes was drawn to the twinkling lure, and she went all the way over to Bob's table. He made no move to get up. It was as if he was a magus or a mesmerist, exerting some potent power of enticement. She presented him with her bare forearm, and let him slide the bracelet over her slim wrist. Then she examined the bangle in satisfaction, and sat in the place he had offered her.

"Thank you, Bob" she said, claiming one of the flutes and taking a sip of champagne from it. She then snuggled against his shoulder, and he put a hand upon her knee. The sight was quite chilling.

"Why, there's good old Squire Windham and the easily led Mr Phinney", Bob stated in vulgar exaltation. It was as if he had only just noted our presence. "This will be the second occasion on which I've been in a position to bestow my hospitality upon you gentlemen. Do come and sit with us." He summoned the waiter again, and ordered more wine and glasses.

Perhaps Bob had cast some spell on us too, for we did sit and sup with them. We had passed a long day, filled with a tiring journey, and were by now in a dazed and disoriented state. Our host saw to it that the drink flowed and gushed. Agnes became uncharacteristically garrulous, twittering and chirruping in an inconsequential fashion, which seemed to gratify Bob. They both fell to swapping vulgarities, and encouraging each other in the practice. She was constantly recharging the glasses, especially the one belonging to him, and rekindling their conversation if it threatened to pall. She did not favour Windham or I with the slightest attention, and she permitted a considerable leeway to Bob's hand as it surveyed her leg.

After a while, our remaining there became so intolerable that Windham and I determined to get up and go. Overhearing our resolution, Agnes shot us a glance so piercing as to absolutely prohibit it. Then she effortlessly resumed her servile bantering with Bob. In fact, she continued to gabble on at him long after his eyes had started to close and his head had started to sink back against the cushion and roll. He rallied once or twice, but when his head slumped forward to nod against his chest she abruptly quieted and snatched the smile from her face.

She put a finger to her lips. "Shush..." she breathed at Windham and me, "shush...".

The pendulous rocker was emitting unmistakable snoring sounds, and Agnes put her ear close by it to test for their tone and timbre. Apparently satisfied that he was asleep, she stealthily reached into his waistcoat pocket. From it she pilfered a small sheath, from which she extracted a sharp stiletto.

"Now you see," she said softly, holding the blade up to the light, "why I must seem to submit to him. He has menaced me with this before. But he can't match me drink for drink, and I knew that he would pass out in a twinkling if thoroughly dosed up."

She returned the knife to its housing and dropped it into her purse. Then she snapped the clasp shut. "I have quite done with Bob. And I have quite done with Antonio too. I want to go home. The hotel can forward my belongings."

"You were ever so brave", Windham advised her admiringly. Then he consulted his pocket-watch. "There's a night-mail with some limited passenger space leaving Lothian Road shortly. But we'll have to put a tremendous spurt on if we're to catch it."

"Let's go then", said Agnes.

We tiptoed somewhat unsteadily from the lounge, and left the stout figure with the tinted glasses to his slumbering. Agnes paused in the lobby to instruct the desk-man to have her things packed and despatched to London before dawn. She said that Giuglini would stay up gossiping and gambling at the theatre until then, and that it would be agreeable to have him return and find her gone.

But Bob's slumber was not as deep as Agnes had reckoned upon. Through the glass door to the lounge we could see him stir, look around, and recover his senses. We hurried outside and jumped into her carriage, but as Danny cracked the whip we saw that Agnes was not the only one with personal transportation at her beck and call. Bob emerged from

Slaney's in an ungainly shuffle that aspired to be a run, and got into another coach that had been idling nearby at the kerbside. Its driver promptly pushed off in pursuit of us. And he kept pace with us all the way through the town, as Danny whipped the pair toward the railway station.

When we reached the Lothian Road terminus our coach rattled at a reckless pace, swaying this way and that on its springs, into its vehicle entrance carriageway. This was inconveniently sited at some distance from the front of the night-mail train, which could be seen standing at steam-up way down the platform. We ground to a dead halt of scraping hooves and creaking leather, and tumbled out. Bob's carriage heaved to behind us, disgorging a thumping great bully with a cosh in addition to his bawdyhouse employer. The hefty thug had presumably hitherto been lounging outside in the coach as some kind of supercargo, waiting on orders. I deduced that their aim was the abduction of Agnes, and that any violence administered to Windham and myself would not be regretted.

The whistle blew and the train lurched forward. Agnes then did something that I would never have expected to see her do. She hitched up the hem of her crinoline and ran headlong at the engine, exhorting Windham and me to do the same. We sprinted alongside her, but as the train gained traction saw that we could not possibly make it to the passenger carriages. These were positioned right at the back of the assemblage, beyond the mail wagons. And it was no use thinking that we could leap in amongst the postal sacks either, because Her Majesty's Mail was strictly conveyed behind locked doors. We ran on nonetheless, with Bob and his burly associate pursuing and bellowing at us to stop.

As we approached the advancing locomotive, the filthy but friendly face of its driver loomed out of its side. "Mr William Frederick Windham of Felbrigg Hall," it hailed my friend in a homely Norfolk brogue, "may I extend you the brotherhood of the footplate?"

"My dear Mr Babcock! Certainly you can."

The strong arms of his fireman then reached down to sweep Agnes off her feet and plonk her up on the metal. The arms swiftly returned, and Windham and I clutched one apiece as we scrambled and clambered onto to the footplate ourselves. Once we were all three safely gathered in, Babcock accelerated the engine past our languishing pursuers. Looking back, we could see Bob distractedly trying the doors of the leading mail vans, before the train's increasing velocity rendered it impossible for him to grasp the handles. His design had been overthrown. Outside the station, darkness, smoke and rain blotted out his receding figure and that of his thick-set accomplice, and only the moon was within vision.

It became plain from the content of his excited conversation with Windham that William Babcock was formerly a guard, then a driver, on the Eastern Counties Railway. They had apparently struck up a friendship on that network at the time. Indeed Babcock proudly flipped a silver watch and chain from his pocket, which he said Windham had given to him on the occasion of his marriage. He invited us all to study the inscription which read, "Presented to William Babcock by W.F. Windham, Esq., in acknowledgement of his civility and attention."

"If you please, Mr Windham," Babcock said, restoring the timepiece to its resting place, "I would be honoured if you would take charge of the engine."

Windham graciously accepted, and as he took hold of the regulator he rolled his head and remarked, "Perhaps I am not entirely without my uses." He drove the train for some distance with great glee and unbounded relish, peering ahead through the circular window in the spectacle plate. Babcock seemed well-satisfied with the competency of his performance. Seeing my friend thus engaged, I congratulated myself that our day's excursion had served some therapeutic purpose after all.

Agnes stood watching with her back to the tender, as Windham drove and the fireman sweated round and about shovelling coal. The glow of the furnace was in her face, and her golden hair and gown were becoming soot-bespattered. Her white stole was being speckled with black patches. Jubilant at the thrill of it all, she raised the offending stiletto from her purse and flung it into the onrushing rain and darkness. I observed, however, that the diamond bracelet that she had been gifted remained firmly entwining her wrist.

Babcock eventually put us down at a coaling stop, and we walked the length of the train by the light of a lantern. I daresay that the passenger apartment's occupants were surprised and astonished to see our bedraggled trio, one dressed for a night at the opera, emerge like ghosts from the trackside gloom. We saw no call for explanations. The car was sparsely occupied in any event, and we found free seats on which we were able to recline. I think that we all fell asleep instantly to the rhythmic lullaby of the wheels' clatter. I was dimly aware that we periodically stopped and stood at one station or another, but otherwise I slept through what remained of the night. The fact that I had drunk a good quantity of champagne added intensity to my dreams, which disjointedly replayed the events of our freakish escape.

We arrived back in London in the early afternoon. Agnes proposed that we go straight to her home for some luncheon. Windham and I jumped at an invitation that would never have been extended in normal circumstances. She lived over on the far side of Regents Park in the locality known as St John's Wood, or the Grove of the Evangelist. The hackney carriage that took us there stopped outside a suburban villa halfway along a tree-lined street named Blenheim Place. The villa occupied its own plot, set somewhat back from the road, and was identical to each of its neighbours. It was a compact two story house in grey brick, with generously-sized windows surrounded by white painted frames. We went up a small flight of stone stairs that led to the front porch.

"Oh, it's good to be back," said Agnes, throwing the door open.

Two little girls rushed noisily at her from along a tiled passage, and buried themselves in her flounces. She introduced them to us as her sisters Thirza, aged thirteen, and Emmeline, aged eleven. Trinette, who had been looking after the girls, appeared also, and there was a day-maid whom Agnes instructed to rustle up some food. In quick time the servant produced a splendid buffet of cold pies and pickles, with coffee and dainties to follow, which we took in the back parlour. We sat at a table by its open French windows, looking out at the girls playing in the garden. It had rained all night, and there was the refreshing smell of damp vegetation that comes after a deluge. Agnes had not yet troubled to change, and she sat wrapped in an embroidered counterpane.

"If I remember it right, Willie," she said presently as she helped a strawberry swirl onto her plate, "you made me a proposal of marriage when we first met."

"I recall that I did."

"Do you stand by it?"

"I believe that I do."

"What terms have you in mind for the accompanying financial settlement?"

PLUCKED FROM OBSCURITY

"It's so blessed quiet in here," commented Augusta Lewellin, "that anyone would think we were fixing to hold a *séance.*"

"And in broad daylight too," added her husband, "and we haven't even closed the curtains." It was actually not long after breakfast had been cleared away. "Whatever would the neighbours think?"

Sitting there at their drawing room table, one could imagine the Lewellins producing a spirit-board and inviting the rest of us to gather around it with our fingers touching a planchette. With her ever-present shawls and bangles one could picture Mrs Lewellin in the role of a medium, receiving otherworldly communications and translating them for everyday mortals. And one could equally well see Mr Lewellin orchestrating some suitably ghoulish bumps and scratches to enhance the atmosphere.

It was the morning of Windham's twenty-first birthday, which was also the morning on which he was due to be wed. We had been specially asked into our landlords' private apartment to toast the occasion with a cheering glass of whiskey. But it was not a good barometer of fortune that none of his relatives had so far consented to attend the nuptial event. And the only guests that had arrived, Mr and Mrs Jeffrey from Felbrigg, had dampened any mood of celebration that might otherwise have arisen. The bailiff and housekeeper were seated leadenly on the sofa, and they had neither accepted any offer of refreshment nor removed their cumbrous outer clothing. Mr Jeffrey was in a coarse tweed overcoat and a billycock hat. A plain, cockleshell bonnet framed Mrs Jeffrey's grey hair and ruby cheeks, and her rough-fibred overshawl was buttoned up to the neck. Their palpable disquiet had given rise to the uneasy silence that Mrs Lewellin remarked upon.

When Mrs Jeffrey did speak, it was indeed to invoke the spirit of one departed. "We don't need the silly rigmarole of a *séance*, Mrs Lewellin," she said in a quivering voice, "to tell us what Willie's poor dear father would have made of this dreadful marriage. He would not have stood for it! Mr Jeffrey and I have been very much distressed since we learned of it. We have quarried our hearts day and night since then, but cannot find the substance within them to bless it."

Tears shone in her eyes, and she pulled a handkerchief from her sleeve to dab at them. She was an unpretending person.

Windham, who was seated by the front window opposite his aged retainers, shook his head with an expression that intermingled joy and sorrow. He was visibly battling his own tears back.

"When I attended Willie's father on his deathbed," Mrs Jeffrey continued, "I promised him that I would give my last breath to keep his boy safe from harm. And though the old squire was fading fast when I said it he heard me, and replied that he was right glad of it. He held my hand and kissed it, there and then. And that's a fact! It's true that the poor old man had a chequered nature, forever shouting and singing and whistling about the house. And it's true that he would swear and rage fearfully when he was put-up, and not spare Willie the fruits of his anger. But he did care for the boy after his own peculiar fashion. And if he could take solid form before us now he would say that this marriage must not go ahead."

Her husband spread an arm around her shoulder, and she burrowed, weeping, into the folds of his coat.

"It's not for us to call your personal arrangements into question, Willie," the bailiff ventured in a more reasoned tone than that of his wife, "and may god strike us dead the day we attach credence to malicious gossip. We are only humble serving folk, and it ill-befits us to hop above our station. But this Willoughby woman...that is to say, lady...of yours is not of good character from all we have heard. She's certainly not been walled up in any secluded sisterhood! Far be it from us to say so, but she is not a respectable person. We've heard that she gets put in funds by society gentlemen, and that she needs a few of them on the go at any one time because she's so blinking extravagant. Can you not find a nice homely girl to fetch back to Felbrigg, Willie, one whom we can welcome with unfeigned gladness?"

Windham was plainly moved by his retainers' entreaties, but he also appeared resigned to his fate and steadfast in his decided course of action. His misshapen mouth opened and closed several times, but failed to funnel coherent sound out.

"She will bring calamity upon us all," bemoaned Mrs Jeffrey, breaking her husband's embrace and turning to face her young master, "and dowse us in dishonour. We have never even stepped on a train before, but have endured a fitful night on the 'parliamentary' to beg you to rejoin your senses."

These trains were so-named because parliament had obliged the railway companies to run a minimum number of services at rates cheap enough to be affordable to all. They also had to consist only of weatherproof carriages, rather than the open rattlers usually reserved for the lower classes. Resenting this interference, the companies scheduled their "parliamentaries" to run at the most ungodly hours, hence the Jeffreys' overnight journey. They had set off late the previous evening and looked intent on scurrying straight back to Shoreditch station once they had said their piece.

"And we have never even been to London before," the housekeeper hurtled onward, "and it seems for all the world like we've fallen into Hades itself. Oh what a mill-race of folk is crammed into her, and not one of them with a gentle word or gesture. Such numberless hoards must be riven with aching pits of loneliness. And what a tumult of traffic! And where do all the rusty beggars come from, and all those wretched infants with nothing for their wares but bird seed or boot laces? Where do they all lay their heads at night? There was never such want in Norwich, I'll be bound. This marriage will have us all in the workhouse, Willie. Oh do say you'll reconsider and call it off."

"My dearest darling Jeffy," Windham at last contrived to splutter, "my heart compels me to act as I do, and if I am a fool then I will be the one to suffer it. I cannot go back on a commitment freely contracted."

This appeal to moral rectitude appeared to find its mark with the housekeeper, and she broke off to consider it.

Strange as it seemed, William Windham had been betrothed to Agnes Willoughby soon after our return from Scotland. Arrangements for their wedding had crystallised thereafter at a bewildering rate. They had visited a solicitor of Agnes's acquaintance, on Russell Square, in order to make terms for the Marriage Settlement. They had paid a call on Mr Emmanuel, the jeweller of Brook Street, where Windham had furnished acceptances for a diamond ring and ancillary desirables. They had spoken with the vicar in his vestry at All Saints Church, St John's Wood, concerning devotional matters. Declaring himself to be fully recovered Windham had thrown over Dr Winslow's treatment regime, which the Lewellins had likewise renounced in favour of assisting his wedding plans. I had been requested, and had consented, to act as best man. We had been measured for the wedding suits we were now wearing at Moses & Son's on New Oxford Street, where it was said you could go in a clown and come out a nobleman.

Wearing their homely country threads, the Jeffreys looked a pair of oddments in the Lewellins' metropolitan front parlour. But, then again, the none-too-fastidiously groomed landlords did not blend all that harmoniously with it either. Their private room possessed an almost antiseptic degree of cleanliness, neatness and order, and so standard were its furnishings that they might have come in their entirety from a catalogue. The carpet was patterned in green and gold, which was matched by the tablecloth, and the wallpaper in grey and purple. The curtains were of the richest red, while the windows were screened by lace hangings. Cabinets, chairs, and stands occupied much of the available space, and a gold-framed mirror hung above the fireplace. The ornamentation consisted of embroidered frames and plants in painted vases, and stuffed birds under glass domes perched on undergrowth and branches. As was often the case in urban dwellings several large canvasses protruded from the walls, depicting solitary stags or herds of hairy cattle in rugged highland settings.

Sensing that they were not far short of exhaustion, David Lewellin now renewed an earlier offer made to the visitors. "Are you sure you won't take any sustenance with us," he asked them, "and permit us to relieve you of your outdoor clobber? It deserts all decency for us to have you stewing there in your hats and coats." He tugged at the crimson bell-rope.

A surly parlour-maid appeared and, at her employer's instigation, stood over the country couple until they disgorged their outer garments. She could see that they were not gentlefolk to whom she owed a show of deference.

"That's the ticket," Augusta directed the Jeffreys, "give them over to her. And will you take a drop of tea and a morsel of nutrition, and perhaps something stronger?" She referred to the whiskey decanter resting on a sideboard. "It's one of Mr Windham's finest malts."

"Well, we're not stopping long, but we have had a most taxing journey," conceded Mr Jeffrey reluctantly, "and precious little slumber. I don't suppose it would go amiss to have our spirits burnished a bit, now would it Jeffy?" He looked at his wife for approval.

She was too tired and upset to stand aloof any longer, and her resolution crumpled. "If the truth be told we'd be glad of some tea and a tot, and a small nibble if you can spare one, Mrs Lewellin."

"You hear that", Augusta said to the girl. "Bring some more plates up, and a pot. And forage them some breakfast leftovers."

While the maid was away, David Lewellin fettled fresh glasses out of a display case and furnished the Jeffreys with a draught each from the decanter. Then he resumed his seat next to his wife at the table. Windham was parting the window lace all the while, scanning the street anxiously for new arrivals. When the maid returned with the requisite refreshments the Jeffreys partook of them timidly, as if the fare was rightly meant for more deserving others.

"Mr Windham's is an uncommon marriage, I'll grant you," Mrs Lewellin said to soak up the ensuing silence, "but you have to credit him, all the same, for landing such a pearl. Mr Lewellin and I are great believers in the state of wedlock, and it's served us well through thick and thin. We've had hardly a harsh word pass between us in all our married years, still less a full-blown quarrel."

"We're very lucky to be able to say that," concurred her husband, "but not everyone's so fortunate. Some just aren't suited to contracting the married condition."

"No, they're not," agreed his wife, "not by any means."

"And we've had some gentlemen roosting here just so as to dodge the marriage peril. That north-country squire we had boarding with us last season certainly wasn't fitted for marriage, though there was nothing wrong with his eye for a pretty face. Can you bring him to mind, Augusta?"

"Oh yes," she chortled, "I can see him now as clear as day, loafing over there where Mr Windham's sat. Roland Leander Stott he was named and it was ever so funny because he rolled all the letters 'r' in his speech, like they do up north, and his friends used to call him "Rollie."

"That's right, so they did. He came from somewhere near Burnley, which he pronounced as 'Burrrrnley', so that it was really drawn out. He had a big house and a great sack of land in that vicinity. And he told us about a girl he met up there, before he came to us, that he might have married. Shall I say what happened?"

"You might as well, Davie. The wedding brougham's not due for a while yet."

"Right you are then. As Mr Stott had it," Lewellin recounted, "this comely schoolgirl, who was called Sissy, had trotted into Burnley on a pony one Saturday afternoon to run some messages for her kinfolk. They were small farmers in the district, and none too prosperous at that. I can't recall exactly how he said he got on speaking terms with her, but they took a shine to one another from that moment on."

"He helped her repack one of the panniers when it fell and spilled," Mrs Lewellin prompted her husband, "and tie it back astride the animal. And it wasn't hard to credit their mutual attraction. Mr Stott was a charming young man and very gay in his manner. There was many a night his comic tales of country mischance had us roaring fit to explode. We never did meet the girl though."

"No that's true, we never did", Mr Lewellin reflected. "Anyway, they'd no sooner become acquainted than Squire Stott whisked her off to an inn and stood her a fabulous dinner. And they got on so famously while they despatched it that Sissy invited him back to the family cottage before the day was ended. Her parents bowed and scraped at the sight of such an eligible suitor, and were as grateful to have him there as you would expect poor folk to be. He supped with the whole lot of them and stayed the night, sharing a bed with one of the girl's brothers. He visited plenty of times thereafter, and he and Sissy spawned a lively interest in each other. The thing even went so far that there was talk of an engagement being hatched when she would come of age. Her kin all thought him a rare catch."

The landlord smirked and rubbed his palms together, apparently relishing what his tale had in store. "Then Mr Stott decided he would take himself off to London for the season. He told Sissy's folks of the plan, and said that he could do their girl a good turn by fetching her along and introducing her to the ways of polite society, in which she was conspicuously lacking. He said that he would satisfy her every expense. She would stay at his family's town residence, where his two spinster aunts were on hand to watch out for her chastity. Well, naturally the girl's parents consented to it. But he had held back from them one tiny little fact."

"There was no posh town-house for the girl to bed down in," Mrs Lewellin interposed gleefully, "and there were no virtuous and vigilant chaperones. Rollie Stott came to us for the season, and farmed the girl out to a room in Pimlico."

They hooted uproariously at this disquieting disclosure. "You might say that he plucked her fair flower up from a country hedgerow," Mr Lewellin proposed, "and replanted it in a mucky town ditch."

They considered this ribald perspective very droll, and laughed deliriously.

"Well, who can blame him," continued Lewellin, recovering his composure, "it was he who was answering for the bills after all. He told Sissy that the town-house was being refurbished in style, especially to receive her, and that it would be ready any day now. And he did give her the chance to make something of herself. Her room was in a respectable lodging and he bought her all kinds of nice things and fine clothing. In fact he got her most anything she asked for, and took her out and about all over town. They troughed at spanking restaurants, and went dancing at the Casino and the Argyle. He took her to the opera and the theatrics, and spun her around the Serpentine in a carriage." Lewellin made a circular motion with his forefinger.

"Well, our Rollie was well-pleased at the way his wheeze had turned out, all things considered, as he had this Sissy girl right where he wanted her. That is to say he was so, until she asked to know for sure from him when they would be married. What a nerve to raise such expectations, after all he'd done for her! She was so far below his rank that there could be no question of an actual betrothal. Mr Stott began to see her as a cadger upon him thereafter, and grew to resent it. And then she told one of his friends that he'd ruined her maidenhood, which he swore on his mother's soul was an atrocious falsehood. In the end he bounced back up north to be shot of her, and sponged her clean from his thoughts. And so it was that all her high-hopes were stillborn."

"Pay good heed, Mr Windham," Augusta counselled my friend, chuckling, "it's not too late for you to stand your own little bird up. Her type of creature doesn't really feel it, and she'd look a fine sight pecking round the altar all on her lonesome."

The Lewellins laughed some more at the thought. "Mr Windham knows I'm only teasing him," Augusta assured the Jeffreys, "and will allow me my trifling familiarities."

The visitors had stopped picking at the plates on their laps some while ago, and had been absorbing their hosts' tale of abandonment with mounting incredulity.

"If I understand you right, Mrs Lewellin," said Mrs Jeffrey, her sense of propriety so affronted that she found herself defending Agnes Willoughby's honour, "you'd be content for Willie to behave as grubbily to his betrothed as this despicable man 'Rollie' would have done? Your Mr Stott sounds like a scoundrel of the first description."

"Hold on Missus," Augusta responded, "there's no call to take it like that. We're only having a jolly with you."

"So you may say, but how 'jolly' do you suppose this poor Sissy lamb felt when she found herself all alone in London and unsupported? And if he had ruined her, as he might very well have done from all you've said of him, she'd never be welcomed home again."

"That was her look-out, wasn't it? She wasn't slow to latch on to him in the first place."

"But he fooled her into it under a false pretence. And I don't suppose that you and your husband sought her out in this Pimlico place to see if you mightn't do something for her?"

"We run a gentlemen's boarding house, not a casual ward for the unwary," Mr Lewellin weighed in belligerently, "and being parked on our sofa doesn't give you the right to bleat at us."

"I'll get off it then, if my sitting here makes you salty." Mr Jeffrey jumped up, seemingly contemplating some sort of physical remonstration with Lewellin. His wife followed him to her feet.

While this dispute was brewing Windham had been observing the scene outside, and he suddenly sprang from his chair in exultation. "Uncle Charlie is coming", he cried. "There is his carriage. I knew that he would support me in the end, despite all his sourness. Now this truly will be a joyous day."

I looked out of the window to observe General Windham's polished vehicle scrape to a stop alongside the pavement. The door opened and its owner got down, looking solemn. He turned his head this way and that, as if sniffing the wind to see if it favoured whatever was in prospect. Mr Portal emerged behind him, followed by Dr Winslow, and all three made for the Lewellins' front door. Judging by their everyday costume, they did not plan to attend a wedding. As they rang the bell, a second carriage pulled up. Its bright adornment of foliage and flowers announced it to be the wedding brougham, come to convey Windham and me to the church in St John's Wood. It was hitched to a pair of grey horses and governed by a portly coachman in jolly costume. A groom jumped off to stand sentry by its door, which he then opened before rolling out a strip of red carpet.

The newcomers were admitted to the house and shown straight into our company. Windham was so overtaken with delight that he misread his uncle's demeanour, and rushed at him with his arms spread wide.

"Uncle Charlie," he exclaimed, slurring heavily, "your presence today is the best wedding present I could possibly have."

But his uncle did not return the expansive gesture, nor make any reciprocal statement of affection. Windham was left standing high and dry before him, his arms uselessly outstretched.

"A wedding present?" the general responded in a tone of quiet disbelief. "This really is too bad, Willie. Have you sustained a violent concussion that makes you act so preposterously? I am coursing around to find something that might explain your truculence, but come up empty-handed. No gentleman marries on the day he comes of age, and no day is right for a gentleman to wed a vulgar popsy. Let's have an end to this absurd nonsense. You're to come with us directly to Outram's on Bedford Row, and sign those legal papers as you agreed. We have a longstanding appointment with Mr Outram senior who's made everything ready to receive us."

"That he has", agreed Mr Portal, his whiskery face peering encouragingly at Windham from beneath his brown bowler hat. "And you needn't fear that skipping your appointment at the church will land you in a breach of promise action. Any pledge made by you before today is unenforceable at law, as it would have been made by a minor."

"And you have only recently suffered a bout of severe mental upset," Dr Winslow chimed in to buttress the gathering tendency, "which I anticipate may not yet be fully ended. This is surely not the right time to undertake the most momentous step of your life, one on which your whole future contentment may pivot."

"Come along now, Willie," the general resumed, with an attempt to strike a chummier note, "and when we've finished our bit of business at Bedford Row we can go forward to Simpson's on the Strand. We can savour one of their tasty spreads and rinse it down with some velvety vintages. You'd like that wouldn't you? And now you're squire, we can have a jaw about Felbrigg matters. Mr Portal and I are looking forward to hearing your views on estate affairs." One could, perhaps, discern a hint of suppressed rage lurking beneath these blithe pleasantries.

Windham's arms had returned to his sides, and he looked as downcast as if he had not one friend on the face of the earth. "It does not suit my convenience to visit Outram's today," he stated evenly, making every effort not to slur, "because I have a compelling reason to be elsewhere."

On receiving this rebuff, the general exchanged a knowing glance with Dr Winslow.

"Will you at least consent, my good Mr Windham," the doctor requested, "to step round the corner to my consulting room before you go there. It's only as far as Albemarle Street and I believe we have sufficient time. You see it is my professional impression that you are not yet quite well, and I gather that you have ceased taking the medication I have previously prescribed for you. I fear that, as things stand, you may fall into actions that you will bitterly regret when you are restored to full health. It has, for example, been suggested to me that no sane gentleman would contemplate making the marriage you propose to make. I cannot say for certain that this is so, which is why I wish to examine you properly under controlled conditions. It will not take above one half-hour, and will amount to no more than your answering a few simple questions. The law would require this much of me before I might attest any resultant documentation."

"You intend to certify him under the Lunatics Act, do you not?" I put it to the doctor. "And have him committed to your asylum at Sussex House." It was standard practice for patients to be admitted to such institutions on a doctor's signature, but these were generally cases where their mental incapacity was glaringly apparent to all.

"Only if a diligent examination renders that course inescapable", Winslow returned hotly.

"You can't think to have Willie thrown in a madhouse, general," Mrs Jeffrey protested, "you'll have the old squire, your own dear brother, spinning in his grave."

"Mind that you keep to your place, Mrs Jeffrey. I will do whatever I think best, however harsh it may seem to the uninformed. Now then, Willie, are you going to accompany us peaceably to Albemarle Street?"

"As I have already had cause to state," Windham replied with steady resolution, "I will not be accompanying you to Albemarle Street, or to Bedford Row, or to any other address it may occur to you to invoke. I have a prior engagement in St John's Wood."

"I've had my fill of this buffoonery, Portal", the general said, losing his temper at last. The pair of them advanced swiftly upon his nephew and tried to crowd him over to the doorway.

A farcical tussle ensued, during which Windham resisted their efforts to take hold of him. The three of them shuffled backwards and forwards in perilous proximity to the densely arrayed furnishings, emitting grunts and guttural exclamations.

"Careful now", David Lewellin warned.

"Mind out for my valuables", his wife added, as they both leapt from the table in alarm.

"Please, gentlemen, no rough play", Dr Winslow cautioned. "I urge you to desist. My examination must be wholly consensual and cannot be actuated by force."

But they did not desist, and the inevitable mishap duly occurred. The victim was a large and leafy aspidistra, nestling in a willow-patterned ceramic pot. The grappling trio overbalanced backwards to barge against its tall stand, and the plant wobbled precariously and then toppled over. Its container smashed open on the green and gold carpet, flinging damp, matted mulch far and wide.

Mrs Lewellin threw up her hands and squealed, "Don't tread it in", as she bounded across and separated the protagonists from the contagion. Her husband jerked feverishly at the bell-rope.

The same parlour-maid as before entered, and Mrs Lewellin pointed to the debris on the floor as if the girl herself had created it. The maid exited again to obtain the appropriate purging devices.

"There now," Dr Winslow pronounced self-righteously, "coercion should only ever be employed as a last resort. It often has unintended consequences, as we have just seen demonstrated."

"And we mustn't knock your precious scruples off *their* pedestal, must we doctor?" the general replied with a scathing look. "In the Guards we are accustomed to act decisively when a situation merits it. What's one broken pot when weighed against all that Willie stands to lose by this marriage?"

"It was one of my favourite pots when it was all in one piece," Augusta Lewellin objected, "and it came in at ten shillings from the Floral Hall at Covent Garden."

"You'll be fully recompensed, madam," the general reassured her, "don't concern yourself."

Accepting that he had bungled the attempt to bully his nephew, General Windham now addressed him in terms that were more sorrowful than angry. "You don't comprehend the enormity of the error you propose to commit, Willie. Apart from any other consideration, you will be blackballed by everyone of note in the neighbourhood of Felbrigg so that the very servants and tenantry will hang their heads in shame. You will be excluded from every facet of county society. Even close relatives such as I will be prevented from visiting. And sooner or later the woman will tire of country life and go off somewhere more exciting. But not before she has run your solvency into a furrow."

He walked over to the door and held it open. "I give you one last chance to accompany me, Willie. We need not involve the doctor if you will sign the legal documents voluntarily."

"I am truly sorry to disappoint you, uncle," Windham responded after a long pause, "but I will be travelling in the other carriage."

"So be it, then, if you are quite decided." The hardness of teak had crept into the old campaigner's tone. "But do not imagine that our dealings may continue to be cast in any genial mould. If you make this match then I must conclude that you are mad and act accordingly. Mr Portal advises me that I may get up a Commission of Lunacy to have your mind ruled unsound. If I succeed then your marriage will be struck down, and so will your freedom of action. Be in no doubt that this course will engender untold unpleasantness, if you force me to adopt it."

The maid reappeared in league with a dustpan and brush, and knelt on the floor to sweep the mess up. Some stubborn looking stains had, however, soaked into the fabric. General Windham lingered at the threshold for some moments, fixing his nephew with a lightship stare in a final bid to require his compliance. Then he was gone, with the doctor and attorney following on. They climbed into his carriage, and it circled round before creaking down the slope towards Pall Mall.

Amid a flurry of tears and sentimental declarations, the Jeffreys now consented to attend the ceremony after all. Windham insisted that they ride there with us in the wedding brougham. I cannot say for certain what it was that made them relent. It may have been the example of the north-country squire's inconstancy, or perhaps it was the depth of his uncle's hostility that decided them to take their young master's part. I think it most probable, however, that when it really came to the rub they simply could not bring themselves to forsake him.

Windham made a show of discounting his uncle's threat, though I could tell that it had gravely wounded him. "Uncle Charlie will think better of going to law," he informed us, assuming the certainty of a seasoned lunacy practitioner, "when he recollects that I am the sanest man living." We all laughed at this attempt to make light of the spectre his uncle had dangled.

Once the Jeffreys had retrieved their cloakroom deposits, and made up their quarrel, reluctantly, with the Lewellins, they boarded the wedding brougham with Windham and myself. They evidently felt that, whatever insult had been given, now was a time for graciousness. Standing at the carriage window in the street, the Lewellins wished my friend their most heartfelt congratulations, and prayed that we would both return to visit them often. They also apologised for any misunderstanding that may have arisen between themselves and the Felbrigg serving folk. With glistening eyes, Augusta confided that she would miss us most frightfully. We were due to go on to Felbrigg that night and had ended our tenures at Duke Street.

We ambled off to the church, which was located on the busy Finchley Road that ran through St John's Wood. The party assembled at its porch was few in number, and Windham made fast work of the introductions. It emerged from these that his bride maintained a small professional entourage. There was a doctor of Guildford Street, who was stated to be her personal physician, and there was the solicitor of Russell Square who had been responsible for drafting the Marriage Settlement. These two shrewd looking gentlemen, in their middle age, were apparently named as its trustees. They escorted Windham into the vestry to attend to its signing, which had to precede the ceremony. The other persons present were principally the bride's friends and relations who all hailed from her birthplace near Alresford, in deepest Hampshire. There was her older brother, and several men and women of various ages who were dressed sufficiently for the occasion, but were rather primitive in their speech and manners. There were also some rather fast female friends of the bride.

The groom re-emerged in time to receive his intended. Agnes arrived in an undecorated open barouche and got down with a stooped woman whom I understood was her mother. The bridesmaids, who were her two younger sisters, followed them out. These were attired in the sort of miniature crinolines that little girls wore for best in those days. Made of lace-trimmed white muslin the frocks ballooned out to just below the knee, with hooped stockings on view from there downwards. Agnes was dressed quietly in a green velvet gown and a balmoral bonnet wreathed with snowy blooms. Windham folded a tiny trinket into each bridesmaid's palm, and presented a luscious bouquet to Agnes. She smiled her acceptance, and he bowed in return.

This tender scene was observed by a passing gaggle of street lads, who had been clowning and tumbling to attract small change from the rattling traffic. "Strike me pink," one of the scruffy gamins hollered at Windham and Agnes, "talk about beauty and the beast. How much tin is he payin' yer to get with him missus?"

His cheerful insolence provoked laughter all round, and Windham picked a coin from his waistcoat pocket and spun it with great precision for the heckler to catch. A little procession was then marshalled in which our company went into the church. The physician acted as father to the bride, walking her arm-in-arm up the aisle to give her away. The marriage was solemnised by the Reverend Mr Maddock. Agnes radiated serenity, while Windham appeared unruffled and not at all melancholy. I produced the ring, and at the prescribed time he kissed his wife, tentatively. Having done this, he beamed with undisguised pleasure.

We went through to the vestry to sign the register, and then the newly-weds were cantered round to Agnes's villa in the wedding brougham. The rest of us walked the short stretch to Blenheim Place. At the house a long table and benches had been laid in the back parlour, ready for the wedding *déjeuner* to commence. We took our places, and I was seated next to the vicar and the two professional men at the garden end. The happy couple sat halfway along the hallway side of the table, each flanked by a bridesmaid. The bride's mother was at the table's further end, with Mr and Mrs Jeffrey to either side of her. The dinner was served by a number of red-faced men in aprons whom I was told were also up from Hampshire. They were none too particular about their language, but neither was anyone else once the beer and porter had begun to foam. And the fare was as rusticated as the chatter, having for its centrepiece a haunch of beef roasted with potatoes in the oven of a baker on the Finchley Road. Steaming rhubarb pie with custard was hurried from the same shop for seconds, and there were shrimps, cresses and muffins to close.

Watching her nearest and dearest demolish the repast, I wondered whether they expected Agnes's good fortune to brush off on them. Conversing with the doctor and solicitor, I also wondered at how someone of her simple origins could enlist the services of such sophisticated types as these. They had apparently met her whilst out riding to staghounds in Buckinghamshire, and both were very respectably connected. I do not think that I was deceived in supposing that she was their client rather than the other way about.

Once the feast had been reduced to slops and crumbs, and the health of the couple had been roundly toasted, the prevailing demand was for a concert party to be got going. At this, Agnes herself stepped up to the piano stool. To her own accompaniment, she proceeded to sing a cradle-song that she introduced as being of her own composing. Her singing voice was more tremulous than that which graced her speaking, but it had a nicely fluttering tone all the same.

"*Good night sweet Babe good night to thee and ere the morning light*," she crooned, "*may your sweet face resume its smiles so happy and so bright.*"

Her mother joined in tearfully with the remainder of the maudlin lyric, listing so far over to one side it seemed she might capsize. Mrs Jeffrey, who was getting on swimmingly with her, propped her up whilst mopping a copious stream from her own face. The close of the refrain was met with a gale of vociferous appreciation. Acknowledging it graciously, Agnes then rose from the stool and took up her bridal bouquet from the table. She picked a red carnation out from it, before handing the remnant to her sister Thirza to whom it fell, as eldest bridesmaid, to bestow one bloom on everyone present as a wedding favour. In the language of flowers, the particular variety given them carried a special omen for each recipient. The carnation chosen by Agnes, for herself, denoted romantic love of a passionate kind.

Leaving Thirza to make her rounds, Agnes walked over to the opened French Windows where I was leaning against the frame. She enquired whether I would care to take a turn in the garden, as it was growing horribly stuffy inside. I agreed, and she linked her arm in mine as we began our perambulation. The sound of one member of the party launching into a humorous recitation in Hampshire dialect drifted out on the breeze. I felt quite light-hearted myself and thought to pose the hostess a mischievous question.

"Do you by any chance keep a dog, Agnes, which answers to the name of Fluff? One that is perhaps an example of those small, furry breeds that's inclined to yap a lot?"

"No, I much prefer cats. You might see Mattie and Tilley skulking around in the undergrowth hereabouts. Whatever made you think so?"

"It's just that Lady Listowel said you would have a dog like that. I think she regarded it as the height of vulgarity."

"And who might Lady Lis-Whatsit be?"

"She's one of Willie's snooty aunts. We were in her carriage at Hyde Park the day we first saw you. She seemed to know quite a bit about you, and disapprove of it."

"The fact that I've not heard of *her* while she's heard of *me* values her disapproval at its right price. But what business could she have to abuse me? What else did she say?"

"She knew that you came from the country originally, though she didn't know from exactly where, and that your true maiden name was not Willoughby. By the way, when we signed the register just now I happened to notice that it's actually 'Rogers'."

"What a keen eye you have."

"May I ask why you changed it? Did you assume the name from some lordly line, such as the Willoughby's de Broke of Compton Verney?"

"Perhaps I did. Or perhaps I pinched it from the

alias a Swell Mob of thieves give when they're up before the Bow Street beak."

"No, tell me seriously. I'm genuinely interested to hear about it."

"Well, if you must know, George, it goes back to when I was first in London and sometimes walked up and down Regent Street on an evening when I had time on my hands."

I refrained from probing into how this peculiar circumstance might have arisen. "Oh really?"

"Indeed. And I would peek in the shop windows as I wandered, and watch the great ladies shuttle about with their shopping. They always had a flunky trolling after them laden high with parcels and what-not. And when they came out of one shop they would get back in their carriage just to be driven to the one next door, or the one straight opposite. I thought it quite amusing. The best time to watch was after dark, when all the shop fronts were lit-up like gin palaces with great diamond-shaped crystal lanterns."

Agnes pointed out a bluish-grey cat as it slunk out from under a bush, crossed the path in front of us, and then vanished under another. "Tilley", she informed me, and we both laughed.

"There was one huge dressmaking salon that looked just perfect," she resumed, "with its heaps of coloured silk and velvet rolls in endless racks of numbered alcoves. A great lady would no sooner have stepped in than a host of showroom women would dance around her with samples. And when she'd chosen her fabric and her pattern, one of them would have to go back home with her to discover her measurements in private. 'Willoughby & Co' was the salon in question. You may find it hard to comprehend George, but I was an impressionable girl once and thought that adopting the name would make me sound cultivated. None of the clothes I was then wearing were my own. I realise now how simple it was of me, but since then I've just stuck with it."

"You named yourself after a drapery shop?"

"You may mock if you like, but it hasn't turned out as idiotically as all that. I had this very *trousseau* made at Willoughby's, *and* I had one of their show-women trundled back here with a tape measure. I make it my practice to be a client of such houses, and not to be one of the poor needlewomen they pay a pittance to actually run the dresses up. That would be worse than forever skulking understairs and being summoned by bells from above. And now I'm Mrs W.F. Windham Esquire and not plain old Miss Willoughby!"

The path we were on curled around the modestly sized plot. Having reached the back hedge we stopped, and looked back over the garden to the house.

"You don't love Willie do you?" I stated starkly. "You've only married him for his wealth and position."

"You don't mind what you say to me do you?" She gave me one of her faint frowns and fell silent for a second.

"No, I don't love him, but I certainly don't loath him either. I think he's awfully sweet and I wouldn't do anything to harm him. Besides, love is the least part of it. And as for acquiring myself wealth and position, it would be insufferably seedy if that were my sole consideration. I was not at all anxious to enter into the married state, I don't mind telling you. What weighed mostly in my mind was the benefit I might derive for my two sisters, whom I wish to bring up and educate as ladies. I don't want them squinting all night, sewing fine gowns they'll never afford by candlelight. And I don't want them making the acquaintance of the likes of Bawdyhouse Bob."

"Will you be safe from him at Felbrigg?"

"I should think so. He's not troubled me since we gave him the slip in Scotland. Anyway, he's an urban parasite and I doubt he even knows where Norfolk is."

"There are such things as trains."

She looked away and bit her lip. "He won't dare to bother me now I'm a lady."

"What about Antonio?"

"Oh him? Well, I might have him along to sing at one of the musical *soirées* I mean to throw at Felbrigg, but he's not gentlemanly enough for a country lady to entertain. From now on my life will be perfectly settled and respectable."

I did not find this entirely convincing, and decided to broach something else that had been troubling me. "When we were in the tent at Ascot," I said, "you claimed that you were the daughter of a clergyman who had fallen foul of an appalling miscarriage of justice. And you said that some moneyed man had then taken you under his wing and sheltered you. That was absolute gammon, was it not?"

She thought this very funny indeed. "Oh Georgie, you are hapless sometimes! Don't you know that it's standard practice to say something of the kind? One doesn't expect anyone to believe it. I just said it for fun, to see what reaction I'd get."

"And you also alleged that your mother had passed away, but there she is as large as life." I nodded towards the house.

"The same applies. The less cluttered one's family matters are made to seem, the more it puts a gentleman at his ease. He isn't led to feel that he will have to cope with all sorts of surplus relatives and sentimental complications."

There was something else about that afternoon at Ascot that I wanted to learn the truth of. "It was no accident that Bob came across us when he did was it? Someone had told him where Willie would be, and that he had caught a passion for you?"

"You make it sound like a nasty infection", she replied, tinkling with laughter. "Well, there will always be some men who wish to be entrapped. And *you* might assume that duplicity is everywhere rife, George, which is a common fault amongst attorneys, but I prefer to think better of human nature. I daresay that your condition may be cured, given time and attention."

She looked petite and demure and inscrutable, just as she had when I saw her lounging on the ottoman at the racecourse. It would have been dishonourable to mention the damning conversation I overheard her have with Bob in the opera house colonnade. And our discussion was now cut short, as Thirza ran out of the house displaying empty palms to show that she had completed her allotted task of parcelling the bouquet out.

"Is there no bloom left for Georgie?" her elder sister asked. When the girl shook her head, Agnes reached for one of the strands of honeysuckle that were growing out of the boundary hedge in profusion. The sweet smell of them was all around us. She broke a flower off and handed it to me with a chaste little curtsy. According to my limited appreciation of the floral code, honeysuckle foretold lasting bonds of affection. That was all well and good so far as it went, but it was not a presentment of romance and passion. I thought of Felicity and felt an acute pang of melancholy. A bawdy song was underway noisily inside.

The celebrations were soon concluded, as we planned to catch the afternoon Norfolk train. Our travelling party was eight in number, being Mr and Mrs Windham, the two girls, the Jeffreys, Trinette the maid, and myself. The long trip to Norwich proceeded without undue incident and it was after dark by the time we reached there. On the train, Agnes had mentioned her understanding that certain facilities at Felbrigg were well below what she considered an acceptable standard. She said that she had contracted for a particularly indispensable item to be installed, to bring things up to scratch. Her meaning became plain when we exited Norwich station. A large porcelain bathtub was strapped to the roof of our awaiting coach.

As was proper, the interior saloon was given over to the girls and womenfolk. It was fortunate that the vehicle was capacious, but, even so Windham, Mr

Jeffrey and I had to squash on the seat behind the driver and his mate, the rearward outdoor seating pen being crammed with luggage.

Our arrival at Felbrigg came long past the bedtime of regular folk. Everyone there was awoken and put to work readying the rooms and bringing in the bags and trunks. The bathtub was lifted and swung through an upstairs window by means of a pulley. Agnes then expressed it as her intention to put the novel object to immediate use, as she felt herself somewhat travel-worn. This occasioned considerable organisation, consisting of every available servant being formed into a snake to pass buckets of hot water from the kitchen up to Agnes's dressing room. The human snake spiralled round the stair hall past portraits of ancestral Windhams, costumed in assorted backward styles. In the guttering lamplight, their faces seemed to grimace at the noisy disturbance.

I did not know what had become of poor Sissy in her lonely Pimlico room, and did not expect to find out. But I could say with certainty that Agnes Rogers, or "Willoughby" if you like, had been plucked from her obscurity to become the Lady of Felbrigg.

THE SHOOTING PARTY

Shortly after their wedding the Windhams departed for the South of France, where they would spend their marriage jaunt. They generously offered that I might remain at Felbrigg in the meantime, and the Jeffreys were as willing to have me stay as they were glad to see the back of Agnes for a few months. But I felt uneasy about living off the largess of others, and reluctant to linger where I had no occupation or companionship. My life had been fractured so that I was unsure of where I belonged. I even entertained the ludicrous notion of signing onto a merchantman at Yarmouth, and putting out to sea. But since this was pure fantasy I actually drifted into Norwich and contracted casual work, outdoor clerking for a firm of solicitors in the town. I took humble lodgings at the Hen & Chickens Inn, along a sooty yard near the railway station.

One evening towards the end of November, Windham paid a call on me there. He was a little stouter and swarthier than before, though time had not much changed him otherwise. As we supped together in the select he gave a glowing account of himself. He and Agnes had enjoyed a terrific nuptial jaunt, he proclaimed, and she had settled splendidly into

Felbrigg now that they were come home. So much so, he ventured to suggest, that the arrival of a small nursery dweller might soon be expected. For himself he was greatly enjoying the return to wholesome rural pursuits, though he was denying himself the pleasures of locomotive junkets or mail-cart driving. This was on account of a pact he had made with Agnes, whereby both were to renounce their former foibles and become paragons of respectability.

It was only when we were several fathoms deep into our conversation that he told me of something that was blunting his contentment. It seemed that, far from simply vapouring about lunacy proceedings, his uncle had actually gone ahead and begun them. Not only that, but the old soldier had succeeded in dragooning his nephew's fourteen other uncles and aunts into joining the suit. My friend handed me the lunacy petition that Mr Portal had served upon him, so that I might peruse it while he crossed the flags to refill our jug. The petition cited him as a "supposed lunatic", and described him as being of "unsound mind". General Windham was the leading petitioner, followed by all seven of his surviving siblings. These numbered his brother, who was a naval captain, and their six sisters, led by the Dowager Countess, Lady Listowel. The husbands of four of those sisters who were still living had signed also. And on the maternal side, the paper bore the noble scrawls of the then Marquis of Bristol, and his brothers Lord Arthur and Lord Alfred Hervey.

Windham was inclined to make light of this apparent unanimity when he returned with the beer. "Mama's brothers will catch it from her when she hears that they've strapped on their gaiters and enrolled in my uncle's shooting party", he predicted confidently. "You'll see that she's declined to add her own signature, and I happen to know that she cordially disapproves of the whole business. The only reason she hasn't scotched it already is that she's been too ill to do anything much of late. I'm going up to London to see her tomorrow, and then she'll make sure that the legal grouse-beaters are called off."

He went on to explain that his mother Lady Sophia, and her second husband, Theodore, had been obliged to swap Torquay for London on what they hoped was a temporary basis. They had taken a short lease on a superior villa out in Old Brompton. This was so that her ladyship might have access to a specialist physician in the West End, who was treating the severe neuralgia with which she had recently become afflicted. Windham's outward mood was one of heedless optimism, and he placed great faith in the potency of his mother's hoped-for intervention. But underneath, his feelings had clearly been singed by the patent hostility of his family's move against him. And I had good reason to be more pessimistic than he about what was to come. I knew that, once a lunacy petition had been issued, a lunacy inquisition would go ahead whatever his mother said. I also knew that these trials hardly ever returned a finding of sanity. They were almost invariably foregone conclusions, just as the one I had attended at the Norfolk Hotel after I first met Windham had been.

Though unreservedly sympathetic to my friend's plight, I have to confess that a grain of self-interest entered my thinking at this stage. The fact that he would contest his inquisition meant that it would be a very unusual one, which was likely to involve scores of witnesses on both sides. This would in turn make it exceedingly protracted and abominably costly. The solicitors entrusted with his defence would stand to profit handsomely from it. As a junior solicitor lacking regular employment I could not take conduct of his case myself, but the principal of a firm like Praed & Pumicestone might, if it were offered to him. And if I were to be reconciled with her father and restored to his employ, then tender relations with Felicity might also be resumed. I must record that my motives were not entirely selfish, however, as I sincerely thought myself best placed to do justice to Windham's cause.

I put my proposal to him right away and he agreed without demur, saying that he had earnestly desired me to suggest it. We toasted our common endeavour, and finished the evening talking brightly of better things. After boarding overnight at the Hen & Chickens, we travelled up to London on the next day's express. The cab we hired outside Shoreditch station dropped us off at Lincoln's Inn Fields, where the Lunacy Office was located. I wanted to visit this branch of the Chancery Court to obtain some further information. Once through its doors we engaged the attention of the grave desk-clerk, who sported a long two-pronged beard of silvery grey. We ascertained from him that Windham's case had already been up before the Lords Justices in Chancery. These two judges were only required to read the evidence presented to them, and had no need to see the "supposed lunatic" or hear anything in his defence. They had duly ordered that an inquisition take place, and this was listed to commence some three weeks hence, at the Law Courts abutting Westminster Hall. The venerable desk-clerk gave us copies of the two medical affidavits that the petitioners had been obliged to submit with their application, but he also made it known to us that Windham had been ordered to undergo formal psychiatric examinations in a fortnight. When we notified him of our intention to offer a contest, he confessed that it would baffle him to recall the last successful respondent. And he added, with funereal glee, that dozens of witnesses had already been summoned to appear for our opponents.

The doctors' affidavits set out the grounds on which the allegation of lunacy rested, and I was curious to learn what they had sworn to. I therefore put it to my companion that we squat somewhere and read them before going on to see Lady Sophia. We did not want to remain in the musty Lunacy Office, where one was not encouraged to set up camp anyway. Lincoln's Inn

Fields is one of the largest squares in London, and as the weather was unappealingly drizzly we decided to shelter in a small octagonal kiosk at the centre of its spacious garden. When we were installed there, I proceeded to review the medical evidence, which I did with increasing perplexity.

Neither doctor was a known psychiatric practitioner, nor had either conducted a recent examination of their subject, both relying for their findings on meetings with him that had occurred long ago. One swore that he was first called to see Windham when he was a boy of four years old, at which time he found him slavering idiotically and unable to speak. He blared inordinately and behaved like a savage. The other agreed that the subject's intellectual powers had been non-existent since early childhood, and stated that they had hardly improved since. Indeed his manners had, if anything, deteriorated. This latter observation was based on some trivial social encounters, at a ball or a matinee and so forth, which were several years out of date. The evidence was insubstantial, but unmistakable in portraying Windham as an imbecile from birth.

I could hardly keep this disturbing fact from him, so I handed him the offending documents once I was done with them. He considered them for some time, and then sat silently for longer while they rested in his lap. Rain was pattering on the glazed kiosk ceiling, and late afternoon darkness was coming in fast.

"No doubt there is a class of person," he remarked at last, "that has been entrusted with my care in past days and had cause to wish that they had not. I know that I have often been a crude and insensitive youth, and that I have led some unfortunates on a breakneck ride. Do not suppose that I am proud of my juvenile years, George. I do not expect to be shouldered through the streets of Norwich and showered with confetti to hymn my humane attainments. But now I am of age, I can at least claim that I strive always for self-improvement. It is only after a very great effort that I have conquered the slavering and foaming that so offended these medical gentlemen. And as to my general behaviour, I believe that I am more mindful of others and less capricious than in times past."

He spoke with the same intense deliberation as he had when he was slumped in the derelict coach at the stable yard. I think that he now had an inkling of what was before him, and an understanding that its woes could not be wished away.

"I can barely recall the men who authored these unkind statements," he continued, "and cannot imagine why they formed such an evil impression of me."

"The charge of imbecility is nonsense," I told him with Alpine authority, "as anyone who knows you will instantly tell. And even 'supposed lunatics' aren't obliged to lie supine while the law runs them over. I'm sure we can find any number of honest souls lining up to speak for your sanity. Let's make our visit to your mother meanwhile, and see what she can do to help us. It's getting late, and it's a fair trek to her villa."

"Yes, let's go and see Mama," he replied with sudden vim and vigour, "and she will put everything back in its right place."

But it was not the best timed moment for us to make a bend, as the light patter had transformed into a heavy shower. Pulling our collars up and our hats down, we dived out of the little refuge and strode smartly to the eastern end of the square. From there we entered Lincoln's Inn itself, through a gateway in its high encircling wall. This is one of the ancient "Inns of Court" that govern the barristers' profession and house its members. Ducking through the Carthusian seclusion of its precincts, we soon attained the renewed shelter of the medieval Gate House at its further side. This gives out onto Chancery Lane, where cabs are to be had, and we halted there in the dry while we awaited one. The narrow thoroughfare was thronged with sluggish traffic and a slew of distracted City types. It threads through the mosaic of legal London, with the premises of multiple quill-drivers crammed into it and the passages leading off.

It was obviously going to be some piece of work to attract a cab, given the brisk demand for any means of escaping the rain. A number of groups and individuals were roosting vigilantly under umbrellas at different points along the kerb. The pubs and shop fronts shone with an inviting fluorescence, and many pedestrians were standing under their awnings or swishing through their doors. We were not ideally placed to make ourselves seen, and, despite jumping up and down and gesticulating when appropriate, we kept losing out on looming prospects. A carter's wagon drew up across the road and began unloading barrels into a cellar, so blocking the downward flow of traffic. Then a hansom cab pulled up behind it, disgorging a top-hatted eminence onto the pavement.

"Now for it", Windham resolved impetuously. Though I tried to dissuade him with a touch on his elbow, he dashed recklessly across the nearside carriageway towards the hansom.

But its driver was a sprightly one, and he swung his lamp to show vacant before goading his horse to pelt round the stationary wagon. Though he had seen the smallest gap in the oncoming traffic, the cabbie had not seen the oncoming Windham. The horse saw him soon enough though, and it reared up as they nearly collided in the middle of the lane. Windham dodged and crouched, and the animal struggled for its footing on the slippery setts.

"Mind yourself, jolthead!" shouted the cabbie, as he was hurled precariously back on his high chair behind the two-wheeler. It was not far short of overturning. Windham stood his ground tenaciously, and the horse shied and struggled before coming to anchor at last. The traffic heading in both directions stopped dead, and a chorus of impatient bellows cut through the splashing of the deluge.

Amazing to relate, the cabman allowed Windham his hire after a spirited debate and much flapping of arms. No harm had been done, after all. I, who had been watching in a state of impotent alarm, joined my friend and we got into the cab and pulled the hatch shut and the window down. He explained that the offer of a tidy tip had decided the cabman in favour of taking us on, despite the fact that he had been uncommonly riled. The thus placated driver then set off trotting towards the Strand, and the traffic unblocked.

"I've spent many happy hours in company with the cab fraternity," Windham told me with a shrewd expression, seemingly oblivious to the hazard he had manufactured, "and so can boast a fair knowledge of their practices and peccadilloes. I used to ride about with them quite a lot when I was first in London. Not because I wanted to go anywhere specially, you'll understand, but just for the pep of the expedition. You'll find that cabbies are carved from the same timber as the rest of us, really. Some are accommodating fellows, while some are the opposite. A good one will discount you the going rate if you hire him for the whole day, and a fine one will toss you a turn at the ribbons into the bargain. I've been all over with them, to some pretty unsightly spots, and to some jolly nice places as well."

At the foot of Chancery Lane, we turned right into a drove of jingling teams jostling to squeeze through the narrow gateway of Temple Bar. It is an unqualified blessing that this impediment to free passage between Fleet Street and the Strand has since been dismantled.

"I've been up and down river on the steamboats too", Windham burbled on, as we cleared the obstruction and joined the flow along the Strand. "I've been east to Greenwich and west as far as the gardens at Kew. You can steam in either direction from Hungerford Pier near here, though you'd have to be an admiral of the fleet to swing yourself a turn at the helm. On a nice day you have to mix with great crowds while you await the boat, and it's packed to suffocation when it does heave to. I bet that our cabman would have charged us a whole shilling if we'd asked him to take us to Hungerford Pier for a steamer, even though it's only sixpence a mile and the distance is about that. Any cabbie worthy of the fraternity will make sure that he inches over the next mile mark, so that he has his second sixpence. The rate is only sixpence a mile while you're within a quartet of Charing Cross, but it goes up to a shilling beyond that. I can't say for certain if we'll be within the limit when we get to Mama's. And we'll have the cabbie wait outside for us, even though that's another sixpence per quarter-hour. Then there's the fourpenny tip on top."

His mood was oscillating between elation and agitation, and he abruptly looked glum. But where the Strand reconstituted itself after forking in two around the island of St Clement Danes church, Windham pointed excitedly to the web of narrow streets and alleys leading through to Drury Lane. This entire locality has recently been demolished, to make way for some grand avenue up to Holborn. But it was then notorious for slums, and for boarding houses as murky as the weather we were scything through.

"It's a very picturesque *arrondissement*," Windham gave it as his considered opinion, "despite its shady reputation. It has lots of wooden buildings that cheated the great fire, their gables leaning halfway across the street like they did in medieval times. It just goes to show that one shouldn't be put off from exploring somewhere interesting on the say-so of cloddish Jeremiahs."

At Trafalgar Square we passed the statue of the King Charles who was beheaded, and this spurred him into further exploration of historical themes. "You'll know of course that Norfolk was dead-set against the king in the Civil War? The Windhams then living were red-hot for the parliamentary cause, and one of my ancestors fought in its victorious army. Felbrigg got off quite unscathed because there was wasn't much trouble thereabouts. And a later forebear of mine, a William like me in fact, was in the government during the French revolutionary fighting. The library at Felbrigg is all down to him, but it's not much used nowadays as we've all been pure dunces since."

He proceeded to outline his own educational shortcomings as we rolled up the Haymarket and along Piccadilly. The traffic was dense, fractious, and slow-moving in the poor visibility occasioned by the downpour. The cab's wheels groaned and rasped. It seemed from his account that Windham had been a very poor scholar and had been held back in the fourth form at Eton when he was fifteen, despite having had a private tutor. "I could not be made to admire," he admitted, "the classics that were supposed to equip me to be a gentleman. And as to what they termed the 'lesser ingenuity' of mathematics, I found it grotesquely obscure."

By the time we skirted Hyde Park and turned into Knightsbridge, he was skittishly endorsing the doctors' view of himself as an imbecile. But his garrulous outbreaks tailed off as we left these populous parts and headed for the undeveloped fringe. His mood became pensive, and as the houses fell away so did his chatter. His mother's villa, Sidmouth Lodge, was located some distance along the Old Brompton Road, where West London finally shaded into countryside. There were only a few large and secluded residences scattered thereabouts then, in a district that is now deep within the maw of the metropolis.

On finding the house, which was off Bolton Gardens, we asked the cabbie to wait as Windham had suggested. It had stopped raining, but the air was cold and foggy, which gave rise to a spectral atmosphere. We went through a garden gate and along an overgrown path to reach the main frontage. An oval pool of stone steps led to a very tall door, between two Greek columns that ran the whole height of the building. The liveried footman who answered our knock looked ready to dismiss us with a routine rebuff. Then he recognised the only son of his mistress, Lady Sophia. At this he let us into a large hallway, with the stairs that it encased hardly visible in the prevailing gloom. He disappeared though a creaky door leading off it, and muffled voices were audible from within. The oil lamps meant to provide illumination were so dim that they seemed only to make the space darker.

The footman returned to bleakly inform us that his mistress was far from well. It would, he said, be a mercy on our part if we were to restrict her exposure to ourselves to the briefest possible duration. His expression seemed to scold us for disturbing them in the first place. He showed us into the chamber he had just exited. It was difficult to make out clear features in this gloomy room, which seemed to house little more than a four-poster bed set in the far corner. A nearby grate was glowing red with embers.

We went over to the bed to observe that its curtains were not drawn, and that Lady Sophia was sitting on its counterpane propped against a bank of pillows. She had a well-knit frame and bore the vestiges in her countenance of having once been winsome. She was not old and the hair that hung disarrayed about her shoulders was more black than grey. But her face was pallid and drooping in the flickering light cast by a mass of candles on a bedside tallboy. She was wrapped in a man's thick dressing gown over a long nightdress, and wore a tasselled head-dress of lace. A pack of cards and a selection of periodicals were scattered within reach on the bedding.

"How nice to see you, Willie," she said, "I do hope it's not a chore for you to visit. And who's this quaint little fellow you've brought along with you?"

Windham introduced me as a friend and his solicitor, and gave his mother a peck on the cheek. She twisted this way and that, and then stretched out her legs uncomfortably. "I suppose it's horrid outside is it?"

"It is pretty filthy", her son agreed.

"I do miss balmy Torquay and detest shivery London," she shuddered, "and I so miss all our gay friends there. Theo and I were never short of company for games or music or a party. They were such a bohemian crowd, and not at all stuffy or stuck up. And now I'm virtually manacled to this bed, and haven't even left the house for weeks. My physician prescribes rest, but unrelieved rest is sheer monotony. It's as if I were transported back to wretched Norfolk, with only your poor father for my companion."

Lady Sophia leniently refrained from elaborating on this over-personal subject matter. "I know what we can do now that you're here," she said in an abruptly girlish manner, "we can make up a foursome at whist. Come and sit round me on the counterpane. You can partner me Willie, and it'll be just like old times at Felbrigg. And Pringle can twin with your lawyer friend."

The footman looked about as keen on this proposal as I was, but everyone acceded, nonetheless, to his mistress's whim. We climbed up onto the mattress and allowed ourselves to be positioned according to her direction. "Oh, won't this be fun!" she said.

We must have made for a strangely assorted lot. There was the daughter of a marquis, her footman and her allegedly insane son, playing cards with a process pleader on a four-poster bed. So far as I can recollect Windham and his mother had the best of the contest, though they were able to tap into a mutual familiarity unavailable to Pringle the footman and myself. She chided and chivvied Windham if his play was not to her satisfaction, and she kept up a crackle of chatter which gadded from here to there and back again. We were treated to a generous slice of gossip concerning members of her Torquay circle, though their successive names were introduced with so little explanation that it was impossible to follow who was who and what was what. We were also acquainted with the activities of her husband Theo, who was described as a marvellous man and a miraculous musician. Interspersed with these comments were subsidiary dicta, concerning the outrageous prices charged for everything in London and the insolent surliness of metropolitan tradesmen.

Through it all Lady Sophia made no mention of the legal nuisance menacing her son, and I saw him angling to raise it several times only to find his opportunity gone. She presently tired of her exertions and declared that the game in hand would be the last one.

"Well, goodbye then Mama", Windham said, as we rose from the bed and readied ourselves to be on our way.

"Goodbye Willie. Do keep sending me all your news, if it's not too much of a fag to write. I so look forward to receiving your letters. Your trip to France sounded such an idyll."

Windham fiddled with the brim of his hat. "They say I'm mad, Mama," he proposed with a little laugh, "but you don't think that, do you?"

"Of course you're not mad, dear. And you're so much better than you used to be."

"I can't tell you how relieved I was to hear that you would have nothing to do with it."

"It's hardly an occasion for relief when a mother refuses to condemn her son. I told your Uncle Charlie, and his creature Portal, that I'd no time for their silly law suit. Never you fret about that."

"It's such a shame that you had to miss the wedding, for if you were only to meet Agnes I'm sure you'd find her as wonderful as I do."

"I expect I would, dear, but this beastly illness has prevented it. I don't blame you for your marriage, Willie. Everyone's entitled to follow their heart at least once in a lifetime. I did when I married Theo, and goodness knows the trouble it landed me in with the family. God preserve you from their sanctimony."

"George here will write to you, Mama, when he needs you to come and speak up for me at my trial. It seems that it will be sometime in the middle of next month, close by Westminster Hall. He'll order you up a nice big comfortable carriage to whisk you there and back."

"Oh I won't be going to any courtroom, Willie, and certainly not in wintry December. I can hardly get out of bed, let alone climb in and out of a carriage or risk stairs. You can see for yourself that my condition quite engulfs me. I wriggle about so much nowadays that it becomes distracting for everyone concerned, and I won't be ogled at from a public gallery. I've told Charlie that I'll have no part in his folly, and that's that. You'll just have to manage without me."

Windham looked at his mother balefully, and I understood that this was what he had expected of her all along. Any hope that she would orchestrate his deliverance had been exposed as a dried husk. She put her head back against the pillows and closed her eyes against a sudden twinge of pain. The footman, who was hovering solicitously, cleared his throat in a manner suggestive of our immediate departure.

Windham pecked his mother on the cheek again, and she took up the cards and began playing a game for one on the counterpane. As we were shown out, I noted that we had been inside for barely an hour and-a-half.

"Well at least that's not so many extra sixpences for the cabman's wait", Windham observed with a dry chuckle, though his temper was not really humorous at all.

We set off for Trafalgar Square, where my friend had booked a suite at Morley's Hotel for the night. He insisted that I share it with him, but there was one more call I wanted to pay that evening.

Once the cabman had let Windham down at the hotel, I asked to be taken on to Red Lion Square. I had the driver drop me at its western edge, as I was shy of showing my face at the Pumicestone residence and thought that the short stroll would calm my nerves.

The fog was now quite thick and the square was very silent. I walked slowly around it, and just as I was coming upon my former address saw that a grand carriage was stationed outside it. As I drew close I saw its passenger, a tall man of military bearing, disembark and advance to the front door. The door yielded to his knock, and the figure of Felicity Pumicestone could be seen framed in the gaslight. She was festooned in a ball-gown, and her whole attire was far more sumptuous than anything I had previously seen her inhabit. She radiated grace and elegance. The man offered her his arm, and as he turned to escort her to the carriage his own resplendent dress uniform became apparent.

"Felicity," I stammered as they approached me, "there you are. I was hoping to have a word with your father."

"Who's this paltry entity?" the lofty officer asked her. He looked down his nose at me and then laughed heartily. He had the same handlebar moustache and side-whisker combination as General Windham, though he was very much younger. I must have looked shabby indeed alongside these two opulent socialites, and I was at once conscious of having let my standard of appearance slip of late. I felt mine to be a dull and doughy presence next to theirs.

Felicity performed the required introductions, though her embarrassment at having to do so was all too plain. "Oh this is George, who is a former acquaintance," she told her escort, "and this is Ralph, or rather Major Fenning. We're going to his regimental ball, George, and I haven't a moment to talk with you just now. But father is within, and will no doubt receive you if you wish it."

My sudden materialisation from the fog had clearly flustered her, but her appearance on the arm of this hearty suitor had made me truly sore of spirit.

The officer handed her up into the carriage, which was emblazoned with a swirling gold livery, and got in beside her. It then skated them off to whatever glamorous venue they were attending. But Anna, who had been holding the front door open, took pity and called for me to come inside. She expressed herself overcome with delight to set eyes on me again, and complained that everything had been topsy-turvy since I'd been gone. The master was at home, she said, and she added that I did not need her to show me the way upstairs.

I duly went up to the front parlour as she had invited, and found Patrick Pumicestone just where I expected, reading his newspaper in front of the fireplace. My entire reason for offering him Windham's case had just been exploded by the sight of Felicity's beau. But I went ahead and did so all the same, simply because I could not think of any better course of action. I was ready to play the penitent supplicant, but in truth he did not need much convincing. I had said very little before his eyes began to gingle at the fee income Windham's defence promised to generate.

"This will certainly be a lucrative matter for the lucky firm that takes it on, George," he said, "and a decidedly prestigious one at that. I was hasty in letting you go, I'll freely admit. I'm sure we can come to terms, if you want to get back with me."

It turned out that Mr Pumicestone had been having a torrid time of it of late. The new junior whom he had hired to replace me was parsimonious in his abilities, and Pumicestone had found it necessary to oversee the novice's every word and action. This had curtailed the frequency of his leisurely attendances at his club. We agreed upon terms for my return, and sealed our bargain with a handshake. But these did not include my resumed residency in the Pumicestone household. Out of deference to his daughter's feelings he could not countenance that. He disclosed that this Major Fenning was courting her ardently, and was a gentleman who boasted a snug competency in his private estate. He was often taking her out and about, and she had much more colour in her cheeks as a consequence. Indeed, their betrothal might be expected any day now. To spare her blushes, my presence would be confined to the downstairs office during business hours under our new arrangement.

Our transaction also allowed that the Windham case would have first call on my attention, and that I might therefore travel as the needs of its preparation might dictate. After our overnight stay at Morley's Hotel, I therefore accompanied Windham back to Felbrigg with a view to amassing sympathetic testimony from those at the estate and its environs. But on our arrival there, Mrs Jeffrey ran out to greet our trap in a state of some excitement.

"Oh Willie, you won't believe what's happened," she exclaimed breathlessly, "Mrs Windham's only gone and flown the coop."

We followed the housekeeper hurriedly into the morning room, where she said that Agnes had left a note on the table. Windham sliced it open and scanned its contents.

"She calls me 'dear darling' and says that she is racked with remorse," he related flatly when he had finished reading, "but she has run off to Ireland to be with her paramour. It seems that Signor Giuglini is to perform in something called *A Masked Ball* at the Theatre Royal in Dublin, and that her feelings compel her to join him there. She has sent the girls back to St John's Wood with Trinette."

His following words were heavily freighted with emotion. "I know that I have not made a good marriage, but I had an infatuation for my wife. I knew that she had not led a moral or respectable life, but I hoped that being married we would be happy together. However the thing is done, and there is no use speaking further of it."

THE EYES OF ENGLAND

I set up shop in Mr Jeffrey's office at Felbrigg in order to begin the task of assembling Windham's defence. The bailiff's room was halfway along the corridor of the servants' range, which contained the estate workshops as well as the servants' hall and the chamber in which the tenants gathered to tender their rents. Windham and I made a schedule of anyone and everyone who might conceivably be willing to swear to his sanity. I then dispatched a missive to each, requesting their participation and offering expenses for their attendance at the trial. Mr and Mrs Jeffrey volunteered favourable statements, as did Knowles the butler, and all three pledged themselves willing to give verbal evidence. They also saw to it that I received a steady supply of prospective witnesses to interview from the house and its surroundings.

As I met with these unassuming servants and cottagers, I discovered a reservoir of affection for their young master. One would naturally expect his dependants to be loyal to their squire, but their devotion struck me as genuine nonetheless. It seemed all the more so, coming as it often did accompanied by knowing allusions to his manifold eccentricities. It was notable that, whether they worked in or outdoors, most had been at Felbrigg all their lives and many had seen Windham grow up. And they displayed a degree of familiarity with their squire that was uncommon in proprietorial relationships. Though some were moved to hilarity in recounting tales of his boyhood frolics, there was not one who doubted his essential presence of mind. Indeed several of the tenants attested to his level-headedness in the line of estate business. I also became aware of the existence of a marked protectiveness toward him. He was frequently described as having been a lonely child, and his parents' wayward treatment of him drew many a disparaging remark. Questions about Agnes tended to incite a glance at the heavens and a broad guffaw.

When I extended my researches to encompass tradesmen, clergy, and gentry of the wider locality, the picture became less sure. There had clearly been occasions on which Windham had been an embarrassment in public, to say the least of it, and a downright terror to say the most. And more than one of the persons whom I approached replied with an affronted denunciation. But on my forays into Norwich, and through other regions of the county, I still found goodwill toward Windham not hard to uncover. There was general agreement, amongst those who knew him best, that he had calmed and steadied during a spell in the East Norfolk Militia the previous year. He had apparently been commissioned as a subaltern by the Lord-Lieutenant of the county, and both the militia's colonel and his own company commander had been impressed by the standard of his application and deportment. There were also a good few shopkeepers, and other persons in trade, who considered his dealings with them to have been perfectly correct and were prepared to say as much in court. It was not long before I had built up a numerically impressive portfolio of parties pledged to uphold Windham's sanity upon their oath.

But trials are not decided on a balance of numbers, and I was conscious that most of the principal actors had eluded me. I had none of my friend's relatives to call to the stand, and was most glaringly missing both his mother and his wife. Nor had I managed to put any of those closely involved with his education into my pocket. It soon became discouragingly apparent that, when it came to prospective witnesses of real consequence, Mr Portal had always got there first. All four of those who had apparently acted as "tutor" to the adolescent Windham were promised to our adversaries, as were most of those who had encountered him at Eton and in earlier periods of schooling. A flurry of the accused's own retainers and acquaintances made for a faint counterweight. I was also frustrated in collecting likely prospects from his more recent time in London. My appeal to the Lewellins received a polite but negative response, written in Augusta's hand. She wished her former lodger bountiful good fortune, but regretted that she and Mr Lewellin had endured some unhappy experiences at law which precluded them from ever again entering a witness box.

The formal psychiatric examination ordered by the Chancery Justices was held in due course at Dr Winslow's consulting rooms in Albemarle Street. Windham was questioned there for over three hours by Dr Thomas Mayo, President of the Royal College of Physicians, as well as by Winslow himself. This pair threatened to constitute a formidable panel of experts against us, and their interrogation was conducted on an uncomfortably adversarial footing. Windham had also to submit to two further examinations, this time instigated by myself. The first of these took place at the Chiswick asylum run by Dr Thomas Harrington Tuke, and was conducted by Tuke and another alienist of high repute whom I had contacted, Dr E. J. Seymour. This session succeeded in enlisting these two gentlemen as expert witnesses for our side. Dr Tuke had been in the news a few years earlier when there had been an inquest into the death of Mr Feargus O'Connor, who had lately been an inmate of his asylum. O'Connor had led the "Chartist" agitation for votes for the working man, which had long since fizzled out in failure.

Sir Hugh Cairns Q.C. conducted the second examination that I organised, in his New Square chambers at Lincoln's Inn. Though not far on in his middle years, Sir Hugh was already a leading barrister and a rising parliamentarian. I was on good terms with the Chief Clerk of his chambers from previous dealings, and it was this that gave me an *entrée* to the great man. He was, by reputation, solemn and tightly-wound, and deadly if roused to disparagement. When I presented Windham to him and showed him the lunacy petition, he trained the gaze of his thin hawkish face upon the offending document. It seemed that the illustrious names it bore did promise to provide an inviting bait for him to swoop upon.

"Well, well," commented Cairns in his dry Ulster brogue, "it looks to me like an old-fashioned family council has been in session, and their fiat has gone forth across the land. Let us put their allegation of idiocy to the immediate question, Mr Windham, and find out if you tread a straight path of sound judgement or a winding track of incomprehension."

Sir Hugh proceeded to interrogate Windham crisply upon a range of commonplace items. He asked after the names of certain prominent public figures, such as the reigning monarch and the incumbent prime minister. He had Windham identify what date he thought it was, and where in the world he supposed we were sitting. He touched briefly upon his subject's comprehension of such matters as politics, religion and popular entertainments of the day. Finally, he invited Windham to name the essential difference between the human figures on view at Madame Tussaud's Wax Exhibition and those to be found thronging a public arcade.

My friend submitted to all this probing with stoic resignation, and his answers were cogent and consequent throughout. "Unless Phinney here is an exceptionally skilled ventriloquist," his questioner was driven to conclude, "you're no imbecile Mr Windham."

Sir Hugh then agreed to take Windham's brief, and undertook to wipe his calendar free of less intriguing obstructions. He also declared himself mystified as to how the petitioners intended to substantiate their contention of madness. When he asked me who was to try the case, I gave him the answer that it would be Master-in-Lunacy Samuel Warren. "Oh, not that prosy thickhead", was his disconsolate response.

Master Warren had some minor fame as a novelist, his best known work, *Ten Thousand a Year*, having been published two decades previously. I suppose that one must concede a place to the picturesque in literature, but this story concerned the nonsensical adventures at law of a character he called "Mr Tittlebat Titmouse", employed at a draper's shop he named "Tag-rag & Co". I had intended to skim it through with a view to furnishing you with an epitome of its plot, but regret that its stony prose grounded me before I had leafed many folios. By way of illustration the following are the first thoughts of Mr Titmouse at the outset of the tale, as he awakes in his attic garret on a Sunday morning. "Heigho!—Lud, Lud!—Dull as ditch water!—This is my only holiday, yet I don't seem to enjoy it!—for I feel knocked up with my week's work! (A Yawn)." A yawn indeed, as the character chatters on to himself for pages in the same exclamatory style. Though literary tastes are said to revolve in cycles, I cannot think that Mr Warren's cannon will ever return to vogue.

Sir Hugh Cairns' objection to Warren's notoriety was less literary and more practical. "Men of affairs like Master Warren," he maintained disapprovingly, "have no business being known to the public for reasons unconnected with their official duties. Fame arrived at in frivolous ways only tends to decrease their gravity and inflate their vanity, and Samuel Warren has a formidable surfeit of the latter. If this case attracts even half the attention I expect it to, what will prevent him from playing to the gallery? And he has not the smallest notion of how to hold the ring in a genuinely contentious matter, as he is a mere commissioner and not a judge. I fear that the trial will slip his grasp, and drift rudderless for the want of a guiding hand."

It was a surprising curiosity of the then state of lunacy law that its cases were not presided over by actual judges, but were instead divided between two "Masters-in-Lunacy". Warren was one of these, and his colleague Francis Barlow, who had conducted the lunacy that I had attended in Norwich, was the other. Both were experienced barristers, but neither was an experienced judge because lunacies were so rarely contested. And their burden of work was not unduly taxing, there being only fifty or so lunacies all told in any given year. The truth of it was that their position amounted to little more than a lucrative perquisite.

The normal form was for whichever of them had been assigned a particular case to travel to wherever the supposed lunatic was residing and examine the unfortunate at a local inn or asylum. Regular lunacies only required the master to read the medical affidavits that had been filed in advance, and then ask a few pertinent questions of the sufferer before agreeing with the doctors that he was of unsound mind. But Windham's refusal to go meekly into this bind would oblige Master Warren to empanel a "special" jury of twenty-three members. There would have to be so many because a minimum of twelve had to concur in the verdict. And each juror had to be of very high social standing. Separate registers were maintained at county level of those who met the qualifications set by parliament.

As I have described at the commencement of this memoir, Windham's inquisition got under way on a Monday, two days after the untimely demise of Prince Albert. Windham and I again shared a suite at Morley's on Trafalgar Square, which was conveniently placed for us to base ourselves for the duration. Given that the masters were required to be mobile in their duties, there was actually no special courtroom set aside for them to hold inquisitions in. The Lunacy Office had accordingly begged the use of a temporarily vacant room at Westminster, which belonged to the Exchequer Barons. This was in the old Law Court building, which had turrets and battlements like a medieval castle and has since been demolished and replaced by an even more gothic pile on the Strand. The old Law Courts were separated from the Houses of Parliament by Westminster Hall, and entered by way of it.

Once sworn, the jurors elected Sir George Armytage as their foreman. This Yorkshire baronet was the sort of sporting gentleman who notches up frequent mentions in the press for attending fashionable race meetings. He was glossy and urbane, with black hair parted to one side and a finely trimmed beard. The substance of the petition having been read out by the clerk, Armytage and his similarly well-groomed colleagues sat forward in their crowded box, ready to receive Master Warren's direction as to the law applicable to the matter. So did everyone else, crammed as they were into a bank of benches which ascended in front of the master's raised dais. Despite the warmth generated by our numbers, the room was so cold that I could see my breath condense before me.

An intimation of how far out of his depth he was came when Samuel Warren broke the expectant silence in a tremulous voice. He was clearly overawed by the intense attention, delivering his initial remarks in such a low and indistinct tone that they were quite lost to his listeners. His grey and crumpled face peered at his notes through tiny oval spectacles, and it looked as if he was struggling to remain sat upright against the weight of horsehair pressing down upon his head.

"Will you speak up, M'Lud?" an uncouth voice at last boomed from somewhere near the back. "We must have our money's worth!"

Received as it was with widespread cries of agreement and shouts of laughter, this knockabout episode set the tone for much of what was to follow. I understood the monetary reference to signify that the doormen were already sponsoring an informal ticketing market.

Perhaps encouraged by the bogus elevation of himself to a judicial lordship, Warren coughed and made an effort to be audible. "While I am responsible for the conduct of this inquiry," he was heard to warn the jury waveringly, "you and you alone are responsible for its outcome. Any miscarriage of justice on your part, precipitating an erroneous verdict, might be attended with disastrous consequences for the public interest."

Having thus transferred the blame for any error onto the jurymen, the master appeared a little more at his ease. But his peroration continued to be delivered in such a broken and faltering fashion, that I will summarise its effect as follows. Warren directed the jury that they were there to inquire into whether William Frederick Windham was of such unsound mind that it rendered him incapable of governing himself and his property. They must start out with a presumption of sanity, and be sedulously on their guard against predisposition or bias. The law would not deprive an individual of his liberty and property without proof of some "morbid condition of the intellect", or some "deranged facility". Mere weakness of character or liability to impulsiveness, imprudence, or extravagance would not suffice. The jury might entertain evidence relating to any period of Windham's life, to determine whether or not it was inconsistent with soundness of mind. And they should not regard the opinions of the medical experts as necessarily conclusive. They should instead attend to all witnesses alike, to consider whether the opinions expressed were rational and feasible in relation to their own experience of life.

Warren finished his oration with obvious relief, and gave the floor over to Montague Chambers Q.C., leading counsel for the petitioners, so that he might open their case. Each side fielded a leader and two junior barristers, and these occupied the front bench immediately facing the master. Chambers was positioned next to his principal client, General Windham, at one end, while Cairns sat with the subject of the inquiry at the other. I was placed immediately behind the great man, on the second row bench which was reserved for solicitors, ready to assist him as required. The whiskery face of Mr Portal bobbed forward and winked at me from the bench's furthest reaches. He was accompanied by several men from the offices of Outram's, his London trial agents.

Chambers was elderly and had wiry white hair outgrowing his wig, but unlike Warren his vocal pitch was even and assured. He began with a lengthy and detailed account of Windham's family background and the scope and nature of his Felbrigg inheritance. "I have also gone through a great mass of information," he then reported, "relative to Mr Windham's state and condition of mind. I have done so for the purpose of placing before you the history of the alleged lunatic from early life, in order that you may decide, after hearing all the evidence, whether he is, or is not, unfit to govern himself and his affairs.

"I have to inform you that the inescapable conclusion of these researches is that, from his earliest infancy, Mr Windham was not as other children are. He simply had not the usual intellectual powers. His case is not one of absolute raving mania, or anything of that kind, but one of simple mental imbecility. The father of the supposed lunatic noticed the weakness of his intellect early in his life, and was so concerned about it that he consulted several medical men of skill and knowledge. Once he had examined the boy, one of these doctors predicted that, far from being improved by the progress of time, the malady was more likely to increase through its passage. I mean to demonstrate that the prescience of this abhorrent premonition has since then been fully borne out.

"And in considering this contention of mine, I would caution you to beware of false lights. It is a matter of common knowledge that deficiencies of mental power, in persons who are the very next thing to idiots, are not infrequently accompanied by a peculiar sort of cleverness. But the existence of such superficial cleverness does not necessarily contradict their overriding incompetence of mind. So it is with Mr Windham. There is a sort of low cunning about him so that he is able, on occasion, to put forward some proposition which might seem at first sight to indicate a glimmering of reason. But when it is examined closely, it turns out to have nothing to do with the matter in hand and be just words and nothing more than that.

"While yet quite a child, Mr Windham became fond of low company and base pursuits, a predilection that has walked with him into adulthood. He would go among the servants and perform acts inconsistent with his position as a young gentleman. He wished to wait at table, and even to wash the dishes. At one junction of his life his father, indulging him as one might a person of unsound mind, purchased for him the livery of a footman so that he might act as the menial he desired to be. His manners at the first school he was sent to were peculiarly childish, being exceptionally rude and boisterous. He was removed to Eton in the hope that the discipline of a public school, and the opportunity of mixing with others of his own age and station, would affect an improvement in his mental capacity. But his conduct there was so inconsistent with the power of taking care of himself that it was deemed desirable to augment his supervision with the appointment of a private tutor.

"He was, accordingly, placed under the particular care of Mr Cheales, a local curate and a man of great experience in the education and management of boys. Mr Cheales soon found that he had undertaken a most difficult and disagreeable duty. Mr Windham played the part of the buffoon, and his manners were so extraordinary and irrational that the Eton boys christened him with the name of 'Mad Windham'. They frequently amused themselves by setting him to perform strange antics. He was taken into good society at Eton and elsewhere by Mr Cheales, but his behaviour was always wanting and was often made the subject of complaint to his tutor. He visited the kitchen whenever he could and continued to court base company. At an evening party he seized a stranger by the whiskers and ran him up against a wall, raging and howling!

"Upon being remonstrated with he would utter a loud, unmeaning laugh which showed at once that he was not responsible for his actions. When spoken to sternly he would cry and blubber like a child, allowing the tears to roll down his cheeks and never attempting to wash them away with a pocket-handkerchief. And he would slaver from his mouth, and leave the resultant discharge pitifully unattended. Mr Cheales tried a variety of ways to reckon with the unfortunate youth, but discovered that very little could be instilled in him in the way of education. He could introduce only a very small amount of knowledge into his head. First he tried kindness, then he tried reasoning, then he tried punishment. The result was that the only means of operating upon Mr Windham was found to be actual personal chastisement. After ill-success in his attempts to cultivate a barren soil, Mr Cheales resigned his tutorship in despair, and Mr Windham was withdrawn from Eton.

"Colonel Bathurst, who had served with his uncle in the Guards, was then induced to take him abroad. But the colonel had no sooner landed on the Continent when he realised that he might as well have taken charge of a wild animal. Mr Windham was subject to unprovoked fits of passion, had an utter ignorance of the value of money, and behaved ungallantly in the presence of ladies. On one occasion the colonel was obliged to strike him sharply with his stick, to keep him in anything like good order. When they returned to England Mr Windham was placed under the charge of Mr Edgworth Horrocks, another military acquaintance of his uncle who had been an officer in the Highland Borderers. He tried every possible means to work upon his charge's mind, but all in vain.

"One of Mr Windham's enduring fancies was to go with railway trains and work the brake as a guard. He would go onto the platform and take the luggage from the passengers and travel with the train as far as he pleased, repeating this performance at every station where a stoppage took place. He would even get upon the engine, and work up its steam, and drive it along as if he were an engineer or stoker. On more than one occasion, he nearly caused a frightful accident in consequence of this hazardous propensity. And while on a visit from Felbrigg Hall with Mr Horrocks, he drove at a furious rate into a neighbouring village and overturned their dogcart. Mr Horrocks, like Mr Cheales before him, found that the alleged lunatic could only be acted upon by extreme severity. Mr Horrocks was occasionally extremely severe, though in point of fact his conduct was unexceptional in the circumstances. From Mr Horrocks he passed into the hands of Mr Peatfield, who took him on a tour of our native isles, though he again proved unmannerly and resistant to all improvement.

"In the spring of this present year General Windham, the chief promoter of this action, and a much decorated soldier, returned to England from India. His conduct towards his nephew, the alleged lunatic, has always evinced the utmost affection. His desire has always been to consult his nephew's interest foremost, and to prevent the necessity of any public inquiry or exposure. General Windham has made every effort to treat his nephew as a rational agent and protect the inherited property, but he might as well have been hammering at the hide of a rhinoceros. When he first beheld his nephew on his return from abroad it was to see him drive a mail-cart into a mob of showmen in a market square, and then brawl with them in a most ignoble display.

"General Windham accordingly proposed that his nephew go to London, to be educated in governing himself through exposure to the gentilities of the season. But his conduct there continued the same as before. He abused the good, kind, virtuous aunt who tried to take him under her wing and cultivate him. Instead he became well-known to the police as a drunken sot in and about the Haymarket, and he even exhibited a desire to act as a policeman himself. He had a particular liking for taking prostitutes in charge, and ordering the nearest officer to move them off to the station house. You will also learn of some other instances that are too revolting for me to relate while women are present. It will be necessary at some stage of the evidence, I anticipate, for me to request that the room be cleared of members of the fair sex, to spare them knowledge of matters that are unsuited to womanly ears."

A cawing of female voices indignantly disclaimed the suggestion that any special consideration should be shown to their ears. Persons of both sexes then resumed listening attentively, to catch any titillation that might not be fit for half of them to hear. For myself, I was concerned as to what awful matters Chambers might have been referring to.

"While residing in London," the petitioners' barrister continued, "Mr Windham met a woman at the races who passed by the name of Agnes Willoughby, but whose real name was Rogers. That taste for low and disreputable society which was seeded in him from childhood, led Mr Windham's feeble mind into a grubby fixation upon this 'pretty horsebreaker'. He fell into the company of her and other designing scoundrels, such as her patron Mr James Roberts, a Mayfair brothel keeper. He was no more able to protect himself from these blackguards than a ten-year-old child might. Though she heartily detested him, a marriage was hastily and hurriedly contrived and a settlement was prepared that greatly favoured the bride. She had got possession of her young man and meant to use it to full advantage. I think you will agree that, if this marriage and its attendant matters stood on their own, then no one who gave it their impartial consideration would hesitate to say that it was the act of an imbecile. And you may not be surprised to learn that 'Mrs Windham' has now left her beloved quite alone to pursue her own caprices, safe in her receipt of a settled allowance from his estate income."

Chambers looked around and nodded earnestly, as if this estimation of Agnes was beyond anyone's reasonable doubting.

"Like that first doctor who examined him," he then resumed silkily, "I will seal these remarks with a modest prophesy of my own. If you find Mr Windham of sound mind, then the whole of his property will fly out of Felbrigg in the beak of this predatory bird. She is a careless spender and will no doubt ruin him if she is allowed to. Mr Windham will at length be turned from Felbrigg's doors and become an outcast in this world. His ancient haunts will not receive him. Within a year, or within a shorter time, he will be deprived of even a sixpence with which to drink at any of those Haymarket night houses where he has in times past spent his money so freely. You will surely decide that Mr Windham can and must be saved from this fate. He *must* be saved from the destruction of his wealth and character, and from society's scorn, revulsion and disgrace. And he *can* be saved through the instrumentality of those principled relatives who have come forward to do their duty by him, and by the verdict that this noble jury pronounces."

This appeal stirred the spectators into stormy applause, flattering them into supposing that they were participating in some great work of public benevolence. I had to confess that Chambers had done his work more than tolerably well. He had succeeded in implanting a grotesque marionette version of Windham in his listeners' minds. Over the following first days of the trial, a procession of witnesses sought to marry the man to the manikin. This puppet Windham was garishly painted and clownishly dressed. It slavered from its mouth and drew a costumed arm across to wipe away the spittle. It danced stupidly, exclaimed involuntarily, and ran up and down to no purpose. Its actions were punctuated by wild shouts of laughter, and its every statement was riddled with palpable untruths. When it was chastised for its misdeeds, it sank to the floor in a sobbing heap of self-pity.

And yet, despite all this, Windham did not have cause to feel too ill-used over the course of the trial's first days. Not all of the petitioners' witnesses were received sympathetically, particularly not the "tutors" whose interrogations took the greatest chunks of time. The Reverend Cheales was dour-faced and much complaining. He, and a supporting cast of Eton schoolmasters, certainly described Windham as having been atrociously behaved there. But they also inadvertently portrayed an isolated and unhappy boy, who met with bullying from his fellows and ruthless suppression from his elders. And the atmosphere of Eton sounded cruel and barbarous. Colonel Bathurst, who had overseen Windham's European grand tour, came across as bemused and ineffectual. He had clearly been unable to guide an adolescent's burgeoning spirit, and the more he tried to stamp on it the more he sowed resistance. Several witnesses attested to angry scenes between them at continental hotels, which were unseemly but little else. The Highland Borderer named

Edgworth Horrocks, however, was pinched in his face and caustic in his patter. It emerged, during Cairns' cross-examination of him, that he had actually been dismissed by Lady Sophia on account of the excessive physical punishment he had dealt out to her son. Indeed, there was widespread shock at the degree of violence inflicted in general upon Windham by those entrusted with his nurturing.

Isaac Peatfield, the fourth "tutor" put up by Chambers, had not resorted to physical coercion and seemed to have rather enjoyed his spell spent with Windham. They had been much nearer to each other in age, and had obviously engaged in a fair amount of dissipation together on their meanderings. So much so that it was often hard to distinguish from Peatfield's account which of them had been leading the other on. Though he strove diligently to present Windham as an oafish companion (recounting, for instance, that the young heir had once addressed a gaitered bishop as a "silly duffer" in his own cathedral cloister) it was plain from the amused glances they exchanged that any misbehaviour had been a collective enterprise.

Most, in fact, of what was aired against Windham in that first week simply described the gambolling of an immature youth who had grown up lacking sound parental control. Windham himself found little to disagree with in it, though much to be sorry for. The petitioners' evidence was more often laughable than damning on the whole, and added up to nothing so much as a carnival of irrelevance. A distilled instance of this came when Lady Sophia's brother, Lord Alfred Hervey, recounted an experience of dining with Windham when his nephew was but a small boy. The child had wanted some tart, and, instead of using a spoon, had thrust his hands into the dish and scooped up crust, fruit and juice together. His mother had then told him that he might have no tart, and had whipped the backs of his hands to make him drop what he had purloined. He had then seized the pudding-bowl and run round the room with it, wailing, until Lord Alfred felled his legs with a hearth-broom, at which he bawled. Though Windham could sometimes be seen to cringe at such compromising anecdotes, he just as often joined in with the generalised laughter that they provoked.

And this was not always at his own expense. Another maternal uncle, the Marquis of Bristol, gave especially good value by displaying a comic level of ignorance of his nephew. He admitted that he had only met with Windham a few times since his boyhood, and that in these instances his nephew had actually seemed perfectly rational. His only lapse had been to fall asleep once after dinner and snore, with a funny expression on his face. There was a great howl at the absurdity of this fact being advanced as evidence for madness. The testimony of Mr Thomas Atkin, a gentlemen's bootmaker of the Opera Colonnade, also attracted unintended hilarity to itself. He said that he had made several pairs of boots of assorted kinds for the supposed lunatic and had always supplied a single set of boot-trees with each. But bless him if the lunatic had not suddenly insisted he provide an extra set for every pair, excepting dress boots, which being of patent leather did not require trees. Challenged by Cairns in cross-examination, the bootmaker conceded that a gentleman might very reasonably order two sets of boot-trees, provided he intended to use one in the country and the other in town.

But on the sixth day of proceedings, a Saturday morning, Chambers made his forewarned request that Master Warren clear the court of women. This was granted by the timorous master, much against their wishes, and the females in the audience got up and trooped out with mutterings of bad grace. Their seats were immediately resettled by men, who had been loafing in the queue that spooled out around the Exchequer corridor.

Given that he had just been at pains to have the room cleared of women, it was strange to observe that the witness Chambers then called upon to appear was herself one. It was stranger still to see that she was Augusta Lewellin. I only slowly perceived her identity, because the spruce individual that was led in and handed up to the witness box was almost unrecognisable as the Duke Street landlady. She had left off her usual multiplicity of clashing shawls and bangles, and was clad in a modest frock of sedate pattern. Her habitually untamed red hair was smoothed to either side of a middle parting, within the frame of a plain bonnet tied with a broad ribbon. And her expression was devout and long-suffering. One might have mistaken the witness for a ragged-schoolmistress, striving to impart scripture to disobliging slum-boys. She locked her gaze upon Montague Chambers, and avoided catching mine or Windham's eye.

Chambers began by asking her to state who she was and how she came to be acquainted with the alleged lunatic. When she had supplied the desired information he gently enquired, "Would you say that the period Mr Windham spent in your house afforded you a full opportunity of observing his conduct, habits, and manners?"

"I should say that it did."

"What opinion did you form of him as a result?"

"That he's not in his right mind."

"Can you tell us what it was that impelled you to arrive at that conclusion?"

"Well," she paused as if it offended her conscience to speak ill of him, "in the first place we just supposed that Mr Windham was somewhat backward, like an overgrown child. He slurred when he talked which made us think that he wasn't quite with it."

"What infantile characteristics was he was wont to exhibit?"

"He was a very restless person, Sir, always on the fidget and scratching himself in a nervous manner. He was forever getting up and going to the door, as if he were afraid of something coming upon him, and then sitting down once more. And he would converse at a crooked angle, as if he had no right understanding of the world at all. He would call my husband 'Old Bob Ridley', after the darkie in that minstrel song he was forever singing. He would say, 'you're blooming like a cotton-bud this morning old Bob, what say we take a jog round the plantation and see what's what?' He would sit down and blather like this one minute, and then start up and rush out of the house the next as if he had not another hour to live. He would jump from stair to stair, and leap from one landing place to another in terrific peril of his neck. We never knew where it was that he went, but he stayed out all hours and sometimes it was days before he fetched up again."

"Did these irregularities occasion you inconvenience?"

"Not so much to start with. Mr Lewellin and I reckon to run a free and easy house, within the bounds of propriety of course. But then Mr Windham started to order dinner and not come home for it. I always made sure that there was a meal ready for whenever he had asked for it, but sometimes he didn't turn up and it would spoil. When I talked to him about it his usual reply was, 'Oh sorry, I forgot'. And one evening he ordered dinner for a party of guests and nobody came, not even himself. When he did finally flop in I said to him, 'Mr Windham, nobody has come to dinner', and he just laughed and replied that he had mislaid to invite them."

"What were his gormandising propensities when he did coincide with a repast of your devising?"

"I beg your pardon?"

"I mean to say, what did he like to eat?"

"Well, he had a very big appetite. Breakfast was his favourite meal, and he would spend a long time over it. His favourite dish was poached eggs, of which he consumed a large number. Sometimes he had as many as four or five."

"He could manage that many in one sitting?"

"Yes, and sometimes more. And when he dined with us he always ate in a ravenous manner. He would gorge himself and devour enormous quantities of food, more like a starving beast than a rational being. And he was in the habit of eating with the carving knife and fork instead of those that had been laid for him, and he never took a meal without beating out some tune with them on the crockery and singing loudly. He is not the most honeyed of vocalists I have to say, and what with his harelip and all it was quite a revolting performance."

"How did you try to deal with him, in the main?"

"We found that the best way of handling him was to beef him up, telling him he was a very handsome young man and one of great strength and promise. When we praised him thus he seemed very pleased, and laughed in a silly sort of way and strutted about. Then he would show his superiority by drinking his beer from a larger glass than anyone else."

"What sort of glass?"

"It was a soda-water siphon with its squirter unscrewed. Sometimes he requested me to call him 'Captain Windham', while at others he solemnly said he would thank us to address him as 'My Lord'. And he was very careless of cash as if he didn't have the sense of it. I have seen him take coins from his pocket and throw them to beggars in a lordly manner, as if he had all the money in the world."

"How did you view these patent absurdities?"

"Once we twigged that he wasn't all there, we felt it our bounden duty to humour him. We generally considered laughter to be the most fitting response, and tended to see each new bout of clowning as no more than a passing shower."

"But in time the skies darkened for good, did they not?"

"That is correct." Mrs Lewellin pursed her lips and shot her erstwhile boarder a glance like a dagger.

"And he came at last to repay your solicitude with foulness?"

"So he did too. It was after he met that 'pretty horsebreaker' at Ascot that his capering took an ugly turn."

"You refer to the former Miss Willoughby, now Mrs Windham?"

"I do."

"How did his behaviour alter after he had fallen into her orbit?"

"He became more agitated in his mind, and uneven in his conduct. He told me that he'd seen her first in the park and had had a jolly row with Skittles about her."

"May we take it that 'Skittles' is the *sobriquet* of another notorious woman?"

"So I am given to understand. She's really named Catherine Walters and is a rival in the same line of work. He said that he'd bullied Skittles well and had her turned out of the park. He spoke of Miss Willoughby as if she was the very best person in the world, and said that they would be married. I told him that she was no such thing and that it would be a very wrong act for him to marry such a woman."

"What did he reply?"

"He told me to mind my own business. It was better not to contradict him. If I did he would call me an 'old hog', or an 'old bat', or another name of that description. Then he became subject to violent fits of rage without cause. When he went into one of them he used the grossest language, and frothed at the mouth. Upon one occasion, because his dinner was not ready the very instant he wanted it, he threw open the window and caterwauled so that the whole street might hear him. There were times when he would just not be quiet, constantly screaming and shouting. It was an indescribable noise."

"How would you account for this disquieting behaviour?"

"I should say that he was so obsessed with Miss Willoughby that it made him ill. On passing her house one afternoon, he saw another man there and came back quite inconsolable. Then he took me down to the kitchen, and said that he would put his hand into the fire if I would do the same. He sat on the servants' table, with the ring of a toasting fork up to his eye like a monocle. Then he called himself 'Agnes' and writhed about on the edge of the table as if he were a woman riding a horse in the park."

The landlady had up to now been heard in respectful silence, but this gem brought forth a lewd cackle from some quarters.

"And his table manners grew ever more disgusting. He would cut up joints and throw the pieces about the cloth, while he sang and rapped on the cups and saucers. In eating he made a snorting noise like a pig. Sometimes he would draw the carving knife across his throat, as if he were cutting it, and at the same time make a gurgling noise."

A bark of laughter went up at this, but it was stilled by the horrified expression on Mrs Lewellin's face. "And that's not the worst of it. One day, when we were at luncheon..."

"You can speak freely here, madam." Chambers nodded at her invitingly.

"One day...he ate so much that he sicked his food right back up into my lap."

There was a gasp of outrage.

"How did he react when you remonstrated with him about this atrocity?"

"His reply was 'Never mind about that, missus', and he carried on eating while I had a girl wipe the muck up."

"Did you not consider barring him from the house there and then?"

"Of course we did. But Mr Lewellin and I decided to pocket the affront, concluding that Mr Windham could not help himself."

"It seems to me, my dear lady, that you and your husband are people of unusual tolerance and fortitude."

"We adhere to the bible's urgings, Sir, wherein we're taught to loath the sin but love the sinner."

"You plainly live out the tenets of godly Christian faith to an exemplary extent. Did Mr Windham remain at the heightened level of agitation that you have outlined for long?"

"No, he sprung off in the opposite direction altogether. When Miss Willoughby flitted to the continent with her opera singing man, he was so pulverised with grief that he had to be put under the doctor. He was so afflicted with care that he would slouch around, if he got out of bed at all that is, dragging his feet behind him and making strange noises as he went. We had the mad-doctor round any number of times, and were at our wits end to know what to do with him."

She paused and looked apprehensive. "And it made him less than scrupulous in his personal habits."

"Forgive me madam, but may I ask you to elaborate what you mean by that?"

"Well, Mr Windham became very dirty and would not wash himself. His hands and face were frequently filthy. My husband used to put him in a hot bath, when he could persuade him into the tub. But one evening, when he was soaking there..."

"Do take your time, dear lady."

"He suddenly jumped out of the bath and ran as far as the front door, perfectly naked. The bathroom is on the ground floor you see, and perhaps he thought he heard the street-bell go. When this happened, my husband rushed after him and got him into the bathroom again before anyone saw him. And there were three female servants in the house at the time as well as myself! Mr Lewellin was so taken aback that he almost struck him, but he's a temperate man and he soon thought better of it. He did tell Mr Windham that he would not allow such conduct in the house, and that he would send him away if it persisted."

"And did it persist?"

Mrs Lewellin blinked rapidly, and then reached for a handkerchief. "I don't know what I've done to have to repeat such vile things in general hearing", she replied, dabbing her eyes.

"I am sure that you can count on the untrammelled sympathy of every right thinking person present."

"Well, all I can add is that the housemaids have sometimes found Mr Windham's bed in a filthy state. The sheets are given out to wash, but the washerwomen would not see to Mr Windham's linen unless I gave her a double price. Because..."

"Yes?"

"He soiled his bed like a child might, in both ways, despite the fact that there was a water-closet down the landing. And one morning, a girl of ours named Sarah Raymond came to me and said that Mr Windham would not get out of his bed. She said that it must be stripped because she had smelled a foul odour. When we entered his bedroom to make him get up, he threw the blankets off, leapt out, and exposed his unclothed person to us. He was unwashed and unshaved, and he presented the most dreadful sight. We threw his bedspread around him right away and spoke to him in the sharpest language. Then he replied with some bad words, as he had done on several previous occasions, and he took up his cut-throat from the washstand and held it before me, saying that he would rip me up with it."

"Were those his exact words?"

"He said 'I'll rip your bloody guts up if you say another word to me, and I'll horsewhip old Bob Ridley.' But then he mewed and whined and pleaded with us not to tell my husband after all."

These incendiary revelations sparked an uproar that was only with difficulty restrained. "We cannot have such ebullitions of feeling," Master Warren ineffectually maintained.

"I am most grateful to you madam", Chambers resumed when the court clerk had restored order. "You have, I think, been through the trials of Hercules today, and have shown dauntless bravery in speaking candidly of troubling matters."

"We care for Mr Windham despite all that he's done, Sir. It is only in the belief that being found of unsound mind will be to his benefit in the long run that we have consented to appear against him."

Sir Hugh Cairns then subjected Mrs Lewellin to a close cross-examination, but it failed to shake her testimony in any important particular. The current of feeling flowed strongly against him. The average Englishman will despise any fellow who cannot be trusted to behave himself around females. The honour of one such had apparently been defiled, and Cairns had to be careful lest he compound the offence by means of an overly aggressive interrogation. He was not assisted, in toeing this delicate tightrope, by her tendency to wax tearful every time he came near to suggesting that she lied. As she was finally helped down from the box, I thought I detected a twinkle of satisfaction behind her red-rimmed eyes.

Our cause was promptly mutilated further as first David Lewellin, and then the housemaid Sarah Raymond, and then the querulous washerwoman of bed linen herself, a Mrs Babbage, appeared to corroborate the essentials of Mrs Lewellin's account. Her husband, who was also uncharacteristically smart in his appearance, added some additional indelicacies of his own invention. And before the afternoon was ended the taciturn War Office clerk called Corbellis, whom I had occasionally bumped into on the stairs at Duke Street, turned up to lend weight to those aspects of the landlady's story that were allegedly within his own observation.

These sensations, and the week's proceedings generally, received the most fervid attention in the press. Full daily transcripts were carried by all the national titles, accompanied by columns of spiky commentary which were then syndicated throughout the land. *Punch,* or *The London Charivari,* started running a regular humorous feature satirising the inquisition's idiocies entitled "Diamonds from the Windham mine". Piquancy was added by the peppery fact that Agnes's cohabitation with Giuglini in Dublin was also being widely reported at the time. She was said to appear nightly at his performances, exquisitely dressed, and to cherish a *penchant* for the celebrated Italian tenor that was steamily reciprocated. Fascination with Agnes and her absence propelled the affair's mystique, so that some journals were labelling their coverage "The Windham Romance". Portraits purporting to be of her, in a range of poses and outfits, were on sale for a small pecuniary outlay throughout the West End.

After the evidence of Mr Corbellis, Master Warren adjourned the case for Christmas which was then only four days away. He was, perhaps, not completely without justification when he was overheard to remark as he rose, "The eyes of England are following my pen."

A CHRISTMAS PANTOMIME

"I may have sung *Old Bob Ridley* from time to time," Windham was prepared to allow, "and I may even have tapped out its rhythm on the tableware with a knife and fork. If singing is a sign of madness then I'll gladly confess to it. But as to all the lunch-regurgitating and razor-twirling and nude-exposing nonsense, I beg to acquit myself."

We were standing at the landing stage on Westminster pier, having walked the short distance there from the Law Courts after the case's adjournment. Though chilly, it was a calm and crisp night, and the lamps along Westminster Bridge beamed wavy reflections across the rippling waters.

"What possessed the Lewellins to say such horrid things about me," he continued incredulously, "when I had believed that we were friends? It seems that I have been terribly mistaken about them. And you'd think they'd be a touch more adventurous in their fictions, would you not? They did, after all, omit to make out that I imagined myself to be Lady Godiva or some other fantastical figure."

I could not help laughing at this and Windham did so too, despite the pickle that our former landlords' testimony had dropped us in. Untruthfulness is an all-too-familiar emblem of villainy, but they had shown themselves well-versed in the art. Mrs Lewellin, in particular, had been received by the jurors with an alacrity of attention and a warmth of approbation not necessarily bestowed elsewhere. So much so that, before we left the court building, Sir Hugh Cairns had warned us that her credibility must not go uncontested if we were to retain any hopes of success.

Sheltering us from hostile elements in the seclusion of counsels' robing room, Cairns had urged us to ransack our brains for anything that might undermine the Lewellins. This had prodded Windham into suggesting that Augusta's younger sister, Eliza Dignam, and her brother Conway, might be ill-disposed to their relatives as there had always been discord when they had appeared at the Duke Street house. I remembered Eliza as the sweet-faced and personable girl who was sometimes put to making beds there, and Conway as the tramp who was sometimes turned away from the door. But Windham informed Cairns and me that Eliza Dignam was to his knowledge a pleasure garden *lorette*, whose periodic visits to her sister's house were made when business was flagging. It was in search of Eliza that we were awaiting a steamer to take us up-river to Cremorne Gardens in Chelsea.

There is no use in expecting a steamboat, or indeed any other conveyance, to transport you to the marvels of this pleasure garden nowadays. Its joys are unrecoverable. In later years it was deemed too disorderly for the peaceable residents of Chelsea to suffer, and its glorious landscaping was uprooted and built over. It was, in its time, a versatile attraction, boasting a respectability during the day that vanished with the light. The nature of Miss Dignam's occupation there hardly qualified her to discredit anyone else's moral character, but Cairns had directed that we must try to find her all the same. I was sceptical about the enterprise, and considered that we were about as likely to chance upon her as to meet a crocodile on the Serpentine.

"How do we know that Eliza will be there tonight," I questioned Windham, "and how will we go about seeking for her when we arrive?"

"I can hardly think that she will neglect her lucrative pitch on the last Saturday before Christmas," he declared, rolling his head and holding his lapels, "the garden is bound to be bulging with revellers. And as to ascertaining where her station lies, we'll just have to trust to good luck."

"But even if we do succeed in tracking her down, what can she possibly have to say that may assist us? And how do you propose to get her to treat with us in the first place?"

"She was always a picture of affability with me at Duke Street and I see no reason for her to go back on that now. I propose that we tender her the customary tariff for an immoral act by way of an inducement to conversation. And then, once we have fed word to her of our intentions, we can see if she has anything useful to say and whether she is up to reciting it in public."

This all sounded highly improbable to me, but far from being depressed by the turn of events against him my friend was in unaccountably high spirits.

He looked to be correct in guessing that Cremorne would be well-attended, judging by the numbers of people waiting beside us for the next up-river boat. The temperate nature of the evening made it an ideal one for outdoor entertainment, and the festive time of year furnished folk with an extra inducement to step out. One of the pigmy steamers that were such stalwarts of river transit soon snorted into sight. Reaching the pontoon it juddered and squeaked against it, and was lashed into place with its great paddle-wheels dripping and its tall funnel sputtering smoke.

"Let's go below", Windham proposed as we crossed the lowered gangplank, "and have a swill of grog as a nerve-stiffener."

We descended a narrow stair into the close and low-ceilinged saloon, which was so packed with thirsty pleasure seekers that the small platoon of waiters was being run off its feet. Orders were being shouted from all quarters, and trays slopping with drinks were being handed, gliding and swooping, amongst the tippling hoards. We managed to squash onto two stools pressed tight against a bulkhead, next to a party of wing-whiskered swells out on a lubricated jag. An especially unsteady one of their number was weaving to rejoin them, having by the dishevelled look of him just been aloft to heave the contents of his stomach over the rail.

The steam-hooter blasted, and the listing motion announced that we had cast off against the current. This caused the returning swell to lose his footing and land flat on his bony buttocks, which was his fellows' cue to squawk like buzzards at his discomfiture. He sat there blinking dazedly at his surroundings. "There's no call for your silly eyes to pop out of your silly heads", he slurred petulantly at his mocking companions. "I'm only having a little rest."

"Hark at 'Mad Windham' over there," one of them taunted his beached confederate, his eyes streaming with tears of laughter, "the dolt don't even know whether to stand up or sit down."

This drollery was rewarded with convulsions of jocularity from everyone within earshot, all quite unaware that the genuine Windham article was close at hand. He laughed along with the rest, and winked at me to keep mum. I could not help but suspect that he was not wholly averse to his sudden notoriety.

A pair of painted maidens, in taffeta and lace, rustled over to grab the drunken masher by his elbows and winch him upright. As they held him there one of them slid her card smilingly into his top pocket and patted it, which sparked off another round of jocular pandemonium. The inebriate swell grinned stupidly as they escorted him to his stool, and then he almost missed it and hit the boards again as they lowered him down.

The resultant cackling of his familiars melded irksomely with the pounding of the engine in that airless and vibrating space. But the atmosphere grew instantly more endurable as we secured, and then sank, a couple of strongly spirituous drinks. Our steamer called in at Lambeth on the south bank, and then over and again at further points on alternate sides of the river. It acquired a net gain in passengers at each berth, until we arrived at Cremorne Pier in Chelsea where almost everyone got off.

Families with children, their day's recreation done, queued patiently on the pier to board the vessel that would restore them to their hearthsides. Some of the youngsters cuddled dolls or toys, won at the hoop-la or bagatelle or some other such "Walk on up!" attraction. Those disembarking, however, did so with a rowdy disregard for standing in line and a clear wish to counteract the discouragement of cold with adult pleasures. All were got up in their very best rig, and those who worked for a living had their weekly pay, and the prospect of tomorrow's rest day, to encourage loose indulgence.

We pressed with the crowds through the garden's wrought iron gatehouse, and parted with the one shilling price of entry. An avenue, lit along its length by coloured Chinese lanterns, stretched ahead through tall trees and low shrubberies. Lighted poles were wound-around with mistletoe and holly to give them a seasonal aspect, and their red and white berries sparkled endearingly. The distant lilt of dance music grew more insistent as we advanced along the path. At its further end the avenue let out onto a large clearing fringed by refreshment stalls, with a dancing platform in the middle. This round wooden deck was slightly elevated, and entered by way of gaps placed at regular intervals in its surrounding balustrades. It was awash with twirling twosomes in wide dresses and tall top hats, bounding along to a frisky musical selection. The uniformed bandsmen were arranged some distance above the dancers' heads, halfway up a giant pagoda which formed the centrepiece of the platform. There were perhaps fifty musicians in all, surrounding a conductor whose every gesture was expressive. Such a concentration of gaslight burned within this oriental bandstand that it shone like a yellow furnace. Successive arcs of lamps strung around the edge of the platform bathed the whole in a sulphurous twilight.

Many debonair pairings milled about the clearing, dancing for a while and then retiring from the platform to stroll, or to sit with friends for a drink and a chat. But at the outer tables by the refreshment stalls, where drink flowed most freely, there was a mixed crowd conducting itself with unrestrained gaiety. And though courtliness was as yet generally prevailing, one could predict its decay as the evening progressed. A hot-air balloon was meandering overhead, presumably at the dictation of a mechanical tether somewhere on the ground. Below the basket a harness dangled into the void, from which an actress with feathered wings and costume was suspended. She was floating in imitation of a bird in flight. We were enchained by the vision and lost ourselves for a while in contemplating her. Then our attention was arrested by a fabulous burst of fireworks from near the riverside.

"She could be anywhere," I said to Windham, when the fusillade was spent, "where do you suggest we try next?"

"Well, we could drift over to the King's Road side I suppose", he replied without much conviction.

We were continuing to debate how to locate the proverbial needle in a haystack when we heard a measured cough from behind us. We turned to see that its progenitor was a policeman.

"You seem lost, gentlemen", he observed. "Is there anything in particular that you are you requiring? Can

I point you in any especial direction, or spring my rattle for you in any respect?"

Though the wooden ratchet they formerly used to attract attention had even then been replaced by a whistle, constables were still prone to hark back to it in their colloquial patter. The officer's face was shaded by his tall pot-hat, and beneath its brim were bushy eyebrows which met in the middle. He waggled them suggestively at us. Though he was draped in the long official overcoat of the metropolitan force, a muffler wound round his neck concealed the serial number on the collar of his uniform jacket.

"You can call me 'Mr Policeman T'," he added, seeing me notice the irregularity, "all the gentlemen in the garden know me as that."

"We are engaged in saving the souls of fallen women," I informed him in a sudden spasm of invention, "and are functionaries of a charitable society devoted exclusively to that object."

"It does you every credit, gentlemen", the policeman said. "We often have Mr Gladstone himself traipsing about here with that very same purpose in mind."

I found it hard to comprehend this statement. Surely one of the greatest statesmen and moralists of the day would not parlay with vice on any pretext?

"He was, indeed, here only a few nights ago," the officer confessed, "asking after a very fair fallen soul whom he was set on saving. Are you set on saving any particular spirit, gentlemen? If not then I can steer you in the direction of several with the temporal virtues of a nice face and a rounded figure."

"We *are* looking for someone in particular as it happens," Windham ventured, stoutly replicating my fiction, "who is in urgent need of our ministrations. She's named Eliza Dignam, and we have reason to believe she may be somewhere hereabouts."

"Well," the public protector returned enigmatically, "you'll not find her by tilling the land or trawling the ocean. The garden is a sizable proposition. She could be at the gypsy's grotto or the rustic fountain. Then again, she could be at the bowling saloon or the fairground patch."

He removed his pot-hat and held it against his chest, sweeping a straggle of displaced hair back across his bare scalp with his other hand. He again waggled his bristling eyebrows. Windham took the hint and threw some coins from his waistcoat pocket into the hat. The policeman looked down, and then up again, apparently finding the donation insufficient. When I supplied some more from my own pocket, he tipped the hat's contents into his palm and restored it to his head.

"That Eliza Dignam's soul must need an awful lot of saving tonight," he reflected, "as there's already been a man here enquiring after her."

"What sort of man?" I asked.

"He was a countryman by my estimation, with a whiskery face and a brown suit and brown bowler hat. You'd better hurry along, gentlemen, if you don't want him to whisk Miss Dignam off to a lodging house before you get there. You'll find that she keeps her salon in the maze, over through the stand of trees on the further side of the platform. It's a desirable spot, but then again she enjoys the best of protection."

Our informant turned to move off. "Have yourselves a *very* good evening, gentlemen", he said, with a theatrically sly inflection.

"But where precisely," I called after him, "are we to locate her in this maze?"

"Discover the central compartment, Sir," he threw back, "and then follow the goddess's gaze."

Having despatched this cryptic instruction, Mr Policeman 'T' faded away. Windham and I exchanged anxious glances, unsure as to whether or not we had just been efficiently duped. But we hastened along the route the officer had mapped out for us all the same, around the dancing platform and through the silent copse beyond. Here we found ourselves at the entrance to the foretold labyrinth, which was fashioned from green hedging. There was no one else around, and after some little consideration we dived in along a narrow passage chosen at random.

It is a fine thing for a maze to offer puzzlement to the young as they attempt to find a sure path to its middle. I must say, however, that my temper was distinctly frayed by having to negotiate this tiresome obstacle. It contained the usual quotient of blind alleys and sudden reversals of direction. As we went round and back again we first drew nearer to, and then further away from, a hazily-lit central section. By the simple device of dogged persistence, rather than by any particular navigational brilliance, we at last reached the central compartment. The policeman's goddess was now revealed as a Venus de Milo statue, standing on a plinth encircled by a wide enclosure of hedging. This had a series of alcoves leading off, each apparently containing a gas lamp though its interior was concealed to the outside viewer. Lacking arms with which to point, the goddess was staring straight at the entrance to one of these arbours.

As Windham and I went cautiously across to it, we observed the protrusion of a brown bowler hat above its boundary hedge. The wearer was obviously standing, and conducting a conversation with a woman who was seated. Their exchange was taking place in such a low tone that only its rancorous nature was apparent. Ardent discussion, and intermittent giggling, could be heard issuing from some of the other alcoves. The argument swung back and forth for some time, and at one point the bowler hat ducked down and a yelp from the woman indicated that its wearer had tried to take hold of her. The hat then reappeared and its owner's voice acquired a wheedling quality, but this approach found no more favour than the earlier disputatious one. The man was eventually nettled into outright anger, delivering what sounded like a stinging curse before storming out of the alcove.

Our eyes could now verify the fact that he was Mr Henry Portal, a solicitor from Aylsham, though he did not see us. We let a safe interval elapse while he vacated the scene, before stepping into Eliza Dignam's "salon" in his place. As well as a containing a gas lamp it was furnished with a bench, upon which she was reclining in a lavish crinoline. The bodice had a graceful curve below the neckline, and her reddish hair was arranged in corkscrew tresses beneath a pork-pie hat perched high upon her *coiffure*.

Seeing our entrance she smiled sweetly and said, "What can I do for you two nice gentlemen?"

"Hello there Eliza," Windham replied joshingly, "we're here on a mission to save your soul."

"Heavens above," she exclaimed, now recognising us both, "is there not one single honest customer in the garden tonight?"

Once she had got over her surprise, we outlined our true purpose. We offered her the price of her time if she would agree to speak frankly with us of her sister and Davie Lewellin. She sighed at the mention of them, and said that no payment was needed as she was a truthful person who was thoroughly disgusted with them both.

"They've been nagging at me without rest" she complained, "to say wrong things about you, Mr Windham. And that bloodhound Portal, who you'll have just seen stalking away, is forever on my trail. He says that I don't know when I'm well catered for. He asks how I can turn down cash that'll make it so I don't have to sit out here freezing my toes off. And it's not just myself I'm cheating, he says. What about my poor brother Conway? Wouldn't I like to see him coddled in a nice clerking place and a steady lodging? Well of course I would, but I answered 'no' just the same. I told Mr Portal to bury his suggestion, because I will not lie on oath. My good name means more to me than avarice."

The irony of someone in her profession valuing her reputation above all else was touching, and, I think, the sentiment was genuinely meant. I could see by the glistening of his eye that her nobility of spirit had deeply affected Windham.

"Will you come away somewhere convivial with us," he entreated her, "and let us stand you a nice warming drink?"

"Well I might as well, Mr Windham, as there seems little chance of me earning my keep tonight what with one thing and another. I know of a snug place we can go that's not too far off."

She got up and led us out of the alcove, and we followed through the rich scent of perfume that succeeded her. There was, apparently, what might be termed a "tradesmen's entrance" to the maze. Eliza took us through an arc of passages, which eventually terminated at what looked at first sight to be a blank brick wall. But she pulled back a thatch of vegetation to expose a concealed door, which she unlocked and pushed open. Stepping through it we landed upon a riverside track, outside the perimeter of the garden. A short terrace facing the river was adjacent to where we were standing, some of its boards advertising lettings of the hourly kind.

The nearest end of the row was occupied by a pub called *The Harlequin,* into which Eliza breezily conducted us. She was hailed in there as a house-familiar and she claimed a table at a bow-window in the front parlour, overlooking the river. Water could be heard lapping against the foreshore, and we could see the far bank's twinkling lights. The room was panelled in a brownish wood, though a series of sections by the entrance had gaudy life-size figures daubed upon them. These represented the characters of the old Harlequinade pantomime, which was much loved then but it is seldom staged these days. There was Harlequin himself, in his multi-coloured, diamond-patterned suit. Then there was fair Columbine, striking an acrobatic pose in the tutu and tights of a ballerina. Clown wore an absurdly puffed costume of doublet and hose, embossed with jagged shapes. Aged Pantaloon was a sour greybeard, leaning on a stick and bent at his knees.

Desultory groups of real-life characters were dotted around the parlour, wearing outfits that were more mundane and less well-presented. From the pinched looks on some of their faces, I considered that it was only the passport of Eliza's presence that kept us free from insidious interference. She nodded a waiter over to attend us, and Windham ordered a round of whiskey and hot water. When it was served, we toasted the season with this welcome sustenance.

"Are we to assume, then," I questioned Eliza now that we were comfortably settled, "that Mr Portal has been trying to persuade you and your brother to bear false witness against Mr Windham?"

"You may assume just so", she replied.

"And are we to further take that he has paid your sister and brother-in-law money to perjure themselves in court?"

"He has certainly paid them," she confirmed, "and if they have told lies in court then that is what he has paid them for."

"They said some ruinously atrocious things today," Windham reported solemnly.

"I am injured to hear it, Mr Windham, and can only be sorrowful on their account. And no doubt Sarah Raymond, and Babbage the washerwoman, and that grasping lodger Corbellis, all said the same?"

"Indeed they did", my friend lamented.

"Well then, they will all have been granted payment too."

"What was your relatives' manner of approach," I asked, "when they tried to get you in on the deception?"

"My sister Augusta came to my lodging in a carriage with her fancy-man, Colonel Broughton, saying that I had to go to a solicitors' office to make an affidavit about you, Mr Windham. The Colonel is her dear old baby, you see, and it's a fact that needles

Davie no end. My sister said to me, 'that blackguard Windham has married a worthless woman and she might bring him a child. I know of a capital thing you can do. His uncle, the general, wants to bring him in mad, and if you will swear for the general it will be the making of you.' "

"Bring him in mad?" Windham repeated the phrase slowly and quizzically, as if struggling to fathom its full meaning.

"That's how my sister put it. And she wanted me to go along with the most grievous inventions, but said that I must keep it quiet. I replied that I would not tell lies for her or twenty generals. She then said, 'You are very foolish if you stick to that line. Will you not at least go to the solicitor with me?' Well I agreed to go, to see more of what she was up to. Mr Portal was waiting when we got there, and he looked me up and down and said, 'This little woman could serve us very well, if she can be trusted to hold up in court.' Then he started telling me that I would be doing you a goodness, Mr Windham, if I swore that you made bad noises and behaved in mad ways. 'You don't suppose,' my sister then said, 'that I am doing this for nothing do you?' And after he had taken down her statement, Portal looked at it and said, 'I am glad you have put it like this, Mrs Lewellin. I have never heard the half of it before.' Augusta replied, 'No, nor have I', and they both fell about laughing. He thanked her and said that he was highly delighted and extremely obliged."

"But you would not oblige him in likewise fashion?" I enquired.

"No, I would not. Mr Portal asked what it was to me if I swore to some non-existent doings, but I said that I would not injure a fellow being that had done me no harm. Then he said to my sister, 'She might have helped us too, but she is nervous and would most likely break down in cross-examination. I'm sure her statement would be just like yours and so it will not be necessary to have it in writing.' With that we left, and when we were on the pavement I said, 'Oh Augusta, what lies you have been telling! How can you swear to such terrible untruths?' And she said, 'I dished it out to him pretty strong, didn't I, and to his lady-love too.' "

"I suppose she meant Agnes by that", Windham deduced.

"Yes, she must have done." Perhaps to draw the sting from these troubling revelations, Eliza added "I do hope that you and your wife are not on strained terms these days, Mr Windham?"

"As George here will confirm," he replied haughtily, "I have not seen her to speak to recently, and therefore cannot say whether we are on good terms or not."

"Oh dear," Eliza commiserated, "and it was such a good match. We all thought she'd landed on her feet with you, Mr Windham."

"So you're acquainted with her?" Despite their estrangement, Windham leapt eagerly at any chance to discuss Agnes.

"We are familiar with one another, given that we come from the same fold as it were."

Seeing our blank looks she added, "We have both been shepherded by Mr James Roberts, who is better known as Bawdyhouse Bob, though Agnes is beyond all that now. It is only by virtue of his good offices that I enjoy my privileged position in the garden, and have a private key that enables me to sneak in and out. Augusta and Davie think that I am worthless, you see, because I am supported in my living by kind friends."

She looked at us primly on uttering this prissy formulation, and shifted uneasily in her seat.

"They say that Conway and I have never earned an honest sixpence in our lives, and they only ever have me in their house as a maid of drudgery and not as a well-met guest. But Davie swindles people in the wine trade, if the number of times he's been sued to judgement in the county court is anything to go by. You'll hear him claim that his counsel sold the cases, but I don't believe that. They both cheat people, and then swear blind that they'll die in their presence if they've not been straight with them. They're not averse to double dealings, as their efforts to turn me to the bad demonstrate."

"And you say that your brother has also resisted their blandishments," I stated, "despite his impecunious state?"

"They've been on at him any number of times, but he's stuck out as contrary as I have. Davie tracked him down to a flop-house in Hoxton one day, to try and talk him round. I'm afraid that Conway cannot get a suitable situation even though he's a moderate scholar. Sad to say, there is something wrong with his mind. Davie told him that he would see him right with an official position, if he would swear he has seen Mr Windham acting indecently. My brother replied that he would not help put a sane man into a mad-house, at which Davie beat him viciously with a stick! Poor Conway has been in hiding ever since, lest his own brother-in-law comes at him with more violence."

"Will you appear at court and help Mr Windham by repeating all this?"

"I'm ready and willing to stand up and say my piece, but I'm quite certain that they'd mash me to paste. I'm not exactly perfect witness material, any more than Conway is, and we don't have the learning to joust with a brief. I'd like to go to finishing school and qualify as a governess, if I can save up enough, but fine intentions won't eliminate my taint."

Someone had just wound the cylindrical music box in the corridor into motion, and it began to plink out a popular tune from the Harlequinade.

"Oo it's just like in the pantomime," Eliza said, "and being as it *is* Christmas that makes it all the more fitting to the fix you're in, Mr Windham."

"In what way, precisely," he asked, "is it fitting to myself?"

"Why, don't you see? You're in the part of Harlequin trying to win the heart of your Columbine, who's Agnes. And your uncle is miserable old Pantaloon, doing all he can to thwart you. Mr Portal is the Clown, assisting the old man as trickily as he is able to."

Windham liked this flight of imagining. "Or maybe you're Columbine, Eliza" he contributed, "and I'm pursuing you. And George here is old Pantaloon."

They both rocked with laughter at this suggestion. "Who then," I objected testily, "is the Clown in this fresh scenario?"

"I really can't say," Eliza retorted brightly, "but you mustn't expect everything to be in perfect trim, like a festive display in a shop window would be."

We commenced to spend an agreeable evening together at that waterside inn, and were introduced to some fellow patrons that arrived later on but whom I can barely remember. I think that they were mainly people who plied their trade at the garden in one way or another. I do recall that the same tune was played over and over again, as the machine only appeared to have the one cylinder.

Sufficiently agreeable was the night, in fact, that it was not until the early hours of Sunday morning that Windham and I returned to our hotel on Trafalgar Square. And it was well after midday that I stumbled out of my bed and tottered into our suite's drawing room. There I found Windham sitting at the table in his dressing gown and grinning broadly. He was clutching a telegraphic message in his hand, from which it appeared that Agnes had read yesterday's court proceedings in one of this morning's papers.

"So sorry, Willie," the message read, "that the case fares ill. I have something vital to impart. Meet me off the Dublin packet at the Irish steam wharf, St Katherine's dock, at two pm the day after tomorrow." It seemed that Agnes meant be home for Christmas.

A PARALYSIS OF THE MORAL SENSE

The waterborne commerce of London is a fabulous thing. It washes in and out of innumerable quays and stairs and basins. It is carried by every conceivable vessel, from the tiniest oar-powered lighter to the largest ocean-going steamer or square-rigged ship. It consists of almost any article or commodity that can be named, bound to or from almost any region of the world that can be dreamed of. It is shuttled through acres of warehousing, and warrens of underground vaults. And there is a constant tide of human traffic too, ebbing and flowing wherever boats touch the shore.

Agnes was due to put in at the Belfast, Dublin & Cork passenger wharf, which was one of several steamship berths running east along the riverside from the Tower of London. Windham had responded to her telegraphic message by stating that he would be there at the appointed hour on Christmas Eve to collect her. Anxious to make a good impression on being reunited with his errant wife, he had hired a smart brougham to mark the occasion. And, being a forbearing soul, he had declared himself ready to forgive her apparent infidelity if she was just as ready to be contrite. We were both eager to hear what vital thing it was that she had to tell us, so we set off from Trafalgar Square on the afternoon in question with him at the reins and me at his shoulder. Once past the Tower we spun eastward to course along the marine parade. The warehouses of St Katherine's dock lined it to the landward side, whilst the seagoing steamers were loading or discharging along the riverside to our right. Owing to the hectic demands of the yuletide season many travellers were swirling across the cobbles, and a nearby cab-rank was enjoying a continuous turnover of custom.

We approached the road bridge that spanned the shipping channel leading from the river into St Katherine's dock. One of the dock's inland basins was thus opened to our sight, revealing the bare masts and rigging of the wooden hulks sheltering there. Its enclosing warehousing rose up sheer from the basin's waterline, and bulky loads were being raised or lowered from high platforms on hoists. Just as we were about to cross the channel, a steam-whistle sounded and a barrier was brought down to halt us. The road bridge was then set to tilt upwards away from us. This was to allow a large sailing barque, which was currently being lowered to river level in the lock, to be tugged out into the stream.

"What a blessed nuisance," Windham complained of our summary detention, "and there's the Dublin packet coming in now."

The Irish liner could indeed be seen emerging from the hazy river and steaming for her berth, which was on the far side of the dock entrance channel. We could only watch as she reached the quay and heaved alongside it. Passengers thronged her deckside gates as the labour of docking was begun, but their numbers were too great for us to make out Agnes in particular. A string of assorted goods wagons was interspersed with private carriages along a traffic lane that arced through the quayside compound. These privileged places would have been reserved for company-authorised vehicles only, with all others left to take their chance of parking out on the dock road. An honourable exception to this exclusivity had apparently been made in the case of a hearse. This sombre coach, with black-feathered plumes sprouting from the seams of its stately roof, had been put at the head of the traffic queue nearest the exit, no doubt to facilitate a speedy uplift for the deceased.

We observed the liner's moorings being secured. Cranes then set about hauling luggage overboard in large netted bags, and the passenger gates were unchained. This prompted a general exodus down the ship's ladders, spilling out into a crush at their foot.

"You'd think they'd let the coffin off first", I remarked to Windham.

"So one might suppose" he replied vaguely, without really hearing what I had said. The protocols of mortality were a long way from his mind, and they are beyond the comprehension of ordinary mortals in any event. He was weaving his head around, trying to catch sight of Agnes, and his sole concern was to make good his reunion with her.

While our attention had been fixed upon the further quay, the lock gates of St Katherine's dock had opened to let the barque nose out. A tug now steamed slowly from the river and reversed into the channel in front of us to take on the barque's towrope. But the cable snagged tight in the sailing vessel's bow-winch, and the strenuous endeavours of several hands failed to prise it loose. The little tug's paddles churned frantically as she battled to hold her position in the choppy waters.

"My goodness, what a topping jamboree", Windham commented sarcastically in his frustration. "How long must it take for these rogues to unpick a simple hitch?"

Amid a professorial lesson in salty bad language, more seamen were summoned forward to the barque's bow to lend their brawn to the collective enterprise. The lock-master poked his head out of his stone hut and appraised the scene with smouldering discontentment.

"Can you spot Agnes over there?" Windham asked me. "She'll think we've neglected her and stomp off in a frightful huff."

I returned my gaze to those disembarking from the liner. In a short while I did see a womanly figure, reminiscent of his wife, standing atop of a ladder amidships. She was mantled in a dark, fur-edged travelling coat, which was broadly cut so as to cover her crinoline. A round, furry hat was warming her ears.

"Is that her, Willie?"

"Why, I do believe that it is."

Windham sprang up and started waving excitedly, and I found myself impelled to do the same. Agnes was looking downward and preparing to descend the walkway, and it seemed unlikely that she would notice us. But then she glanced up and did see us after all, as we jigged about on the brougham's box as if dancing a Highland fling. She waved back, smilingly, and then began to descend the ladder most cautiously, with one hand clutching its rail and the other hitching her skirts. She then vanished from our sight, into the crowds swarming about the quayside and streaming out onto the dock road. We could see from the wobbling of the carriages waiting at the quay that they were receiving their passengers. The waiting carts were also being busily freighted with goods. But the hearse remained at a standstill, penning the others back.

Due to the continued difficulty in connecting towrope and tug, the lock-master now emerged from his hut and set about haranguing all and sundry through a speaking-trumpet. This made the seamen escalate their efforts at the bow-winch, as if their backs had been lashed by the cat. When I next looked over at the steamship quay it appeared that the coffin had finally been let down and stowed, because the hearse was now rolling out onto the dock road. This enabled the previously boxed-in drivers to twitch their own teams forward. As the hearse turned so as to lead them towards us in an impromptu funeral procession, the barque's deckhands at last managed to free her towrope. This was then thrown onto the tug with a resounding cheer and tied fast, and the sail ship's scarecrow bulk was towed through the channel in front of us. Once she was clear, the road bridge was lowered and the barrier was lifted.

But the restoration of the roadway enabled us to see that the hearse was now facing us on the opposite side of the channel, waiting to come on. Its top-shelf was tenanted by a sable-hatted, dark-suited duo, both of whom were seated expressionless and ramrod upright. They certainly did not lack for the mournful garb and demeanour of the undertaker. The one who was driving was tall and heavy-set, while his associate was short and stout. The differing elevation of their respective top hats was so comic that I almost disgraced myself by laughing. I mused that their conflicting heights must have made for an awkward spectacle when they were supporting either end of a coffin.

Despite his impatience, Windham's sense of propriety informed him to beckon them onward in priority to ourselves. The crossing could take only one conveyance at a time, since it had only a single carriageway. As the hearse clattered onto the newly horizontal bridge, we doffed our hats in deference. And as it approached with closed curtains, I reflected on how respectful it was that the squat undertaker was wearing dark tinted glasses. I also regarded the fact that he lifted his topper at us as being more than decent. Then he raised the specs and winked an eye at us from within a puffy socket. He was Bawdyhouse Bob, and his driver was the thumping great bully with a cosh whom we had eluded at the Edinburgh railway terminus.

I still had it somehow pegged in my head that nothing was amiss, even as the hearse rattled past us. My thoughts churned at the extraordinary happenstance of Bob coinciding with us at the riverside today. I hoped that Agnes had found an attentive porter to oversee her baggage while she waited patiently on our arrival. My mind was palsied by the puzzling medley of events.

But Windham was not so docile. "The damnable slinks," he cried, trying to bring our brougham round to give chase, "they've snatched her off!"

Hearses are not generally built for pace, and few would have backed the lumbering funeral contraption in a straight contest with our nippy brougham, despite its head start. But the line of oncoming traffic that came in its train now rendered it impossible for us to turn. Having waited so long to be away already, none of the carters or coachmen was minded to lend us precedence. We were thus rendered utterly stuck, as we watched the hearse's black plumes recede along the dock road and dwindle to nothing somewhere in the region of the Tower.

I had heard of the nautical crime known as "crimping", whereby sailors, fresh ashore from a trip, would be rendered drunk and insensible by a tavern girl and then taken to an improper lodging. Next morning they would awake to find themselves manning some pestilential vessel embarked on an interminable voyage halfway across the world. But it was a curious style of crimping that abducted a Norfolk squire's wife from a marine promenade in broad daylight.

When we were at last able to progress, we naturally visited the Irish wharf and enquired after Agnes. The company's office could confirm that she had boarded at Dublin, as per her booking, and that she had seen out the passage. But as to her present whereabouts it could help us no further. Had a coffin been put on board at Dublin, we enquired, or had there been a death at sea? They had no record of either, as such, they said, but they had granted a special dispensation for a hearse to stand in readiness at the quay.

"The ruffians have got hold of Agnes for a bad purpose", Windham said despondently, as we stood on the office step. "She could be anywhere by tomorrow night, just like that hoary old tramp."

He referred to the vessel that had occasioned our delay, which had now been set adrift on the river and was getting under sail.

I did my best to contradict my friend's dour prognosis. "She may just as well, as you yourself said, have simply got tired of waiting and flounced off in a pique. She could easily have inveigled herself a lift in one of those carriages. And I wouldn't be surprised if there isn't a message arrived from her by the time we get back to the hotel."

"Perhaps so," Windham conceded without convincement, "but what are we to do if there is not?"

I suggested the interim measure of swallowing a steadying drink on the journey home, but Windham was uncharacteristically out of countenance with this proposal. We drove straight back to Morley's instead, where no telegraph from Agnes awaited us. There was still no word from her when we asked again in the lobby, having taken some supper in the lounge. I was expecting Patrick Pumicestone to call later on that evening, and so I tried to persuade Windham that we lawyers would together contrive some clever scheme for finding his wife. But he declined to be reassured by these platitudes and absented himself, saying that he would take himself off for a stroll, perhaps to the Haymarket. I was, to say the truth, much concerned for his welfare.

When he was shown into the suite's drawing room sometime later, Mr Pumicestone himself appeared to be in sickly fettle. I was going through some trial papers at the table, and left off them to observe that there was an uncared-for aura about his person. His scant remaining hair was sticking up even further from his head than was usual. What with this and his antiquated swallow-tail coat, he seemed almost baffled by the times we lived in.

"Would you in all honesty, George," he asked as he sat with me at the table, "say that the trial is going well?"

"There are some significant obstacles for us to contend with," I flannelled, "but once we are able to put the defence case across then I am certain that they will be dispelled."

"That is your considered opinion, is it?" Pumicestone had been consulting with me as the trial progressed, which had necessitated my renewed submission to his pernickety collaborative method. I must, however, openly state that he had advanced several suggestions that were not lacking in practical merit. I informed him of the events concerning Agnes that afternoon, and of the fact that we had thus been prevented from receiving some intelligence she had to convey.

"You will," Pumicestone presumed after due consideration of these developments, "have cause to remember Inspector Holden?"

"Indeed I do." I could hardly forget that most loquacious of policemen, and felt an arctic chill at the very mention of the man who had been instrumental in estranging me from Felicity.

"Don't excite yourself, George," Pumicestone soothed me, "he has nothing new to bring against you, so far as I am aware. But he does have his ways and means with the criminal classes. He may be just the man to worm out the whereabouts of Mrs Windham, so that we might find out what it is that she has to tell us. It just so happens that I will be dining at my club tomorrow and the inspector will be there also. You and Mr Windham might step along and join us?"

"But surely you'll be spending Christmas Day with Felicity," I objected in amazement, "at home in Red Lion Square?"

"Not a bit of it", he returned with an aggrieved air. "It is to avoid being alone *myself* at Christmas that I am obliged to seek company elsewhere. My dutiful daughter is contracted to celebrate the day with Major Fenning at some frivolous function in Knightsbridge. She will not even be condescending to attend chapel with me in the morning."

It was not my principal's practice to take me into his confidence on personal matters, but his resentment at this state of affairs had clearly got the better of him.

"She apportions so little time to be with her father of late," he moaned onward, "that I can hardly expect Christmas Day to be any different. It obviously attracts no unique distinction, such as would compel her to spend it indoors. It is my lot to be alone this year, and in many more to come, I shouldn't wonder. Fenning has proposed to her, though I must admit to suspecting that his people are not all he makes out." Pumicestone waved this last thought away no sooner than his lips had shaped it. "But you need not be concerned with any of that, George."

I could not, on the contrary, have been more intimately concerned with what he had said, but I held my peace all the same.

Once we had concluded our business, he directed me to appear with Windham at his club the following afternoon for two-thirty. He then took his leave.

Windham had not returned by the time I retired to my bed, but he was huddled in a drawing room easy-chair when I arose from it. It was my clear impression that, if he had dozed at all, it had been in the place he was now occupying. His hair and clothes were disarrayed. He had no zest for celebrating Christmas, or for digesting a filling meal. But under my coaxing he agreed to attend at the club, though neither of us felt any expectant pleasure. The possibility of Felicity's betrothal to Fenning had curbed any festive wonderment on my own part.

The *Gibbous Club* occupied a former merchant's house, being part of a terrace lining one flank of a narrow paved courtyard running alongside Staple Inn. The Inn's tall outer wall loomed opposite. As Windham and I entered the building we encountered a decorative style, of bare panelling and varnished boards, that was more solid than opulent. The club was named after the gibbous, or humpbacked, phase of the moon, and I had always understood that this was because its members saw themselves as incorrigible misfits. This had led me to suppose that all sorts of esoteric practices went on there, and that its patrons were men of unconventional habit and inquiry. But as we were seated on benches at a long table in the first floor dining room, I perceived that nothing could be further from the truth. Our dining companions were incorrigibly ordinary, if they could be remarked upon for anything. They wore no unspeakable peg-top trousers, no colours or checks in the cloth of their suits, and no impudently-sculpted neckties. And their general deportment was similarly unnoteworthy.

There were not more than a dozen others present, and we all sat at the same table in the sparse and echoing chamber. I was placed opposite Mr Pumicestone, and Windham was put across from Inspector Holden. The policeman nodded briskly at us in turn and shook our hands, he and Pumicestone having already been present before our arrival. We engaged in an exchange of sociable niceties, and then picked our way through the various courses that were served.

Despite the seasonal delights on offer, it was a glum little feast really. All of us gathered there seemed to be missing the warm glow of family and home. Windham's disposition was scrupulous and correct when required, but was otherwise taciturn and unforthcoming. Mr Pumicestone was no more cheerfully inclined than he had been the previous night. And it turned out, as we enquired after his domestic dispositions, that Inspector Holden was a widower who had lost his only child in infancy. There was a small Christmas tree by the front window, but the crackers and sweetmeats it bore went largely unmolested. It occurred to me that we were all suffering from a gloom that I thought to christen, "the gibbous condition."

"Pumicestone here has been telling me all about your wife's unfortunate disappearance, Mr Windham," Inspector Holden said after we had finished eating, "and I have been following the progress of your case with considerable interest."

Windham smiled weakly in acknowledgement, but was too downcast to reply.

"Mr Phinney is aware," the inspector continued addressing my friend, "that I have spoken uncharitably of Mrs Windham on at least one past occasion, when she was in her earlier incarnation as Miss Willoughby. But now that you are married to her, Sir, I need look no further than the fact that she is a Lady."

He dabbed his mouth with a napkin. "And with reference to yourself, Mr Phinney, I need look no further than the fact that you do seem aligned with the forces of good after all. It may be that I misjudged my earlier intervention between you and Miss Felicity, though I think you will admit that I had fair cause at the time."

This, I thought, was the closest he was likely to come to tendering me an apology, and so I nodded my acceptance.

"I am not the one," the inspector propounded in his precise and deliberate manner, "to say where your wife is, Mr Windham. But I do have my tendrils of investigation, and I can promise to flex them to the full in order to locate her."

"That is more than handsome of you", Windham granted in a bleary and emotional voice.

"Might you not begin, inspector" I proposed, "by searching all of Roberts' illicit gaming houses and bordellos? I assume that you possess a reasonable knowledge of their whereabouts?"

"Ah, but some nice conundrums arise in that respect. Certainly we have a good idea of where his places of low resort are located, and you can rest assured that we would like nothing better than to blunt

Roberts' criminal pencil. You may ask me why we do not raid these benighted addresses as a matter of routine. My answer, in the first place, is that there is nothing illegal in itself about running a brothel. And my answer, in the second place, is that the law is an unseaworthy vessel when it comes to gambling. Our legislators allow leeches like Roberts to maintain the fiction that they are merely running a social club, and that they reap no profit from the games they stage. And when their clientele includes a fair admixture of noble names, as it invariably does, these will always second the proprietor in his falsehood. My superiors are reluctant to see their betters wrung through a police-court mangle, and therefore nothing is done."

The inspector spread his lean fingers in a gesture of impotence. "And besides, you can't be certain that Roberts is responsible for the abduction, as you did not witness its actual commission as such."

"That's true enough," I admitted, "but if he *was* responsible, then that would unarguably be illegal?"

"That it would, Mr Phinney. Abduction, false imprisonment and slavery are all forbidden under the criminal law and can attract lengthy penalties of imprisonment, even coupled with hard labour. And if we could sew the offence onto his jacket then we would also have to consider how Roberts set about stealing Mrs Windham from such a public forum, with so many potential witnesses present. If chloroform or some other noxious substance were administered, then that would be a compounding felony."

Holden's words offered little comfort to Windham generally, but this thought put an especially unhappy look on his face.

The petitioners' case was resumed at the Law Courts on the following morning (there not yet being provision for a public "Boxing Day" holiday) when the popular appetite for it remained undiminished.

Observers of Windham's charioteering into Aylsham market square, and of our subsequent altercation with the menagerie showpeople, described what they had seen. I was relieved to discover that none of them seemed to have identified my own part in that debacle. Half-a-dozen metropolitan policemen, including the one from whom Windham had borrowed the whistle and hat at the Haymarket, testified to his capacity for tomfoolery when in drink. The hansom cab driver, whose horse my friend had faced down on Chancery Lane, turned up to recount that incident and draw an uncharitable inference from it. A bilious Norfolk gentleman complained that, when once entertained as a guest at Felbrigg, he had asked Windham for a glass of sack, but his host had given him a glass of brandy instead saying it would do him more good. "Have you come all the way from Norfolk," Sir Hugh Cairns enquired of this witness in cross-examination, "to tell us so little?"

Railwaymen of assorted grades and experience attested to the supposed lunatic's regular unauthorised stints as porter, guard and engine driver on the East Anglian network. This intelligence, and the oft repeated suggestion that Windham was not the only gentleman given to tipping railway officials to one illegitimate end or another, inflamed outraged letters to the press. The Secretary of the Eastern Counties, now recast as the Great Eastern Railway, eventually penned a pompous corrective to *The Times* averring that no civilian was ever permitted to interfere with the conduct of a train. And this was only one of several strands of published correspondence triggered by the inquisition. A certain Mr James Roberts of Piccadilly wrote to *The Times* complaining that he had been "fearfully calumniated" in the courtroom. "I pledge my sacred word," his contribution read, "that not only have I never been an owner of brothels, but I have not even entered one for many years."

Mr Portal took the oath to testify to estate financial matters and to what he characterised as the "iniquity" of Windham's Marriage Settlement. Under this arrangement Agnes received a generous annual jointure, which was no more than one would expect. But even I had been surprised to learn that the document provided for her payments to endure even if their marriage did not. Portal also painted an estate contract Windham had entered into as something that no rational landowner would have accepted. The contract in question was for the felling and sale of surplus Felbrigg timber, and the allegation was that Windham had received well below the going market price. Miscellaneous timber merchants were then called upon to support this contention, and the evidence in this connection ate like wood-weevils into a whole day's sitting. This was especially galling to me, as I was obliged to engage some rival timber merchants with a view to them advancing the opposite viewpoint for the defence.

Before Mr Portal left the stand, Sir Hugh had put Eliza Dignam's accusations that he had suborned witnesses to him. We were on treacherous ground with this, in view of the nature of her profession and the fact that hers was a lone voice against a number of ostensibly upstanding citizens. And I had not been successful in my search for her brother Conway, so that he might corroborate her allegations. Portal was unimpeachably cool in responding to Cairns, and he pooh-poohed the barrister's every hostile suggestion. "I believe that her sister may've mentioned your saintly Miss Dignam," he recalled at one point, "in relation to a court summons for indecent conduct."

A week had soon passed since Christmas, with no sign of anything useful having been suckered on Inspector Holden's tentacles of intelligence. The petitioners' psychiatric evidence opened on the first day of the New Year of 1862, with testimony from the doctors who had sworn the affidavits we read in the kiosk at Lincoln's Inn Fields. These two medical men relayed their recollections of Windham's sorry state as an infant. Cairns made short work of then, however, by making each admit to having no meaningful recent knowledge of his subject.

But the principal medical expert for the petitioners was Doctor Forbes Benignus Winslow. Ascending the witness box stair he was, as always, exquisitely mannered and groomed, and he sported an extravagant white bowtie. He owned up to the equally resplendent catalogue of his professional distinctions that Montague Chambers then recited for the benefit of the jury. At Chambers' behest, Doctor Winslow went on to relate that he had first met the supposed lunatic at his Hammersmith asylum for male patients, sometime the previous summer. He added that Mr Windham had only been visiting then, and was in no way under his professional supervision at that time. It was the occasion on which my friend and I had been driven to Sussex House with his uncle and Mr Portal.

"Did you have sufficient chance," Chambers wondered, "to observe Mr Windham closely on that day?"

"Certainly I observed him, as I observe all those persons whom I am given to greet. And General Windham, with whom I have been acquainted for many years, requested me to pay special attention to his nephew."

"Did he tell you why?"

"He said that he was anxious about his nephew's competency to become squire of Felbrigg, which he was soon due to inherit."

"And was there anything that caught your eye about Mr Windham's appearance and demeanour that might seem to disqualify him from assuming that honour?"

"I saw that there was a peculiarity about his expression and laugh, and that he had a speech impediment arising from the oral deformation which this court has already noted."

"Did you attach any psychological significance to these observations?"

"A close study of his physiognomy suggests a man of weak intellect, one who perhaps exhibits some characteristics of imbecility, and is to a degree afflicted in that way from birth."

"Does that same close study suggest a man of unsound mind?"

"I would not necessarily conclude that Mr Windham has an unsound mind, judging merely from his outward appearance."

"But you have had subsequent opportunities to gain an insight into the inner man, have you not?"

"Indeed I have. Sometime after our first meeting, Mr Windham submitted himself to my formal care as an outpatient, through the agency of his uncle."

"What occasioned his uncle to refer him to you?"

"There had been a breakdown in his nervous state, following a perceived romantic reversal. I treated him for debilitating melancholia at his Duke Street lodging, and he recovered in due course."

The doctor went on to describe Windham's then condition in some detail, and outlined the remedies he had seen fit to prescribe for it. Chambers then enquired whether he had been able to draw any inferences from the episode as to Windham's state of mind.

"I thought him vulnerable to pendulous swings of mood, beyond any normal being's propensity for the same. And this opinion was immediately reinforced when he veered off in the direction of unreasoning glee soon after his recovery."

"Did you think that he continued to be in an unsettled condition then, despite the fact that he had ceased to consult you?"

"Yes."

"And is it your view that he was still in that condition when he contracted his marriage?"

"I believe that he was, though I do not consider his unstable state wholly responsible for that misguided decision."

"Thank you, doctor. We will revisit the marriage in due course. Let us now turn to the psychiatric examination of Mr Windham ordered by this court. You conducted the session in tandem with Doctor Mayo did you not?"

"I did."

"And you regard that gentleman as an outstanding practitioner?"

"I do."

"May I ask how you prepared yourselves in advance?"

"By all means. Mr Portal, the solicitor for the petitioners, showed us some of the witness affidavits that had been sworn in their cause, and suggested certain questions to be put to Mr Windham which he had written down on a sheet of paper. Dr Mayo and I had a short consultation about how to proceed beforehand, and we agreed to question Mr Windham upon some of the points arising therefrom."

I had been present at this examination, and had found their approach more accusatory than clinical at the time. They had confronted Windham with what was little short of a charge sheet against him, and had switched their questioning from one to the other as if playing a game of tag. Why did he wait at table in his boyhood? Had he not led his tutors on a merry dance? Was it right to interfere with the railway and put the lives of others at risk? Was it not for the official police force to wear a pot-hat and blow a whistle to round up disorderly elements? Why had he married a woman of misconduct and impurity? Was he not aware that she had previously consorted with a monsoon of manhood? And so on. This interrogatory method had jarred Windham into adopting an increasingly flippant habit of reply.

Chambers led Winslow through the notes of this examination that the doctor had taken at the time. As he did so it became plain that Winslow had entered each charge advanced by Mayo or himself, and each unsatisfying reply given by Windham, as a debit in the insanity ledger. When asked, for instance, what opinion he would hold of a man who paid to have improper relations with his wife, Windham had replied unabashed, "I should consider him rather a scamp." Chambers sifted through all this at very great length, and it was not until well into the second day of Winslow's evidence that he at last asked the alienist to particularise his conclusions.

"I regard Mr Windham's as a very remarkable condition", Winslow began in response. "In medical language it may be characterised as one of *amentia* as distinguished from *dementia. Amentia* is not downright idiocy but is something between idiocy and lunacy. It resides in the failure of a crucial mental faculty to develop. In cases of *amentia,* one should pay more attention to the actions and appreciations of the alleged lunatic than to any ticks that one might observe in conversation. From what I have learned of Mr Windham it strikes me that he is not able to realise his moral obligations. He has no apparent sense of shame. I could not get him to accept that it was an act of indecency to marry a woman whom he knew to have had immoral relations prior to their engagement. In Mr Windham's instance we have a form of moral retardation, which amounts to a paralysis of the moral sense."

"A paralysis of the moral sense," Chambers repeated, looking significantly along the line of attentive jurors, "that is a most telling turn of phrase, gentlemen." He was, perhaps, signalling to these men of repute that their verdict should encapsulate their disapproval of impure romantic liaisons (whether or not their private habits justified such a stance).

He turned back to Winslow. "I think that you have been in court for much of the case so far, doctor?"

"I have attended the greater proportion of it."

"May I ask whether the evidence you have heard tends to strengthen or weaken your opinion as to the state of mind of the supposed lunatic?"

"It has strengthened it in many regards, particularly in relation to his depraved behaviour in the Lewellin household."

"And is your conclusion in any way inconsistent with Mr Windham being able to write a rational letter, conduct a coherent conversation, or to make sensible bargains to a limited extent?"

"Not at all. The cunning of the insane is proverbial. I have patients under my charge with whom you might converse for a whole day without guessing that there was anything the matter with them, whereas if I were to once give you a clue of it you would detect their infirmity straight away."

"Is Mr Windham's affliction one that calls for him to be subjected to any degree of personal restraint and control?"

"I should say so, on the whole, though not necessarily in the form of his committal to an asylum. Mr Windham might be able to conduct himself with propriety if he had some suitable person to take care of him, though we have heard of his stubborn resistance to external influence. I think that anyone appointed to his care might supervise him daily, and be taxed with threshing out his moral indifference."

"Is it your judgement that Mr Windham should retain any powers in relation his estate?"

"He might be permitted to go abroad for the purpose of making small purchases, but it is my considered opinion that Mr Windham is, at present, destitute of the capacity to conduct his financial affairs prudently and with diligence."

"And is it your definite conclusion that, within the legal language employed by the petition, Mr Windham is of 'unsound mind so as to be incapable of managing himself and his affairs?' "

"That is my overriding conclusion."

Thus we reached the culmination of the petitioners' case, whereon Chambers gave the witness over to Sir Hugh Cairns. There followed a titanic, but studiously polite, contest between them. During this protracted encounter, Cairns revealed himself forensically effective at isolating and chipping away at each pillar upon which Winslow rested his opinion. Was it not commonplace, he asked, for a child to be unruly and to like dressing up? Did the doctor believe that amateur engine driving, if it stood alone, would be proof of insanity? Had it not been shown that perfectly sane gentlemen were given to misbehaving on the railway? Surely Mr Windham was not the first country squire to be unwise in love? And was not his marriage, however misguided it may seem to others, his own business in any event? What was actually meant by the term *amentia*, and had it not been discredited by recent scientific enquiry?

It seemed to me that Sir Hugh had by far the best of these exchanges, repeatedly forcing his opponent to concede that each factor he relied on was not persuasive in itself. Did such elements, Cairns at length made to suggest, really amount to no more than "a basket of fragments?" Winslow was obliged to fall back on the contention that they must all be taken in combination nonetheless. Cairns then moved to criticise the witness for founding so much of his reasoning upon an unquestioning acceptance of the petitioners' case. He put it to him that this was especially unsafe in relation to circumstances that were in dispute, such as those alleged by the Lewellins. Was not the doctor, in presuming to do this, usurping the functions of both judge and jury? "If you were to evaluate Mr Windham's state of mind," Sir Hugh postulated, "solely upon your personal and professional observations of him, would you still reach the same finding that you have given here?"

"I should be loath to form the opinion that I have expressed if that were so", Winslow conceded. "The truth is that, independently of the *data* supplied to me by Mr Portal, and of certain circumstances which I assumed to be correct, I have had no means of testing

Mr Windham so as to determine his true state. The opinion I have supplied is founded upon the assumption that certain beastly and irrational acts which I have heard attributed to him were really committed by Mr Windham."

"I am grateful for your candour, doctor." Securing this admission was, on the face of it, a notable triumph for Cairns. But it was also a double-edged blade. One could see that Doctor Winslow's frankness and fair-mindedness had commended him to the jurors. It also left the field open to them to reach exactly the same conclusion as he had, based on the same evidence that he had heard.

Doctor Mayo corroborated his colleague's account of the examination, and seconded his essential findings. But he was less prepared to give ground than Winslow, which made his eventual tussle with Sir Hugh an increasingly ill-tempered one. I regarded the honours in this struggle as shared evenly between them. Once Sir Hugh had let the witness go, Montague Chambers declared the petitioners' case closed. This was greeted with widespread astonishment because it could only mean that General Windham himself, despite having initiated the whole farrago and been present throughout, was not going to give evidence in his own suit. He remained immobile, seated next to Chambers with his arms folded and his eyes perusing the skylight, which was his customary pose. Perhaps he was shy of being implicated in suborning witnesses? Perhaps he was reluctant to denigrate his nephew in person? His face betrayed nothing of the considerations within.

Now it fell time for us to mount our defence, which came to last, I freely admit, too long for its own good. It went well enough to begin with. Cairns made an opening speech of surgical exactitude, garnished with withering phrases concerning the shortcomings of the evidence produced to date. He pointed out that it was mostly irrelevant and inconsequential, and he assailed the testimony of the Lewellins and their acolytes as being simply incredible. He read out a sheaf of eminently fluent business letters that Windham had written to diverse persons, and asked if they could have been penned by an imbecile. Mr and Mrs Jeffrey then gave favourable evidence at length, and so did Knowles the butler. A woman called Henrietta Voysey, whom I had contacted, gave a touching account of Windham's days at Eton. She had been his lodging house keeper (or "Eton dame") there, and she described a boy who was acutely homesick but entirely sane.

Doctor Harrington Tuke and his colleague Doctor Seymour swore to Windham's manifest sanity, and resisted all Chambers' attempts to drive them from that position. Tuke was mild-mannered, dapper and avuncular, with a precisely cultivated thatch underscoring his jaw line. When Cairns asked him to comment on Winslow's conduct of the psychiatric examination he said, "I think it is a great mistake in such cases to put special questions. In my interview with Mr Windham I merely conversed with him as I would any other gentleman." When Cairns asked for his view on Winslow's expert findings he remarked, "I hardly know what the term *amentia* signifies, and I do not believe in 'moral insanity'." And when Cairns sought his clinical opinion of Windham's eccentricities, he declared, "No amount of what is commonly called eccentricity would in my view amount to madness. If, for instance, a young nobleman were to choose to act as a sweep, and carry a soot-bag in the street, I should not therefore consider him of unsound mind. And I have never met an imbecile who displays the smallest fraction of Mr Windham's character and awareness."

Sir Hugh and I had pondered long over whether to subject Eliza Dignam to the glare of the inquisition, before deciding that we could not do otherwise. As she had promised, Eliza stood up and courageously repeated all that she knew to the discredit of Portal and the Lewellins, and by implication that of General

Windham and his co-petitioners too. She had made a good effort to dress suitably, and she responded collectedly to Sir Hugh's questioning. But when it came time for her to face Montague Chambers he simply stated, "I have no instructions to cross-examine this witness, whom I understand to be a common gutter prostitute." Eliza took this humiliation stoically, having herself predicted that the court would pay her no mind.

The endless stolid persons, whom I had induced to speak up for Windham, were then paraded forth day-upon-day with eulogies to his sanity on their lips. These were the Felbrigg servants and retainers, the estate cottagers and tradesmen, the Norwich shopkeepers and merchants, the county clergymen and gentry, and the officers of the East Norfolk Militia. Most of them performed more or less creditably in the witness box. But it is an unfortunate truism, concerning any drama that outstays its welcome, that fickle public interest will all too soon fester into contempt. And the endless repetition of dull fact will always be trumped by colourful sensation. Our witnesses did not grip the imagination like those who had gone before them. As our defence dragged on deep into January, public interest first waned and then wilted. This, in its turn, excited a search for whom to blame.

Cries of "folly", "waste" and "shame" were now increasingly heard from all quarters. Some organs attacked General Windham and his co-petitioners. The *Daily Telegraph* denounced them as "those who have not scrupled to drag the sickly particulars of their kinsman's life into the light of day, to ravage slum and stable for repulsive evidence, to weary and shame the English public in their desperate yearning for the oaks and broad acres of Felbrigg Hall." Charles Dickens's periodical, *All the Year Round*, poked an accusing finger at the medical men, finding that "the case for the imbecility of the mad-doctors has been made out. One eminent authority cries Sound! Another equally eminent cries Rotten!" *The Saturday Review* admonished Master Warren, reckoning that "an abler president would have kept some check upon the counsel who appeared before him."

It may not surprise you to learn, however, that lawyers were the ones most liberally targeted for excoriation. "Worse than the JEZEBEL who led Windham along the path of misery," one *Telegraph* editorial fumed, "worse than the poor foolish debauchee himself, are those wreckers who tarnish a respectable profession and disgrace the law because they call themselves lawyers." *The Times* complained that all concerned were "eating like caterpillars into the estate", and asked, "Are there no means of deciding a rich man's sanity as you would decide a poor man's sanity?" A full-page cartoon in *Punch* depicted the blindfold figure of lady justice standing behind a trestle table with an oyster barrel resting upon it. A set of barristers, in their wigs, gowns and tassels, were gorging themselves on the seafood and lustfully dolloping vinegar on. The caption read, "Law and Lunacy: Or, A glorious Oyster Season for the Lawyers."

I tried not to take these squibs to heart, consoling myself, in relation to the cartoon at least, that solicitors were not actually represented in it. I suppose that I must accept some measure of culpability for fielding so many mundane and repetitive parties, but I was still relatively inexperienced in my profession. Cairns exempted himself from examining most of our witnesses in favour of more pithy engagements elsewhere, leaving his juniors to take the strain. Chambers delegated his own cross-examinations to lesser beings, in similar fashion. Windham himself ceased to attend at the Law Courts, and the jurymen's sentiments became quite unfathomable aside from their palpable boredom. One of them had already excused himself from further involvement, on the ground that it would be dangerous to his health, possibly to his life, for him to continue.

Our stock of witnesses was finally exhausted on the second to last Thursday of January, which was the thirtieth day of the inquisition's sitting. "Everyone must be aware," Master Warren said when the defence presentation was declared ended, "of the extremely difficult nature of this case. I fear that my exertions have sorely affected my nerves and made me very poorly. I trust that I will receive the sympathy of both sides if I vacate our sittings over the forthcoming two working days, and we resume as usual on Monday for counsels' closing statements." The *Telegraph* declined his invitation to be sympathetic, opining in its next issue that "Judges who carry 'nerves' into court are apt to leave brains outside it."

When I returned to Morley's Hotel following the adjournment, I found the thin, purposeful face of Inspector Holden awaiting me in the lobby there. "I have something of substance to convey to Mr Windham", he announced. "Would you be good enough to lead me to him?"

THE MIRACLE OF PHOTOGRAPHY

A good many of us would not regard January as a month overly besprinkled with joy. It can seem unrelentingly cold and gruesome. But even so Windham had become acutely apathetic and fatalistic of late, and had taken to brooding in our hotel suite for days on end. He had grown indifferent to my reports of the goings-on at the Law Courts and sceptical as to the merits of prolonging matters there, even through the contributions of sympathetic witnesses. He had ceased to keep abreast of the press commentary on his case, which had flattered and fascinated him in its early stages. His notoriety had, by now, thoroughly lost its sheen. And the wide publication of his likenesses had thrown him open to crude lampoonery if he did set foot abroad.

When I fetched Inspector Holden up to our suite Windham was bundled on the settee still clad in his dressing gown, though the afternoon was drawing on. He stirred only so far as to offer the visitor a grunt and his hand, but he did not get up. He was not really in any ready state to receive callers. After their taciturn greeting, Holden showed us a press cutting that he said might offer a clue as to Mrs Windham's whereabouts.

As I read it then handed it to Windham to do the same, the inspector sat on the sill of our window that overlooked Trafalgar Square from an upper floor. The curtains were not yet drawn, though dusk was in the offing, and he gazed out at the milling citizenry as if no opportunity for surveillance was to be passed up.

The press item in question was clipped from the "Persons Wanted" column of pink sporting weekly *Bell's Life*. "Wanted," it read, "Photographic Portraitist, to Capture Ladies Fashions for Paris Exhibition: Would suit gentleman of Holywell Street." A postal box number was given for applicants' ease of response. The Holywell Street named was a narrow thoroughfare running parallel with the Strand, well known for its numerous small publishing houses, book-selling shops, and artistic studios. It was also infamous for the unblushing vending of candid jottings and prints. The street was located in that lowly and decrepit region between the Strand and Drury Lane, now recently levelled, that Windham had hailed for its old-world charm on our drive out to Brompton to see his mother. Its mention in the notice clearly invited responses from men of indifferent morals. But any relevance to Agnes that the notice might contain quite escaped me.

Windham was not in the sort of leisured condition that is receptive to puzzles. "Civil of you to bring this snippet to my attention, inspector," he remarked with grim satiric intent, "in case I decide to set up shop as a pornographer once the lunacy court has deprived me of my inheritance."

"I do hope that won't be necessary, Mr Windham", Holden replied with an indulgent smile. Then he assumed a very serious expression.

"Let me set out my reasoning", he said. "You see, *Bell's Life* can sometimes serve the seasoned observer as a kind of underworld almanac. It lists race meetings and competitive fixtures of allsorts, and where there are spectators there will also be pickpockets and undesirables of more ambitious types. I think that you two found this out at Ascot, did you not? It can be helpful to know where this or that blackguard may be snacking on a given day. But there are some more specialised 'sporting' activities, and I don't refer here to a game of croquet on the front lawn, that require more discreet advertising. This is due to their abhorrent and illegal nature. The sponsors of, say, a bare-knuckle fight or a savaging between dogs, have need to publicise their impending atrocity in advance. They often do so through cryptic notices in the *pink 'un*, to use its colloquial title, the real meaning of which is instantly recognisable to those 'of the fancy'."

Still resting on the windowsill, the inspector turned to face Windham directly. "And there are certain more fleshy opportunities, Sir, having precious little to do with sport, which are also semaphored in *Bell's* classified pages."

Windham unbundled himself, and sat upright on the settee with an expression of foreboding on his face.

"I have no wish to alarm you, Mr Windham, but you will, perhaps, have read of a trade in beautiful women who are abducted and carried off to a life of confinement in Parisian brothels?"

"I may have done," Windham confirmed anxiously, "what of it?"

"Well now, I would invite you to review the advertisement's words, 'Capture...for Paris Exhibition', and reach your own conclusions. The promoters of some allegedly high-class Parisian establishments will keep only the most desirable of women, as their reputations depend upon it. They are always on the look out for the same, and are careless about how they procure them. And they are reluctant for the goods to arrive 'sight unseen', as one might term it. Thus, I would surmise, the need for an unscrupulous photographer arises. It would be reasonable to suppose that whoever is behind the advertisement has previously employed the services of an artist, and is now seeking to tap into the more lifelike possibilities of photography."

"And you have an inkling," Windham guessed, "of who that advertiser is?"

"We have long suspected a certain James Roberts, alias 'Bawdyhouse Bob', of involvement in this odious cross-channel commerce. And, forgive me for taking the liberty of saying so Mr Windham, we consider few women to be as marketable as your wife."

An image crossed my mind of Agnes playing canasta, and making polite chatter, with a lot of other wasp-waisted abductees awaiting deportation.

"Do I understand you to be suggesting, inspector," Windham asked gravely, his mind probably plagued by more disturbing images, "that the bawdyhouse bloodsucker has that fate in store for Agnes?"

"I cannot, for sure, supply the answer, and my suspicions are insufficient to support a round of orthodox police intrusions. If he still has your wife in his custody, Mr Windham, then Roberts will certainly have seen to it that she is not to be found by means of conventional searching."

"But you think you know where she is?"

"I would hesitate to commit myself that far, but I have set some machinery whirring that has put an address into my notebook. A genuine photographer of Holywell Street has been persuaded to respond to the printed box number and advance his credentials. After some postal negotiations with an anonymous party, the photographer's offer of service has been accepted and his discretion vouchsafed. He has a standing instruction to present himself at an address in the Shepherd Market area of Mayfair, one that is already referenced on our blacklist of Roberts' suspected dens."

"What good, though," I cavilled, "will the intelligence do, since you have already discounted a frontal police raid?"

"Ah but I have a very subtle sort of raid in contemplation, one that I would describe as more of a 'swoop'. If he is indeed the originator of the advertisement, then we must insinuate ourselves into Roberts' confidence so that he willingly betrays the concealed place of detention. And if we do discover Mrs Windham, and any other women held there without their consent, then we shall whistle up a squad of uniformed bluebottles. Some rudimentary subterfuge will be needed to attain this end, including a slight element of disguise on your parts, since you are both known by sight to the targeted individual."

"You allude repeatedly," I pointed out, "to 'we' in this connection?"

"So I do, Mr Phinney, for I am counting on your assistance. I propose that we accompany my tame portraitist to the Mayfair address he has been given early tomorrow afternoon. Master Warren has obligingly vacated the court's sitting, and I believe that it will be as fine a day for light as any at this time of year. Once there, we will pass you two off as the photographer's artistic assistants and myself as his general dogsbody. I suggest that we foregather at his studio on Holywell Street, at midday tomorrow, and that you arrive in your most secondhanded of sartorial combinations."

It was hard to know whether to regard all this as a harbinger of hope or despair. Windham was more than capable of yawing to either extreme in response to much lesser stimuli. He scratched his unshaven chin and ran a hand through his tousled hair. He made to speak several times, before thinking twice of it. Then, at last, a kernel of resolve hardened in his soul.

"I may appear an idiot to some", he said, getting up from the settee and practising his head rolling and lapel clutching mannerism. "Some say that my countenance is unprepossessing, my habits are filthy, and my very existence is a curse and a burden. But I am not without my redeeming qualities. I care deeply for my wife despite her inconstancy, and I am not at all the stingy, sulky fellow that they make out. We will go with you tomorrow, inspector, and see to her release."

I saluted his optimism, while hoping that it would not turn out like the proverbial bulb that stalks in winter but never sprouts a flower. Windham's propensity to soar, in a second, from black disillusion to blind faith was always something to behold. But he could just as quickly dive back down again.

Come the next morning, my friend and I assumed our most nondescript clothing as the inspector had outlined. We strolled east from our hotel along the Strand, and into Holywell Street beside St Mary-le-Strand church. We found the shop we were seeking at the street's nether end, nearest St Clement Danes, where there were only narrow pavements and a cart's width between its mouldering terraces. One would have considered it a rather dingy setting for a studio except that, in common with many of its neighbours, the building wore angled mirror-boards to reflect light into its upper stories. Whatever licentiousness might be enacted upstairs, the shop displayed only conventional landscape studies and the usual stiffly posed portraiture in its window.

The door was opened to us by a tall young man with long hair and a fulsomely silken beard, both of which were jet black without a streak of grey. They contrasted strikingly with the kaleidoscopic colouring of his waistcoat. He was E.A. Seafield, the artist who had conducted the *conversazione* at the Hanover Gallery, and these were his commercial premises. He recognised me from our previous meeting and was clearly primed to expect our call. Unnerved by bumping into him again without warning, all I could think to do was ask how his daubing was coming along.

"Oh painting is so *passé* these days," Seafield replied as he showed us in, "and photography is very much the medium of the moment. I engaged these rooms some months ago when I took the profession up, so as to duck the attentions of my erstwhile West End clientele and the blinkered art critics. The old fossils of the art market wouldn't dream of straying into a district of real character like this one. But I'm sure you're not intimidated by it, are you gentlemen?" He beamed broadly as though it would gratify him greatly if we were.

"Certainly not," Windham assured him, "we are perfectly at ease in the locality."

Further photographic *tableaux* were arranged inside the shop on low tables with lacy cloths, and there were lines of oval-framed portraits hanging from long wall-strings. There was very little space to spare, but a stack of partially completed canvasses in one corner suggested that Seafield had not abandoned painting absolutely. He was possibly hedging his bets as to future trends in the visual arts. Windham twitched a curtain that divided the shop from its back parlour, perhaps picturing Agnes herself posed behind it in a *tableau vivant.* But it was I who was in for a thrilling when Seafield drew the curtain back.

"Good afternoon, George," said Felicity Pumicestone, awarding me with a nervous smile, "and a good day to you too, Mr Windham."

She was reclining in a rocking chair, to one side of the fireplace range, and Inspector Holden was sitting in its twin to the other. He was roughly dressed. The room was coarsely, but cosily furnished, and crates of what looked like technical accessories were open in the middle of the floor. Rather than fashionable crinoline Felicity was in the dowdy skirts a girl serving in the shop might afford, and her auburn hair was brushed back and wound in a plain coil. I was perplexed by everything to do with her presence here, not least by the fact that she was apparently sipping from a glass of fortified wine.

"Major Fenning has a noggin now and then, George," she saw fit to excuse herself by saying, "and I think it churlish not to keep other people company in their pastimes."

She looked as prim on saying this as Eliza Dignam had when talking of being supported in her living by "kind friends". In the light of my own imbibing, I could hardly complain that Fenning was proving to be a bad influence. My feelings at seeing her once again were a compound of excitement and dread.

"Miss Felicity is to be the costumier," Holden intervened by explaining, "of our little escapade. And these modern marvels," he spread out a hand to indicate the crates of photographic hardware, "constitute what one might describe as our theatrical props."

"You'll readily appreciate," Seafield put in knowledgably, "that I have to pack and carry my own 'camera obscura' when working apart from the convenience of my studio. The process I employ requires that the exposed glass plates are developed straightaway while still wet. It is the latest 'wet collodion' method, do you see? I usually have my own dedicated handlers along with me, but I'll have to make do with novices today. There's nothing to it really, just a little messing about with chemicals and the suchlike, and the hazards are quite trifling."

He casually upturned the palms of his hands, which were straggled with burns and stains. "Everything you see here has its slot in the creative jigsaw, and all these accoutrements can be acquired for cash at any Philosophical Instrument Maker. There are the plates themselves, and the bottles of chemicals, and the 'safe light' red lanterns. And then there's the camera, of course, and the tripod, and the hood to make for a closed canopy. We'll have to heave it all about between us. Will you take a strengthener yourselves, gentlemen," he lifted the wine decanter from where it was warming by the hearth, "to render you a notch more valorous?"

We agreed, and he obliged us accordingly.

"And I have a terrific range of costumes in stock," Seafield resumed, "that I use for dressing my sitters. Some like to be captured in the guise of an Admiral on the high seas, or an Arabian princess, or some other romantic likeness. I believe, Miss Felicity, that you have something suitable set aside for our friends, do you not?"

"Why, indeed." She got up and knelt on the floor before a large basket containing a mass of old clothing and assorted accessories.

"Since you're to go in character as Edwin's assistants," she said, lifting a little stack of things from inside the costume box, "I thought that we might fit you out to emulate your supposed employer."

She got to her feet bearing two brightly hued waistcoats, a couple of very full and black false beards, and a pair of matching wigs. Then she apportioned these between Windham and me for us to put on.

"It was my bright idea," she recounted as we did as instructed, "to contact a photographer, after papa told me of the notice in the sporting press that Mr Holden had spotted. By a delightful coincidence the commercial directory threw up the name of Edwin Seafield, and it is by my persuading that he has consented to help us."

"We must," Seafield contributed, "do everything possible, Mr Windham, to liberate your wife."

When we were both 'in character', Windham glanced from me to Seafield and then back again. "I thought it was your intention, Miss Pumicestone," he remarked facetiously, "that we were to emulate Mr Seafield not to ape him? Let us trust that Bawdyhouse Bob can't tell the difference through those muddy specs of his."

It must be admitted that the whole thing was an immensely baggy conceit, and we all burst into giddy laughter. Felicity then evicted Holden from his rocking chair and sat Windham and me to either side of the range, while she attempted to perfect our disguises with the assistance of brushes and greasepaint. Our close proximity to one another, as she attended to mine, fizzed with unease.

"I wonder what excitements," she said with some brio, "await us in Mayfair, George!"

"You're surely not coming with us," I protested warmly, "to what will almost certainly be a house of ill-repute?"

"I surely am, as I have my role of costumier to play."

This Fenning ogre had plainly kneaded her sense of womanly propriety into a perilously elastic state. "But that would be an affront to decency," I appealed to the inspector, "will you not ban it?"

"It is somewhat improper, I'll grant you," the policeman conceded, "but I judge that the presence of a female dresser will enhance our credibility. And the lady is most insistent."

Her resolute expression told me the same. One might almost have suspected Holden of willing Felicity and me into each other's society.

Seafield had hired a carriage roomy enough to transport all five of us, the camera, its tripod, and three containers of equipment to Mayfair. We waxed skittish as it drove us over there, but Holden cautioned us to gravity as we turned off Piccadilly and penetrated Shepherd Market. As the carriage set us down at our destination, I reflected that vice and respectability are often found to reside cheek-by-jowl. Mayfair, with its lordly accommodations, harboured a lump of grit in the shape of Shepherd Market. The buildings in this enclave were poorer than in its immediate surrounds, and a few unkempt individuals who were out and about eyed us with hostile glints.

Our party had arrived in a cobbled close that gave every impression of being residential. And when the portraitist rapped on the knocker of one of the terraced houses, the door was answered by a surly but apparently ordinary housewife. The rest of us held back as Seafield parlayed with her, and then followed him inside as he won admittance. We lugged the gear along a passage and into a tatty back room where the woman brusquely told us to amuse ourselves, before leaving us to it. There was something alien in her attitude and in the pervading atmosphere of the place. The greying lace curtain over the window was nailed to the frame so that it was impossible to see out. A number of leather couches, lining the walls, were pretty much the room's sole furnishings, and they were oozing stuffing and sagging in patches. The disguise that I was in now felt totally ridiculous, and the thought that I was exposing Felicity to danger disturbed me greatly.

Five or ten minutes passed without anyone materialising. So, not wishing to test the couches, we sat down variously upon our crates. You could vaguely hear the distant crash, thud and tinkle of piano, cymbals and drums, periodically augmented by hoarse voices and cackling, though it was not certain where these sounds came from. Once in a while the background hubbub would abruptly swell, and then fall away again, suggesting the opening and shutting of a door. This would be followed by footfalls on the stair, and bursts of loud, unvarnished language. These would be joined in the corridor by the drab tones of the woman that had admitted us, who always seemed to appear to order. She would satisfy demands for hats and coats, and then see their owners out of the front door. Sometimes she would receive newcomers, and the process would be reprised in reverse.

We waited there for what seemed like ages, though it was probably not more than half-an-hour all told. Then we again heard the gust of sound rise and fall, this time to be succeeded by the slow and jerky gait of a bulky individual descending the staircase. The portly shape of Mr James Roberts then assumed human form at the door.

"Upon my word," he said, lifting his specs and blinking at our company, "you look like a bunch of buskers pestering for tips along Oxford Street. And what a lot of gear you've dragged in."

He lowered his spectacles, the prevailing lack of illumination perhaps tending to our advantage. "Which one is Seafield then?"

"I am he," the portraitist responded, getting to his feet, "and I did inform the gentleman with whom I corresponded that I would need to come adequately equipped and assisted. The miracle of photography is accomplished by technical sophistication, not by mere slight of hand. May I have the honour of knowing whom I am treating with?"

"You can think of me as Mr Punch for the time being. And you can have the honour of remembering that my commission is a delicate one, requiring complete discretion on your part. I usually hire an artist, and he's no trouble and doesn't litter the place up half as much. There'll be well-rewarded work in it for you if you please me and take good care what you are about. But a howling dog's no good to anyone, and might as well be throttled."

"I am fully aware that your terms are ones of secrecy."

"See to it that you remain so, and that these others take it to heart too."

Roberts lit a cigarillo. "Now then, I am about to show you into the presence of a young lady who may harass you with this or that fantastical claim. She might maintain that she is held here against her will, or blab some equally hysterical piffle. Young women will trill out whatever passes between their earlobes, without regard to truthfulness or logic." He gave a dry, dismissive laugh, "And this one is more than a little touched." He tapped his forehead. "So be assured that I have her best interests in contemplation, and ignore anything she says to the contrary. Now follow me."

We marshalled our lumber and manhandled it into the passage and up the stairway. Once on the landing, our guide took a small star-shaped keyring from his waistcoat pocket and unlocked a door. This gave out onto a balcony that wrapped itself round a small concert floor. We could now hear the pianist and drummer at first hand, and see that they occupied a stage elevated to one end of the space below. Their efforts were sprightly but largely tuneless, though some of those present were dancing. The outlandish scene revealed from the balcony described a fairyland for the rakish gentleman. There was a welter of gallants with "puffy-outty" whiskers, and a lot of lavishly crinolined women. The menfolk were seated round hazard tables, set with cards or ivory counters and a wheel, their faces glowing red as if warmed by a witch's cauldron. The women drifted about them, replenishing their drinks or leaning into their expensively tailored sleeves. The air was dense with choking tobacco smoke.

"Just a few old friends enjoying a companionable rubber of bridge", Roberts commented, clarifying the situation for us.

We accompanied him round the balcony, past a series of shut doors. One of these opened suddenly, spilling out a man and a woman who weaved their way light-heartedly past us and our encumbering boxes. They descended a spiral stair near to where we had come in and then parted, the man rejoining some fellow hearties at one of the tables. The balcony terminated in a curtain, beyond which we were led into an area that was dark and an apparent dead-end. But after Bob had fiddled about with something unseen, a wall panel gave way and we issued forth onto a landing much like the one we had started from.

We were then ushered into a drawing room, where the clock seemed to have spun from daytime to night. The shutters were closed, and there was only lamplight. Mrs Agnes Windham was seated on a sofa, reading a stage periodical. Her demeanour contrived to be languorous, despite her straightened state, and her appearance was as practiced as ever. She watched detachedly as we filed in and lowered our cases to the carpet.

"What have we here," she enquired in a world-weary tone, "a troop of travelling players booked to entertain me? How thoughtful of you Bob. I suppose I would be wasting my breath if I told them that you are holding me a prisoner here?"

"Quite squandering it," her gaoler confirmed, "they'll not mark a word you say. They're photographers, and they've come to take your picture." He stooped over her and leaned close-in to her face, "Now won't that be dandy?"

Agnes did not seem to think so, and she returned her attention to her reading matter. Roberts then waddled over to a closet door at the far side of the room and banged upon it sharply. Two cauliflower-faced confederates promptly emerged and assumed watchful stances.

"Don't drag your feet, then," their boss instructed Seafield, "get your clobber set up and go about your business quickly."

"There is the small matter of the shutters," Seafield pointed out, "we can hardly proceed in unnatural light."

"Very well then," Bawdyhouse Bob responded irritably, "there's no need to climb on stilts about it!" He had one of his men unlock and unfurl the slats. "Does that satisfy you?"

I was uncertain as to what our next step might be. We had found Agnes for sure. But the balance of force did not favour our rushing Roberts and his men, who were no doubt armed and resolute. There were none of Mr Holden's "bluebottles" to hand, and we were not able to escape the building in order to "whistle them up" as he had proposed. And I was worried that Windham's mounting agitation would betray us. I could see that he was bursting to make himself known to his wife, and barely containing the urge.

Now with the benefit of daylight, Agnes made a closer study of us. Her inquisitive stare eventually rested upon me.

"Oh Mr Assistant," she asked me, "don't you think that a sprig of honeysuckle would complement your colourful waistcoat most splendidly?"

"I haven't given it a moment's thought", I returned, struggling to attach significance to the peculiarly inconsequential remark.

"Well you should," she said, regarding me intently, "because the overall success of an ensemble depends upon its every tiny detail."

It was a funny time to be offering fashion tips, but touching on the subject seemed to perk Agnes up.

"Oh, I'm so glad you've hired the photographers in Bob," she said, sitting up in sudden animation. "They'll be much more fun than those fussy sketchers who expect you to sit still for eons. And I must look my best for the Parisian gentlemen! They'll be a frenzy of expectation when you send my pictures on. I can't wait to go. And when I get there, and they see that my charms hold good in person, they'll be vaulting over each other's backs to be near me."

"That would be the desired effect", Bob drawled slowly, clearly taken aback by her sudden enthusiasm for the project.

"Where do you want me," Agnes sprang to her feet as she asked this of Seafield, "over by the window, perhaps?" She assessed the atmospheric conditions quizzically. "But is the light strong enough? I'm scarcely qualified to pronounce upon it, but that must be rather the point when it comes to photography?"

"It's a perfectly bright day," Bob said, "so far as I can judge." He lifted the tints and peered about him. "And you can keep away from that window, or there'll be trouble."

"I don't doubt that it's luminous outside," Agnes countered, "but there's not much of it trickling in here. The windows are too small and facing in the wrong direction. And that ghastly wallpaper damps everything down, and the horrid carpet simply drinks in the light."

"She's quite right", Felicity ventured, catching onto Agnes's objective while the rest of us floundered. "If we take her portrait in this dim surrounding then it will only make her look frumpy. I was thinking of putting her in a nice velvet gown, and its raised braiding must be allowed to show up. And we might wreath her hair in flowers. Why don't we go back to Edwin's studio, where everything is perfectly ordered for the enhancement of appearances?"

Felicity squeezed my wrist, and I now realised that Agnes had been trying to signal that she knew me. It was, in fact, surprising that anyone who had seen me before might not.

"It would be a poor do indeed," I said, attempting to camouflage my speaking with a gruff voice, "should we fail to record the lady's true beauty."

"And that would sell me *so* short," agreed Agnes, "and shamefully disappoint the Parisian *boulevardiers*."

"Well now," Seafield cogitated, "if we do go back to my suite then the results will certainly be superior. I have a comfortably furnished atelier there, with mirror-boards to assure ideal lighting conditions."

"The thing must be done here," Bob insisted in exasperation, "for the sake of discretion. Now stop complicating matters with girlish niceties and get on with the job!"

"Ah but," Holden piped up cunningly, "we are *very* discreet at Holywell Street, and very well up in the ways of the world. We have a singular selection of racy backdrops and revealing outfits. Why, I can picture our pretty lady here standing in front of a fountain draped in half a toga, with an urn on her shoulder, or sitting in a seashell without a stitch on!"

"Hmm," Bob was not allergic to considering this lewd suggestion, "you mean she'll do for us what the Duchess of Ferrara did for Titian?"

"Just so." Holden made a good job of licking his chops lasciviously. His lowly attire added spice to the impression.

Agnes made an even better job of recoiling at the proposition as if she had been given civet to smell. "Only a great beast," she exclaimed, "would put a woman up on a mantelpiece for such ripe amusement!"

This made Bob's mind up for him. "Come now my flickering glow-worm," he said, "don't be so bashful.

You were quite content to go to this man's studio a moment ago. It would be good for him to have such a woman as you for his model, and there need be no misapprehension as to the propriety of the thing."

"My carriage will still be waiting at the front pavement", Seafield remarked encouragingly.

"Very well then," Bob resolved, "we'll push off. But we'll grab a bottle of good brandy at the downstairs bar first. It'll make the afternoon go with a spurt."

He told the cauliflower-faces to bring Agnes along, and led us through the dressing-closet entrance out of which the stocky pair had first popped. We all packed in there, hauling the apparatus, pressed together in an unwanted degree of intimacy. The closet betrayed no obvious alternative exit. But, as before, some fumbling with something unseen on Bob's part induced a wall panel to swing ajar. We thus emerged partway up a staircase which, once descended, opened into a small lounge off the main hall. Some military men were lazing around in there, enjoying drinks and female company. In a short while we could hope to be outside, as Agnes had intended, and the tables would be turned on the bawdyhouse *voyeur*.

Roberts instructed a big, tall man, who had been overseeing the room from a corner, to fetch the desired vintage of brandy. But, instead of obeying, the man strode across to Windham, leant over him and squinted hard into his face. I recognised him as the thumping great bully who was Roberts' usual roughhousing helpmate. "This human article," he said, whipping the false beard and wig from my friend's head, "smacks to me of Mad Windham."

Bob shuffled sharply to his side. "I see," he said angrily, "this has all been a masquerade has it, designed to guy me? And what are the true identities of these other pretenders?"

He pulled off my beard and wig. "Ah, it's the ever-present Mr Phinney." He then advanced upon Seafield.

"I would thank you not to tug mine," the photographer requested, "as they are genuinely connected to my head."

Bob accepted his assurance, but was plainly ready to lay violence on somebody. "Who's this labouring type then?"

"I am Inspector Holden of the Metropolitan Police."

Roberts received this news with so much alarm that he omitted to find out who Felicity was. "We must get that floosie back into her hidey-hole," he declared of Agnes, "before someone spies her. But I'll need to consider what to do with the rest of them meanwhile. Maybe we'll throw them into the keel of a coffin-ship, and kick the inspector in headfirst. Clear the lounge," he instructed his more keen-eyed associate, "so I can have some quiet while I think."

The bully gestured to the women disported roundabout that they should take their partners into the main room. Registering this spectacle, it was Felicity's turn to have her composure tested. One of the martial loafers in that lounge was Major Ralph Fenning. He was seated a little way off sporting a supercilious expression, and blowing smoke-rings into the face of the girl on his lap. At her enticing, he took her hand and let himself be led into the other room.

Once the couples had left, Bob's bully slid a knuckle-duster onto his fist and Agnes's two minders immediately imitated him.

Her arms now freed by their resort to weaponry, Agnes glided over to where Roberts was standing. She then reaffirmed her endless capacity to surprise. She reached her arms about his well-nourished circumference in a sort of hug. "Our association has not been without its moments," she told him, "but I have far more congenial things to do with my time and really must tootle off now."

She offered Windham the crook of her arm. "Come along Willie, we shall be on our way."

Windham gladly joined his arm with hers, and they sauntered out of the lounge and into the gaming room as if taking up position for a waltz. Felicity and I followed in likewise fashion, while Seafield and Holden formed the rearguard of our little flotilla. The musicians raised their tempo a little, perhaps thinking that we were all about to dance. Reaching the room's further shore, Agnes produced a small star-shaped keyring with which she unlocked a set of double doors. She certainly had an easy way about her with Bob's waistcoat pocket. Her former pimp and his henchmen were starched stiff with astonishment.

Once through the doorway we discovered ourselves back in the hall that we had first entered, where the surly chatelaine was blocking our path. "Make way," Agnes directed, "for Squire and Mrs Windham."

The woman must have been in service at one time or another because she not only made way, but also dropped a curtsey as she opened the front door. The Norfolk gentryfolk breezed past her, and we all billowed out onto the pavement.

Inspector Holden then blew his whistle, whereupon a police wagon he had apparently stationed nearby drew up and disgorged a squad of uniformed officers who scuttled straight inside. The invasion must have caused a panic within, as a broth of gentlemen was soon boiling out onto the pavement and hastening to quit the scene. There had been a wet snow flurry whilst we had been in Bob's den, though that had now given way to a shaft of sunshine. The absconders slithered in the slush without benefit of their hats and coats. It seemed that Holden had no intention of questioning any of the escaping patrons. One of these was Major Ralph Fenning, who grimaced awfully at the sight of Felicity, before struggling through the slurry in the others' wake. He attempted no fugitive excuses or explanations, and I saw from Felicity's wintry expression that her feelings for him were extinct.

Without a word, she walked to Seafield's waiting carriage and climbed aboard.

Holden hurried indoors to supervise his men, and Seafield followed to make safe his equipment. Soon Roberts, and the three underlings of his who were complicit in Agnes's detention, were led out in chain-bracelets and hoyed into the police van.

"I'll give you such a clout if I get close enough," the Bawdyhouse man hissed at Agnes as he passed her.

"Shut your slimy beak," she sang back vehemently, "you'll never get near me again." Then she turned to Windham, with a tender expression and her arm still linked to his. "I want you to know, Willie, that I have renounced that petulant child Antonio forever. I am sorry I abandoned you. I resolved to return as soon as I read those sulphurous stories circulated about you in court, before I was so rudely prevented. I will stand by you from now on, and will have something very particular to tell the lunacy court next week. But I have had a thick time of it of late and want to go to Blenheim Place directly and be with my little sisters."

When the surrounding commotion had died down, and the tools of Seafield's trade had been restored to his carriage, the photographer offered to transport us all home. We said *adieu* to the inspector. The atmosphere on the journey was more subdued than celebratory. Felicity was far too prickly for conversation, and Agnes's silence suggested that her usual vitality had been more drained by recent events than she cared to admit. Having dropped Agnes off at St John's Wood, then Felicity at Red Lion Square, Seafield let Windham and me off last of all at Morley's Hotel. Though Windham visited his wife next day at Blenheim Place I did not want to intrude on their reunion. And he kept whatever she may have told him to himself.

A CABRIOLET ON A CORDUROY ROAD

I arrived early for the hearing's resumption on Monday, and decided to await the opening of the courtroom on a wall-settle in Westminster Hall. This august setting has seen any number of exalted trials down the ages, most notably the one where King Charles I was condemned to lose his head. And Windham's was, of course, far from being the only cause currently underway at the adjacent Law Courts. In those days, before the old Law Courts' demolition, the parties for listed cases swirled about an area of Westminster Hall at its northern end. As I waited, I observed the ebb and flow of these interactions. Solicitors met their clients, and introduced them to their barristers. These, in turn, sought each other out to chatter or negotiate. Documents were produced and examined. Groups formed, then coalesced or dispersed. And all the while a monastic hush prevailed.

At one instant I saw General Windham some way off, standing talking to Montague Chambers. This occasioned me to reflect that the general had been roughly handled by the press during the trial. As I described near the start of this memoir, his heroic Crimean reputation had revolved into that of a pariah during the Indian Mutiny. Some commentators wrote that his former fame was undeserved, and that his generalship had been found lacking in the latter. I am ignorant of military matters and so am in no position to express an informed opinion. Whatever the merits of the relevant arguments, the general was removed from active field command after his perceived failure at Cawnpore. He then endured three further years of separation from his wife and children, in a humiliating posting at Lahore. It was this that he was newly returned from when I first met him at Aylsham, and some columnists had been taunting him with it throughout the trial. He had had a series of rejoinders published in the letter pages that attempted to fumigate his name, but which read more like a gnarly compendium of his grievances.

These circumstances disposed me to give the general the benefit of the doubt concerning his complicity in the malicious mis-statements of the Lewellins and others. While pondering this, I was admiring Westminster Hall's oaken hammer-beamed roof which is such a miraculous survivor from medieval times. The beams were hung with banners, and their ends were beautifully carved. But when I lowered my gaze from this scrutiny, I caught General Windham himself in the act of lowering his frame to sit beside me.

"You've put in a creditable effort, Phinney," he said, "but it's all been to no avail I'm afraid. I know how these jurors, and more particularly their wives, think. You may be assured that I'll not be too hard on Willie when it's over, and I shall spare him the indignity of committal to an asylum at any rate. You will have no ground to oppose my appointment by Chancery as custodian of his person and property. My wife and I, and our little ones, will live at Felbrigg and so preserve it intact for the rightful pedigree. We'll accommodate Willie there, and arrange for a daily superintendent to be in attendance to keep him out of harm's way. But there will be no place for the grasping and promiscuous Miss Willoughby. Once their marriage is annulled, I mean to ensure that they never meet again. And I put you on notice, Phinney, that I will not tolerate any difficulties made by meddling legal muffs in relation to these arrangements."

"You rather assume," I responded, "that the verdict is going to come down on your side. And you disregard the fact that, even if you do win, a victory assisted by lies is a dishonourable one. I observe that you have not taken the stand yourself, and can only deduce that, as a man of honour, you are embarrassed by the false evidence concocted in your corner by Mr Portal."

"The need to delegate," he replied, "is one of the great drawbacks of command. And it is all-too-often the case that those whom one uses are not equal to their allotted tasks. Portal overreached his brief, certainly, and his excessive zeal produced some unfortunate and potentially counterproductive results."

This was, by any yardstick, an ambiguous response. "May I ask, then, to what effect you did brief Mr Portal in preparing the testimony of the Lewellins and the other witnesses from their house?"

"Permit me to reply," he returned obliquely, "with a pertinent tale for the connoisseur of portents. Incidentally, I wouldn't bother to repeat anything I say as I'd only call you a slanderer."

His tone had gained a sharper edge.

"You'll be aware," he went on, "that in the Crimean War we set out with our allies to stop the Russian bear from mauling the Turkish Sultan to death. So, with the worst campaigning season of the year coming on, we shipped an army halfway across the world to the Crimean promontory to bait the bear in the port of Sebastopol, his fortified lair. Our men squatted for a year, throughout a fearful winter, in the bare heights above the town like a tribe of ragged scarecrows, pitifully provided for from home throughout. Right from the off the error in the campaign was a want of transport and supply, and there was a serious outcry against the blundering government and army high-ups. Everything had to come in by sea though Balaklava harbour, an inlet that was quite unsuited to the task."

His face assumed a faraway look.

"Well, while the men languished without basic provisions and foodstuffs, sometimes without basic shelter even, an officer could have any frippery he liked sent out on his own account. Some would order anything a man could think of, from marmalade to a musical-box. One staff officer, who should have worn the cap of a dunce rather than that of his regiment, had a cabriolet shipped all the way from England! I daresay he imagined it spinning him nimbly from this muddy entrenchment to that."

He made a scuttling movement with two forefingers. "At first there was only a corduroy road up the slope from Balaklava harbour, made from the planks of a foundered ship, though later the engineers built an entire railway all the way up to the front. I can see that numskull staff officer now, driving the cab up that corduroy road in the pouring rain. He was whipping the poor beast pulling it, and the cab was swaying drunkenly as it slithered in the grooves between the planking. Eventually the inevitable happened, and the cab went over and was smashed to smithereens."

He looked at me significantly, and nodded his head slowly as if the import of this apparent parable was witheringly obvious.

"Your meaning is obscure to me", I returned impatiently.

"Is it really?" He advanced his face nearer to mine. "Well then, let me assist you. Willie's state of mind has, from birth, always swung between elation and despair just as that cabriolet swung from side-to-side. And he has always trodden a slippery and uncertain road. It has only ever been a matter of time before he overturns and shatters for good. What of it if he is given a little push?"

I think that he was about to add more to this chilly analysis, but just then a swell of excited voices from near the hall's entrance perturbed its prevailing calm. Like a whipped-up sea, those who were idling there waiting for the case to start surged to gather around the door and witness the arrival of Agnes Willoughby. I mean, of course, the arrival of Mrs W.F. Windham Esq. Most of those present would never before have seen her in the flesh. Ever the actress she had timed her entrance impeccably, to coincide with the door to the Law Courts being opened. As she glided though the swiftly parting crowds towards it, General Windham watched in goggle-eyed astonishment. Inspector Holden had seen to it that her liberation had gone unrecorded by the press, and the general gazed at her as if he were seeing a sorceress just surfaced from the underworld.

Agnes led the way through the corridors into the Exchequer courtroom, and I lost the general in following her along with everyone else. She took a seat at the front on counsels' bench without much regard for its lawyerly exclusivity. The room was soon filled to overflowing. When Sir Hugh Cairns appeared he and Agnes had a short, but intense conference in low-tones, the sense of which I was frustratingly unable to catch from my seat behind them. Windham then appeared and sat beside me, just as Master Warren was assuming his podium and the clerk was appealing for all present to quiet-down and take their seats.

Cairns sprung straight to his pins and applied for the master's leave to examine one final witness. Though he was very loath to allow it, since our evidence had only last week been declared closed, Warren had no choice once he heard that the witness was none other than the supposed lunatic's wife. Agnes was dressed expensively, but tastefully, and she ascended regally to the witness box. Cairns trotted her though the preliminaries of establishing who she was. He then questioned her briefly and uncontroversially about her married life to date. Her answers evoked a diorama of normality and domestic contentment, and she attested with surety to the soundness of her husband's mind.

Sir Hugh then jumped into the thicket. "I think," he presumed, "that I would be doing you no disfavour, Mrs Windham, if I were to acknowledge that you have in the past been a member of a certain disreputable profession?"

"I have never made any secret of that fact", she declared with brazen assurance. "Any defenceless child may have their innocence corrupted by designing individuals, and yet return by their own decision to purity in sentient adulthood. I have been privileged to hear the clarion call of redemption, and I have not let it go unheeded."

"That speaks of a high moral character, Madam. Do you have anyone particular in mind when you refer to 'designing individuals'?"

"I refer to my former 'protector', or I should say my former corrupter, James Roberts."

"Is he the person whom this court has heard described as 'Bawdyhouse Bob'?"

"He is."

"Has this individual ever communicated to you the substance of any discussions he may have had with General Windham, the chief petitioner in this case?"

"Indeed he has, on several occasions, though I have never met the general himself."

"In what terms did he relate the content of these discussions?"

"Mr Roberts said that he had made an arrangement with the general, whereby..."

"Conversations between the witness and another party," the vigilant Montague Chambers leapt up to object, "cannot be admitted as evidence in this case. The sole issue here is Mr Windham's state of mind.

This witness has every reason to try and tear General Windham down, and that gentleman has already endured an attempt to blacken his good faith through the allegations of another immoral woman."

"I am entitled," Sir Hugh replied, "to place before the jury evidence of conversations that relate to the conduct pursued by General Windham in the getting-up of this case. Suppose I could prove that he was ruled by motives of self-interest, surely that would be relevant to the current enquiry?"

"We are not trying General Windham here," Chambers persisted "but rather the sanity or otherwise of his nephew."

The general examined the skylight as if completely indifferent to the outcome of the dispute.

Master Warren sank his chin into his hands. Up to this moment, he must have felt that the inestimable release of seeing the proceedings end was close at hand. But, instead, he was suddenly being forced to make a critical judicial ruling. "I think that the question is a doubtful one," he said with an agonised expression. "Ordinarily," he continued uncertainly, "I would be bound to reject evidence of collateral conversations concerning General Windham as tending to raise issues beyond our scope. If collateral issues are to be continually raised, then we may not finish our deliberations until Easter."

He looked unhappily at Agnes, who returned him an unwavering gaze of the utmost sincerity. The jurors caught her expression too, and I think that they found it hard to square with Chambers' description of her as an "immoral woman."

"Given that the witness is patently a Lady," Warren directed hesitantly, "I would consider it uncivil to refuse to attend to her statement in full. I therefore rule that her evidence is admissible, and require that you do not press your objection further Mr Chambers."

Chambers spread his palms in a gesture of impotence upon being rebuffed with a ruling so clearly grounded in sentiment rather than law. He sank back down beside the general, whose expression remained stonily impassive.

"What arrangement," Cairns asked Agnes, now that he had been cleared to put the question, "did this Roberts individual say that he had made with General Windham?"

"Mr Roberts said that the general would see to it that my husband was at Ascot races on a given occasion, and that Mr Roberts would know where to find him."

"Was that the occasion when you and your husband first met?"

"It was."

"And where was Mr Roberts to find him?"

"It was to be underneath the paddock clock. Willie's landlords the Lewellins were agents of the general, which was why he boarded Willie with them in the first place. It was they who told him that Willie had gone gooey-eyed over me. Mr Lewellin was formerly a guardsman, you see, and had actually been the general's camp orderly in the Crimea. Mrs Lewellin had been in service at his house. The general helped Mr Lewellin to set up in the wine trade, and later helped establish them both in their boarding house. They were paid to bring Willie to Ascot and make sure that Mr Roberts might bump into him, so to speak. He then brought Willie along to his marquee to meet me."

"What earthly purpose could General Windham hope to serve by having his nephew introduced to you?"

"Oh well, that was his grand plan. The general told Mr Roberts that the idea came to him from the sorry example of an old army chum of his. This poor chap was called Freddie, I believe, and he was sent mad many years ago by some woman blowing hot and cold over his affections. I was to perform the same trick on Willie, by feigning interest and then stringing him along. His uncle told Mr Roberts that Willie's mind would be wrecked by this as surely as poor Freddie's had been. It was my part to agitate Willie into such a weak state that the general might take control of him. The general even took him along to see the unfortunate Freddie at an asylum, to scare him into a bendable condition."

"But the stratagem failed, did it not?"

"So it did. In all his cleverness the general did not reckon on my breaking with Bob and refusing to play my part, or on Willie and me actually marrying."

She looked sweetly in her husband's direction. "And I could never have done him harm in any case." Windham returned her affectionate expression. "So General Windham had to think again," she resumed, "which is why he resorted to these legal proceedings."

"And what was the prime object of the general's restless manoeuvring?"

"Why, having Felbrigg for himself and his brood. What else? He was incensed by the thought that all the family property would go to Willie. He told Mr Roberts that, as a younger son, he had received but little in his own life and had always been destined to be 'shot for nothing' in the army."

"I assume that Mr Roberts planned to profit from your husband being delivered into his hands, but what monetary consideration did he give to the general in return to satisfy his own side of the bargain?"

"He forgave certain gambling debts that the general owed to him. And, when I steamed-in from Dublin a month ago to say my piece here, he had me chloroformed and stolen from the landing stage! Mr Roberts has held me a prisoner to prevent me from speaking the truth, and he planned to despatch me to Paris in immoral servitude. But I have been freed by the intervention of courageous friends!"

Her attentive public responded to these revelations with startled gasps. "And," Agnes added without further prompting, "Mr Roberts said that General Windham always had it as his aim to 'bring Willie in mad' one way or another, whatever the true facts."

The phrase had a familiar ring to it. It seemed that bringing his nephew in mad dovetailed not only with General Windham's purpose but also with his desire. I discovered that any lingering respect I might have had for him had been snuffed out. He was no better than a marauding highwayman from the old coaching days, laying in wait for innocent travellers on Hounslow Heath. Perhaps it was the ruination of his military reputation that had sent him to the bad. I remembered Windham commenting that his uncle seemed to have caught a severe dose of dyspepsia out in India. Whatever the truth of it, the general's face did not betray so much as a twitch in response to the several vocal denunciations that were now shouted in his direction.

Windham heard his wife out calmly, having obviously been aware already of what she was going to say and having presumably already forgiven any initial involvement she may have had in his uncle's plot. How the jurors received her statements I was unable to guess. They still had to chew their way though the closing speeches of counsel that were pasted over the trial's final three days.

It is in the nature of these perorations that much disposable rhetoric is expended, to which my professional experience already rendered me largely immune. Sir Hugh Cairns, in particular, excelled himself with a day and a half's address that climaxed with a reference to Virgil's *Aeneid*. He invoked a story recounted therein of a tyrant who tortured a prisoner by chaining him to a dead body, thus leaving the living man to die and both to decompose together. He warned the jury that it would be a far crueller fate still to chain Windham to the "icy and corpse-like embrace of legal incapacity and lunatic restraint."

Montague Chambers steered clear of the classics, but reprised every colourable chapter of Windham's life in graphic detail. The highpoint of his oration was a curious one though, being a spirited defence of a man who was not himself on trial. "It is deeply to be regretted," he lamented, "that General Windham should have been so coarsely assailed for the purpose of withdrawing attention from the real merits of this case. He has never skulked in the hour of peril. Sufferings and hardships almost unexampled he has endured, like his brave comrades, with manly fortitude. While we were sleeping in our beds in comfort and happiness he was at the post of danger, and it was there he won his glory."

On the morning of the Thursday, the thirty-fourth day of the inquisition, Windham dressed soberly for the personal examination that it was his lot to face. He was nervous, but quite composed. At eleven-o'clock Master Warren took his seat, and said that he was ready to read his complete note of the proceedings out for the jurors' benefit. This proposal was greeted with expressions of horror from the jury box, and their foreman Sir George Armytage hastened to his feet to say that such a Herculean labour was entirely unnecessary. Warren then informed the jurors that, once the court had been cleared of strangers, they would be at liberty to put questions to Mr Windham in a friendly way. There was no telling how long this private examination would last, and so I drifted back into Westminster Hall. Cairns retired to the sanctity of counsels' robing room along with his juniors.

As the hours wore on without word coming from the courtroom, Westminster Hall became increasingly filled with expectant sightseers. I was pleased to have my isolation at last relieved by the coming of Mr and Mrs Jeffrey, who had once again braved the parliamentary train and London's vicissitudes to be in at the close of their master's ordeal. They were followed by Felicity and Mr Pumicestone, so that we formed a select little group of Windham's supporters. Then Inspector Holden appeared, and so too did Eliza Dignam with an unkempt but genial young man who was plainly her brother Conway. Agnes swept in just as

I heard from a court-runner that the jury had retired to deliberate. It was approaching three-o'clock and Windham's interrogation had lasted for nearly four hours. Cairns had sent out for me to return to court, and I brought the others along with me.

Windham was overjoyed to see us, though his nerves were stretched so taut that he could barely utter a word. We all sat at the front with Sir Hugh. General Windham was at the other end of the bench in his usual pose of staring up at the skylight with his arms folded. He was flanked by Mr Portal and Montague Chambers. We had to endure a gut-churning wait for the jury's return, but, as it happened, they came back after only half-an-hour. In answer to Warren's question as to whether they had reached a verdict on which they were all agreed, Sir George Armytage stood up and confirmed that they had. "What is it, then?" Warren further enquired. It was, "That Mr Windham is of sound mind, and capable of taking care of himself and his affairs."

This verdict was received with loud cheers and celebrations, which rose to a crescendo when William and Agnes Windham joyously embraced. I, and his other well-wishers, gathered around and congratulated him mightily, patting his back and pumping his arm. My friend's triumph was so complete that he was quite inconsolable with tears. It was not his own, but his uncle's cabriolet that had been justly overturned.

THOSE ANCIENT HAUNTS

The events I have described took place long ago, and I see that it has taken me two and a half more years to record them in writing. We hurtle along in life's reckless ride across the rocky fells, tossed in a creaking brake, with scant chance to pause and savour our surroundings. Many previous certainties are now almost gone from present memory. The old two-wheeler hansom is, alas, fading out of regular use. The acrid stink of petrol is replacing the fruity whiff of horse dung. The cheery splutter of yellowish gas is giving way to the sterile glare of electricity. The "merry sixties" of last century leave a ghostly imprint on my mind, like the faint figures left by passers-by on long-exposure photographs. An inquisitive little girl stood over here by a barrow until she got bored and moved off, and a shoal of shoppers stopped to examine some wares there, before strolling out of frame.

You might assume that the trial's losers, being also its promoters, would be made to bear the strain of failure by having to pay their nephew's legal costs in addition to their own. But this was not so. In the then state of Lunacy Law, the legal expenses of a "supposed lunatic" could only be funded from the property at issue. As a result, Windham teetered for some time on the edge of bankruptcy. And this was not the only inequity exposed by the trial. Soon after its conclusion, Sir Hugh Cairns saw to it that a bill of reform was enacted by parliament. This provided that a supposed lunatic might be awarded his costs against unsuccessful petitioners. It further ensured that contested cases would henceforward be heard by a Judge of the Queen's Bench, rather than by a vain and vacillating master. It also established that evidence pertaining to things happening more than two years before the date of an inquisition would henceforth be subject to a strict test of their relevancy.

What of myself and Felicity? Well, I picked a fine day, not long after the trial had ended, to take her on an excursion to the Crystal Palace in Sydenham. The splendid edifice had been reconstructed there, having housed the Great Exhibition in Hyde Park ten years earlier. We had visited it together as children, when all our respective parents had still been living, and I hoped that the happy memory would be conducive to good-fellowship in the present.

We travelled by train from the Victoria station in Pimlico. Walking up from the local halt Felicity took my arm, and, on reaching the palace, we shared our astonishment at seeing the incredible creation in glass and iron anew. Modelled as it is on a cathedral's pattern, and surely dwarfing older creations of that name, we entered what one could regard as the nave. A breathtaking vista opened before us, narrowing towards the distant central transept. Amid abundant foliage and statuary, whole villas and labyrinths of ancient civilisations had been structured to scale in pigmented attire. Pompeii, pickled in time by the Vesuvian ash, led us to the temples and tombs of Ancient Egypt. The ornate Alhambra gave onto to the human-headed bulls and winged lions of antique Assyria. Past the mosaics of a Byzantine basilica, we found ourselves in the pillared walk of the Greek Parthenon.

The day was cloudless and serene. And as we dawdled, or swept, according to our inclination, through the ambulatories of ancient and modern creations, Felicity's jewelled soul was illuminated to me in the revealing sunlight. I remarked to her that visitors might, one day in the far-distant future, find here a memorial to the "Pretty Horsebreakers" of yesteryear. Under a plaster facsimile of the Achilles statue, I suggested, they might discover a carved and painted Agnes Willoughby in chiselled crinoline, entertaining a mounted wooden gentleman from a threadbare barouche. Felicity was much tickled by this fanciful invention of mine. We went outside, and I gave her my hand to ease the passage of crinoline and slippers down the stairs leading to the gardens. She linked my arm afresh as we promenaded along the winding pastoral paths, resplendent with trees and plants and fountains and nymphs. Despite the leaflessness of the branches everything seemed fragrant and bright, like a broad field of lavender. Reaching the lake at the bottom of the gardens, we rested on a seat overlooking the giant models of antediluvian creatures that inhabited its islands. There was a *Megalosaurus*, and an *Ichthyosaurus*, and various other unpronounceable monsters. It was hard to imagine that such leviathans ever truly bestrode the earth.

"You see," I said to Felicity, "we can live adventurously without journeying very far at all. We can travel through time and space right here at the Crystal Palace."

She smiled, and I put an arm around her shoulder.

"I suppose," she volunteered after a while in thought, "that we all somehow contrive to survive our own idiocies. In our different ways we have each confused the attractiveness of something with its real suitability. You went in search of enlivenment, and found that it stole what you had in the first place. I was deceived into considering Ralph exciting, when he was actually no more than a cad."

"And you were just as certain that I was unutterably dull?"

"Perhaps a measure of dullness is not an entirely bad thing, George. Steadfastness in another is, perhaps, enrichment enough. And I should reassure you that, before he was found out, I had already decided to reject Major Fenning's proposal."

We had, it seemed, managed to knit our romance back together, and I made a marriage proposal of my own which she accepted.

So why did I set out to write this memoir? One reason is that, since retiring from my profession, I have enjoyed the leisure to do so. Another is that Windham's was my first court case of any real consequence. But the true precipitating cause was the more sorrowful one that, after almost fifty years of our life together, Felicity had passed away. This current year, being 1912, would have marked the half-century of our marriage. I believe that the quality of our companionship consistently outshone any minor botherations that might have arisen between us now and then. Though she had been ill for some while, there is nothing that can prepare oneself for the blow of bereavement. The Red Lion Square house, where I still reside, remains oppressive in its stillness. I constantly think I hear her moving about, and expect her to appear from moment to moment. I do habitual things that assume she is here, like shooing the cat from her favourite chair, and that have no logic since she is not. Without the agitations engendered by my encountering Windham, I do not believe that our happy union would ever have come to pass. That is why I wanted to set it all down, potted for posterity, and to caulk the leaks in my memory before all recollection sieves away.

During his opening trial address, Montague Chambers predicted that his "ancient haunts" would not receive Windham if he were to be found of sound mind.

Chambers was not alone in thinking that Windham would slide into ruin and dissolution, if left to his own devices. I fell out of touch with my friend not long after the inquisition, absorbed as I was with my wedding to Felicity and my new dignity as business partner to her father. Intelligence concerning the Norfolk couple occasionally filtered through, however. One learned that their match was not without its stormy patches, and that Agnes spent frequent periods away from rural Norfolk. But one day I received a card from Felbrigg inviting Felicity and me to attend a *fête* there in celebration of the birth of their son, the grandly named Frederick Howe Lindsay Bacon Windham.

Felicity and I travelled to Norwich on the *fête's* preceding afternoon, with an overnight stay booked at Cromer. The stage coach headed to the coast, which was named *The Ocean*, was boarding when we arrived at the Norfolk Hotel's coaching yard. "Find your places ladies and gentlemen, quick quick", shouted its driver in a thick rustic burr. He helped modest parties and their battered boxes onto the roof with the same solicitations that he lavished on squeezing gentlefolk inside. Everyone was treated to a gracious bow and a "Good daaaaay Sir", or a "Good daaaaay madam", and no one was required to consult purse or pocket for a compensating tip. William Windham was in his element, just as he had been when I first observed him on that railway platform. The broad-accented coachman asked us to sit beside him on the box. Once we were off he reverted to his best Etonian, though it emerged in a rather slurred fashion. We congratulated him upon the birth of his son, and nattered cheerfully as we barrelled along the country lanes. He was, he disclosed, now the coach's proprietor and regular driver, and he dropped us at the Belle Vue Hotel in Cromer which was its terminus and the place where Felicity and I would spend the night.

Under a clear blue sky, we walked the short distance to Felbrigg the following morning. A handsomely decorated marquee had been erected in the parkland outside the hall's south front, and there were numerous guests present. It looked, in fact, like the whole district had turned out. An enormous bullock was being spit-roasted, and a band was playing *The Roast Beef of Old England* while weaving in and out of the merry-making hoards. Hurdle races, and pole climbing, and sack jumping games were underway. There were jingling matches, wherein a person ringing a bell was dogged by blindfolded pursuers who attempted to tag him. At length, a procession was formed and led by the band into the tent. The ox was carried in on the shoulders of eight men, and everyone took their appointed places. Mrs and Mrs Windham came in, Agnes cradling the baby, with Thirza and Emmeline, who were really young women now. They joined their weightier tenants and neighbours at the top-table, and settled the infant in a crib. Felicity and I were seated at a long table populated by traders and persons from the professions, and hundreds of diners of all classes, from the estates and beyond, were seated at many more. The tent was bedecked with flags and balloons, and at one end a banner bore the legend, "Long live the Youthful Heir."

An opening chorus of welcome was sung by a choir of schoolgirls, clad in nice neat frocks. Grace having been said, a company of carvers then filled plates for us all from the huge carcass. Gigantic provisions of food and drink were served, and tackled with gusto by everyone in sight. When the feasting was done, a man introduced by Mr Jeffrey as the estate's oldest tenant proposed the health of the infant arrival, which was drunk amidst respectful celebration. Windham got up to deliver a generous reply to the whole company, which in turn received a roaring response. In obedience to a general call the Lady of Felbrigg, Mrs Agnes Windham, then stood up and scattered some pious sayings around. Bestowing a bountiful smile upon the gathering, she spoke of no longer being a stranger to a spirit of Christian humility and grace, as might have once-upon-a-time been the case. Introducing a balding cleric sat nearby as the Reverend Mr Vetch, she extolled his virtues while he looked upon her adoringly. "From the moment he planted the sign of the cross on the forehead of my baby," she said of the reverend gentleman, "I have been in thrall to his gentle ministration."

Once I had absorbed the initial shock of hearing her speak in such conventional terms, I reflected that it was not as surprising as all that. There was, as I have previously stated, something of the actress about Agnes. She may be said to have assumed a number of roles, to the public eye, in these pages. There was Agnes Rogers, the innocent peasant girl, fetched up to London and led astray into vice. Then there was Agnes Willoughby, the pretty horsebreaker and daring society courtesan. There followed Agnes the Jezebel, a designing corrupter of inexperience and predatory harlot. Now here was Mrs Agnes Windham, the Christian lady and gentle font of charitable largess. She remained, throughout her various incarnations, petite and demure and inscrutable to me.

Standing at high-table by her son in his cradle, she looked every inch born to Felbrigg's ancient haunts. She was draped in custard-yellow velvet, which harmonised well with her golden hair and heightened the brilliancy of some splendid ornaments. I still have the honeysuckle flower that she gave me at her wedding *déjeuner* in St John's Wood, pressed flat between the browning pages of a memento book.

AUTHOR'S NOTE

This book is a fictional adaptation of the real-life Windham lunacy trial, based upon an illustrated transcript published in pamphlet form by W. Oliver of the Strand soon after it ended. The cover portrait of Windham himself is reproduced from that source.

My aim has been to maintain as great a degree of historical accuracy as is possible within the framework of a novel, but many small, and several key elements have been altered to make for a rounded and flowing narrative. George Phinney and the Red Lion Square household are entirely fictional, as are Mr Portal and his Aylsham law-firm. The other main characters are taken from life, albeit subject to my reading of their essential natures. At the trial William Frederick Windham was indeed found to be of sound mind, though things did not end-up quite as I have described.

The research materials I have consulted are too numerous to cite individually, but I would particularly acknowledge the useful archive concerning the case held at Norfolk Record Office. A short, but fruity factual account is "Mr & Mrs Windham, A Mid-Victorian Melodrama from Real Life" by Donald MacAndrew (The Saturday Book, 1951). A bizarre fictional treatment is

"Agnes Willoughby: A Tale of Love, Marriage and Adventure" by William Stephens Hayward (1864). There is also "Redan Windham: The Crimean Diary and Letters of Sir Charles Ash Windham" (London, 1897).

A readable, and fair-minded, account of the background to the case and its known facts appears in "Felbrigg, The Story of a House" by R.W. Ketton-Cremer, first published in 1962. The late Mr Ketton-Cremer was the last resident-owner of Felbrigg Hall, which is now a property of The National Trust. Under the trust's auspices the house and its surroundings can be visited in season, and the special atmosphere of the place experienced in person.

Russell Croft, 2012

22317765R00177

Made in the USA
Charleston, SC
17 September 2013